Praise for …

Glamorous Illusions

"Bergren, award-winning author of nearly 40 books with two million–plus sold, launches readers into a sumptuous world of wealth and world travel with the first in the Grand Tour Series featuring Cora Diehl Kensington. Cora learns she is the illegitimate daughter of Montana copper baron Wallace Kensington, which sets her on a journey of discovery and healing when she joins her half siblings and their wealthy friends on a Grand Tour of Europe. Will McCabe, their guide, worries over the precarious family dynamics and his own developing feelings for Cora, who must face her own demons when her siblings sabotage her every move. The family must come together, however, when danger threatens all of them. Readers will come to love Cora as she struggles over her feelings for Will and the dashing Frenchman Pierre de Richelieu, and they'll delight in the scenes of England and France in pre-WWI Europe. This is a worthy beginning to the series."

Publishers Weekly

"A fascinating mix of travel and intrigue, heartache and romance, *Glamorous Illusions* sweeps you away on the Grand Tour, exploring London and Paris through the eyes of a young woman who longs to find her place in the world. The title captures the story perfectly, as Cora delves beneath all that glitters to discover what is real and true, while not just one man but two vie for her affections … ooh, la la! A grand start to a new series from a seasoned author who writes from the heart."

"Who am I and where do I fit in this world? These are just two of the important questions addressed in this poignant story that takes the reader from an impoverished farm in Montana onto an opulent cruise across the Atlantic to stately England and finally to the city of love, Paris. With fresh characters, a touching story, and plenty of adventure and romance, you'll get swept away in this lavish world of the young and wealthy."

"From a bankrupt farm in 1913 Montana to the glitter and glamour of a European Grand Tour, *Glamorous Illusions* is the trip—and the read—of a lifetime. Absolutely one of my favorites ever, this book is a stunning adventure from first page to last. A truly masterful storyteller, Lisa Bergren has penned a magical journey of the heart and soul that will leave you breathless and longing for more."

"A Cinderella story lingers in the pages of *Glamorous Illusions*. Open the book and be swept into a story of heartache, strength, and romance. Add in the sweeping beginnings to a Grand Tour of

Europe, and I found all the ingredients for a story I couldn't put down."

Cara C. Putman, author *Stars in the Night*
and *A Wedding Transpires on Mackinac Island*

"Here's a new historical series with something for everyone: romance, mystery, and family issues. Bergren brings the Grand Tour season of the wealthy of the early 1900s to life, and her characters jump off the pages. This series is sure to land on readers' keeper shelves."

Romantic Times

GRAVE CONSEQUENCES

GRAVE CONSEQUENCES

THE GRAND TOUR SERIES

LISA T. BERGREN

David C Cook®

transforming lives together

GRAVE CONSEQUENCES
Published by David C Cook
4050 Lee Vance View
Colorado Springs, CO 80918 U.S.A.

David C Cook Distribution Canada
55 Woodslee Avenue, Paris, Ontario, Canada N3L 3E5

David C Cook U.K., Kingsway Communications
Eastbourne, East Sussex BN23 6NT, England

The graphic circle C logo is a registered trademark of David C Cook.

The website addresses recommended throughout this book are offered as a
resource to you. These websites are not intended in any way to be or imply an
endorsement on the part of David C Cook, nor do we vouch for their content.

This story is a work of fiction. All characters and events are the product of the author's
imagination. Any resemblance to any person, living or dead, is coincidental.

LCCN 2012955795
ISBN 978-1-4347-6432-4
eISBN 978-0-7814-0878-3

The Team: Don Pape, Traci DePree, Amy Konyndyk,
Nick Lee, Caitlyn Carlson, Karen Athen
Cover Design: JWH Design, James Hall
Cover Photographer: Steve Gardner, Pixelworks Studios

Printed in the United States of America
First Edition 2013

1 2 3 4 5 6 7 8 9 10

123112

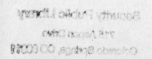

We are ever striving after what is forbidden,
and coveting what is denied to us.
—*Ovid*

Part I

~PROVENCE~

CHAPTER ONE

~Cora~

A shiver of fear ran down my back as I looked to the busy train platform outside my window. *It's only your imagination, Cora.* Silently, I counted to thirty, watching businessmen shake hands before parting. A young husband tenderly bussed his wife on the cheek as she anxiously wound a handkerchief in her hands. A man caught my eye in passing. He smiled and tipped his hat in my direction and I hurriedly glanced back to my lap. But when I lifted my eyes, the blue eyes of the dapper blond gent inside the train car with me were locked on me again. He was clearly watching me over the top edge of his newspaper.

I sighed and glanced at Nell, beside me.

"Cora?" she asked, studying my face. "What is it?"

"That man three rows up," I whispered, careful not to look his way. "Don't look right away. Wait until I look back to the window. Then see if he isn't studying us."

"All right," she said, a bit wan. Our near escape from kidnappers in Paris had left us all on edge. Even now, on this train bound for

Provence, we had no idea if a telegram from our fathers, demanding we purchase passage on a steamship bound for home, would soon turn us right back around.

I looked back to the platform. The train whistle blew, and those few remaining boarded or departed. Our car lurched and then slowly began rolling forward. A man came up outside my window, keeping pace with us. It took me a moment to realize who it was.

"Pierre!" I whispered in sweet surprise, knowing he couldn't hear me. He smiled and tucked a red rose in the crevice just outside the window, then kissed his fingers and placed them against the glass.

I smiled as Nell and Lil both giggled in excitement beside me and Vivian shushed them. I put my fingers to the glass and stared into his green eyes, mouthing the word *good-bye*. He was practically running now, and neared the end of the train platform. He mouthed the word *adieu* and stopped, lifting a hand. A wave of sorrow washed through me, surprising me as I craned my neck to see him as long as I could. I wouldn't see him for a while, and this was the first time we'd been apart since I met him. His gesture had been undeniably moving. I knew for a fact he'd had several appointments this morning. Whom had he ignored in order to see me off?

"That might have been the most romantic thing I've ever seen," Lil said with a dreamy sigh, settling back in her seat once all we could see were city buildings and streets with countless people going about their days.

"I would quite agree," said a man, suddenly at the edge of our row. All four of us looked up at him—the blond man I thought had been watching me earlier. Will and Antonio rose behind him, concerned since he'd approached us without introduction. "That was Lord de Richelieu, wasn't it?"

"It was," I said before I'd thought it through. "Do you know Pierre?"

He gave me an odd smile. "Indeed. We have spoken on a number of occasions."

Will and Antonio eased back a half step with this revelation. But they did not leave. The man glanced over either shoulder at them, smiled again, and resettled his hat in the crook of his arm. "Gentlemen, ladies," he said to us all with a smart nod, and with that, he made his way down the aisle of the car, presumably heading toward the water closet.

"I told you we should have arranged for a private car," Vivian grumbled toward Will.

"And as I said," he returned benignly, "there were none to be had." His eyes followed the man. "Did you catch his name?"

I shook my head. "He didn't introduce himself. But if he knows Pierre, he can't be all bad, right?"

Will's eyes narrowed and flicked toward the window, where the petals of my rose were fluttering in the gathering breeze. "I would imagine Lord de Richelieu knows a great number of people," he said, almost to himself, then looked down the empty aisle.

"If we're to continue this journey," I said lowly, "we can't be looking over our shoulders the entire time, worried the kidnappers have returned."

"And he hardly seems the type," Viv added, equally as quiet. She lifted a hand and waved toward the end of the train. "So boldly approaching us."

"Quite," Will said, turning away then. But I could tell by the gingerly way he took his seat—as if poised to spring back up—that he didn't entirely agree.

I watched Will out of the corner of my eye as he leaned forward, arms on knees, to speak with his uncle, our tour guide, or "bear," who sat beside Antonio Lombardi, his fellow guide and guardian for our group. They had risked much, taking us to our next destination before we received the blessing of our fathers to do so after the attack at Pierre's chateau. As if he sensed that my gaze was still on him, Will glanced my way. I hurriedly turned my attention to the view outside my window, thinking of how he had saved me during the attack—and how that seemed to make Pierre jealous....

I shifted uneasily as I stared at Pierre's rose stubbornly clinging to the crevice in the window. It was actually timely, this parting. I needed some days to sort out just what I felt for Pierre de Richelieu. Or didn't feel. Accepting his sister's hospitality by staying in her Provençal chateau in Tarascon made me feel further...entwined. And yet the promise that we would literally be staying in a defensible fortress might very well be the only thing that would keep our fathers from sending an armed horde to collect us and cart us back to America. We were willing to do anything to continue this tour across Europe. Whatever it took.

Behind Vivian sat her beau, Andrew, reading a newspaper, sitting next to his younger brother, Hugh, who was already in the midst of a hand of gin rummy with Felix, my half brother. The rest of the car was filled with twelve others. Two of them—Yves and Claude—were private detectives our bear had hired to ensure our safety, the remaining number a mix of Parisians and tourists. The blond man had not yet returned. Thoughts of him made me wish for the private car, as Viv did. Not that it mattered all that much in terms of finery or comfort when comparing it with our first-class cabin. Deeply burnished mahogany graced the tables and trim. Rich, autumn-hued toile covered the cushions. Matching drapes were tied back beside each window. At the bar at the far end of the car were crystal decanters and goblets rattling and clinking as we crossed rough patches.

All in all, it was much finer than anything I'd ever experienced in my former life. It caught me...that odd sense of experience, understanding. A year ago, I would have been wide-eyed in wonder at such lavish surroundings. Now it felt more like I belonged within it. I wasn't sure whether or not I liked it, that I felt that way. What would happen to me when I returned to my normal, simple life? To school? A small town? Much of it beckoned to me. But never had it felt more distant than it did to me now.

Over the next hour, we slipped away from the last vestiges of the city and eased into hills ruled by French vintners and farmers. There were rows upon rows of spindly grapevines stubbornly making their way out of rocky soil; orchards of silvery-green olive trees; fields full of sunflowers not yet giving way to their heavy, yellow hats. The sun, rising hot and shoulder high, shone across my lap like a brilliant, golden blanket. Overcome by sudden weariness, I unpinned my hat, leaned my head against the window, and gradually succumbed to sleep even as Lillian and Nell, the youngest of both families, giggled beside me.

I cared not whether they laughed, nor whether there was any impropriety in my head rolling to one side or my mouth hanging open. As long as I did not end up snoring like a drunken sod, I figured a rest was warranted. Given the events of the day before, none of us had slept much, and we were all tired. Besides, the long train ride south was to take all day. If I could sleep away an hour or two of it, all the better.

When I awakened from my nap to find the girls now fighting sleep beside me, I smiled, stretched my neck a bit, and then picked my way past Lil to make my own visit to the WC. There were private water closets, or "WCs,"—one for men, one for women—on either end of the car. Vivian smiled at me, her green-brown eyes shifting to the girls. I was almost past the young gentlemen in our company when Hugh grabbed my wrist. I frowned down at him in irritation. "What's this?" he said, dropping my hand and shrugging as if unfairly accused by my look alone. "Come now. I only wanted a word." He flipped his brown hair out of his eyes.

I sighed. "What is it, Hugh?" I asked, schooling my tone into something civil. I seemed to be on a new, fairly even path with my half siblings and their friends, and I didn't wish to ruin it.

He smiled, catlike, and folded his arms, glancing at Felix, then back to me. "I only wished to know what our Parisian host meant by his grand gesture as we departed." He pointed toward where the rose had been, now long since blown away with the wind.

"I don't see how that's any of your affair."

"Oh, but it is, actually. As you dozed away the morning," he said, gesturing toward my seat, "I was thinking of a new import business Pierre may be interested in discussing. When shall we expect him to next join us?"

I eyed my brother, and Felix gave me a little shrug as if to say a joint venture wasn't *impossible*. I straightened. "Pierre was going to do his best to see us before we finished our week in Provence and moved northward. He does intend, however, to meet up with us in Venice, if not before."

"Ahh, yes. Venezia." Hugh picked up his hand of cards again. "A fine place for romantic trysts."

"Hugh," Felix warned.

"Forgive me," Hugh said, arching a brow, but with no trace of apology behind the words.

I sighed, rolled my eyes, and moved on toward the WC. As I reached the end of the car, the thick-necked, barrel-chested private detective, Yves, set aside his paper and rose, pulling aside the curtain that led to the tiny alcove. Feeling the heat of a blush rise up my neck, I looked into his small eyes. I knew he was only there to look after us, but did he intend to stand outside the WC door? What possible trouble could I encounter there? I ignored my impulse to protest, knowing this was a necessary evil if we were to continue on the Grand Tour. And after the events at Chateau Richelieu, I supposed it would be better to find comfort in the detectives' presence rather than protest it.

Yves rapped on the WC door before me, paused, and then turned the knob. Two steps away, the train steward's eyes widened. Yves glanced inside and, apparently mollified that no kidnapper lurked atop the sink, gestured inward. I entered and closed the door behind me, knowing before I saw myself in the mirror that a mortified blush now covered my face. But as I stared at my reflection I giggled. "Well, now you can say you've been escorted into a restroom, Cora," I muttered to myself before beginning the complicated process of seeing to my business in frightfully tight quarters. I shuddered to think what the second-class cars' WC might be like. While they could not be any smaller, they were likely more rustic.

Afterward, I filled the basin with a bit of water, splashing my face. I'd become accustomed to the noise and sway of the train, much as I'd found my sea legs aboard ship, but here in the WC, the clack of the wheels crossing sections of rails was much louder than anything upon the sea.

A knock at the door startled me. "Mademoiselle?"

"Oui?" I said, leaning close, using some of the little French I knew.

"Êtes-vous bien?"

Was he inquiring after me? Heavens! One would think I'd been in here for hours! Was there a time limit in French train bathrooms? "Oui, oui!" I called, hoping my tone said, *Leave me be.*

I wiped my face with a soft, Egyptian cotton towel and set it to one side, knowing the steward would replace it after I left. Then I straightened my traveling suit's periwinkle jacket and exited, barely glancing at Yves as I passed him. It was one thing to keep an eye on someone and another to invade their privacy. I'd have to speak to Will about just what was appropriate.

I made my way to my seat just as another steward flicked out a white linen cloth across the table I shared with Lil and Nell. They'd awakened and stretched luxuriously, blinking with wide-eyed anticipation for the pot of tea and delicate pastries awaiting us on the cart.

"That suit complements your eyes, Cora," Lillian said, greedily reaching for the first pastry, a luscious-looking croissant filled with a berry jam.

"Thank you," I said, as I took my seat. Again, I marveled at the idea of having more than a couple of dresses. Now I had trunks full of them.

Without asking, the steward poured each of us a cup of tea before moving on to the next table. I stirred a spoonful of sugar and some milk into mine and waited for Nell to choose her pastry before taking my own. I tore off a bite and slid it into my mouth, the delicate layers practically melting on my tongue. If there was one thing the French knew how to do exceedingly well, it was baking. Never in my life had I had such delicacies.

"So," I said, taking a sip of my tea. "Pierre told me of his sister's chateau. Would you like to hear about it?"

"Oh," Lillian breathed. Then she clapped excitedly. "Yes, please."

Nell nodded enthusiastically, her coils of hair bouncing.

"Apparently, the chateau sits directly upon the Rhône River, on the site of an ancient Roman castle. Its presence has long taunted its enemies across the water in Beaucaire, but, reportedly, people of both cities shared a fear of the Tarasque."

Both girls stared at me with rounded eyes. "What is the Tarasque?" Nell asked, as if half afraid to know the answer.

I shook my head and pursed my lips as if vacillating in my decision about whether to tell them. I glanced at Vivian, and she gave me a small smile, already well versed in the game of older siblings.

"Please, Cora, tell us," Lil pleaded.

"All right, then. I know you two are quite grown-up ladies. So promise me, if we go for a swim, you mustn't fear the monster."

Nell narrowed her eyes at me. "Monster," she said flatly.

"Indeed. For many, many years, both those in Beaucaire and Tarascon feared the Tarasque, a river monster that ate both cattle and children."

"Well, fortunately for us, we are neither cattle nor children," Lil said primly.

"I'm sure you're quite right," I said, nodding and taking another sip of tea. The blond stranger passed by us then, and Vivian's eyes met mine. How odd that he had been gone, all this time. Or had he slipped back in while I slept and left again? I consciously kept my gaze on my tea and croissant, never looking his way.

"Perhaps the old monster's eyesight isn't what it once was," Felix said over his shoulder as he played a card.

"Yes," Hugh said, joining in as he studied his hand. "I've heard tell that his teeth have fallen out and he simply gums his victims, breaking their bones until they're a mushy mass he can swallow."

"Ewww," Nell said, wrinkling up her pert little nose. Then her eyebrows lifted. "Do either of you want that last pastry?"

I shook my head, as did Lil, and the round-faced girl eagerly scooped the pastry onto her plate.

"What else do you know of the chateau?" Lillian asked, tilting her head.

"It's lovely and has survived through the ages, mostly as a prison. Pierre's brother-in-law purchased it some time ago and restored it for his new bride. There is even a moat and drawbridge on the side that isn't guarded by the river herself."

"And both square and circular towers," Will said, across the aisle. He gave me a gentle smile, nodding in obvious appreciation for my knowledge. "My uncle and I have admired it from afar in previous years but have never been inside. We very much look forward to the opportunity."

"As do I," I said, meeting his intense gaze.

His look made my breath catch in surprise. Because if I wasn't mistaken, he wasn't just talking about architecture and history.

Our hosts were not in their magnificent home when we arrived, but an attentive staff greeted us and showed us to our rooms, which were spread across two floors of the ancient castle. At first, this alarmed Will, but his uncle intervened, assuring him that we would be watched over by the detectives on guard in the hallways through the night. My heart pounded when I found I was one of only two downstairs, fearing I'd once again been relegated to lesser quarters since I was only half Kensington, but when the butler opened the door for me, my heart slowed to a quieter, yet bigger *ka-thump* as I looked around.

"The castle was once, uh, how you say…prison," said the butler soberly, in halting English laced with a thick French accent. A thin smile grew across his lips. "But zee mistress of zee house has a way with making one thing into another. Her brother asked that you be given this suite."

"I should say she is quite gifted," I muttered, gazing open-mouthed at gothic arches rising in one dome after another above me in the L-shaped suite. I chose to ignore his revelation that Pierre had thought to assign me this room. I had no idea what the other rooms looked like, but I knew this was indeed special. One window looked out along the length of the Rhône River. A small balcony led to a private alcove directly above the water. On the far end, in the en suite bathroom that held a huge, claw-footed tub, was another window that showcased miles of rolling farmland.

"Merci," I breathed as three stewards and Anna arrived with my trunks and valises.

"But of course, mademoiselle," the tall, thin man said with a genteel nod. His keen eyes studied me a moment longer, and I wondered if he knew who I was…or rather, who I was to Pierre. I detected nothing but idle, bemused interest in him, even as he reluctantly turned and headed toward the door. Yet given the way he'd spoken of Pierre, he struck me as a servant who had known him for a good, long while. "If there is nothing else, mademoiselle?"

"No, thank you. I will be quite content."

"Very well. I shall send down a tray of refreshments. Dinner shall be served at eight o'clock." He gestured upward, apparently forgetting the English word for *upstairs*. He turned to go, thought better of it, and turned back to me. "While you shall be dining out-of-doors, you might wish to dress as if you are dining in the formal dining room, with eh…As it becomes, eh, later, it can be…" He rubbed his upper arms, as if cold.

"Chilly," I said, supplying his missing word. "I'll need a wrap. Thank you."

He gave me another faint smile and left, then. Anna and I shared a look. "Servants' quarters in one castle, a queen's in another," she said, lifting a trunk lid and shaking out an icy-blue gown. "I was thinking you might wish to wear this tonight, miss. It has that smart lace jacket that matches so well."

"That's fine," I said, going to the French doors and slipping out onto the balcony. I brought a hand to my mouth. The platform was about eight feet long and only a couple of feet deep, with a roof, one of only two on this level, the only variations in the smooth, straight stone wall. Clearly, the balconies were later additions to a side of the castle that had been meant to be impossible to scale. The ancient wall rose straight from the water below, to a height of perhaps thirty or forty feet. Here and there bits of grass and moss sprouted between the gray stones, but she looked as sturdy as she had likely looked when she was built.

Down below, the river moved past slowly, a luxurious flow of liquid green.

"Miss Cora?" Anna said. "Do you wish for me to turn down your bed? Would you care to take a rest before supper?"

"Indeed," I said, reluctantly turning back and peeling off my gloves, feeling the weight of our long train journey. I left the door open, liking the scent of the water and fresh air. "And perhaps a bath afterward?"

"Of course," she said, going behind me to help me out of a jacket that clung to my arms, then unbuttoning the gown beneath. As it slipped away, I breathed a sigh of relief. A knock at the door revealed a steward carrying a silver tray laden with grapes, apples, a wedge of cheese, a hunk of bread, and a pitcher with two glasses. Anna set it on a small table. "Would you like me to pour you—"

"No, no, Anna," I said, slipping under the incredibly soft sheets and fluffy down-filled cover. "You must be as weary as I am. Please.

You've done enough. Go and take your own nap, if you wish. Just be sure I rise in time to get ready. Otherwise, I'm liable to sleep through the night in this haven."

———◇◇◇———

She shook me awake a couple of hours later. I bathed and dressed, and Anna put up my hair in a clever twist, adding progressive sections of hair until it wreathed my head. "Where did you learn to do that?" I asked, turning one way and then the other in the mirror.

"A maid on the train showed us," she said, obviously pleased that I was pleased. She tucked a small ivory-colored feather on a comb into the folds of my hair and patted my shoulders. "You'll be the prettiest on the porch," she said proudly.

I smiled at her praise and rose to follow her to the bed, where she'd laid out my lace jacket. "It'll hardly keep me warm with all those holes," I said as she slid it over my shoulders. "It's more for show."

"Pish," she said. "France has lovely, warm evenings, even this close to the water. You'll be fine. I'll check in on you in an hour or so. Give me the signal, and I'll fetch you another wrap if necessary."

"Thank you, Anna."

"Of course," she said, staring at me as I hesitated.

I looked down. I was wringing my gloved hands.

"Miss?"

"It's Pierre's *sister*," I whispered.

"Ahh. She'll be as delightful as m'lord, no doubt. Go in with your head held high. Give her no corner to push you around. You are her guest. And her brother is smitten with you. That will either raise her ire or make you immediate kin. Either way, you'll win her over, I know it."

"Thank you for the vote of confidence." Still, I stood there.

"Well? Go on, then. You'll do no winnin' of her here, hiding away."

I laughed under my breath and turned to do as she asked. Outside, Will waited, looking handsome even in his too-short pants and tight black jacket. He wore a crisp white shirt and a perfectly knotted tie. His hair was slicked back in dapper fashion, giving him a refined, decidedly distinguished appearance. "William," I greeted him with a smile.

"Cora," he said, raising a brow. "You look lovely." He offered his arm, clearly his reason for waiting at my door—to escort me upstairs.

I took his arm, quietly assessing his strength in the bulk of it beneath my fingers, and we began climbing the two flights of stone stairs to the upper floor.

"Miss Kensington?" I paused and looked over my shoulder, and Will did the same.

It was the blond man from the train. His bright blue eyes flicked from Will to me and back again, the hint of a smile again on his lips. He was dressed for dinner, and he emerged from the suite across the hall from my own, obviously an honored guest. We turned fully around and waited for him to reach us.

"We didn't have the opportunity for proper introductions on the train," he said. "I'm Arthur Stapleton. Art, my friends call me." He reached out a hand to Will.

"William McCabe," he said. "And as you've already guessed, this is Miss Kensington. Miss Cora Kensington."

"Cora Diehl Kensington," I said, quietly correcting, offering Art my gloved hand. "What a coincidence that we were headed to the same household here in Provence."

"Quite," he said, that smile quirking the corners of his lips again. "Celine and Adrien are lovely hosts. You're in for quite a treat." We turned and walked up the stairs, with him hurrying to come up on my other side. I resisted the urge to sneak a look at Will. Was it only my imagination? Or was there some hidden story with this one? I knew Will wouldn't like it that a man had been put into a room directly across from mine. It was hardly suitable....

"The Bellamy dinners above the Rhône are renowned the world over," Art said. "Or am I speaking out of turn? Perhaps you're well acquainted, and we simply have not yet crossed paths."

"No," Will said, "this is our first time. We were the guests of Lord de Richelieu in Paris. He sent us here to his sister."

"Fine company you keep, then," Art said.

"Indeed. A blessing. And you, Art?" Will said. "Clearly you're an American. How did you come to sojourn here above the Rhône?"

"Business," he said easily. "Sometimes you have to go places you'd rather not. Sometimes you go places you wish you never had to leave."

We reached the top of the stairs and moved down a grand hallway with stone floors and a thickly padded red carpet that ran the length of it.

"How long will you be here in Provence?" Will asked.

Art shrugged. "A week, maybe two. I'll see how things progress."

"From where do you hail?"

"Washington, DC."

"Long way from home."

"No farther than any other American in the south of France," Art said. We entered the main dining room then, and others in our party came up to us, the girls gushing over my hair and their fine rooms. Art slipped away and went to greet a couple that looked like a matched set, each trim and about the same height, equally handsome. Salt and pepper, I thought, or pepper and salt. He had jet-black hair. She had blonde hair, a shade lighter than her brother's.

Art watched as we neared them. I had the distinct impression he was observing my every move. Was it simply paranoia? Or my fear of the moment, feeling unready to meet Pierre's sister? My fear that she'd look me over and find me wanting before I even opened my mouth? I squared my shoulders and met her steady gaze as Art introduced us, noticing she did not share Pierre's green eyes; hers were rather a warm brown that made her blonde hair all the more exotic.

"Adrien and Celine, this is Cora Diehl Kensington, and William McCabe, her tour guide."

My eyes went to Will's for a moment. We'd never said Will was our group's guide…but maybe Art had met with others in our company and found that much out. I quickly returned my gaze to Celine's, wanting her to recognize only quiet confidence in me, not doubt or fear. That was one thing I'd learned about the aristocratic crowd to date—if you gave them any edge, they pushed it.

"Ahh, Cora. *Belle, belle*," Celine said, smiling as she looked me over in an invasive and yet completely warm manner. *Cora, beautiful, beautiful*, I thought her words meant, given her pleased expression as she assessed me. "I see why you've stolen my brother's heart," she said, leaning toward me as if sharing a secret. Then she leaned back and looked at her husband. "Is she not?"

"Indeed she is," he said.

"I, uhh, thank you," I said, feeling the heat of my blush and wondering what Will was thinking.

"And according to Pierre, you have a beautiful heart, too," she said, taking my hand and tucking it into the crook of her arm. "I'm certain we shall be fast friends. If he loves you, then so shall I."

I stiffened. No such declarations of love had been shared between myself and Pierre—it was far too soon. I struggled not to cringe as we walked away from Will. And then I wondered why I was so concerned about him. Far more had transpired between me and Pierre than between Will and me....

Celine led me outside and onto an expansive stone patio that might have once been the roof of the castle. The edge was rimmed with a wall that reached up to my knees, leaving an expansive, sumptuous view of the river, the woods across from it, another castle, and here and there, the glow of other homes. In the center of the patio was a perfectly formal table, complete with candelabra, sterling, china, and crystal. Celine deposited me at her husband's right. He pulled out my chair as his wife directed others to fill in around us. Will was several places down from me, on the right, past Andrew and Lillian. And Arthur Stapleton was directly across from me, with Vivian on his left.

"Your name is so familiar to me," Vivian said to Arthur as soon as we were seated. The footman handed us each a cloth napkin. "Have we met before?"

"It's unlikely. I would have remembered such a fine acquaintance as you," he said, casting a respectful eye in Andrew's direction. "The Stapletons cut a wide swath," he said. "The family runs a vineyard in California—"

"A fine vineyard," Adrien interrupted from the head of the table, lifting his empty glass as a footman filled it.

"And they have holdings in several mines in Colorado. Perhaps my uncle and your father have done business together?"

"Perhaps," Vivian mused, but her brow knit in confusion, as if she were trying to puzzle it out. "Is that what brings you to Provence? Your family's vineyard business?"

"In part," Arthur said, lifting his own glass—admiring the color, I guessed. "I never refuse an opportunity to partake of Adrien's wines."

"Nor any other opportunity," Adrien said with a laugh. "Don't let him fool you. His business is to imbibe among the world's finest citizens, gathering stories."

"I do enjoy that," Arthur said with a smile, meeting my eye again with that particular quirk teasing the corner of his lips. "I meet the most engaging people as I travel about. Andrew, be a good fellow and tell me about your travels. I hear you're on the Grand Tour."

All our champagne glasses were filled, the golden bubbles apparently from the Bellamys' vineyards, and a toast was made to "our new American friends." And then the food was served. Course after course…canapés, cream of asparagus soup, watercress salad with roasted squab, then poached salmon with cucumber and fresh dill. By the time we paused for a delicate rose water and mint sorbet, I was feeling the strain of my corset's ribbons.

As they served the sixth course—a tender filet mignon, topped with foie gras and truffle drizzled with cognac—Andrew's recounting of our Grand Tour moved from Paris and to our intended itinerary ahead.

"Come now," Adrien said, lifting his goblet of red wine and taking a sip. "Tell us more of your adventures at Chateau de Richelieu. From what Celine and I've heard from Pierre, you were lucky to escape with your lives." His eyes drifted over me, as if he hoped I might pick up the story where Andrew left off. Andrew paused, clearly caught and wishing to avoid the topic—not wishing to upset the younger girls, who trembled any time it was mentioned. I glanced at Hugh and Felix, who had clearly been overly imbibing, accepting glass after glass of champagne and wine, with little water in between.

"We'd all be dead if it weren't for Cora," Felix said, lifting his goblet in my direction. "Which certainly calls for a belated toast. To Cora."

The others reluctantly followed his lead and lifted their own goblets. "To Cora."

When I dared to look around, I found that Art was studying me. I shifted in my seat and looked down at Felix as he went on, willing him to look my way again so I could shush him. "Really now, Felix," I cut in. "It was a combined effort."

"Don't let her fool you," he said, his words slurring. "They taught her well on that Montana farm. Raised her up strong. She's a scrapper, I tell you. A scrapper. All dolled up, you wouldn't guess it. But she's a scrapper. My other sisters couldn't've done what she did that night. I'm proud she's one of the Kensingtons now."

Andrew rose and walked around the table.

"Uh-oh," Felix said, eyes big and laughing. "I'm in trouble," he said to Hugh, who lifted his own brows in delight over this latest turn of events. "What? May I not compliment my sister? I was simply answering our host's question!" He lifted his hands up, feigning defense as Andrew reached him. Andrew paused a moment until Felix lowered his hands, and then he bent to say a few words in Felix's ear. Chastened, Felix quieted and raised his hands. "Forgive me," he slurred. "I quite forgot myself."

"No, no," Celine said, leaning back against the high back and one arm of her chair in languid fashion. "This is exactly what we look for in dinner conversation, no? An exotic, exciting story? It's just the sort of thing Arthur relishes."

I looked over at Art as he smiled down at our hostess. "Your table is always rich with lore, Celine," he said, lifting his goblet in a silent toast.

"It was Cora who led the girls out," Hugh said, picking up the story that I had hoped would die. "She was the one who found the hidden passageways and pulled them out." He shrugged his shoulder. "Of course, I would've done the same, had I not been tied up."

"You were tied up?" Celine said. "In my brother's home? How is this possible? Such a travesty!"

"Indeed," Hugh said. "But Will and Cora managed to turn the tide, and sent a maid running for help. The intruders had cut the phone line. Murdered the butler."

Celine gasped. I glanced down at the girls. Both were quiet, hands in their laps.

"Really," I said. "Might we turn our conversation to more palatable topics? The girls—"

"Who would do such a thing?" Arthur asked, picking up on Celine's indignation, making me feel as if he were on our side. "What were they after?"

"We think they wanted to nab the girls," Felix said. "Lucky Cora and Will got to Lil and Nell before the intruders could."

"They came after us with axes," Lillian said, her voice shaking.

Celine gasped. "Truly? What a nightmare!"

"Really, Lil. You don't have to relive it," I said. "We can converse about something else."

"No," she said, her eyes meeting mine. "It's true. You saved us. You and Will. If it weren't for you..." Her eyes welled up with tears, and she swallowed hard. She shook her head.

"Did they catch them all?" Art asked, fiddling with his sterling spoon, straightening it, and then meeting my eyes from under a concerned, hooded brow.

"All but two of them," I said. We had to move on from this if the girls were to get any sleep at all tonight. "Happily, we're far from them now."

"And in a castle, an ancient stronghold," Adrien said with a warm, reassuring tone. A footman cleared my half-eaten plate, and another delivered a delicate custard drizzled with a golden sauce and several gigantic raspberries. "We shall pull up the drawbridge and release crocodiles into the moat this night," he said with a gentle smile. "No one will get to you here. Trust me on this." His eyes moved to my sister and to Nell, reassuring them as well.

"Merci, Monsieur Bellamy." I took a tiny bite of my custard, but my stomach roiled. From thoughts of the attack? Or simply because I was miserably full?

"Forgive me, Cora," Art said, watching me set down my spoon. "I didn't mean to upset you by egging him on."

"Oh, it's all right." I forced a smile to my face. "It's all behind us. Only hardships like this for us to endure now," I said, waving about.

Art smiled and then laughed. "Your brother's right, Cora," he said, taking a sip from his glass. "You are an uncommon sort of *society* girl."

Was it my imagination, or did he intend to goad me? Did he already know of my parentage? Had the story made the rounds among European society? Adrien had said Art enjoyed such stories....

Fortunately, the bear picked up his own tale, and the whole table listened as he shared of one tour group's misadventures aboard a Greek yacht, years ago. "From then on," he finished, "we cut Greece from our itinerary." He shook his gray head.

"Much to my dismay," Will added. "I'd dearly love to return."

"Well, my boy," his uncle said, patting him on the back, "when the business is yours, you can take your clients where you wish. The world will be your own oyster."

Will smiled and winked for effect. "Do I detect a dare in those words, Uncle? Do you not think I have it in me?"

"Ah, no, son. I think you have more than enough mettle to take it on. It shall be a delight to see how you make the tour your own."

I loved their relationship, the way the bear could be the tough taskmaster one moment and the doting uncle the next. It made me long for my own papa, who was now in Minnesota, and wonder how he was faring since his stroke.

First thing tomorrow, I'll see about sending a telegram, I thought. I needed to know how he and my mother were doing—and, likely, they hungered for word from me as well. It struck me that I hoped I wouldn't hear from Wallace Kensington at all. Because it'd only take one sentence from him or Mr. Morgan for this whole Grand Tour to end. And as much as I missed home, there was much, much yet here for me to discover.

---◇---

~William~

Will luxuriated in the rare opportunity to have some space to himself as he watched the warm rays of a dawning sun stream through cross-mullioned windows.

He yawned and forced his legs out from under the fine, warm covers. He sat up, resting his feet on the Turkish carpet, the chill of the stone beneath seeping up to meet his skin. *This place will be frigid come winter.* He shivered at the thought of it, glad they'd arrived in summer. He knew that as the sun climbed, baking the arid Alpilles region, he'd likely be sweating, wishing for the cool of morn, but for now he rubbed his arms and rose to hurriedly dress.

But when he entered the dining hall for breakfast, he saw Art, Felix, and Hugh, soaking wet and shivering, standing on the edge of the far wall, their host beside them in a similar state. Celine, their hostess and the only other person up yet, lifted her china cup in welcome. "Bonjour," she greeted him.

"Bonjour, madame," he said with a nod and partial bow.

"Shall you breakfast with me, monsieur, or do you favor a dip in the Rhône as my husband is fond of doing each morning?"

"Each morning, madame? Even come winter?"

"Even come winter," she said, shaking her head as if the man were beyond reason. "He says that it gives him, ahhh, *la vie*."

Life. Will smiled and looked out through the French doors to the vast patio beyond it. Felix was stepping up on the wall again. "By your leave, madame, I'd best see to my clients," he said.

"Please," she said, gesturing outward as if he were merely the latest lost cause.

Will's heart skipped a beat as he shut the door, even as Art and Felix leaped together, hollering all the way down. Adrien Bellamy and Hugh exchanged a delighted look and laughed as the sound of a splash rose from the river. "Hugh!" Will called.

The man glanced over his shoulder. "McCabe! Quickly! Find your bathing costume and join us."

Their host nodded and put his fists to his chest. *"Il va mettre les cheveux sur votre poitrine,"* he said, nodding and smiling, encouraging him. *It will put hair on your chest.* "It is what you Americans say, no?"

Will laughed and walked up to the wall beside them and looked down. Thirty feet below, Felix was swimming toward shore. Will laughed and shook his head. It looked incredibly dangerous. As well as overwhelmingly fun. The only chance he'd have to join them was if he leaped before Uncle Stuart arrived for breakfast. As much as the old man preached about joining the locals in whatever exercise they had planned—in order to "better experience a place"—Will highly doubted he'd endorse this particular adventure.

Quickly, he unknotted his tie and unbuttoned his shirt, peeling both away.

"Bon, bon!" their host praised. With a salute, Adrien dived off the edge, his arms outstretched and feet together, before bringing his arms together and slicing through the blue-green water below.

Will whistled lowly. "That takes some chops. And it has to hurt." Far below, their host reached the surface, bubbles still rising from his entry.

"You're going in nothing but your trousers?" Hugh asked, his teeth chattering.

"It's more than you have on," Will said, yanking off his shoes and then his socks.

Hugh shrugged and looked down at the water.

"How many times have you jumped?" Will asked.

"This will be my third. The key is to break the surface tension with your hands or feet. Slice it. Otherwise, it'll feel like you've just slammed into a wall. Trust me."

Will gave him a grim smile and stepped up beside him. The drop seemed far longer than it had a moment before.

"Scared?" Hugh taunted.

"I'd be a fool if I wasn't," Will said, rubbing his hands together.

Hugh laughed. "Just don't land on me," Hugh said. And then he leaped.

CHAPTER TWO

~Cora~

I awakened to shouts and laughter coming from outside my window. As I turned over in the wide bed, I heard the clang of a hallway gate and the sound of footsteps passing my door. I fought the urge to peek out the door to see what was happening, remembering that Arthur Stapleton was right across the hall. What if he peeked out at the same time? I thought about his blond hair and piercing blue eyes. It wasn't that I sought him as another beau...I had my hands full already with Pierre and...

I groaned and rolled over, forcing Will's face from my mind, concentrating on the fine bones of my room's architecture instead. Which inevitably led me right back to Will and his love for architecture. I sighed and again forced him from my mind, thinking instead about the people this room had once contained. Each wall echoed of memory, of struggle and strife, but also of triumph and release. I'd walked the perimeter of the whole thing last night, tracing my fingertips over the etched lines of graffiti, the names of men long dead, dates long past. *1732. 1649. 1810.*

The Bellamys had refurbished these rooms with care. Thick tapestries adorned the walls. Warm, wide, finely polished planks covered what I assumed were stone floors. And through the far arch, around a corner, was that lovely bathroom with the view of the Rhône Valley.

When I heard another shout and then, a second later, a distinct splash below, my curiosity got the better of me. I threw back my covers and went to the door, and leaned against it to listen. From the hall, I heard the clang of a lower gate, then the one on our level, then footsteps running past again, slapping as if wet and barefoot. *What on earth…?*

I reached for my robe and wrapped it around me, then eased out onto the balcony. But just as I did so, a body fell, not ten feet away. I gasped and drew back, but then heard the splash and the laughter of others above me. I stepped forward again and scanned the water, smiling as I discovered what they were up to. They were jumping! From above! Even from where I stood, below them, it was a good twenty feet to the water. From their launching point, a good forty. Who was up to such shenanigans?

I stepped closer to the stone rail and peeked over, watching as the man surfaced and took a deep breath, grinning widely. *Will.* With firm strokes, he swam toward the beach below. He wore no shirt; the muscles in his back were broad and toned, reminding me of some of the statues we'd seen in museums. I had no business watching him, admiring him. And yet I couldn't seem to do anything else. He reached shore, grabbed hold of the rocks, and tentatively, shakily moved up them. I heard the clang of a metal gate at the shoreline. I stepped into my room, then over to my door. A moment later, I heard the muffled voices—an exchange between a guard and Will?—another gate, then more slapping footsteps of a man passing by.

I eyed my window and smiled. Before I left this place, I wanted a try at that jump. Even if I just did so from my small balcony. That was likely daring enough. And would give me a taste for what the men in my party were clearly so enjoying.

Hurriedly, I shook out a sleeveless gold dress, not waiting for Anna to rise and come tend me. I was eager to get above and see if I could watch at least one of the men leap before they tired of their game. What a thrill to be a man! What freedom! Should I decide to take such a jump, it would most assuredly have to be under cover of darkness. I slammed several pins into a quick knot of hair at the base of my neck, wincing as one scraped along my scalp, then turned toward the door. I'd last heard a man pass by and jump five minutes ago. But I'd been around the corner, in my bathroom. Were they done? Was I too late? I rushed to the door and opened it—

Right as Yves let Will come through the gate, five feet away.

"Will," I said, smiling and studiously keeping my eyes on his, rather than on the wide expanse of his muscled chest and narrow waist below. Dripping wet and plainly freezing, he hugged himself, but his grin was sheepish as well as wide. "Was your bath inside the chateau not acceptable?" I asked.

"This is far more invigorating," he said, nodding back toward the gate and running a hand through his wet hair.

"I can imagine," I said, turning to close the door.

"Wait," he said, stepping forward, right beside me. I held my breath. But his eyes were on my room, not me. "May I?" he asked, barely glancing down at me, already moving past.

"Of course," I said, gesturing in. I remained in the hallway, rolling the big key in my hands. It'd hardly be proper for me to be in there with him. I could already feel the detective's eyes on my back. But I watched him, dripping on the fine, wood floor. "What is it, Will?"

"It's this *place*," he breathed, looking up and around. His eyes followed the lines of the ceiling, and then he moved to the wall, his fingers tracing the lines of some of the graffiti I had traced the night before. It was silly, really. But in that moment, I felt as if we had touched, rather than merely touching the same etchings in wood and stone. I looked away, aware that my eyes were drawn too often to his skin, rather than to the things he was so clearly admiring.

He appeared beside me then, perilously close. "Forgive me, Cora," he said. "I forgot myself when I saw those arches." He reached up and slicked his wet brown hair back again. "I wager you were assigned the finest room of all. This place is fantastic."

"Indeed," I said, hoping he'd move on. "It's a veritable suite."

"Do you mind if I bring Uncle down to see it?"

"Not at all."

He went to the door and wavered, gesturing to his soggy trousers. "I'm hardly in a state to escort you."

"No," I said, hurriedly, thinking it could not get any more uncomfortable. "Please. Go on. I'll see you up top."

"I fear my leaping is done for the day," he said, rubbing his arms again, drawing my attention to biceps and triceps that rippled with each movement…. "I'd best get to my room and change before Uncle finds out what we are up to. At least, if I hope to take part again tomorrow."

I nodded, keeping my eyes to the floor. "I'll see you in the dining hall."

"All right. Should I send someone down for you?"

"William McCabe," I said, looking up to meet his warm brown eyes. "I think I'm capable of walking a couple flights of stairs on my own. Besides, Yves is here."

"Good," he said, smiling at me, glancing over at the detective, then back to me, a wet lock of hair falling toward his eyes. Never, ever had I thought he looked more handsome. I found myself wishing we were alone. That I could say…what? Something to keep him there. With me. For just a second longer. But then he smiled, turned, and took the stairs, two at a time.

The clang of the gate shook me out of my reverie, and I turned to find Hugh, Felix, and Arthur coming through, Yves locking it behind them. At least they were in proper bathing costumes, adequately covered from neck to knee. "Well, well, well," Hugh said, a laugh on his breath as he looked up the stairs to see Will disappear. "Keeping company in the hallway?"

Arthur smiled and ducked past us, as dripping wet as the others were. "Good morning," he said, giving me a friendly wave before opening his door across the hall.

"Truly, is there not something between you and our Will that might give Pierre a run for his money?" Hugh whispered, nudging me.

I caught Art's blue-eyed gaze as he shut his door, clearly hearing every word.

"Hugh, leave her be," Felix said, grabbing hold of his friend's arm and yanking him past me. "Come. We need to change and get to the breakfast room, or the bear will skin *us* alive."

"I'm coming," Hugh said, yanking his arm from Felix's grip. My brother led the way, and Hugh made a polite offer of his arm.

Resignedly, I climbed the steps with him, suddenly more than ready to be in the company of our hosts and guardians.

"You should try it, Cora," Hugh said, lifting one brow in a subtle challenge. "The jump, I mean. Adrien leaps three times each morning, rain or shine. It's quite bracing."

I nodded noncommittally. If I were to jump, the last person I wanted watching me was Hugh Morgan. He'd seen me once in my bathing costume. And I sincerely hoped it would never occur again. Even the memory of his wolfish eyes running over me from head to toe sent a shiver down my back.

"What did you think of your mad jump into the Rhône this morning, Mr. Stapleton?" Lil asked him, casting him her best attempt at a flirtatious smile.

I frowned. Arthur was much too old for her. That wasn't quite fair—there were plenty of May-December romances—but there was something about him that made me hesitate…something I couldn't quite grasp. It nagged at me.

"I thought it was perhaps the most sane thing I've done of late," he returned.

"Oh? How so?" I asked.

He sat next to Will in the backward-facing seat of our rented motorcar, across from us. The two shared a smile. Their hair was not yet quite dry, and their faces held fresh color.

"Sometimes a man just needs to remember he's alive," Arthur said to me, his blue eyes sweeping over Lillian, too. "You step off a ledge like that, and every second feels like a minute. Your whole life runs through your mind as if it's about to end, and you have the maddest desire to turn and try to catch yourself, claw your way back. But then you're falling, piercing the water, going under, under, under. You reach for the sky, kicking for all you're worth, desperate for air, and when your face breaks the surface..." He took off his bowler hat, ran a hand through his blond hair, and then settled it again. "There isn't anything quite like it. Wouldn't you agree, McCabe?"

"Indeed," Will said, a glint in his warm eyes. "I can see why our host jumps each morn. It's quite the way to start the day."

The motorcar's engine roared to life, and the driver got in at last. We joined the caravan of three other vehicles carrying the rest of our traveling party, servants, and guardians off to visit the town of Saint-Rémy-de-Provence, which had its own Roman ruins but was more famous for being where the seer Nostradamus was born, and where van Gogh painted *The Starry Night* during a stay in a place for the mentally infirm.

"Perhaps I'll have to attempt a leap myself," I said, thinking over the hot, dry day ahead of us and how welcome a swim would feel.

"I think not," Will said, his brow lowering. "Uncle Stuart nearly had a fit of apoplexy when he learned we had attempted it. He would never hear of our fairer companions doing so."

"Pish," said Lillian. "If the boys can do it, so can we!"

Arthur smiled in his catlike way. "It's a different thing, being on the edge of the precipice. Ten dollars says you won't get farther than thinking about it."

"Ten dollars!" I said, outraged by both his attempt to lure my sister in to the jump and his unseemly, costly bet.

His eyes widened at my response. "I only propose a gentlemanly wager," he said. "Forgive me if I've offended you or your sister." He seemed sincere.

"Not at all," I said, my tone lower, less defensive. "It's only that—"

"I'll take your wager, Mr. Stapleton," Lillian said, reaching out her hand to shake his in the manner of men.

"Lillian."

"No, Cora. I'm a woman grown, with quite a generous bank account. If I wish to make it ten dollars fatter with Mr. Stapleton's money, I shall do it."

Art threw his head back and laughed at her playful audacity. "We shall see, Miss Kensington. We shall see."

I sighed and cast a helpless glance in Will's direction, but he only gave me a shrug. I looked away, out to the rocky landscape beside us. Part of me wanted to stop her. But how could I do that when there was a part of myself that wanted to do the same? Leap, fly, plunge… for a moment, aware of little other than the feel of the wind in my hair and the rush of adventure to tell me I was truly alive.

My life…I shook my head and thought about how mad this whole adventure was. A girl who'd come from a dirt-poor farm in Montana now dressed in such finery, riding in luxurious motorcars, guarded by fierce men determined to keep others from ever attacking us again. That I'd even been involved in such an attack was monumental in itself. I could never have imagined such a dramatic turn of events. And thinking it through, it made me so weary I wished

I could hop out and somehow run across these foreign countries, across the sea, all the way home.

I stared up at the white, chalky cliffs, wishing, for the moment, that they were the blue, snowcapped peaks of my youth.

"Are you yet with us here in France, Miss Cora?" Arthur asked over the roar of the engine and the wind from the open window.

I looked up at him in surprise. Were my thoughts so apparent?

"In part," I said, not missing Will's slight scowl. Was it my imagination, or did Arthur's faint flirtation irritate him? "I miss my home in Montana."

"Ahh, yes. I hear the Kensingtons have a fine manor in Butte."

"Or is it the farm?" Lillian asked, looping her arm through mine. "I bet you're homesick for your farm."

"Farm?" Arthur said with pleasure lighting his eyes. "I thought Felix misspoke last night...I hardly imagined the Kensington clan residing in anything short of the world's finest abodes."

"You might be surprised," I said, giving him a sly smile for once. *Let him wonder over that*, I thought. "So, tell me," I said, clapping my gloved hands together. "William, what say you of our mighty prophet Nostradamus? Was he a godly prophet or an evil hack preying upon innocent medieval minds?"

"You know of Nostradamus?" Will said, his eyes warming as they met mine.

"A little. We studied the Medicis and learned that Catherine was quite the admirer of the man, making him her son's physician."

Will nodded. "He called himself a doctor, but he was thrown out of medical school. He was largely self-trained, after traveling for years, studying the art of herbal medicines. The plague took his first wife and children from him. In subsequent waves of the disease, he did his best to save others."

"But it was his prophecies that made him most famous, correct?" Arthur asked.

"Indeed. Some say he wrote of the great fire of London in 1666, as well as of the rise of Napoleon."

"How thrilling!" Lillian said, clapping her hands together. "What else?"

Will shrugged and shook his head. "You mustn't give it too much credence, Lillian. He attached no specific dates, lending plenty of room for loose interpretations to be 'proven' in time. He wrote of floods, wars, famine in the years ahead of us yet."

"How did he learn of such things so far in advance?" she pressed. "Séances? A trance?"

"No, no. And you mustn't consider such things glamorous," Will told her gently. "The man himself feared the Inquisition, and for good reason…. He was in tenuous territory. It was fortunate for him that prophets and astrologers were exempt from the hunt for heretics."

"But do you believe he had the gift? That he was a true prophet?" Lil asked.

Will gave her a kind smile. I liked that he seemed to be able to show that he cared even as he corrected. And it was always wrapped in a quiet strength. Being around him was reassuring. Calming. "I personally think he was a student of human nature and history, watching the rise and fall of rulers and kingdoms, the rhythm of nature in drought and flood. His predictions were merely recitations of those observations. But you can decide for yourself."

————◇◇◇————

~William~

Will wasn't certain what Stapleton's game was, but there was definitely a game in play. Hugh had invited him along on their excursion before Will had had the opportunity to intervene. His uncle preferred that they travel with only their clients. It was a common issue on the tour—once acquaintances latched on they were difficult to shake loose. But Kensington and Morgan were paying for this tour, not Stapleton, so while an afternoon together was acceptable, Will hoped the man would have the good sense to bow out in the coming days.

Will picked at a loose thread around the button on his jacket, electing to wrap it around the base of the button rather than risk pulling it and sending the button flying. He felt God's nudge and knew his Father was asking him about his real agitation over Arthur's presence.

Truth be told, it was because he was finally free of Richelieu. Or at least, Cora was free of Richelieu for a few precious days, and he'd hoped he'd be able to find more time with her. He hadn't expected another man to enter the picture, more than nominally curious about the newest Miss Kensington.

But he had no right to such feelings. He was her guardian, her tutor, her guide, nothing more. To lay claim to anything else would endanger every future goal he'd ever held. If Wallace Kensington thought for a moment that Will held any illusions that something might come of his friendship with Cora, the consequences would be grave indeed. He'd be dismissed on the spot; his uncle would have to carry on without him—and Will doubted he had the stamina to do so—and the family business itself would be in jeopardy. Who would send their daughters on future tours if word got out that the guide preyed upon innocent young females given to his care?

His eyes narrowed as they pulled to a stop and Cora leaned forward to admire the Autographic Kodak camera that Arthur pulled from his pocket and carefully began to wind.

"Oh, take our photograph!" Lillian said, leaning toward Cora.

"Gladly," Arthur said, stretching out the lens and leaning over the viewing piece, then clicking the button at the end of a wire. He opened a small window on the back and wrote with a special pen, reading his words as he did so. "Two of the loveliest women in all Provence—Cora and Lillian Kensington."

"Indeed," Will muttered, not waiting for the driver before he opened the small door and escaped, stretching out his long legs and brushing out his trousers. He lifted his hand to Lillian, helping her step down, and then Cora. Arthur followed, and Felix came alongside him, asking about his camera.

"I should pick up one myself. It'd be an ideal way to document our travels," Felix said.

"Of course!" Arthur said. "It's a shame you haven't had one to date."

"I'm afraid my uncle doesn't favor them," Will said regretfully, coming up on Arthur's other side. "He prefers our clients catalog their own memories. Or sketch or journal."

"Perhaps it's time for your uncle to embrace the future," Arthur said lowly, as the old bear lumbered toward them.

Will bristled at his words. Over the course of the afternoon, Arthur took three rolls of film—thirty-six frames—of the Kensingtons and Morgans attempting their hand at pétanque with old men in berets beneath the slim shade of dry, city-bound trees, on hard dirt ideal for the rolling-ball game. Will resented Art's continual demand for the group to hold still as he documented the moment, and Uncle Stuart's jowls began to grow red with irritation as it went on.

Art took photographs of them listening to Uncle Stuart sharing a legend of Nostradamus's burial—that the Provençal-born prophet had a brass plate on his chest with the date his body would be disinterred, even when he'd left explicit instructions never to disinter his remains. Art took photographs of them exiting the Roman ruins of the mausoleum. And he took photographs of them sitting in two rows before blank canvasses, attempting to re-create van Gogh's famous painting of a night sky as afternoon shadows grew deep. It seemed he had no regard for the cost of the film, or the coming cost of developing, telling the group that the photographs could be printed out on special paper and mailed home as postcards.

More often than naught, Cora was at the center of his compositions. Will was certain of it. His eyes narrowed, and for the first time, he sincerely hoped Richelieu would show up this week in Provence.

I'd rather take the devil I know than the devil I don't.

———◦◇◦———

~Cora~

I resisted the pull of the dive for the next couple of days. At first my resolve was to give Lillian a good example, after she hovered on the brink of the castle wall and ultimately had to forfeit ten dollars to

Arthur—which he graciously tried to refuse. Will had insisted he accept it, because he wanted Lil to remember that she ought not wager at all.

But after another dry and dusty day about in the countryside, I found the pull increasingly difficult to ignore; I caught myself constantly daydreaming of my leap, especially after watching the men pierce the water for three days in a row from my secret view on my balcony. Our suppers, shared on the sprawling stone patio of the chateau with a pleasant breeze off the river, eased my angst some. We dined together outside on the wide porch, eating roasted chicken with lemon and sprigs of fresh rosemary and crepes filled with mushrooms and cream. But the river seemed to whisper to me, and I looked to her again and again. When dinner was done, we milled about, sipping at champagne with raspberries bobbing in the bubbly depth, posing for a new round of photographs by Arthur. We admired the setting sun, which cast the river below us into a deeper hue of teal, and it seemed to call to me again, enticing me in.

Plus, I simply wanted to prove it to myself. That I could do it, regardless of Will's views that it wasn't an exercise for the "fairer sex." I wouldn't halt where Lillian had. I'd practice on my own tonight, under cover of darkness. Would they not be surprised, come morning, when I made my leap with confidence? I'd step into the air and remember to breathe on the way down so that I could hold my breath until I broke the surface again and—

"Penny for your thoughts," Will said, sitting down on the wall as I stood gazing at the river. He sipped at his champagne, his eyes shifting over the others, then sidling back up to me.

"Oh," I said, wondering if I dared to tell him. Would he try to stop me? "I was just considering putting on my bathing costume and joining you gents come morn for a leap into the Rhône."

He studied me with slightly narrowed eyes, as if he knew I wasn't telling him the exact truth, but then he turned and looked over the edge. "It's a big jump. Are you not scared?"

"Aren't you?"

"Every time," he said with a conspiratorial grin. "But that's part of the thrill."

I peered over the edge with him, watching as the river swirled here and there in minor eddies and a leaf-laden branch drifted by. "Is it cold?"

"Not as cold as the lake. Not as warm as the sea."

"And is it deep? There are no rocks to watch out for?"

"If you can get several feet out, it plunges straight down a good thirty feet. I've never seen or touched bottom." He eyed me. "Maybe it's best you skip it. Or if it's a swim you crave, simply walk down the stairs, through the gates. It's far more ladylike."

"Maybe," I said lightly. "Though I'm still more farm girl than a lady." It chafed, the idea that we couldn't do as the men had without being censured, judged. I took a sip of champagne. "Will, what do you think of women having the vote?"

His eyebrows lifted. "What? Where did that come from?"

"Where has it not come from?" I returned. "It's a part of conversation, in newspapers, everywhere. Just today, Vivian and Lil were talking about it."

He studied the river a moment, apparently gathering his thoughts. "I think women should have a say," he said carefully. "And giving them a vote is a fair and prudent call. That said, women need to put their heads to understanding the issues before they cast a vote."

"As should men," I said.

"Agreed. Far too many don't. They vote by party alone, never really paying attention to what a change might do. They get swayed by a speech, a man's charisma, rather than forming their own opinion."

I nodded, wondering if Will had ever been swayed on any front. I admired that about him, his fortitude. He was steady, like a boulder in the river—the water went by, but it was never pulled under.

"Would you vote, Cora, if given the opportunity?"

"Of course. I'd imagine we women would appreciate the opportunity more than men. It's like me being here on the tour." I glanced over my shoulder at my traveling companions. "They enjoy it. But how many other journeys have they been on? This is one of many, I'd wager. I've never been anywhere other than Normal School."

"And that mitigates some of their appreciation?"

I shrugged a little. "I can't know for sure. But that's what I'd guess."

He lifted his chin, and I studied his profile as his eyes scanned the castle and woods of the far side of the river. Then his eyes shifted to mine. I forced myself not to look away, allowing him to know I'd been watching him. "You and I are in agreement," he said softly. "We appreciate the things we have to fight for."

A chill ran down my back. He did not look away. What was he saying? Why did I get the idea that he spoke of fighting for *me*?

"What're you two conspiring over?" Felix said, edging near with Arthur in tow. We both looked to them with some relief.

"Your sister believes she's ready to vote. And leap into the Rhône."

"What? A suffragette diver among us?" Felix said in wonder, smiling at me. "Perhaps you're more a Kensington than I imagined. Though heaven knows I can't convince Lil to make the jump now that she's stared down the executioner's blade. And Vivian believes it to be the last thing you women should be doing."

"Maybe the Diehls are more hearty stock than the Kensingtons," I whispered to him.

He hooted and ducked his head. "Don't let the girls hear you say that."

"I won't." I smiled. I saw that Arthur's eyes darted from my brother to me and back again. Had he overheard my whisper? I knew I was blushing, and I turned to study the river again, sipping from my glass of champagne.

"If you jumped with me tomorrow, they might follow," Felix said.

"Maybe. It's a far piece," I allowed, gesturing toward the water. "Best for everyone to make their own decisions and not feel undue pressure."

"Agreed," Will said. "But be advised that once the women get involved, Uncle will likely put a stop to it. He was very relieved when Lillian turned back yesterday."

"If everyone will simply refrain from getting killed, all will be well," Felix said.

"Yes," Will said with a smile. "It would be most helpful if everyone abided by that rule."

I covered a pretend yawn. "Well, gentlemen, tomorrow is a new day. I believe I must turn in. After the long day and heat of the sun, I confess I'm most eager to return to my novel."

"Are you reading Lawrence's *Sons and Lovers?*" Hugh teased, enjoying my look of dismay.

"Pish," Andrew said, coming alongside him, "that book is nothing but an Oedipal indulgence for the working classes."

"That's exactly what makes it so engaging," Arthur said, perching on the chateau wall and bending to light a cigarette. He passed a box around, offering cigarettes to the others, and then lit Hugh's as well, tossing the stub of his match over the edge, letting it fall to the river below. "I'd think you would find it uniquely engaging, given its mining backdrop."

"You'd think wrong," Andrew said.

"Perhaps you'd enjoy *Autobiography of an Ex-Colored Man,*" Arthur said, eyeing me and blowing smoke slowly from the corner of his lips.

"Oh?" I said, throwing him a confused look. "Why would you say so?"

"It's quite an engaging read. The main character is of mixed race. He must decide between embracing his Negro culture by engaging in ragtime music or passing as white and living a mediocre existence as a common man." He took a steady drag on his cigarette, never releasing me from his gaze.

I stilled even as the men about me shifted uneasily. So…he knew. About my history. Had Pierre told Celine and Celine told him? Or Hugh? Felix, even? I straightened my shoulders. It mattered not. Right? I was through with hiding. I lifted my chin. "It does sound engaging," I said, staring right back into his eyes. "I'll have to find a copy the next time we're in a bookshop."

Will and Felix straightened and nodded in my direction, bidding me good night. I passed by the others, saying good night to each of them, as well as thanking our hosts. Yves followed me at a distance of ten feet, my silent guard. At first I'd believed he never slept, but over the last couple of days I learned that Claude relieved him on duty by the gate below at midnight.

In my suite, Anna helped me undress and put on a fresh night-gown, then she brushed out my hair. I lifted my hand, irritated to see it trembling. I thought it was past me—my desire to keep my parentage a secret. I thought I'd embraced who I was. Accepted it. I thought about my teasing words to Felix, about me being of sturdier stock than my half sisters. His drunken comment that I was a scrapper. Why was all that permissible, but a near stranger's discovery of the truth enough to set me to trembling? "Lay out my bathing costume, will you, Anna? I wish to make the leap with the young gentlemen in the morning before we begin our day."

"Ach," she said. "Don't tell me you're to be a part of that nonsense."

I forced a smile and looked at her reflection in the mirror. "I'm most certainly going to be a part of that nonsense. Don't you wish to give it a go yourself?"

"Not a'tall, miss. Never been one for more than a shallow bath-tub full of water."

"Do you know how to swim?"

She shook her head. "No call to learn, anyway," she said, cutting off my next question.

"You don't know what you're missing." I winced as she hit a knot and dragged the horsehair brush through it.

"We mustn't always pine after what we think we're missing, miss," she said, cocking a brow and nodding toward me. She set down the brush and then swiftly wound my hair in a long, thick braid. "Some things are just not ours to be had."

"Or they *are* ours, if we simply reach out and take them."

"Hmm," she said, eyes on my hair.

"Are you afraid? Honestly?"

"Honestly, yes," she said, tying the end of my braid with a tight knot of string. "Sometimes fear is something we must battle through. Other times it's something the Lord gives us to warn us to take heed." She left me then, going directly to my third trunk at the side of the room, and pulled out my bathing costume. She laid it on a sitting chair. I thought I saw her shaking her head a bit.

"Thank you, Anna."

"Good night, miss."

She closed the door behind her, as carefully as if I were already slumbering on and might be disturbed. Twilight still clung to the skies, and so I climbed into bed, taking my novel from the side table and turning up the flame on the lamp. But my eyes refused to focus on the words on the page. Again and again, my eyes went to the chair and my bathing costume and then the window.

I had to wait until dark. Under cover of darkness, by the light of the moon, I'd leap.

CHAPTER THREE

~William~

The men sat in a line of chairs, watching as a full moon rose over the horizon, smoking the last of their cigars. The women had long departed, and twilight had just given way to navy sky. The air was still warm but blessedly cooler than the heat of the day, and Will found himself looking forward to the morning's plunge, just as surely as Cora was. Or perhaps she'd elect to take the more conservative route and wade from the shoreline.

A smile tugged at his lips. He knew enough about Cora Diehl Kensington to know that wasn't possible. And what was that look about this evening? When he'd turned to find her bright blue eyes studying him, not looking away. It had made him itch to take her hand in his. Her delicate fingers…fingers that other men so easily handled, kissed in greeting, even. And yet he had no right. *No right. Get it through your skull, McCabe*, he told himself. *It can't be.* Had they been two normal people, not client and guide… But tonight, before the others joined them, when it had just been the two of them…

He shook his head and stared up into the stars above them, wondering if he might be slowly going mad as van Gogh had in this same countryside. He told himself it was all his imagination. But then he thought again of that moment together. Out from under Pierre de Richelieu's watchful gaze, Cora had turned a few degrees in his direction. If he turned a few degrees too…

He rose and walked along the wall, looking below to the river, warm cream stripes of reflected light from the chateau dancing in it—from Cora's suite below? He tried to drive away his traitorous, treacherous thoughts. After a while, the others said good night, and his uncle came to join him. Stuart took a deep draw on his cigar and then slowly blew the sweet smoke out. It drifted around Will and past him on the breeze. Stuart stamped out the stub of his cigar on the wall and casually let the remains fall to the river.

"I heard from Wallace Kensington today," the old man said at last.

Will froze. So word had finally arrived. "And?"

"He applauds our clients' fortitude and tenacity, as well as our astute choice to add more guardians to our traveling troop."

Will dared to take a breath. "And?" he repeated.

"And he wants assurances that we left the kidnappers behind in Paris."

Will considered that a moment. "There's no way to know. You know as well as I that those two escaped."

"Chances are that they've gone underground, though. Without the element of surprise—now that we know what lengths they'd go to—we won't be caught unawares again. They'll likely move on to easier targets."

"You hope." Will stamped out his cigar too and tossed it to the water, the taste no longer appealing to him.

"I hope."

"Not many travelers on the road that could fetch the ransom that one of these would," Will said, nodding over his shoulder at the chateau.

"Indeed. Are you saying you wish to take the safe road and return home? Forego our extra pay? Let alone our complete fee for the tour…"

Will studied the water, far below. "In my experience, the safe road rarely leads to growth, depth, edification."

Uncle Stuart clapped him on the shoulder. "Sleep on it. Let's talk, before breakfast, before we put it to the others and make sure they're all game to carry on. Kensington and Morgan are en route. They plan to rendezvous with us in Vienna to make certain all is well before we venture into Italy."

"Ahh." So the fathers were willing to let the chicks stretch their wings, to a point. In Vienna, they would decide for themselves if the tour was to continue.

"Think about it, Will. What assurances can we offer them when it comes time? We have to prepare our argument."

"Best to let the children persuade them. They've done all right so far."

"Perhaps," Stuart said, looking as weary as Will felt. He turned to go, his shoulders stooped and every step a clear effort.

"Sleep well, Uncle."

"You're not turning in?" he asked, looking at Will over his shoulder.

"Not yet. I think I should keep an eye out. Make sure that Felix and Hugh don't get it in their heads that they should sneak out to that cabaret in town. I heard them mention it under their breath. If they do, I'll wake Antonio and tag along."

"If we're down by you four, be certain you alert the guards."

"I will. Good night."

"Good night, Will."

Alone at last, Will climbed on top of the short wall and let his legs dangle over the far side for a while. The moon climbed high enough to spread glittered light across the surface of the water, shimmering like diamonds. The warm breeze covered him, surrounded him, welcomed him. He breathed in, feeling that such a moment ought to bring him only deep contentment. And yet he felt nothing but the roiling of his mind, churning over the events of the day.

———◇◇◇———

~Cora~

I tiptoed out onto the portico and cocked my head, listening for the men above. It seemed they had all retired at last, leaving me alone to appreciate the river on my own. In the distance, across the river in Beaucaire, I could hear singing, and it made me smile. Lights from the medieval castle across from us streamed in wavy, golden reflections over the water, competing with the moonlight, silver and glittering.

I took a deep breath, loving the moment. The perfection of the air—not too hot, not too cold—the feel of the breeze, carrying the scent of the water and reeds and loamy earth.

I dropped my robe to the cool marble tiles beneath my feet and climbed to the edge of the balcony rail. I listened a moment longer, and, hearing nothing, decided that the night was mine alone. How could they all depart? Leave this magnificent hour with none but me to admire it? *Thank You, Lord*, I breathed. *For this opportunity. For the chance to be on this tour. To be in this castle, above this river... Regardless of what it costs me, thank You. Help me to embrace my new life. Lead me to embrace what I ought and ignore what I ought.*

My heart raced. I paused, wondering if it was the Lord, cautioning me. But my perch was twenty feet lower than the others'. What harm could come to me here? And if I couldn't do this now, how could I face Felix come morn and confidently step up to the wall beside him? They all seemed to need a woman to show them what courage looked like. Strength. Not pandering toward social convention or acceptance. I needed to show them all—I thought, remembering their bemused expressions—so that I might gain their respect. True relationship.

I glanced below again to the moving water. Not overthinking the jump was key. Moments belonged to those who acted. Not those who thought about acting.

Remembering how we used to swing from a rope and let ourselves go, dropping into a haystack inside the barn, I shoved off from the portico rail. I milled my arms as my feet moved in front of me. *Oh no.* I wasn't vertical—far too flat. I barely had time to take a breath before my legs, back, and head slammed painfully to the surface.

And then I was sinking, in more ways than one. The dark waters closing in above me. Realizing too late that I felt too stunned to move, to fight for the surface, to even breathe...

———◇◇◇———

~William~

As soon as he heard the splash, he knew it was Cora.

He'd not seen her leap, but the impact, directly below her portico, told him all he needed to know. *Foolish girl! In the dark? Alone?* He yanked off his shoes and pulled off his tie, searching the water, gradually stilling as the bubbles ceased to rise and the current covered all traces of her entry. Where was she? Why had she not surfaced?

He clambered to the wall and jumped, praying she wasn't caught beneath among the rocks and reeds. *Help me, Lord. Help me find her.* It seemed to take forever for his drop to come to an end, and longer for him to rise to the surface. He kicked and used his arms to reach the top. When he did, he gasped for air and looked around. In the moonlight, he could plainly see she had not yet risen from the river's hold. *No. No, no, no...* He dived, kicking and pulling himself down, toward the side. *Show me where she is, Lord. Please don't let her die. Please...*

He felt around madly, stretching in all directions, wondering if she was just out of reach, caught by river reeds at the ankle.... His lungs screamed for air and he rose, anxious to grab a breath and dive again. But just as he prepared to do so, he caught a glimpse in the moonlight of a head, a shoulder, ten feet away. Drifting away from him, facedown.

He swam over to her, turned her over, and, with an arm hooked around her chest, her head resting on his shoulder, he kicked like mad to reach the rocks. Once there, he took hold of a boulder and did his best to get a foothold on the slimy, slippery stones below to heave her up onto it. He managed to do so before slipping, then righted himself and clambered up. Will lifted her and carried her to the small concrete platform before the gate.

"C'mon, Cora. Stay with me," he panted, bending to listen for breath. He took her wrist and felt for a pulse.

No breath. No beat.

No, Lord. No! Help me!

He bent her head and paused a moment, then sealed his lips against hers and blew in, watching as her chest rose. He pressed against her belly, trying to force the water from her lungs, then returned to blow into her mouth. Years ago, his uncle had befriended a Swiss doctor who had told them of such techniques among midwives in the mountains. Last year, a German physician had shared the story of doing much the same thing, saving a young boy who'd been under water until he was blue....

Will prayed he'd not just been telling a tale.

He bent and blew into her mouth again, then pressed against her belly again. "C'mon, Cora. C'mon, sweetheart. Breathe." Over and over again he repeated his task, the fear rising in his throat.

But then she choked, sputtering and spitting water. Quickly, he turned her to her side, and she spewed river water from her lungs and continued to cough. But she was breathing! She was breathing!

Thank You, Lord. Thank You, thank You...

He couldn't help himself. He gathered her into his arms and leaned against the chateau wall, watching her, waiting for her to breathe without coughing. He panted, trying to catch his own breath.

"Will," she whispered, staring at him a moment and then closing her eyes and wincing as if in pain.

"What is it? Are you hurting?" he said.

"No, no," she said, opening her eyes again, her long lashes clumping with droplets of water. "Well, yes, my head hurts. But I'm all right. Will…you saved me."

"I…I guess I did."

"I'm sorry."

He smiled. "That I saved you?"

"That I scared you," she said, closing her eyes, her teeth chattering. "I'm so dizzy."

"Did you hit your head on a rock?"

"I don't know. I don't remember. I hit the water really hard."

He took a deep breath and rose with her in his arms. "Let's get you upstairs. You need to get warm, and I need to call a physician."

"No," she said, resting her head against his shoulder, which Will took to mean she was *really* dizzy. The Cora he knew never admitted to weakness, not if she could help it. "I mean, yes to getting warm. But no doctor."

From around his neck he pulled a key, one the butler had given him the morning they arrived, unlocked the gate, and carried her through it. They stood in the dark passageway beneath the chateau. "Cora, I need to send for a doctor. If you hit your head, you may have a concussion. I know for a fact that you almost drowned."

"And now that's passed. I simply need rest. The dizziness will abate."

He resisted a retort. Climbing two flights of stairs with her in his arms hardly left him with enough oxygen to debate, so he remained quiet, thinking about his options. Once at the top, he kicked at the second gate, looking at Claude, who was dozing in the hall across from Cora's door. He had no key for this one. "Claude," he grunted in irritation, frustrated that the man had allowed her to jump, even if he couldn't truly be held accountable. After all, who would think that Cora might slip out of her room via the river?

Claude leaped up and wiped his eyes, as if he couldn't quite believe what he was seeing. *"Monsieur,"* he said, fumbling for the key in his pocket, fishing it out. *"Qu'est-ce qui s'est passé?"* What happened?

"The lady chose to make the jump alone and landed oddly." Will glanced down at Cora. She was frightfully pale in the light of the hall lamp and shivering. He steeled himself. He needed to get a doctor to her side. Now. "Stay with me, Cora," he said, squeezing her.

Her big blue eyes opened, and she blinked. She looked like a soggy China doll.

"Fished from the Rhône, you're as lovely as ever, Cora Kensington," he said grimly.

"Thanks to you," she muttered.

Claude opened the gate and then her door. Arthur Stapleton peeked out from his room. His feet were bare, his shirt unbuttoned. "Everything all right?"

"No," Will said. "Cora's had an accident." He carried her into her room and set her on the bed, Art and Claude right behind him. "Go and fetch my uncle as well as her maid," he said to the detective.

"Oui, monsieur," Claude said. He scurried out of her suite.

"Will, I don't want a doctor," Cora said as he hurriedly covered her with a thick blanket, wet bathing costume and all.

"If you could see yourself, Cora," he said, pushing back his wet hair. "Your teeth are chattering. Your lips are practically blue!"

"She jumped? In the dark?" Art asked in consternation, moving around to the other side of the bed and lighting a lamp, then a wall sconce.

Will gestured toward the French doors. "Just from her balcony. Still, high enough to knock her unconscious."

"Here's another blanket," Art said, handing it to Will from a rack to one side. He moved to turn on the desk light too—the lone electrical lamp in the room. Light flooded over Cora.

"The chattering…will stop…in a moment." She closed her eyes, her forehead wrinkling as if she were concentrating.

"And your dizziness?"

"It will abate. Promise me, no doctor."

Will frowned at her as he settled the fresh blanket across her and leaned over until he was in her line of vision. "Why not? If ever there was cause it's—"

The distinct sound of a Kodak *click* made him glance up at Art, but the man was straightening as if he was stretching, one hand behind his back.

"Because if my father hears of this," Cora said, "on top of what happened in Paris, our tour will be over. And it will be my fault."

He stilled. She was right. But his heart told him she should be examined. To make certain all was well. She took his hand in both of hers, sending a shiver up his arms, every nerve suddenly at attention. "Thank you, Will."

Will heard the mechanical *click* sound again and tore his eyes from hers, over to Arthur again. But the man was turning. "I'll go and see what's detaining Claude," Art said. "I agree with you, McCabe," he said over his shoulder. "We ought to fetch a physician."

A hundred questions bombarded his mind at once. But Anna entered then, her night cap askew, her robe hastily tied around her waist, and, right after her, Uncle Stuart and Claude. Art hovered in the background, by the door.

Stuart looked at them both with wide eyes as Will hastily rose from the edge of her bed. The bear strode over to their young client, her wet hair strewn across the pillow, and looked over to Will. "She made the jump?"

"But not the landing," Will said.

"I told you that that tomfoolery would come to no good end," Uncle said as Anna shooed them out the door so she could change her mistress out of her wet clothes and closed it behind them.

In the hallway, Will paced. "Right after you reminded me it was good for our clients to do as the natives. This leap to the river is what the lord of this castle does," he said, waving about him.

"It is quite the experience," Arthur put in.

"It's one thing for the young men," Stuart said to them both. "But the young ladies?" He shook his head and settled his chin in hand.

"Come now, Uncle. Such a double standard! This was as likely to happen to Felix as it was to Cora!" But doubt washed through him. Was it his fault? For encouraging her? Not *discouraging* her? Their conversation about the vote came back to him. Had that been a deciding factor for her? Some mad desire for equality?

"Will," Stuart barked. He looked up. Apparently this wasn't the first time his uncle had said his name. Slowly, he followed the old man's gaze to the stairway.

Antonio had arrived. "Unfortunately, I must add to your burdens, Mr. McCabe, William." He paused to meet their gazes. "The young gents have slipped away to the local cabaret. I'll head out after them, but I wondered if Will could join me."

Stuart groaned and lifted a hand to his gray head. "Go," he grunted. "The last thing we need is for another of our clients to come to a poor end this night."

"If I can be of service," Arthur said, "I can go with Antonio." His keen eyes moved to Will. "In case you'd rather remain here with Cora."

"If they've been imbibing, it may take a number of us to bring them home," Will said. "They had plenty to drink even before they left. But I have to change." Will looked down at his wet trousers.

"Then go change!" his uncle erupted. "Get on with it!"

Will felt his cheeks burn, chastened as if he were a schoolboy. Still, he hesitated and lifted a hand. "You mustn't call a doctor. She is cold. Shaken. But she will be fine, come morning."

Uncle Stuart lowered his bushy eyebrows. "You are certain."

"Fairly certain. And as she said, if her father hears of this, so soon after our escapade in Paris…"

Uncle Stuart raised one hand and shook his head in agitation. "Fine! Fine. I shall see to the girl. You go and collect the boys. Please…" he said, turning to Antonio. "Tell me that some of our charges are safely in bed this night."

Antonio gave him a rueful smile. "Vivian, Andrew, Lillian, and Nell are all accounted for. Only masters Felix and Hugh have slipped away."

"Thank heaven for that." His droopy, weary eyes met Will's again. "Well? Why are you still here, son? Go!"

"Yes, sir," William muttered, turning away. But as he wearily climbed the stairs, he wondered if they'd all be best off if the tour was canceled and everyone went home.

Because his heart was at war with his mind, remembering the feel of Cora in his arms, the way her small hands felt in his, the wonderment in her eyes when she said *you saved me...*

Something had shifted in that moment. Nearly losing her had almost stopped his own heart from beating. And bringing her back made it seem as if his heart now beat to a new rhythm of its own.

CHAPTER FOUR

~William~

The closer they got to town, the more frustrated Will became. How long did he have to go, trailing the progeny of the world's rich and famous and hauling them to safety? Where was the justice in it? *How is this fair, Lord? What is Your plan for me in this? Help me to learn it, so I can venture on to some other battle....*

They found Felix and Hugh in the village, in a narrow cabaret that opened onto a seating area and tiny stage; it was so late, the show was over. Will breathed a sigh of relief even as he choked on the thick smoke. The young men were drinking wine out of ceramic cups, a local maid on each arm as they made stumbling attempts to speak to them in French. Antonio laughed and shared a knowing look with Arthur. But Will was feeling anything but amused, only wishing he was back at the chateau, watching over Cora or falling into his bed for some much-needed sleep.

"C'mon," Will said over his shoulder to Antonio. "Let's pry them out of this place, or none of us will get a blessed hour of sleep tonight."

Not that sleep was likely anyway, he thought darkly. Despite his deep weariness, his mind sparked with activity. Over and over, he replayed Cora placing her hands around his.

What was he doing? He'd broken all kinds of his uncle's rules—not telling him all he should know, going against him, in a sense. Holding Cora and wishing he could go on holding her, kiss her... Slowly, he acknowledged the truth. *I've wanted to kiss her all along, since the first day I met her. But I can't. I can't.* To chase that desire might open up a future with her, but it would definitely spell the end of any chance of getting back to school this fall. And without a future, without enough to even secure more than a modest flat and a month's rent, what could he offer her? *My uncle would have me on the first train out of here...to say nothing of what Wallace Kensington would do if he found out.*

He thought about Cora choosing him over Pierre de Richelieu. It made him laugh under his breath. *Whom would you choose, McCabe?* "C'mon," he said, tapping Felix on the shoulder. "We're here to escort you gents home."

Felix's blue eyes, so like Cora's, widened in surprise and delight. "Gentlemen! Excellent! I was just saying we had far too many pretty girls to choose from. Now you can ease our conundrum by taking a couple off our hands."

"*You* can share, Kensington," Hugh said, lifting the chin of one pretty girl and leaning his forehead toward hers with a smile, before smiling at the other, who was pouting on his other arm. "I find the more, the merrier." He caught sight of Arthur behind Will. "Yes, man, yes! I want a picture of this night to remember!" Pulling both of the girls close, he posed for the man as he squared up a photograph.

"Stay very still," Arthur said, peering into his viewfinder. "In this light, I'll need more time for the exposure."

"Fine by me," Hugh said. "Longer to caress their sweet, French curves…"

"You know they're as drawn by your fine clothing and fat purse," Will said. "You smell of money."

"Better to smell of money than the streets," Hugh said, barely moving his lips.

Will turned away, pinching the bridge of his nose between thumb and forefinger. Never had he wanted to punch the man more than he did right then. Cora was back at the chateau after having almost died and here they were—

A hand touched his shoulder, and Will wrenched away. Belatedly, he realized it was Antonio, not Hugh, and he closed his eyes, shaking his head.

"Will," Antonio said, tentatively stepping toward him and frowning in confusion. "Why don't you get some air, outside? Art and I will see to the young gents."

Will ground his teeth and turned, pushing his way through the laughing, chatting, drunken crowd until he was outside, beneath the light of the moon, breathing in deep draughts of cool night air. "What am I supposed to do now?" he said, lifting his hands up to the skies, thinking of Cora's touch, thinking of her staring up into his eyes. He felt utterly lost. "What *now*?"

Hugh and Felix eventually emerged with sour looks but without further complaint, followed by Antonio. They made their way back to the chateau, with Will brooding all the way home. He was so tired of playing guardian. So frightfully tired.

Still, he knew he had to check on Cora as soon as the young men were safely in their rooms. After Anna's whispered, "She's resting peacefully," he dragged himself back up the stairs and down the hall to bed.

Surprisingly, he fell asleep as soon as he hit the pillow.

Now, morning light tugged at his eyelids, urging him to rise. To go up top. Where the men were likely *getting ready to jump*.

He gasped and rose, throwing back the covers. What if one of them hit the water as Cora had the night before? An impact such as she'd suffered, from a greater height... He'd been so angry with the men last night, so agitated, he hadn't told any of them that it would not be allowed today. He rushed to pull off his nightshirt and hurried into his bathing costume, then ran down the hall, through the vast salon, the dining hall, and then out to the sprawling deck.

But when he got there, panting, the only person he saw was Cora, clad in a bathing costume. Her back to him. It was then that he recognized how early it was, the pink of dawn just edging the eastern horizon. Cora's breath fogged in front of her face, and she rubbed her arms.

"Cora," he said lowly, not wishing to startle her and make her fall. Not when she was perched forty feet above the surface of the water.

"William," she said, not looking back.

He strode over to her and climbed atop the wall beside her. "Are you mad?"

"No," she said, flicking a thick blonde braid over one shoulder. "Determined."

"Sometimes there's a fine line between the two," he said.

"I imagine so."

"How's the head?"

"A good, steady throb, but better than last night."

"Don't you think that a leap this morning is rather foolhardy?"

"Haven't you heard? It's best to get on the horse as soon as he's thrown you. Otherwise you might never climb in the saddle again."

"Some horses aren't meant to be ridden."

"This one is." And with that, she stepped out and began her descent.

He shook his head and held his breath as her arms windmilled, steadying her position. Then she pointed her toes, pinched her nose, drew her arms tight beside her body, and plunged into the river, as straight as an arrow. The blue water turned green as bubbles rose, all around her point of impact.

His eyes searched for her, waiting, waiting, his heartbeat tripling in time. And then she popped up, gasping for air and floating onto her back, smiling up at him.

Heavens, she's lovely. A river siren. Grinning, he jumped too, entering the water ten feet from her, and then hurrying to the surface, eager to see her again. Hear her voice.

"Now *that* is how it should've gone last night," she said when he broke the surface.

"Indeed."

She turned toward shore and, with light strokes, made her way there. So different from last night... He followed her, choosing breaststrokes, so he wouldn't miss one second of this moment, just the two of them. She reached the boulder and attempted to clamber out, slipped on a rock, and fell back into the river.

He laughed. "Here. Let me help you." He edged closer and took hold of the rock, an easier span for him to reach across, then offered his hand. She took it and made her way up and over the rocks and onto the platform. He followed and opened the gate for her. Just inside, she paused as the gate clanged shut behind them.

"Will, I wanted to speak to you about last night," she said, her tone laced with apology. She leaned back against the wall and played with her fingers, as if nervous.

"There is no need," he said. But inwardly he wondered what she was speaking of. Of the rescue? Of making him promise not to summon a doctor? Or for reaching for his hands? He started to walk past her, but she reached out and took hold of his fingers with two of her own. Slowly, he turned toward her, the familiar electric jolt jumping up his arm, up his neck, down through his shoulder blades....

"I think there is," she said. She dropped his fingers and lifted a small hand to his chest. He froze and closed his eyes—as if she were about to rip his heart out and he was powerless to stop it. He felt drunk around her. His senses alert and yet slow at the same time. "Will. Please look at me."

He forced his eyes open to see the silent invitation in her gaze. He shook his head, even as he leaned his hands above her, against the wall, rather than pulling her to him as he longed to. She reached up and placed her hands on either side of his face, her brow furrowed, anxious, wondering....

He scraped his fingers across the rough stone blocks, trying to remind himself not to touch her. *She is not yours. Not yours...*

"Cora. What of Pierre?" he asked, each word paining him.

"He is lovely. Almost too good to be true," she said. "But so are you." Her fingers wandered over his brow, his cheeks, his jaw, as if she were trying to convince herself. "And this...this thing between us," she whispered, so quiet he could barely make out her words. "I have to know. Once and for all. Is it real?"

"Don't do this, Cora. I can't resist...I don't seem..." He leaned toward her and breathed in the scent of her skin, washed in the clean river water, making her smell fresh like France itself—honey and lavender and grass and water....

His head was beside hers, and for several long seconds they stayed there, inhaling, intoxicated by sharing the same bit of air. "I can't," he whispered, perilously close to her pert ear, dearly wanting to kiss it, then her cheeks, then her lips.... "You have to know that I would if I could. But this..." He shook his head slightly. "It's against my uncle's principal rule—no courting the clients." He huffed a laugh, without mirth. "Not that I have the means to court anyone, even if I wished to go against him."

She lifted her chin and turned her face closer to his, so close that he could feel her breath on his cheek. "Don't you know," she whispered, "I'm not a woman accustomed to men of means? William McCabe, I'm a simple woman of the plains. Raised on a farm with none but two old dresses and one pair of boots. And I can't deny...I can't deny what I feel. Not after last night. Can you?"

Sick in the belly with swirling waves of both desire and fear, he stared into her eyes. And for the first time, he knew her as his compatriot, another person of simple heritage, simple means, lost in a rich man's world. He understood her. And she, him.

"Cora," he said, leaning closer, her lush lips just barely brushing his as he whispered her name.

"Will," she breathed, her beautiful eyes reminding him of the Mediterranean, the sky just freed from storm clouds.

He wrapped his free arm around her waist and pulled her closer.

Outside, a splash, and then another, sounded. They both stilled, caught. Discovered. Shame washed through him. What was he doing? Compromising Cora's reputation? Her future? As well as his?

He closed his eyes, agonized at breaking the moment. "I'm sorry," he said, pulling away from her, an act as difficult as pushing open a bank vault. "I'm sorry," he repeated, rubbing his neck, not daring to look back at her, doubting his resolve, still wanting to take her in his arms again. "They shouldn't find us in here. Alone."

"No," she said, staring at him as waves of pain washed through her eyes. "They shouldn't." All trace of warmth, heat, was gone from her tone. Only embarrassment. Sorrow. She raced past him, up the stairs, and practically shouted at Yves to unlock the gate, desperate to escape through it and into the safety of her room.

Will stayed where he was, his head pounding with one thought.

I just made the biggest mistake of my life.

---◇◇◇---

~Cora~

I was mortified. What did I think I was doing? What must he think of me, behaving in such a wanton manner? When he'd carried me to my room, I had been so certain there was something more in his eyes. Something I'd glimpsed before, recognized. And he seemed so intrigued by my touch…I thought he needed only a bit of encouragement to express his intentions.

What an imbecile I've been.

I'd been horribly forward. Enticed him, when he meant only to stick to his uncle's rules. Clearly, I'd imagined far too much—the stolen glances, the moments when we connected. Even if he was attracted to me, he didn't intend to act on it. *And well he shouldn't, Cora. What are you doing to the poor man?*

He was the bear's apprentice, my guardian. My protector. The drama and danger had encouraged our intimate connections. Nothing more. *Nothing more…*

A knock sounded at my door. "Mademoiselle? A package for you."

I opened it, wondering how long it would take for the dull thud in my head to quit pounding, obviously the repercussions of my clumsy jump last night. Or was it now from my awkward, embarrassing moment with Will?

A maid offered me two boxes tied with ribbons.

"Merci," I said, closing the door after her and taking them to my bed. I slid the ribbon off the first box and opened it. Above the tissue wrapping was a card with a bold PDR monogram on top. Pierre. Lord of the sprawling estate outside Paris. Politician. Businessman. And in some odd, star-crossed manner, my potential beau. Presumably, all I had to do was accept his pursuit and he would court me in earnest. But truly, how was that ever to work out? A Montana farm girl and a Parisian nobleman? The idea of it was preposterous. And yet, here it was….

Tentatively, I opened the card, feeling doubly embarrassed now. It was as if he knew, had seen me with Will moments ago, even from miles away.

Mon ange, I miss you terribly. I still hope to reach you before you depart Provence. A mere evening together would assuage my heart's need to be with you. In the meantime, I send you this as a token of my affection. - Pierre

With a sigh, I reached for the tissue and then gasped as my fingertips met the smoothest, richest silk I'd ever touched, in a lovely caramel color. Anna knocked and peeked in before I spoke, carrying a small breakfast tray. "Miss? May I be of service to you?"

"Please," I said, since I was still in my robe, my wet hair down around my shoulders. I pulled out the jacket. With an overlay of exquisite lace and beads, it was lightweight, perfect for a day of touring in the hot Provençal weather, but also elegant enough to see me through many daytime occasions with nobles.

"Oh, my," Anna said, as she finished pouring my tea. "Isn't that lovely?"

"Indeed," I said. I pulled out a matching skirt and a delicate lace dickey to go underneath the jacket. "But is it proper, receiving clothing from a gentleman?"

She smiled. "As long as it is clothing such as that, I see nothin' wrong with it. Quick, open the other box."

Obediently, I did as she asked, untying the ribbon on what clearly was a wide hatbox. "Oh!" I gasped, bringing my fingertips to my lips. It was the exact shade of caramel as the new suit. Around the top was lace to match my jacket. I pulled it out and put it on, moving to the full-length mirror. "My goodness. Have you seen anything so glamorous since we left Paris?"

"Hardly, miss," Anna said, peering at me from over my shoulder. "You must wear it today. It's perfect for our trip up the Canal du Midi to Carcassonne."

"Really? You don't think it's too much?"

"*Pshht.* Not at all. I'll just go and give your skirt and jacket a quick press while you eat a little something and drink your tea. But we have to be quick about it. The minutes are ticking away, and we're soon to be off."

"All right, then," I said, drawing hope from her bustling optimism. But as she disappeared behind me and I stared at my reflection in the mirror, I knew my glee wasn't entirely for the right reasons. To be certain, the clothing was grand. Pierre's gesture, beyond sweet. But what brought me ultimate satisfaction was the thought of Will finding out who had given it to me.

I stared at my blue eyes in the mirror. "Being vindictive is not becoming, Cora Diehl Kensington," I whispered. "Not becoming at all."

The youngest girls were saying good-bye to our hosts as I entered the hall, and most of the others were already outside in the touring cars, their trunks loaded and engines rumbling.

"Ahh, Mademoiselle Kensington, *enchanté*. We shall miss your fine company," Adrien said, bowing over my gloved hand and kissing it. "I heard you made the leap this morning. I only regret that I languished in bed and missed it."

"Forgive me, my friend, for rising so early," I said with a smile. "I shall remember that leap forever." *In more ways than one.* I pushed away the memory of Will's wet hair and dripping face, his warm breath on my lips....

I moved to kiss Celine on both cheeks. "Your hospitality, too, will always be a sweet memory for me."

"Come again, mademoiselle," she said, "and next time in the company of my brother. I know he longed to be here with you."

I smiled and looked to the floor, then back to her kind eyes. "He sent me word that he hopes to yet rendezvous with us in Provence. I do hope *our* paths cross again."

"I would like that very much," she said, smiling, and I knew that she was sincere, in the cautious way of a sister guarding their brother's heart.

"Au revoir," they called. I exited, past a line of servants, who nodded and smiled, and noticed Arthur getting into the motorcar ahead of us. Had he officially joined our traveling party?

Will stood beside the small back door of the last vehicle. I immediately regretted my dawdling and my fanciful decision to wear the new clothes.... Now I'd have to sit with him.

I barely took his hand as I picked up my skirts and entered the car, facing Andrew and Vivian. "Good morning," I said to my half sister and her intended, and they greeted me in kind.

"My goodness, Cora, when did you get that new suit and hat?" Vivian said. "It's lovely." She leaned forward to touch my skirt, admiring the silk.

Will entered and shut the door, and our motorcade drove off.

"It was a gift," I said, hoping to leave it at that.

"From Father?"

"From…another." Who was I fooling? There was only one man, other than Wallace Kensington, who would send me such finery. I tried not to enjoy the realization that Will's shoulder stiffened when I said it. And I berated myself for my lack of charity and grace. Regardless of his reasons for turning away from me, it was his right, yes? And who was I to demand his attentions when I had already caught the eye of Pierre de Richelieu? Who was I to mess with any man's affections at all?

All I wanted was to return to Montana after this adventure, to resume my simple life, my simple aspirations to teach, unencumbered by a relationship with any man—my father, Will, or Pierre. They would only seek to pull me into their world, not enter mine. *Honestly, get ahold of yourself, Cora. Remember who you are. Or you'll turn into someone you'd never choose to befriend.*

We drove down the long lane of the chateau and onto a larger road. Viv's keen eyes went from me to Will to me again, clearly picking up on the tension between us, while Andrew asked Will some question I didn't bother to listen to. Mercifully, over the next hour, Vivian didn't force me to an idle conversation of our own. I continued to look out the window, pretending to be absorbed by the landscape, which was growing more green and lush as we approached the sea, where the soil wasn't claimed by wheat and sunflowers rather than olive trees and vineyards.

Will entertained Vivian and Andrew with tales of the Provençal artists, past and present, who had favored this part of the country—Matisse and van Gogh, Cézanne and Renoir. But all I could think about was him gathering me in his arms so tenderly last night, that moment inside the gate this morning, and the other times we'd shared...on the boat crossing the Channel, on the *Olympic*, and before that, in Montana.

And although I kept my eyes scrupulously on the passing landscape, my heart kept whispering, *It's not just your imagination.*

CHAPTER FIVE

~Cora~

After a train ride along the rocky beaches and blue-green waters of the Golfe du Lion, past sleepy, sun-drenched beachside towns filled with fishermen just arriving from their morning toil, we finally reached the canal. I'd managed to appear as if I were napping for most of the two-hour train ride, and the others had left me alone. Such an escape would be far more difficult on the river barge. Still, I moved to the end of the long, flat boat, hoping to find some private alcove in which I could settle.

But there was no escape. There was but one seating area, and clearly, we were all expected to gather together for the bear's lecture on history, canal construction, and the area's architecture. We left the canal landing and set off at a leisurely pace, drifting past quiet villages and under the sweeping branches of huge trees planted decades before. It was idyllic, really. Something I'd normally enjoy. So I tried to settle in and pay attention to the old bear—and *only* to him—for a while.

"The canal was a wonder of its time," said the old man, waving his cane toward the water. "Indeed, it inspired many other similar constructs, including the shorter Suez Canal in Egypt and the soon-to-be-completed Panama Canal in the Americas. This canal took far less expense and political maneuvering, even though it was completed a century or more before those two."

It was most intriguing, this idea of cutting a waterway through the land in order to avoid circumventing hostile Spain—as well as Barbary pirates, back in the day. But I was continually distracted, sensing Will's gaze. And was it my imagination, or did Arthur point his camera toward me more than he did the others? "When did Art become a part of our tour?" I whispered to Lil.

"When he said he'd arrange lodging for us in Carcassonne," she whispered back.

Ahh, I thought. So that was it. The bear would tolerate his company as long as he was useful, introducing us to society as we traveled. How long could that hold out for an American? *Hopefully not long*, I thought, recognizing my own surly demeanor, but I was confused, overwhelmed, and I couldn't seem to dispatch my terrible headache....

I imagined that Will wondered what had come over me, that my forward nature allowed me to flirt with him while Pierre yet pursued courtship. *You are awful, Cora Diehl Kensington. Not behaving at all as your mama and papa raised you.*

Wanton, wily, wicked...

I abruptly rose, and the bear paused in his lecture, looking at me with consternation.

"Forgive me, but I am not feeling at all well. I think I might go to the bow for a bit more fresh air." I was moving away before I thought how foolish that statement was. We moved at a slow pace, and the entire deck was awash with a cooling breeze.

The bear nodded as I passed him, and he continued his monotonous lecture. Will was a far livelier teacher, but I would not have been able to tolerate a single minute of listening to him. I prayed that he would not follow me now.

The old captain of the barge watched me as I squeezed past, along the narrow walkway and out onto a tiny deck at the bow. I gestured to a metal crate—presumably filled with life vests or equipment for the river boat—and he gave me a pert nod, as if to say, *Sit anywhere, you fool. Just get out of my line of vision. And that includes that enormous hat.*

I sat down, feeling the heat of the metal seep through my skirts as well as the heat beating down on me from the sun. I was glad for the shelter of my wide hat. If I were to put a parasol above me, the captain would surely toss me overboard. I had just settled in to the sound of the water, the rhythmic chug of the steam engine, the feel of the breeze on my face, when a girl's voice interrupted me.

"Cora?"

I opened my eyes and looked over to find my younger sister beside me.

"Are you quite all right?"

"A bit of a nagging headache, but I'll be fine." I scooted over, making room for her. "Sit down, quickly, or the captain will have a fit."

Lillian glanced over her shoulder at him and then, safely shielded by her own hat, widened her eyes at me. "I don't know what it is about the French, but they intimidate me."

"You? I thought you adored this country."

"I do, but I'm far less brave than I appear," she said.

I smiled. "I understand."

"Your new traveling suit is so lovely," Lillian said, running her hand down my sleeve. "That silk is completely scrumptious. And that hat…it's simply perfect on you."

"Thank you, Lil."

"Where did it come from? I thought I'd seen all you'd purchased in Paris."

What was the use? The truth would come out, sooner or later, and I was enjoying this brief moment with my sister. "From Pierre," I said in a whisper, leaning closer to her.

"Oh!" she said. Her green eyes rounded in excitement. "That is so romantic. How did he know your size?" Her eyes moved over me from head to toe.

"I suppose from the tailor who created all our ball costumes."

"Of course," she said, clapping her gloved hands. She folded them and tucked them under her chin. "I do so hope that one day I have such a grand romance as you."

"I hope you do too," I said, but my mind was slipping toward Will, rather than Pierre again.

"Perhaps Mr. Stapleton will consider courting me," she said in a whisper.

"Arthur?" I said, carefully forming my response in my head. "Oh, Lil, even if he was, he'd be the start of many. Don't be in too much of a rush to find a husband."

"Do you think you will marry Lord de Richelieu?"

It was my turn to look upon her with wide eyes. "Marry? I think not."

She frowned. "Why not? He is like…" She paused, looking forward, her entire face becoming wistful. "Like a fairy-tale prince. How can you resist?"

I laughed under my breath. "Perhaps that is exactly it. As much as I am enjoying our tour, this is but a chapter in my life. And the rest of my book is not a fairy tale. It's full of very realistic, challenging tasks and people. Children, eager to learn. When I get back home, I'll resume my education at the Normal School in Montana."

"You…" She blinked slowly, frowning. "You're…you intend to go back? But why? You are a Kensington now."

I gave her a gentle smile. "I'm also a Diehl. And my parents worked very hard and sacrificed much to get me to Normal School. Your father only promised me this tour and to finance the rest of my education. I was never to assume life among you."

"Well that…that's ridiculous!" she said. "Of course you should assume life with us."

"Thank you for that," I said. "I will look forward to our relationship in the years to come, Lil, but we mustn't push into such tender territory."

"You mean, push *Vivian*."

"No, no. I mean push everyone. Vivian as well as all the rest of your friends. Don't give me that look. Vivian and I are finding our way. But truthfully, this all feels rather like make-believe. Like I'm acting, rather than being who I truly am."

She frowned at me. "You'll become accustomed to it in time."

"I already am, Lil," I said softly. "Far more than I ever imagined I could be. But I have to keep one foot back in territory I've known my whole life."

"Why?"

"Because I wish to be a content country schoolteacher. I'll look back fondly on this adventure as just that—a grand adventure, with its lovely clothes and fascinating excursions and scrumptious food and lodging." I shook my head, trying to come out of my reveries. "No. This is my present; it isn't my future."

She clamped her lips shut and stared at me, obviously reluctant to continue our disagreement. But her eyes said, *We'll see.*

The engine of the canal boat reversed, and we looked up to find that we were approaching our first lock. "The bear will want to enlighten us as we go through that," I said, gesturing forward. "Shall we rejoin the others?"

Lil nodded, and we rose together, making our way around the captain's bridge and back to the others. It was Felix who approached me with a solicitous, warm question after my well-being, and once again, I fought the desire to look at Will.

To see if he was looking at me.

Wondering after me.

---◇---

~William~

Try as he might, he could not keep his eyes from moving to her, again and again, as Uncle Stuart lectured on what was about to transpire. She was a vision in her classic, camel-colored silk, the hue making her skin a healthy peach, her hair peeking out from under the matching hat all the more golden. But there was pain behind her eyes—from her professed headache? Or from their blunder of an encounter that morning?

The barge settled into the lock and was tied up to enormous cleats at the edge. The captain yelled to the lockmaster above, *"Commençons!"* and the old man nodded. Great metallic clicks echoed around them as a solid gate sealed the canal shut behind the boat, and another gate opened to allow a flood of water inward. The younger girls clapped as the barge began to rise. Cora edged around them in order to better see. *Such an inquisitive mind...*

Hugh and Arthur had retreated to the back of the boat for a cigarette, while Felix, Vivian, and Andrew chatted with Uncle Stuart. The private detectives split up, one going to the bow, the other remaining at the stern.

Will leaned over the rail and stared at the water steadily rising on the far wall with them atop it. Fifteen minutes later, the lockmaster gave them a salute, lowered the next wall, and the captain moved the barge forward. It truly was a remarkable feat of engineering, built in the seventeenth century. *If they could do that then, what could I do now?* He considered the geology, hydrology, and engineering marvel each canal was and grew almost as excited about it as he did about architecture.

Who was he fooling? He'd be fortunate to complete his bachelor's, let alone seek the additional schooling he'd need to become an architect. But everywhere he went, the bones of buildings or canals called to him. *What am I to do with this, Lord? This call? Simply utilize it as part of being a bear? Show me, Father. Lead me to a place of peace and out of this constant...agitation.*

The maids brought out enormous picnic baskets and proceeded to put out bread, fresh butter, salami, cheese, grapes, pears, and chocolate. They pulled out champagne and poured crystal flutes full of bubbling liquid. As one maid passed a flute to him, he took a sip and chastised himself for his foul mood. What a sniveling child he was. How many would wish to trade places with him? Enjoying the life of the rich, even if he wasn't rich himself?

And yet…what good did it do him—his eyes shifted to Cora—when he wasn't free to choose his own steps?

————◇◇◇————

~Cora~

The medieval city of Carcassonne seemed to be the apex of my fairy-tale vision. We were to spend the night in the chateau, a castle within the city's double walls. The chateau had its own protective walls and what was once a moat, now dry. After our arrival, when we were given a scant hour to rest and change into fresh clothes, we went to the grand old Basilica of St. Nazaire and St. Celse and saw the famed "siege stone," a portion of a frieze containing dense images from one of Carcassonne's battles. The bear gave us permission to walk through some of the city, enjoying the market and shopping for trinkets, before returning to the chateau.

Two hours later we were in fine gowns and gloves with our hair dressed, the men in their finest jackets, sitting around a long, elegant table set for thirty-two. Multiple candelabra served as our only light, lending a moody, secretive feel to the room that was lined with oil paintings of nobles long dead. Cut crystal and ornate silver, including more spoons and forks than were remotely necessary, graced settings of Limoges china. By now I was well versed in when to use what cutlery with which course—thanks to Anna—but I still thought it ridiculous.

I forced myself to make small talk with the viscount to my left and the handsome but deadly boring nobleman to my right, while I appreciated the delicate dishes from a famous chef in the chateau's kitchens, coming to us via multiple courses. But as I forced another bite to my mouth and smiled and nodded at whatever the viscount had said—his meaning made vague by a thick French accent and a limited knowledge of English—I longed for my mother's plain meatloaf and roasted potatoes. Carrots gone mushy after too long atop the stove. A simple apple cobbler for dessert. Laughter and comfortable conversation. And no corset beneath my gown. Freedom to breathe. *To breathe.*

The thought of it made me fight for composure. To not rise and run from this room, ripping out my fancy feathered hair dressing and the hundreds of pins in the coils of hair, unbuttoning my gorgeous, horribly constricting claret gown and ripping it off as I tore down the hall. The mad vision made me want to laugh aloud, and I narrowly kept from doing so.

"Did I say something amusing, mademoiselle?" said the handsome nobleman.

"Oh, no," I said, taking a quick swallow of water. "Forgive me. I was just reminiscing over something. I'm terribly sorry."

"Quite," he said, and then in a droning tone abruptly resumed his long, boring story about a trip to New York. I took a sip of wine. And then another.

Somehow, I made it to the end of that dinner. Afterward, we were led to the city walls, climbing stairs to the tops of the towers, then down the other side, tracing footsteps of knights in armor. We walked for fifteen minutes until we looked out over the gently winding Canal du Midi glistening in the moonlight, and an utterly still valley below. Crystal flutes filled with sliced strawberries and champagne were poured and passed along to us.

Over the horizon, the round top of the moon rose, and we cheered, finished our champagne, and allowed the steward to pour more. It was idyllic. It was magical. And I was feeling lighter by the moment. When the steward came around again, I lifted my flute in my right hand, and he filled it.

From my left shoulder came a deep whisper. "Do you think that perhaps you've had enough?"

"Go away, Will," I whispered, looking back out to the valley.

"You look like a princess upon the walls."

I dared to look at him then. "I said, go away. We've said far too much this day, have we not?"

He stared at me for several breaths, clearly debating. "Indeed." He turned to bend down and lean against the wall with his elbows to undergird him.

I waited for him to say more—to confess there was more—until I realized I was holding my breath and at last inhaled. It was silly. And futile. Even if he did admit to having feelings for me.

Will and I were doomed from the start. Wallace Kensington would never allow it. He'd see it as an insult—the bear's apprentice chasing after his daughter. Even if we waited until the tour was over to openly court, Wallace Kensington would sniff out the truth. He wouldn't like how it appeared. How it might look to others that the guide was fraternizing with his long-lost daughter. I knew it as well as Will—Wallace Kensington had the power to end Will's career, his future. The bear's business. And if he caught wind of it now, our tour would be most assuredly done.

But I couldn't help it. More than ever, I wanted to know. To know if Will felt the same for me as I did for him. I turned toward him, lifting my eyes in a studied, slow way that I hoped would be dramatic. And affecting.

"Cora," he growled in a whisper, taking a deep breath, his nostrils flared, as if he was trying to compose himself. Could he not give in? Admit it? At least, to me? In secret?

I waited for a long moment.

It appeared not. And I'd once again exposed myself in a way that burned.

"Good night, William." With that, I abruptly turned and left him, tossing the remains of my champagne over the edge of the wall.

He was right.

I'd had more than enough.

CHAPTER SIX

~Cora~

The next morning, we were up with the sun and into riding clothes, the bear intent on taking us on some mysterious "adventure of the soul." None of us knew of what he spoke, of course, in that we considered the soul best represented in the grand cathedrals and basilicas we'd toured in the last weeks. Riding clothes were hardly proper attire for such a place.

When we'd all gathered by the touring cars, Felix asked again where we were going.

The old bear grinned like a secretive Santa with his bag stashed in some remote location. "Trust me, young ladies and gents. Trust me. Into the motor carriages with you. William shall see you through while I rest my old knees here at the chateau. I shall look forward to hearing all about your adventure when you return."

So we did as he bid, accompanied by Will, Antonio, and the two detectives. And after an hour's drive on dry, dusty, terribly rutted roads—repairing two flat tires along the way—we pulled over beside what looked like five cowhands and twelve mules.

"Oh, they don't intend for us to ride *those*, do they?" Vivian sniffed, looking to Andrew as if he might rescue her.

"I'd wager they do," Felix said, giving her a small grin.

I looked up, above us, to the craggy peaks of the scrub-covered limestone mountains, and gasped. Just barely in sight was one edge of what had to be the crumbling remains of a castle.

Will caught my eye and smiled. He nodded once. "Cora has seen it," he called, as we all clambered out of the vehicles and drew together. "Have any of the rest of you?"

"A castle!" Lil cried, bouncing on her tiptoes and pointing. "Up there!"

"Indeed," Will said. "Two thousand feet above us are the remains of the ancient Chateau de Peyrepertuse, once called one of the 'five sons of Carcassonne,' assisting Aragon in protecting the frontier. Now, if you'll kindly line up here, from biggest to smallest, these men shall assist you in finding the proper mount."

I was the tallest woman in the group, behind Felix and with Vivian right behind me. "Fancy a race on these?" I asked my sister with a smile over my shoulder.

"I think not," she said, rolling her eyes. We'd come a long way since our ride through the English wood and our fateful end in the mud.

A young man led me to a small black mule and gave me a leg up. Then he helped me settle into her saddle. "I feel like a clown at the circus, riding a tiny trike!" I said to Felix, directly ahead of me.

"And you look about as ridiculous," he allowed.

I grinned at him. "As do you."

"Thank you for that, sweet sister."

I turned away so he wouldn't see how his idle comment set a blush climbing my neck and cheeks. He'd never referred to me as such before. Had Vivian and Lil heard? And if so, what was their reaction? I didn't dare look.

I could hear Vivian behind me, chastising Arthur for taking pictures of us, even on mules. I smiled. They might be my very favorite pictures of all he took.

We set off along a small dirt path that zigzagged up the mountain. There was no need to steer the reins of the mules; they simply followed the one in front, as if they did this day in, day out, every day of their lives. Perhaps they did.

The closer we got, the more excited I became. The air cooled the higher we got. But in peekaboo views, we glimpsed more and more of the castle, tantalizing bits of what we were about to see in full. Vertical walls built atop cliffs, extending their height. Round and square towers.

Some five hundred feet below, the best view yet, Will pulled his mule to one side and gestured for us to do the same. From here, we could see the full line of the castle, with some walls that had resisted the ravages of time and others that were barely visible.

"The name, Peyrepertuse, is derived from the French 'pierre percée,' or 'pierced stone,'" Will said, beginning his lecture. "She seems to rise from the cliffs themselves, does she not?"

I nodded along with the others, but my mind was on the name. Pierre meant "stone." That made sense, given that Peter was called the rock of the church. But I'd never bothered to think about it when I was with Pierre de Richelieu. The thought of him and his letter to me made me smile. But did I think of him as a rock? As my rock? Not really.

My eyes flicked to William. He was more of a rock. Stubborn, stuck, stilted. Pierre was…something else entirely. Constant movement, pleasure.

Might he meet with us here in Carcassonne? Or elsewhere? Our days in Provence were dwindling…and there was a part of me that was eager to see him. To see if what had begun between us was merely a fun, passing fancy or something of consequence. And if Pierre were here, it'd help keep my mind off of Will.…

"On the far end is the keep of St. George, which appears completely separate from the castle, given our viewpoint here, but is not," Will said. "Directly above us is the main part of the chateau, a two-hundred-foot–long curtain wall. It looks a bit like a ship, does it not? Sailing the ridge's wave?"

We nodded and then continued our ascent. At the top, Will dismounted to pay a stoop-shouldered, sun-withered old man with gold coins from his pocket. Some ancestor of those who once ruled these lands, now charging admission? A scrawny, skittish dog growled at us as we moved through the gate and into the castle. Whatever we were paying, it was clearly not enough for the man to feed his dog.

The cowboys took the reins of our mules and tied them for us while Will led us to the eastern wall. The view across mountain ridges and valleys was breathtaking. "Over there in the distance, you see the remains of the castle, like a finger, pointing to the sky?" Will said, coming close to me, placing a hand at the center of my back. I shielded my eyes from the glare of the sun and searched where he pointed, pretending I didn't notice his touch.

There. "Yes," I said.

"Where, William?" Lil asked, squinting. I frowned, recognizing that I felt both relief and sorrow when he moved to her, pointing over her shoulder so she could follow. What was going on inside me? I had to stop this and stop it immediately.

"That is the remains of the chateau of Quéribus, the last of the Cathar strongholds to fall in 1255. As difficult as Peyrepertuse is to reach, she's more challenging still."

"Was Quéribus one of the sons of Carcassonne, too?" Nell asked, like a student bent on earning a top grade in class.

"Indeed," he said, giving her a wink.

"And the Cathars…" I mused. "Who were they?"

He studied me. "A thirteenth-century religious sect who grew very critical of the corruption they saw in the church. They flourished here, but their rebellion was soon exploited for political purposes. Peter II of Aragon dearly wished to annex Languedoc, this region in which we currently stand, but Philippe II of France would have none of it, of course. He convinced the pope to declare the Cathars heretics. A crusade was formed, and for a hundred years, the Cathar faith was exploited, her followers routed out, tortured, and killed."

An adventure of the soul, the old bear had teased us. Sounded more like *tortured souls* to me. "What did they believe?" I asked.

"The Cathars believed there to be a duality between good and evil. They thought that if they renounced the world and lived their lives in nonviolence, eating as vegetarians and abstaining from man's, uh…baser desires, they would become closer to God."

Hugh snorted and barely turned to hide his smile. "How did they intend to further their cause if they did not…procreate? In a generation, they would've died out!"

Will's lips clamped shut as he studied the man. Then, "They believed that was up to God. They only knew what they were to do."

"But obviously, God did not honor them," Andrew said. "They were all killed?"

Will kicked at a loose stone before him and then looked to the wall. "Many went into hiding. Thousands were killed. Twenty thousand alone in Béziers in 1209. The pope promised the heretics' land to the crusaders, as well as granting complete forgiveness, even *before* they'd murdered their supposed enemies. By 1244, the Cathars were largely dead or in hiding; that year, their last fortress at Montségur was sacked. As you walk about these ruins, consider what you would do if you believed God had directed your steps...." He faltered, looking my way before regaining his composure. "Consider what it would be to have been in the boots of either Cathar or crusader."

He set us loose after that, a somber, contemplative group as we wandered through the dry, dusty remains, ducking under low doorways, walking still-intact walls like knights on duty, considering how it would appear from here, to see thousands of armed men approaching, bent on taking us down...and then how impenetrable the castle would have seemed back in the day. We climbed the sixty-some rock-hewn stairs that led us to the fortress within the fortress, San Giorgi, the keep. Inside, we climbed to the top and peered over the edge. My eyes followed a pair of falcons that hovered fifty feet away, riding the winds. I thought I'd rather be them than either crusader or Cathar. But what did it mean to follow where God led, even at the price of death? Both sides believed God was behind them. How could that be?

Arthur came up beside me and leaned his forearms on the edge of the wall. "How many men and women found themselves here because it truly was their holy calling, and how many came because everyone around them *told* them it was their holy calling?"

It was an impossible question, so I remained silent. But his words rang in my head. How much did we do in life that was the result of what others around us demanded? Rather than what God was calling us to do? What was God calling me to do? Here? Now?

Lord, show me. I'm Yours. Lead me....

My eyes moved back to the swooping falcons and, beneath them, the rocky valleys. And then I turned and scanned the ruins of the castle until my eyes found what they sought.

William.

⸻◇◇◇⸻

When we all gathered again, sitting in a line along the castle wall, we shared a picnic of cold roast chicken, bread, and fruit. The group was uncommonly quiet, all lost in thought.

"Any questions from you?" Will called, rising. I was both glad and sad that there were four people sitting between us. My mind and heart were whirling as I wondered if what I felt was true, godly. Was He leading me to Will? Telling me that Will was the right man for me, regardless of what others thought? Regardless of our fears?

"So this was originally built as a Cathar castle?" Felix asked.

Will ran his hand down the crumbling corner of the wall nearest him. "They took refuge here, but no, it was built long before that. Many of these sites are symbolic outposts of Charlemagne's ninth-century empire. Sadly, when his feuding sons took over, Languedoc became a scrap fought over by two fierce dogs. France ultimately won, as we've seen."

"How is it in such good condition?" Andrew asked, tossing a rock from one hand to the other.

"It fell by negotiation rather than by force," Will said. "And it was used as a base from which to harass other Cathars in subsequent years."

"So none were put to the stake here?" Hugh asked. His intent look, as if he wished he could see it happen, sent a shiver down my spine.

"No. But over there, in Minerve," Will said with a nod toward the castle on the far ridge, "a hundred and forty were burned. Simon de Montfort, the leader of the crusaders, a devout man following orders from holy men he trusted, was universally hated. Not only for how he hunted the Cathars, but how he took out the legs from beneath the Languedoc. The entire region celebrated when his head was bashed in by a trebuchet stone. They sang songs of it." He gave a shrug.

My eyes widened at that bit of information. Such violence, such hatred, all fueled by faith. This wasn't an adventure of the soul—it was the means to set a hundred trails of gunpowder afire. The old bear loved such sweet tinder. Anything to get us thinking.

———◇◇◇———

That afternoon, when we returned to the chateau in Carcassonne, the bear greeted me in the hall. "A telegram for you," he said gently. The others filtered past, all intent on bathing and resting before changing for our last dinner in this ancient city.

I entered a library, and he followed, sitting down in a big leather chair while I went to the window to open the telegram. I scanned it. "It's from my parents," I said, then fell into reading it in silence. They'd received my own telegram. My father continued to make good strides since his stroke. He still wasn't able to speak, but he seemed to understand much. And he was walking. Clearly, the hospital in Minneapolis was giving him good care. I reread the words twice, then a third time, hearing my mother's voice, smiling at the glad tidings they contained. The hope.

I stared through the chateau window, which boasted a view over the second city wall, out to the verdant green valley below, and thought how far I felt from my parents. Our life together seemed a decade ago, even though we'd parted less than two months ago. So much had changed in that time. I had changed. Was I still the same person, at the core? Or less or more of who I was meant to be?

"Is his health improving, child?" the bear asked.

"Much," I said, folding the thin sheet of paper. "I am very grateful."

"And yet hearing from them leaves you homesick," he said gently.

"Indeed." Slowly, I turned to face him, wondering if I was so very transparent.

"Many start to yearn for home about this time on our journey," he said, waving his unlit pipe in the air. "It is normal. And, trust me, something you can overcome."

"What if..." I began, biting my lip, then walking toward him, perching on the edge of the couch beside him. "What if I did return home now?" As much as I loved the tour, in these last days, things had become almost unbearably complicated.

"To what gain? You'd have no funds for your schooling. And your father…"

"Wallace Kensington is not going to force my papa out to the street. Not now. He got what he wanted. Me, on this tour. An opportunity for me and my siblings to come to know one another, find a measure of trust. But…" I looked to the window again.

"Is it your home that calls you? The familiar? Or the fear of the unfamiliar ahead? Perhaps it is the idea of Pierre de Richelieu once again crossing paths with us? If it is that, rest assured—"

"No. No," I said. "I mean certainly. Pierre complicates things, in good measure." *But not nearly as much as Will.*

"Are you…are you falling in love with him, child?" the bear asked, lowering his gray, bushy brows in consternation.

I choked and brought a hand to my chest, fearing for a moment that he'd read my thoughts about Will. "What? In love?" I laughed and shook my head. "No. Pierre is beyond charming. I think him attractive, enticing, even," I said with a shrug. "But he is not the sort…"

"You imagined as your husband?" he finished for me.

"Exactly." I had always pictured myself with someone far more… average—far less encumbered.

"That is good. Matches made on tours rarely amount to anything good. But what of my nephew?"

He asked it so steadily, I ran back over the words, certain I had misheard him.

"W-William? What of him?" I returned, fiddling with my jodhpurs, too cowardly to meet his keen eyes.

"Is he the sort of man you mean, Miss Kensington?"

"Mr. McCabe, I don't know what you are asking."

"I think you do."

I abruptly stood. What had begun as a pleasant session with a confidant had turned into an interrogation. "I don't know what you've imagined, but—"

"I hope we're not interrupting," Will said, entering the room with three others.

The bear and I both jumped and glanced back to each other. And in that glance we both knew the same thing—I had feelings for Will. Deep feelings.

"Look who has just arrived," Will said, his tone carefully droll. He and Arthur and Felix separated to reveal the other.

Pierre de Richelieu.

CHAPTER SEVEN

~William~

He couldn't bear to watch her go to him. He felt as if his heart were literally tearing in two as Richelieu took her hands and kissed her on both cheeks. He could hear the Frenchman murmuring, the delight in his tone. Cora's meager words sounded bright, excited to see him again.

"Do you mind if I escort Miss Cora for a brief walk on the veranda?" Richelieu asked the bear, after shaking his hand in greeting.

"Not at all," the bear said, gesturing them outward, obviously as eager for their reunion as they were. Will swallowed hard. From the salon windows, they'd be in plain view, giving them privacy, but not beyond propriety. *How can I keep my eyes from straying to them?*

Arthur snapped a photo of the two as Richelieu tucked Cora's hand around his arm, then bent to show Felix something on the back of the camera. Felix had purchased his own Autographic Kodak and was learning to use it. The two excused themselves to continue their tutorial, following Cora and Richelieu outside.

"William Henry McCabe," Stuart said, striding toward him with no shortage of fury, the cane in his hand shaking. "What have you done?"

"Wh-what do you mean?" Will glanced to the empty doorway. He took the red-faced old man's arm. "Sit, Uncle. You know such agitation isn't good for your heart."

"Pour me a drink," demanded his uncle, falling more than sitting down. Had he become so much frailer in the last week? *I've hardly given him a moment's notice*, Will admitted to himself. His attention had been solely…elsewhere.

Will walked over to the crystal decanter and poured a stiff drink for his uncle, then carried it over to him, sitting where Cora had been. "What has you so upset, Uncle?"

The man took a quick swig of the amber liquid and swirled the rest around the glass, studying it. Then he looked back to Will. "I asked Cora if she thought of you as husband material."

Will swallowed hard, now wishing he'd poured a glass for himself. "And…and what did she say?"

"You saw what she *said*! She said as much in what she *didn't* say as what she did! It's as plain as day! The girl's holding Pierre de Richelieu at arm's length because she's in love with you!"

Will's eyes widened, and he glanced over his shoulder to the closed door. A moment before Felix and Arthur's voices could be heard on the veranda; now they'd dropped to silence. "Please, Uncle, keep your voice down."

"Are you in love with her?" Stuart bellowed, ignoring Will's entreaty, his face becoming even more red.

"What? No! I know what the rules are," Will said. "My only intentions are to get through this tour and get back to school. No matter how attractive Cora might be."

His uncle stared at him, searching his eyes. Will stared back at him, lips clamped.

"Are you certain?"

"Of course!" But even as he said it, his heart sank. Because he wasn't certain. Not certain at all…"I know what this tour means to you," he whispered. "The extra money will see us both through in good order."

His uncle let out a breath and sank back against the chair. He rubbed his temples, squeezing them with one hand. "More than you know. And I would have to send you home if—"

"No. *No*," Will said, raising a hand, giving him an exasperated look as if his uncle had imagined far too much. If Stuart sent him home, there would be no increased pay for the summer's toil, possibly no pay at all. What would happen then to his plans to return and enroll in fall session? His plans to finish his degree? He'd never be on his own, never be free to be an adult, out from under Stuart's ever-present watch.

Stuart swallowed the rest of his drink in one enormous gulp and studied him again. "So, you are telling me that there is nothing at all to be worried about between you and Cora?"

"An idle attraction, flirtation, nothing more," Will said, smiling as if it were a painful joke, hating himself with every word. "It's part of my assignment, yes? To make every young lady feel attractive, desirable, while keeping a respectable distance?" *How many times has Uncle said those very words to me?*

Stuart paused for several long seconds and then nodded once. "Good. *Good.* Forgive me, Nephew. But I would advise you to ease back, since the girl seems to be a tad confused on that front. We don't want her leaving with a broken heart." He shook his head and brought his fingertips to his forehead, looking more gray and frail than ever. "That can enrage a father even more than having his daughter fall in love."

"Understood," Will choked out.

"We're to be on to supper at the café in but an hour," Stuart said with a sigh, apparently mollified for the moment. "You'd best go change."

Will nodded and turned on trembling legs while trying to convey utter ease. But what he saw in the foyer stopped him cold. Hugh stood right around the corner, leaning against the wall, arms crossed.

"Hugh," Will grit out.

"William," the man said with a catlike smile. He followed Will up the stairs, and Will instinctively knew the man had heard every word of his conversation with Uncle Stuart. *Every word.* Even if Felix and Arthur hadn't, this one had.

"I thought you were up resting before supper," Will said, hating his own strangled, infuriated tone.

"Indeed," Hugh said, falling into step beside him as they climbed the grand staircase. "I'd come down to see if I might have a word with our bear, but from what I heard, he seems cantankerous." He paused to take a breath. "Perhaps later."

"Catch him right after supper," Will said, forcing some semblance of kindness to his voice. "He'll be in brighter spirits. But you know how sleepy he gets after a meal."

"I shall."

They parted at the landing, Will heading to one wing, Hugh the other. As he walked, he rubbed his neck, thinking it felt as stiff as a rock. He'd failed them all. His uncle. Mr. Kensington. Cora.

And Hugh knew it. Would he tell her? Drop his hurtful words on her at some fateful moment, hoping to get a chance at her himself? To become a confidant of a kind for her? Will's eyes narrowed. He was the sort. Hurt her in order to comfort her.

Will had to get to her first. Say something that would help her understand, if it came up. But did he dare? When he was feeling so… weak?

~Cora~

Our hosts had left for Marseilles, telling Arthur that he could play host in their stead, but he led us to a town café for dinner, rather than have us eat in the massive dining room again. Even in our most simple of touring suits, we far outdressed the locals. I shifted uneasily as I entered. The ceilings were low; the place packed with laughing, mingling people who gave us only a cursory glance before dismissing us; and we were led to a long table in the corner.

I glanced at Pierre, wondering how he'd fare in a café so…base. Part of me relished seeing him here, for once far from his usual environs. More like my own. To my surprise, he looked utterly at ease.

"Oh, it's marvelous. Perfect, Arthur," the bear enthused. "Thank you for suggesting it."

"Not at all," Arthur said, his eyes moving to the others. "It's one of my favorites in Carcassonne. I hope you enjoy it as much as I do."

"Come, Cora, Pierre," the old bear said. "I'd be very honored if you sat with me."

"Of course," Pierre said, moving to follow him, tugging me along. We were at one end of the table, and Will was on the other. I couldn't help but think the seating arrangement was by the bear's careful design.

We settled in, and two waitresses set out long baguettes that smelled like they'd just come out of the oven, as well as *escargot*, snails covered in butter and garlic. I'd still not acquired a taste for them, but I tore off a piece of bread as the others did before me, smiling as my younger sister giggled over the "barbaric practice."

"Oh, no, no, no, my dear," said the bear. "It isn't barbaric. Only customary. These people would surely giggle if they sat down at the chateau table we shared last night."

"All that cutlery makes *me* giggle," I said lowly.

He smiled at me and nodded graciously. "There are charms belonging to each, yes?"

"Yes," I said, looking down the long, country table covered in a clean but worn linen and over to Pierre. "Given the choice, I'd sit at this one most every night of our tour."

Pierre gave me a mischievous look, pulled off his jacket, and settled it on the back of his chair, then unbuttoned his sleeves and rolled them up. His action gave me pause. What was this? He immediately looked more relaxed, welcoming, even if his shirt was made of a finer cloth than anything I'd ever touched before joining the

Kensingtons. He broke off a piece of bread and handed it to me with a grin.

Never had I thought he looked more attractive. Was it because he looked less…formal? More approachable?

Vivian, sitting between Arthur and Andrew, had overheard me. "This might be good, hearty food. But surely you would miss Pierre's chef's preparations. Or what we ate aboard the *Olympic*? Or with the Bellamys?"

"Forgive me," I said. "I don't mean to sound ungrateful. It's only that cafés like this are more…me. Where I'd come if I was just Cora Diehl, traveling on her own."

She stared into my eyes a moment, her own squinting a little as if she was trying to understand such a mad statement. Andrew leaned over and whispered something in her ear while Arthur took a sip of his wine, absorbing every word, every nuance. What was his interest in all of us anyway? I shoved away the idea that Andrew was saying something dismissive about me and concentrated on my crusty bread, trying to rein in my thoughts. We were past all the cattiness. Weren't we?

"I wouldn't mind dinner and company like this every evening," Pierre said in my ear, daring to squeeze my hand under the table.

"Is this like other Grand Tours that people have taken?" I asked the bear, eager to change the subject and shift the attention as my cheeks flamed from Pierre's touch. Had I not been thinking of sharing only Will's kiss, these last two days? But what was this? Pierre seemed…different. Somehow more in reach, *accessible*, than when we were in Paris. More like when we'd met on the ship.

"No. The tours are far more relaxed, these days. Our predecessors of the seventeenth or eighteenth centuries, even the Victorians, would never do something such as this." He motioned to the quaint but rustic room. "But the tour is what we make it, is it not? I want you to feel like you are in these places as they really are. Living them. Touching, smelling, hearing, *absorbing* them."

I smiled over the older man's passion. I loved it when he talked this way. "Today, as we toured the ruined chateau, wandered her walls—I could imagine enemy forces gathering, trebuchet stones battering the chateau. It came alive in my mind."

"Excellent!" the man said, clapping his age-thickened fingers together. "Such memories will stick with you until you're as old and gray as I am. That will serve you as well as the knowledge of nobles and art you gain along our trail."

"It is all well and good," Andrew tossed out, putting a thick pat of white butter on his bread, "but there is a part of me that wishes I was back at home, working with our fathers, learning more about my future than about the past."

"What? No, no," said the bear. "These experiences shall serve to connect you to others and your world, your whole life through. Even if you never meet any of the people you've met here again, speaking with someone in the States who has been in Carcassonne, for instance," he said, waving toward the windows of the café, "in this ancient city, gives you immediate connection. It is much like sharing the same alma mater."

"I suppose," Andrew said doubtfully, stuffing another piece of bread into his mouth.

Just watching Andrew lather the bread with that amazing, creamy butter made me want another, but the trays were empty. Soon after, the waitresses arrived with wide bowls of vegetable soup and, after that, perfectly roasted hens, their skin a lovely golden brown and sprinkled with herbs, and to the side, tiny red potatoes. The chicken was so tender it practically fell off the bones. When we were done, I couldn't remember feeling so full. Or so happy to have eaten what I had.

Afterward, we walked the streets, enjoying pockets of locals singing and dancing. In one small plaza, people walked beside us, speaking rapidly in French, flirting playfully. They gestured over and over to the musicians and others dancing, and at the bear's nod of permission, we turned and followed them. They gave us a brief lesson in a peasant dance, and we split up, several of our group joining clusters of the locals. The detectives—as well as Will and Antonio—did not take part, each moving to a different side of the square to keep watch. It was then I realized that they still worried that we might be trailed…targeted. Here, now, the threat of our would-be kidnappers seemed distant. I disliked that their actions reminded me of it.

It made me sad for them, having to maintain the role of constant vigilance, because to be at the center of the dance was joy itself. Pierre knew the steps—having learned them as a child—and proved a skilled teacher. I let him lead me, enjoying the sway and dip, jump and skip, turn-turn-turn, sway and dip…and only once caught Will glancing my way. In frustration? Consternation? Anger? It was impossible to discern.

I shoved away a sense of guilt. Had he not turned from me in the chateau stairwell when he had his chance? Had he not insisted that it was better for us to stay apart? We traded partners, and Hugh swung me around in a circle, then led me in a broader one.

"Pay no attention to the bear's apprentice, Cora," he whispered. "You are right to welcome Pierre. Will's intentions…" He shook his head.

We parted and turned for three claps, then rejoined for a moment. He left me hanging on his last words, of course. Made me ask. My eyes flicked to Will and then across the circle to Pierre.

"What? What do you know of his intentions?"

"He has none," Hugh said, and for once I believed him. "The bear accused him of loving you from afar. He denied it. Said he only wished to get through the tour, collect his fee, and return to university."

I swallowed hard and forced a smile. "As well he should. I have my own plans to return to school come autumn."

He scoffed and looked at me in disbelief. "A Kensington girl as a country schoolteacher? Ah, no. Likely Wallace has far greater intentions for you. This is but the beginning. And none of your father's plans would include a man of McCabe's low means, regardless of his fine character."

I frowned. "No, Wallace and I only agreed—"

But then we were separated, and I was in Arthur's arms. "Are you all right?" he asked, looking down at me with concern. I missed a step, and he caught me, one hand at the small of my back and the other holding tight to my hand. Within a moment we eased back into the rhythm.

"I am fine, fine," I said, forcing another smile, suddenly wishing to return to the chateau, to my room, to put a door between me and everyone else. "Only getting tired, I think."

"It's been a long, full day."

"Indeed." I peered up at him. "Are you enjoying this? Joining us for part of our tour?"

"I am," he said, searching my eyes. "And you, Cora? Isn't this more a joy than a trial?" He paused as I digested his question. "I take it you've experienced nothing like it. You're like a duck in a new pond. Cautious but exulting in it."

"What a thing to say!" I sputtered in surprise.

He smiled. "What? It's true, isn't it? Couldn't you say those words yourself?"

The song came to an end, and he gave me a little bow as I followed the women in the group, giving him a small curtsy. "Yes," I said. "I suppose I could."

We stayed with the locals for several dances, then the men tossed coins into the musicians' open baskets and we moved on in pairs down the cobblestone streets—past smoky cabarets and empty cafés where waiters and waitresses cleaned tables and swept floors; past storefronts with lovely Provençal linens or brightly painted pottery in the windows; past a young couple caught in a secret embrace; past welcoming old men, three to a bench, smoking pipes; past old women frowning at us as they dumped cold dishwater, silently telling us to go back to where we came from.

At last we returned to the chateau, and the old bear stood by the door, counting as we all entered, like a mother hen making sure all had returned to the roost come nighttime. He nodded, looking weary but content, as was I. Antonio and I held back, and I stepped beside the old bear. "Thank you for one of the finest days of our entire trip," I said, touching his arm.

"You're welcome, my dear," he said, eyes twinkling. "Rest well. For tomorrow is another." He and Antonio paused, obviously waiting for me to say good night to Pierre. So I turned to him.

"Thank you for journeying all this way to see me for but one night," I said, taking his hands in mine.

He leaned forward and gave me as slow and tender a kiss on either cheek as was permissible. "I could do nothing other. I only regret that I must leave you again. The memories of our time together, our dance, shall have to sustain me in the meantime."

I laughed at his dramatic words. "I will look forward to it," I said, genuinely feeling it. Whatever was transpiring between us was not entirely unwelcome. However far-fetched it was, the idea of us being together beyond the summer wasn't *impossible*, was it? I enjoyed his company. And, unlike Will, he made me feel wanted. Worth being pursued regardless of what it cost him. "Good night, Pierre."

"Good night, *mon ange*," he said, reluctantly releasing my hands.

I entered the foyer and saw that the others had reached the landing and were separating to their own wings. Will was not in sight, and I swallowed hard, past a lump of disappointment. But what had I expected? A good-night kiss? A hug? If I were honest, part of me had wanted him to see my tender parting from Pierre. Part of me wanted to spur him with jealousy, drive him to truth.

But it was clearly true, what Hugh had said. Will had made his decision. Regardless of what we'd shared, or nearly shared...

CHAPTER EIGHT

~Cora~

I paced my room like a caged tiger. My mind was swirling with thoughts of Will, as well as of Pierre, of Wallace, of my future. It didn't help that the room was hot, given its placement on the western side of the chateau. All afternoon, the stone walls seemed to absorb the sun's rays, and now they seemed bent on cooking me inside. *I have to escape it....*

I pulled my summer dress back on, easing the tight sleeves over my sweaty skin. How I longed for the light, flowing work dresses from the farm! But there was nothing like that in my trunks; my lightest, airiest dresses were far too formal for an evening's walk. And I didn't want to draw any undue attention. I only wanted fresh air. And space.

If we had still been along the Rhône, I would've taken another dive off the deck into the blessedly cool waters. My best chance for relief was a walk along the walls, where the breeze came up from the sea, through the valley, washing over me and easing my tension. I exited my room quietly, not wanting to disturb Vivian in the room to my left or Lil to my right.

At the end of the hall, Antonio straightened and watched my approach. "Something you need, miss?"

"Yes. Some fresh air. It's terribly hot in there," I said, gesturing back to my room. "Perhaps after an hour's walk, it will have cooled enough to sleep. I hate to impose on you...."

"No, no," he said in his thick Italian accent, frowning and rocking his head back and forth as if my words pained him. "It is no trouble at all. Let me get another man to take my post. You will wait here?"

I nodded and knit my hands together, hoping against hope that it would be Claude or Yves who came to take his post. I wasn't in the mood to see Will. I bit my lip and tapped my toe, waiting for what felt a long time, considering leaving on my own. But that would be foolhardy, inviting trouble.... At last I saw shadows dance at the far end of the hall, entering from the servant's staircase.

I found myself holding my breath as they approached. Every nerve in my body felt alive. I trembled, alternately excited and furious, fighting for composure. Both Yves and Will followed Antonio. Which one of them was to accompany me?

"Master Will says he'd do well with a walk too," Antonio said with a conspiratorial grin in his dark eyes. "I shall remain at my post here."

"Yves will come too," Will said. "Given the hour. And your reputation."

"Of course," I replied evenly. "But surely Antonio and Yves can manage a late-night walk with me? There is no need for you to be troubled, Will."

"My knee is aching," Antonio said regretfully, his dark brow lowering in confusion. Plainly, he thought I'd welcome Will's company. "But I can manage if—"

"No, no," I said, already turning, agitated. "It will be fine."

At the bottom of the stairs, Will closed the gap between us. "Don't let my presence upset you, Cora. You will have the space you seek. I can follow you by five paces, as your guardian, nothing more." Not daring to speak, I nodded and forced myself to walk through the door he opened for me, and then ahead of him.

Yves quickly took the lead, and Will followed me, each five paces from me. We walked down the street and then climbed the turret stairs, round and round, up to the top of the city's inner wall. The wall was dotted with other late-night pedestrians out enjoying the cool of the night and a tapestry of stars above us. I sensed Will close the gap as we passed several gentlemen having a leisurely smoke, then felt him ease back when we passed two young lovers, arms intertwined, caring neither for propriety nor reputation. Even as I tried to push away all thoughts of Will, I longed for such freedom, but it still felt deliciously intimate to be even this close to him. His eyes on my back, my hair. Even if he didn't want me. Even if this was as close as we would ever be.

I'm walking the walls of a medieval city, I thought, striving to remember this moment, absorb it, as the bear had encouraged. I ought to be thinking of it, committing it to memory so that I could share it with my future students, rather than thinking of the man behind me.

Especially with Pierre here in the city, coming all this way to see me...

But again and again my mind went to Will.

Will. William. William McCabe. I wonder what his middle name is.

Two men came directly toward me, speaking rapidly, trying to catch my eye.

Ahead, Yves turned, and Will edged closer to me again. I watched as the men caught sight of Will, and their eyes widened in understanding. They immediately gave me a wide berth, passing me by with a genteel nod rather than engaging me. It made me smile, Will's powerful presence. Other men respected him. Not because of his money or his clothing, but simply because of his presence.

I breathed in the cool night air, feeling more and more calmed the farther I got from the chateau. The farther Will and I were away, together. I stopped at a city tower topped with a steep cone of a roof as the others were and glanced back at Will. I pointed up and raised my eyebrows, silently asking his permission. He tipped his head toward me, assenting, but held up his hand. He gave a low whistle, and Yves turned, saw what we wanted, and then went up to the tower to make certain no one else was there.

Yves soon returned and, with a flourish and a smile, gestured upward. I climbed the stairs, around and around. When I reached the top, my breath caught. I went to the tower window to look out upon the city and beyond it, the mountains in silhouette, blocking the pale stars, competing with the moon. It was beautiful. A fairy tale. And yet if I were the princess, who was the prince? Pierre, back at the chateau, peacefully sleeping? Or the man who had denied me, keeping his distance below?

I paced, moving from window to window, trying to sort out my feelings, my thoughts for a long, long while. When I heard the trudge of footsteps on the stone, I turned and found myself praying it was Will. Then praying it was not. I turned back to the window, unable to withstand the suspense of seeing him arrive.

Was it Yves? Or Will?

He stood behind me for a long moment, and by his hesitation, I knew it was Will. Every hair at the back of my neck stood on end, waiting for his touch. Would he give in? Admit that something was happening between us? Something unavoidable? Or might I finally set it aside?

After what seemed forever, he laid his hands gently on my shoulders and then slowly, ever so slowly, ran them down my arms until he intertwined his fingers with mine, his chest against my back.

I could barely breathe. I closed my eyes and leaned against him, relishing the feel of his arms covering mine, his cheek resting against the side of my head. ·

"Cora," he whispered. Equal measures of frustration and hope in one word.

"It's beautiful, is it not?" I tried, feeling as if I ought to attempt some sort of conversation.

"Not half as beautiful as you," he said, his lips close enough to my ear for his breath to warm it. I shivered, and he released my hands, wrapping me in his arms. I reached up to put my hands on his burly arms and leaned my head back against his chest, still looking outward. *It's true. Despite what he said, he cares. He cares!*

"We only have a moment," he said. "I told Yves I was coming to fetch you." Gently, he turned me around and placed a hand on the side of my face. "I know I should keep my distance, Cora. But I can't help myself. God help me, I can't...." Then he bent to kiss me on the lips, using his other hand to pull me close. He smelled of soap and spice and leather, and his lips on mine felt…uncommonly wonderful. After a while, I nestled against him again, feeling the steady, strong beat of his heart.

"What are we going to do, Will?" I asked.

"This," he said, edging slightly away to tip my chin up so I was looking at him. "Stolen moments until the summer ends. Then, once we're home, I'll be free to go to your father and ask him for his permission to court you properly."

I pulled farther away. "It isn't his decision to make. After you cease to be my guide, and I your client, Wallace Kensington…" I shook my head in frustration. "It is Alan Diehl that you should seek out. He is more my father than Wallace Kensington ever was or will be."

Will withdrew and stood beside me, arms crossed, as I continued to look outward through the window. "You think Wallace will be content to send you off once the tour is complete? You do your thing, he does his?"

I frowned up at him. His words were so close to Hugh's that alarm bells went off in my head. "Why, yes."

"You're wrong. This is just the beginning of Wallace Kensington's plans for you."

"What? What are you talking about? He and I have a very clear agreement. I take this tour, get to know his other children, and he will fund the rest of my education, as well as see my parents to a better place. That was it."

"And you have no interest in getting to know him further?"

"No," I said. "I know all I need to at this point. Alan Diehl is my papa. It is him I miss, think about, pray for. Not Wallace Kensington."

He nodded thoughtfully, then reached out to take my hand in his, pulling it to his lips. "I'd go seek out the pope, if necessary, in order to get permission to court you, Cora Diehl Kensington."

His kisses on my bare knuckles sent shivers up my arm, and I smiled up into his eyes. "I do hope it doesn't go as far as all that," I said.

He lowered my hand, now holding it between both of his. "What of…Pierre?"

That was more difficult. I knew that Will was the one my heart longed for. But I hated the idea of disappointing Pierre, bringing him sadness. He was such a delight, so supportive, so sweet. He'd never done a thing to make me turn from him. But it was unkind to lead him on; I needed to tell him. Tomorrow. Before he left.

But my plans proved impossible.

Because in the morning, the bear was dead.

CHAPTER NINE

~Cora~

I ached to go to Will. To give him a hug, try to ease his pain. Sorrow etched his face. Over and over he reached up and massaged his forehead, staring at the ground, the sky, the mountains in the distance, as if he was trying to accept the truth of the matter. Stuart McCabe was dead.

He'd died in his sleep. A heart attack, the doctor said with a shrug, as if it happened every day. I knew it likely did happen every day. But not to Stuart McCabe. Not to Will's uncle—his only surviving family, that I knew of. Not to our bear, in the middle of the Grand Tour.

Arthur, Antonio, and Pierre saw to all the funeral arrangements. Apparently, the bear had always wanted to be buried where he breathed his last. "'Don't bear the burden of shipping my corpse home, boy,'" I'd heard Will say to Felix, obviously quoting his uncle. Through it all, Pierre was so caring and courteous—to the point that he put off his business at home—that I couldn't summon the courage to tell him what I had decided. The service in the chapel was brief, with the pastor speaking in French so quickly and in such a mumble I doubted even Will could follow what he said. And then the men lifted the simple casket and carried it out behind the church to a cemetery that looked over the green rolling hills, with a view of the mountains in the distance, and the river below.

They'd lowered the casket into the ground, the pastor said a few more words—bored, as if he'd rather be anyplace but with us at that moment—and then tossed a fistful of dirt on top of it. He departed without a further word, and the look of woe on Will's face as he stared after the man made my heart break. I knew there were no words that would make it right. Nothing that would ease the pain. But it made me wish for some, with everything I had in me.

One by one, my siblings and the Morgans and Art went to him, touched his arm, shook his hand. Felix thumped him on the back. Lil gave him a hug, and he clung to her a moment, grateful. How I wished I could do the same! But Pierre was by my side, taking care of me, I supposed. Watching over me. His tenderness moved me as much as it irritated me. We approached Will, and I reached out a hand to touch his arm and then hesitated, pulling it back, clenching it before my belly. "I'm so sorry, Will. It's a terrible loss for you," I said.

He met my eyes and then glanced over to Pierre and back, such pain in his gaze it made me want to weep. He nodded. "It is. I'll miss him forever. He was good to me...." He looked out over the valley and then back to the grave as two men began shoveling dirt into it, not even having the courtesy to let us depart.

"Come, come, my friend," Pierre said, gesturing toward Will and then down the path. Pierre put a hand on his shoulder, and

I walked on Will's opposite side. "It is sooner than the bear likely wished, but he could not have chosen a finer place to end his own grand tour, could he?"

Will smiled then, and I was grateful to Pierre for his kind words. "No, I suppose he couldn't."

We all paused and looked across the magnificent castle rooftops and dual walls of the ancient city and the verdant valley beyond. It was a good resting place. A fine stop.

"He trusted you, Will," I ventured to say. "I mean…if you choose to go on. Your uncle had been leaving most of the guide duties to you this last week. Had you noticed?"

He studied me a moment, as if surprised by the observation, and then nodded. "That's true." He shook his head. "He wasn't himself. I should've known…should've pushed him to see a doctor."

"And then what would've happened?" I asked. I thought about my own papa…about him rallying in Minnesota. It could so easily have gone another way. "God holds our lives in His hands. I think the bear lived it out the way he wanted—on a journey, and now onto the next. He didn't strike me as one who would've been content at home for long."

Will stared at me, and I sensed he drew a measure of comfort from my words. Pierre turned and offered his arm to me. After a moment's hesitation, I took it.

Back at the chateau, after Pierre had gathered his elegant luggage and a footman had brought it to the foyer, I rose from my seat beside Lil and Nell to go and say farewell to him. I wished I had it in me to tell him that this was it—that he shouldn't come to me again—but I felt weak, weary. And knowing Pierre, unless I was quite forceful, he'd only take it as a challenge to change my mind when our circum-stances were less glum.

He offered his hands as I came near, and I placed my own in them. He pulled me close to kiss both of my cheeks, slowly, tenderly, as if letting me go caused him a physical ache, and I felt terribly guilt ridden. *This isn't me. I can't go on this way.* Over his shoulder, I saw Antonio keeping watch at a respectful distance.

"Pierre, I...there's something I ought to tell you."

"Non, *mon ange,*" he said, studying my face, not letting my hands go. "Do not say it now, in the throes of grief. This is not the time to make any decision."

I started, surprised that my feelings might be so plain to him, and he smiled. He squeezed my hands and leaned forward to whis-per, "I know this seems improbable. This romance. But give me a chance. That is all I ask. I shall see you in Vienna. Be safe."

I sighed and gave him a small smile. "Are you certain? Why—"

He interrupted me with a quick shush and leaned forward with another squeeze of my hands. "Until we meet again, *mon ange.* Adieu."

Helplessly, I watched him wait for the butler to open the door, and then he was gone.

------◇◇◇------

~William~

Felix and Arthur sat across from him in the drawing room of the chateau down in the city. Antonio stood by a window, chin in hand.

Will looked out and thought that Richelieu was right—that Uncle Stuart would've approved of this final stop on his lifelong tour, with views of both the magnificent mountains and the castle, like a foretaste of heaven itself.

But now was a point of decision.

"What will you do?" Arthur asked quietly. "Take your clients home?"

"No, no," Felix interrupted. "Pierre suggested we return to Paris for a while. To rest. Gather ourselves. Then decide. Let's not make a rash decision."

Will's furrowed brow deepened. Take Cora back to the Richelieu chateau? Toward their would-be kidnappers? *And Richelieu?* He shook his head. "I think not. My uncle…he'd want me to carry on. I have all the paperwork. I've led this tour with him for years. The very next one was to have been my first, solo." He shrugged his shoulders and dared to look at the men. "Why not simply carry on?"

To their credit, they managed to hide any hint of doubt. And their apparent belief that he could indeed fill his uncle's shoes was all the support he needed. Antonio gave him one encouraging nod. He rose. "We'll move on in the morning."

"Surely you need another day—" Arthur began.

"No. We'll go on to Nîmes. Continuing on will be…therapeutic. I'll see them through to Vienna, then leave it to their fathers to decide. They may very well elect to take them home then."

"I could go on with you for a bit longer," Arthur offered. "Now that you're down a man. I have a couple more weeks before I'm due to return…."

Will studied him. He seemed sincere, and even though Uncle Stuart had hardly been a physical guardian of late, he had been another set of wise eyes and ears. Surely Art could be as much assistance—even if he elected to leave them early. Will reached out a hand to him. "I'd be grateful. Even if you can't accompany us all the way to Vienna, it helps to have another man about."

"Say nothing of it," Art said, shaking his hand.

"Now to tell the Morgans and Kensingtons," Will said, looking to Antonio.

The older man put a hand on his shoulder. "You are already a fine bear, William. I have every confidence in you, as would your uncle."

"Thank you, Antonio. I'm glad you're with me." He felt a wave of melancholy wash through him. A hope that Uncle Stuart would enter the room at any moment. *He's gone...gone forever.*

"Of course! Where else would I be? I shall miss your uncle dearly, but it is as he would have it. You, continuing on in his stead."

But as Will entered the hallway, he wondered whether he would continue if Cora Diehl Kensington wasn't one of his clients, and if there wasn't a handsome check awaiting him at the end of the journey.

CHAPTER TEN

~Cora~

Our touring cars pulled up along an ancient city gate at Nîmes, and Will came back to speak to us, allowing us to remain seated.

"More and more," Will said, gesturing behind him to the ruins, "we'll glimpse the remains of the Roman Empire. We'll drive about the city so you can get your bearings—be sure to watch for the Maison Carrée, a Roman temple. In a bit, we'll visit the Pont du Gard, the highest aqueduct the Romans ever built. And tonight, we'll attend a bullfight in an amphitheater that was erected close to two thousand years ago."

"A bullfight?" squealed the girls.

I felt less enthused. We were to dress to the nines and then sit on stone seats to watch men harass a bull? I'd had far more fun sneaking past the bull in Mr. Hanneman's fenced north quarter back home. That animal had won prizes at the state fair....

Well, I told myself, *at least the amphitheater will be of interest.* My heart skipped a beat. A real Roman amphitheater.

"That gate appears sunken," Vivian said, hands on hips, waving at the Porte Auguste with her fan, then turning the fan on herself again. It was only midmorning, but with the roofs folded back on our touring cars, the summer sun had already set us to perspiring.

"Well noted," Art said after taking our photograph from across the street, looking up at the place. "Over time, the city has been built up and roads paved and paved again. The Porte Auguste is but one of two city gates left. We're fortunate it remains at all. See those two larger arches at the center? They were for the chariots and horses—and the two smaller arches on either side were for pedestrians. Quite organized, don't you think?"

Vivian gave it a dubious look, clearly ready to move on, and Art returned to his vehicle. But my eyes moved to Will, who was presumably sharing the same information with the young men in the car ahead of us, waving back toward the gate, pointing to the far right and then tracing the line to the left. Something Felix said made him laugh, and he was so handsome in that moment—brown hair shining in the sun, eyes alight with joy—that I sucked in my breath. I'd not seen him even smile in the last two days. And to see him laugh…

Vivian looked over at me and frowned. "What is it?"

"Nothing," I said, quickly glancing back to the gate after I sat down beside her again. "I only was thinking…would it not be a delight to travel back in time and see Rome in all her glory?"

"Hmph. Maybe," she said, continuing to fan herself. "Perhaps travel via chariot was cooler than this infernal touring car."

"Be glad we're not in buggies," I chided.

"Or on mules!" laughed Lil.

I nodded, smiling with her, but as I did so, my eyes slipped back to Will. He was striding past to rejoin Art and Hugh in the car behind us. We shared a long, delicious glance.

"What's your secret, Cora?" Nell asked, and my heart skipped a beat as I quickly looked to her, worried she'd caught us. The girl was madly fanning herself, her apple cheeks truly resembling apples, they were so flushed.

"Excuse me?"

"How do you manage to look so fresh while the rest of us perspire?" She dabbed at her forehead with a lace-edged handkerchief.

"Trust me, I'm far from cool," I said, picking up my own fan, relieved to have narrowly avoided discovery and now feeling the heat of embarrassment.

The driver in the touring car behind us beeped his horn, and our vehicles made their way into the flow of traffic. Blessed air blew by us, and we held onto our hats.

Antonio, riding in front with the driver, turned to tell us what we were seeing as we drove. The Maison Carrée, an elegant Roman temple built in AD 2, was "one of the best preserved in the world," shouted Antonio over the noise of the wind. I craned my neck to get a better view of the elegant, finely fluted columns that surrounded the temple. Next, past many stately, grand homes, was the vast Jardin de la Fontaine. Antonio droned on about the eighteenth-century gardens capitalizing on the water source here in the city. "Above them in the distance, the octagonal structure, you see?" he said. "It is Tour Magne, once part of the Roman walls." Antonio shook his head sorrowfully and lifted his dark brows. "One of the best views of the city is up there." Clearly, he regretted that we hadn't time to stop.

We moved on, turning and turning again until the huge amphitheater came into view. "Les Arénas," Antonio said, lifting a proud hand toward it in the distance, as if introducing us to his girlfriend. I brought a hand to my chest and gasped. I'd never seen so grand a structure. If this was so remarkable, what would it feel like to see the Coliseum in Rome?

"She holds twenty-five thousand spectators," Antonio said over his shoulder, looking from us to the arena. "Chariot races, gladiators, and now, tonight, a bullfight."

"I confess I prefer the bullfight to a gladiator fight," Vivian said.

"Not me!" Lil said with a giggle, leaning toward Nell. "I'd prefer to see men in all their...manliness."

"Lillian Kensington!" Vivian said, sounding aghast. But we were all smiling.

We drove out of the city, then, out into the countryside, past farms with neat and tidy rows of lavender, olive groves, and vineyards. An hour later, we turned, and up ahead, we could see greenery that could only mean one thing...a river. We pulled up beside a small chateau that overlooked what we learned was the Gardon River, and the men led us around back to where five rowboats were waiting.

"Oh, a boat ride," Lillian said, clapping her small hands together.

"I admit," Vivian said to me, "it does sound welcome. To be on the water."

I nodded in agreement, waiting for us to be assigned our boats. Will told the younger girls they'd be with him and Hugh. I shoved aside my disappointment, pretending to have nothing but my own assignment in mind. "You, Cora," Will said, barely looking at me, "will join Felix and Art."

"Excellent," I said, turning to take my brother's proffered arm as we traversed across the wide expanse of rough limestone to reach the boats. Was Will avoiding me? Afraid to be too close to me lest he betray his feelings? Angry I hadn't ended it with Pierre? Or was he changing his mind? He hadn't spent any time with me in the days since the funeral, and now with the bear gone...perhaps he was solely thinking about getting us through the tour and getting back to school.

Perhaps *everything* had changed.

"Vivian and Andrew, please go and join Antonio in the last boat," said Will over his shoulder as we walked. They grouped together behind us, and I envied them, the chance to float the river, holding hands, sharing longing looks, without fear of repercussion. Ahead, I could see the two detectives, each in their own boat, already at the oars. As we clambered into our assigned boats, Yves shoved off with his own oarsman, taking the lead in scouting for any trouble...or perhaps, noticing the boulders that dotted the blue water, he only sought the best route down.

Felix offered his hand, and I stepped carefully into the boat while the oarsman steadied it. Felix sidled in, well accustomed to the rocking ways of wood upon water, then Art. "I'm relieved to be in your boat this time around," I said lowly to Felix as he sat down beside me.

"Oh?"

"Yes. Well I remember your expertise with an oar in a water fight," I said.

He smiled and reached out to take my hand. "I think it was in that moment, seeing you sopping wet and still laughing, that I realized you were truly my sister."

I smiled and looked down, embarrassed by our intimate moment.

"Though an oar is a far less effective weapon than a paddle," he said. "Besides," he whispered, leaning close to my ear, "our oarsman appears to want nothing of any fun whatsoever."

I dared to look at the stern man—dressed all in white, with a blue handkerchief smartly tied at the neck—and almost burst out laughing. From his expression, one would have thought this excursion was a form of medieval torture rather than a delightful respite. I ducked my head and tried madly to cover my giggle. But when Felix let a burst of pent-up air out as he turned—pretending something had caught his eye—I was lost. Together, we laughed and laughed.

The oarsman flicked his chin forward, toward us. *"Qu'est-ce qui est si drôle?"*

"He wants to know what amuses you," translated Art from up front, bending over his camera to take our photograph.

"Well, clearly, friend, it is not you," Felix returned. "Is life so horrendous that you should appear like your horse died en route to the boat?"

"Felix!" I cried, aghast.

"He doesn't understand English," Felix whispered, smiling at us both.

"Hmph," said the man, clearly dismissing us. Either Felix was right, or he thought us idiots.

"Ignore him," Felix muttered, and offered his arm. I looped my hand through. "Let's not allow anything to ruin this gorgeous day on the river, even this fine man manning our oars!" he said, cheerfully waving at the man.

Art shook his head, bemused, and we entered the strongest current of the river, moving rapidly down and around the bend. I took off one glove and leaned over to let my hand drag in the water, watching as my fingers left four rivulets behind them. I dipped it lower, relishing the cooling effect.

The other two boats came closer, and we tied up for a bit, drifting and chatting. Art took more photographs of the group.

"May I have a couple of those for postcards, Art?" Vivian asked.

"Certainly. We'll get them developed in Nîmes before we move on, and you can post them."

"Oh, I want one too!" Nell said. "May I have one?"

"Yes, of course."

I looked everywhere I could at the scenery, working hard not to glance in Will's direction. A champagne cork popped, and then another, and glasses were pulled from a basket and passed along.

"Please," Felix said, offering his to the oarsman. "You appear to need it far more than I."

"Non," the man said gruffly, giving his head a stiff shake.

I bit my lip, trying not to laugh. The man looked angry enough to jump overboard and swim to shore. Or deck Felix.

Tiny, perfect strawberries were passed next, and we tossed the uneaten tops in the river, watching as they floated for a while and then disappeared.

Will was half turned in his seat, and when we rounded the bend, I could see why. Up ahead was a triple-level limestone bridge, and we all gasped at the sight of it. At the bottom of the bridge were sturdy arches with columns and breakers thick enough to weather two thousand years of whatever the river brought her way. Above that firm foundation were three levels of beautiful arches.

"The Pont du Gard," our young bear said proudly, turning back to us. "At a hundred and sixty feet, it is the highest bridge the Romans ever built. They considered it a testimony to their empire and took great pride in it, and for good reason. Here we are," he said, gesturing across the river, "in the midst of a waterway that has flooded every spring of every year since that bridge was first erected. And still"—he shook his head—"two thousand years later, there she remains."

The oarsmen separated our boats from the others on the river as we neared the bridge, giving them more room to maneuver, and we all grew quiet, in awe as we got closer and closer, then slid underneath the monolith and past her. "That aqueduct carried water that originated at the springs in Uzés," Will said, "thirty-one miles from Nîmes, and was in use for close to five hundred years."

I couldn't keep myself from it any longer. I looked over to Will, who stared back at the bridge as long as it was in sight. I knew how he loved architecture…the bones of a structure. And I longed to hear him talk about it. See the excitement in his eyes as he explained to me just what a mechanical engineering marvel it really was. But it dawned on me that he wasn't going to be an architect. He was already the next Bear McCabe. And the thought of it made me feel unaccountably sad.

"Already sad to be leaving the Pont du Gard?" Felix asked, putting a knuckle under my chin.

"What?" I asked, trying to focus on what he was saying. "Oh, yes. You got me. Have you ever seen anything like it?"

"I think not," he said, giving his head a little shake, his blue eyes wide with wonder. "Truly, a most magnificent excursion, this," he called out, verbally saluting Will. "More champagne?" He held up a bottle.

Will shook his head, and when Felix turned to me, I did the same.

"Friend? *Ami*?" Felix asked the oarsman, again lifting the bottle. The man practically growled at him.

With a smile and a cock of his eyebrow that said *all the more for me*, Felix tipped up the bottle to his mouth and drained it.

———◇◆◇———

~William~

They returned to Nîmes, and after getting settled into a sumptuous mansion, they separated to their rooms. A light lunch was sent to each suite, where the clients were to rest and change before a quick dinner and then a walk over to the amphitheater to enjoy the bullfight.

With a long groan, Will stretched out atop his bed, staring at the high ceiling and crystal chandelier above him. He checked his wristwatch. He had four hours before they were to meet in the salon downstairs. Will closed his eyes and considered a quick bath. He winced as he thought about squeezing into his light summer suit, tighter than ever, and joining the others in all their finery. Especially considering he'd be sitting in the too-small suit through a sultry summer evening in the amphitheater, on a stone seat.

No. I can't do it. Not one more day, not one more hour.

His eyes popped open, and he glanced over at his armoire. There was an excellent tailor around the corner. His uncle had purchased a suit from him last summer. And had it fitted for him within the hour. Might he find something similar?

The funds in his bank account at home were meager, but he saw no argument against the purchase. He had his uncle's private purse, still full of a wad of bills, even after paying for his burial. And if he were to play the role of a full-fledged bear for the remainder of the summer, ought he not look the part?

---◇◇◇---

Will emerged from his room that night feeling like a new man. He had on a tan suit in the finest weave that, blessedly, breathed far better than the light wool of his old suit. He smiled as he paused in front of his door, straightening his tie along a collar that finally, *finally* fit around his neck. And inside his hotel armoire was a brand-new formal suit as well. It would allow him to circulate among the well-to-do at any function ahead and actually make others turn their heads in admiration rather than cover their mouths and whisper, laughing over him. In addition, the tailor had persuaded him to purchase an extra pair of trousers, two smart, crisp shirts, and a second tie, as well as a belt and two pairs of shoes from the cobbler next door.

Will had spent a fortune, most everything in his uncle's private purse, but what else could he do? Truth be told, if he was to hold his head up high and take Cora's arm like a man, he could not tolerate looking as he had heretofore. She deserved better if they were ever to have a chance to be together....

He strode down the grand marble staircase to meet the others. Cora turned as he entered, as if sensing his presence, and he smiled, briefly allowing his eyes to settle on hers before moving on to Vivian's, as if she and Cora held equal favor in his heart. But he had to concentrate to keep his gaze on Vivian and then move on to Felix, because all he wanted to do was to look back to Cora. To make sure she had noted his new clothes, to make sure she looked happy and…proud.

The thought made him pause. What was that about? He wanted to make her proud? She wasn't the kind of girl who was moved by the finery of her new set. So was this really about him?

He frowned in confusion even as he forced a smile for Lillian and Nell, who were coming to run their hands over his sleeves and coo over his new suit.

"Sir?" said a servant, coming to him with a telegram on a silver tray.

Will reached for the envelope and turned away for a moment of privacy. He slid the telegram out and discovered it was from his uncle's attorney back home.

Unfortunate news –STOP– Bills overdue funds short –STOP– Must complete tour to bring accounts to date –STOP– Will you still get paid your fee without Stuart –STOP– Please advise –STOP– Carlyle Connor

He sucked in his breath and took a few steps away from the laughing, chatting people behind him, feeling almost dizzy. He'd known that Uncle Stuart wasn't flush, but he'd thought he'd likely discover a nest egg in his bank account. After all, the old man had been hoping to retire. But on what? Had he assumed Will would support him?

Will massaged his temple and then ran a hand down his face. *I just spent so many dollars…on clothes. Clothes…*

"Are you all right?" Cora asked in a whisper, suddenly at his elbow. "You look positively ashen."

He glanced down at her and watched as her big blue eyes moved down to the telegram in his hand. He didn't want her to be worried. Not for him. Not for his future. Not when he hoped they might have a chance. Some sort of chance…

"It's fine. A surprise. But I'll deal with it. Come," he said, forcing a smile to his face and lifting his arm to her. "Nîmes awaits."

CHAPTER ELEVEN

~Cora~

We dined upon a favorite of Nîmes, the *brandade*—a salt cod puree with olive oil and milk—and caviar and tiny, perfectly toasted slices of bread. After dishes of the smallest but most succulent raspberries I'd ever tasted, smothered in cream and crystallized sugar, we left for the arena, promenading down the street in pairs.

Daringly, Will offered me his arm again.

"You look exceptionally dapper this evening, Master McCabe," I said under my breath. "New suit?"

"Indeed," he said from the corner of his mouth, then he turned smiling eyes down at me. "But you always look exceptionally beautiful, regardless of what you wear."

I smiled and squeezed his arm, feeling electrified, every fiber of my being awake and alive. I'd never experienced anything like it. I'd had twinges of it with Pierre—but this, *this*...

We turned a corner, and the arena came into view. "People would come from near and far to attend the games here," Will said, speaking loudly enough that all nearby could hear him. "The Roman motto was, 'Give them bread and circuses,' but there weren't nearly enough seats, even in an arena as grand as this one. They distributed tickets, which were collected at the door. The nobles sat below; the poor, up high. There were merchants outside selling food and drink that all were allowed to carry in."

"Where'd they…see to their business?" Hugh asked, inhaling deeply on his cigarette.

The younger girls dissolved in giggles behind him.

"In massive latrines," Will said.

"Thank God for that," Hugh returned with a smile.

"So why not give us a good gladiatorial sparring?" Andrew asked. "Isn't bullfighting a Spanish tradition?"

"Indeed," Will said, turning to walk backward so he could speak to the whole group. "But there's a shortage of men willing to die for another's entertainment, and with the Romans gone, as well as their slaves…I'm afraid bulls are as close to gladiatorial combat as we can get."

We smiled with him. The crowd thickened the closer we got, and Antonio led the way. I took hold of both Will's and Art's arms, making way for the others. Behind us, Lillian was on Felix's arm, Nell on Hugh's, and Vivian on Andrew's. The detectives guarded our rear flank. Even without the bear with us, I felt protected and safe. More so given my proximity to Will.

I fought to keep my composure. The last thing I needed was my brother or sisters catching on. Hugh was already far too keenly aware of the attraction we felt, his eyes missing nothing. Art, too, even so new to us. But it was like yeast causing dough to rise, what I felt for William, impossible to suppress the more I was with him. The raw, physical draw. I felt as though I'd been awakened from a deep slumber and my very existence depended on sharing every moment with him. Our time together on the Carcassonne wall, our kisses, ran through my head again and again, and I hungered for the chance to steal away with him for but a moment of privacy we could call our own.

I knew I would need to find an opportunity to cut Pierre loose once he returned. Memories of his sweet farewell sent a wave of sorrow and shame through me. But I'd tried, hadn't I? At least a little…

The merchants outside the arena sold jugs of wine and bread wrapped in paper, and despite the fact that we'd just supped on far finer fare, Hugh and Felix stopped to purchase both. Reaching into a pocket inside his fine new jacket, Will gave tickets to a man at the ancient Roman gate, and we were pressed from all sides as we entered the melee and moved forward. It was so tight there would've been no option to turn back, even if we wished it.

We walked through a tunnel that rose twenty feet, and when we were through it, we moved up a stairwell at the edge of a grand oval. The feel of it, with people lining every level, took my breath away. At the center of the sand-covered floor was a French flag, as well as two more. "What are those others?" I asked Will, gesturing toward them.

"The community flags from which the bullfighters hail."

He turned, and I followed him up the stairs and then down a row to our seats. When we sat down, he turned to me, concern in his eyes. "This can be a bit bloody. Might you be overwhelmed?"

I almost laughed. "William McCabe, do you forget that I was raised on a farm? That is a question for my sisters and Nell."

His eyes hovered over mine for a moment, and then he smiled. "I would imagine."

We were seated in male-female order so that none of the women in our troop were unguarded. Additionally, the detectives stood on either end, along the stairs, keeping constant watch. I thought it a bit much at this point. We'd not seen the men who had attacked us in Paris once. Obviously the leader was in deep hiding. I would have suggested releasing the detectives from their duties, but I knew Mr. Morgan and my father would have none of it. It was precisely due to the detectives' continued involvement that we were still on the tour at all. Without them, our fathers would have demanded we pack it up and head home. Will stood and met Claude's eye as he guarded the aisle to one side. He motioned my direction, then asked Art, on my other side, to keep an eye on me.

"Honestly, Will, I'm perfectly safe here in the middle of twenty-five thousand people."

"You might be surprised," he said. "Please do not let down your guard." He moved to speak to the others, presumably to warn them of what was to come in the bullfight.

In front of me, a group of young French men were celebrating. Down so low in the arena, they were likely the well-to-do or associated in some fashion with the evening's bullfighters. They toasted with wine—*"À votre santé!"*—and drained their cups together.

One hugged his companion and caught my eye. *"Mon Dieu!"* he said, putting his hand to his heart. *"Au ange! Au ange!"* He hit his friend on the shoulder and gestured to me, and then his companion did the same to the next, until all five looked back at me in wonder, as if I were truly an angel. A guilty pang went through me at their use of Pierre's favorite term for me.

"I imagine you cannot go anywhere," Art said beside me, "without attracting new admirers."

"Oh, I wouldn't say that," I said, then looked at the young men before me. "*Comment allez-vous?*" I asked, one of the few French phrases I knew. *How are you?*

"Ahh, she spoke to me!" cried one in English, collapsing dramatically.

"Tell me, *mon ange*," said the one seated at the center, as Will returned to his seat, "that you do not uh, uh," he stuttered, searching for the English words, then finished, "*lui appartient.*"

"He wants to make sure you do not belong to me," Will translated, his eyes sliding over to meet mine.

Felix laughed and leaned in front of Art, catching the gist of the conversation. "No, no," he said, waving his hand, as if the idea were preposterous. "*C'est ma soeur.*" Felix gestured over to Will. "*C'est notre guide.*"

I needed no translation. His tone was clear enough. I was his sister, and Will nothing more than our guide. In Felix's mind, there'd be no way that Will would ever be with me. My eyes went to the flags moving ever so slightly in the scant breeze that passed through the arena. Was that what Will feared most? Others looking down on him? Thinking he was unworthy of me because my father was Wallace Kensington? But I wasn't that girl! I was the daughter of a farmer, my home a ramshackle, run-down dirt-poor farm in Montana.

To think Will unworthy of me was preposterous. A well-traveled, kind, handsome man I once could have only dreamed of, now struggling to be considered my equal…only due to…blood?

I thought of Will's words of warning. As well as Hugh's. And Lil's reaction to my plans to return home. Was it true? Was this trip only the beginning of Wallace Kensington's plans for me? His means of getting me into the fold, settled, accustomed to luxury and excess, before demanding more of me? Would he truly stand between me and Will at the end of our tour? Well, if he tried, he'd be surprised. A deal was a deal. I'd agreed to this trip in exchange for him helping my parents and sending me back to school. As far as I was concerned, we could part ways amicably, and my life would be my own. Not his to dictate. And if I chose Will…

I turned to watch him. Will and the playful young gentlemen were chatting in French, the men gesturing to the arena. "He says his cousin is one of the bullfighters. He claims he is one of the best."

"I guess we'll see the truth of that sooner rather than later, eh?" Andrew said from down the row.

"You doubt his word?" I asked, leaning forward to look over at him.

"I doubt any man's word, be it cards or bullfights."

"That's rather cynical, don't you think?" I said.

"Not cynical. Wise."

———◇◇◇———

For a while, we traded idle chatter through Will's translation. The men shared their jug of wine with us, passing us chipped, clay cups and insisting, "Drink, drink!" and we reluctantly accepted. We learned the men were from a neighborhood in the city with a long tradition of training the best bullfighters around. We were invited to a celebration party after the fight, which Will tried to decline, but the men would have none of it. "You, new friends," said one in rudimentary English. "Come, come!"

Will looked at me, and I shrugged a shoulder. "It is precisely the sort of thing my uncle adores on the tour," he said. His face fell a little. "Adored," he amended. "Although not with the caliber of people your traveling companions would endorse."

"It will be good for them," I said in a whisper, leaning toward him. I hovered there for a second, simply enjoying his proximity, and he turned his head—just a couple degrees—toward me, clearly appreciating the same. I made myself withdraw before anyone noticed.

Horns blasted, and milling people hurried to their seats. Lovely women dressed in Spanish costume and headdresses processed in two lines to music barely audible over the crowd's cheering. The women danced, their skirts flowing as they turned one way and then another, arms high in the air. A line of men came in, also in Spanish dress, heads held erect and to one side, hands on their hips. They came down the center of the two lines of women, and they all danced together as the crowd clapped in rhythm. Art moved past us and down the stairs to try to capture the moment on his Kodak.

The clapping was so loud, so precise, that it reverberated in my chest. I grinned at Felix and then smiled at Will, glad we could share a moment such as this. It was grand to be sitting in a two-thousand-year-old structure with twenty-five thousand French. I'd never experienced anything like it. The nearest I'd ever come was the county fair back home in Montana, but that typically brought in a mere thousand people for the rodeo.

A woman on horseback rode around the circumference of the arena, and as she passed, the crowd let out a roar of approval. The result was a wave of sound, filled with such joy and excitement that a shiver ran down my neck and back. It was as if they were one organism, all these people....

The couples in the center moved into a second dance and, when they were done, filtered out. The crowd began to call in a collective low hum, which escalated to the most deafening sound I had ever experienced when the bullfighter entered the ring. He strode out, a black hat atop his head, a black and red cape at his back. He had on a perfectly white shirt and tight black pants that were tucked into boots. When he reached the center, he lifted one arm and bowed to each quadrant of the arena, eliciting waves of cheers. Then he turned toward a far door and whipped a red banner before him, back and forth.

At once, the crowd became as silent as it had been loud only moments before. They held their collective breath. Then the gates opened, and out ran a black bull. The crowd was on their feet, shouting and raising their hands, as if an enemy had crossed a boundary line. The bull seemed disoriented, running one way and then the other. He was much bigger and much faster than old Mr. Hanneman's bull from home.

The matador called out to him and waved his red banner like a flag, taunting him. Without pause, the bull turned and ran straight at him. I gasped as he allowed the bull to draw terribly near before whipping the flag away at the very last moment, the red cloth in his hands waving over the fearsome horns and black hide of the passing bull. As he turned, I could see what I'd missed at first—the matador had slid a slender sword through the ridge of the animal's back. I'd not even seen it in his hand. But blood dripped down either side of the bull as he turned, scraped at the ground with his hoof, warning of another charge, and then went after the matador again as the crowd screamed, *"Magicien! Magicien!"*

Again the creature was pierced. I recoiled in horror. It was barbaric, this practice. I'd known the bull was to be killed, and I'd seen animals slaughtered many times on the farm. But this wasn't the quick, respectful death I'd expected. It was slow, drawn out. Torture.

But then a second bull was sent into the arena, and the crowd roared their approval, twice as loud. Felix hooted beside me. "Can you believe this? What a spectacle!"

I shook my head, feeling a little queasy. He wasn't listening for my response.

"Cora, are you all right?" Will asked in my ear.

I looked up at him, about to ask if he might escort me out for a moment, when the men in front of us rose, arms up, cheering with the crowd about us, and then their cheer spread across the masses. We stood too. The matador had apparently dodged both bulls, one after the other, piercing both. Hidden by the crowds, Will slipped his hand around mine as if sensing my distress. Both bulls ran around the ring, the second arrival chasing the first.

The matador strode toward them, calling out, waving his red flag, and one turned, lowered his head, then tore after him. But the other was acting oddly. Frenzied. Jumping up against the far wall, almost as if he knew what was coming and intended to try to escape. The crowd cried out and pushed back in a visible wave, and men ran out onto the floor to distract the bull, waving at him with sticks, and when he charged at them, they jumped to safety themselves. They were like the rodeo clowns back home—incredible, jumping so high so fast that I wondered if their legs were made of springs. All trying to get the bull back into position to take another run at the matador.

But one man didn't quite make it. He fell back to the dirt, just missing being crushed by the passing bull. The animal circled around, and the man took another run at the wall, the bull coming perilously close. He jumped up and over, directly below us. The bull ran past, circling and coming to a stop halfway out. Behind him, the matador called to the bull and regally waved his cape, but the bull was staring at the man below us; he was holding his arms up, shouting in victory about his narrow escape, the people behind him doing the same. And they were all waving bits of red.

Oh no, I thought, looking back and up to see our whole sector mimicking those in front. My eyes went back to the bull even as I grabbed hold of Will's arm in terror. The bull was already in motion, churning toward us, and this time, he jumped up so high, he landed on the top of the front wall. Everyone erupted into screams and shouts, dividing as if the bull were Moses and the crowd the Red Sea. His belly was stuck, his legs flailing, but he was clearly going to make it over. And when he did, he'd likely gore as many of his screaming tormenters as possible.

"Come on," Will said, forcing me to stand as the crowd pressed back toward us. "Keep your feet!" he shouted at me, looking over me to the rest of our group, all of whom were already scrambling to stay ahead of the crowd that was pouring toward the exits in panic. "Keep your feet! Stay together!" he called to the others.

I could see what he feared most. The crowd trampling us. Others were already falling, disappearing beneath. "This way!" shouted our new friends, pulling at us, taking our arms, rushing us onward toward the opposite exit. A thick mass of people pressed past. I could not see the detectives or Felix or my sisters. Had they made it through the exit already?

Will put an arm around my shoulders, his fingers digging in as if nothing could pry me from his grasp. He put up his forearm like a battering ram, bumping into those ahead of us as people pushed us from behind. Yves was there then, on my other side for a moment, but then a woman stumbled, and he stopped to aid her. Will and I could not stop. We were carried with the tide of humanity, pressing terribly close through the tunnel, our feet moving in fast, mad inches as our bodies crushed together.

"Hold on, Cora," Will grunted to me. I no longer feared falling as more entered the tunnel. I feared suffocating. I could practically lift my feet and be carried.

But then the crowd was splitting, like a fissure in the earth, wrenching me away from Will. He held on so tightly I winced. "Will!"

"Cora!" he cried, clenching his teeth. But he finally released me, knowing he couldn't keep hold of me without hurting me. There was no choice in the matter. We were simply flotsam on two raging rivers, now breaking apart, a wave rising between us.

———◇◇◇———

~William~

Over and over, the moment he knew he could no longer hold on to Cora looped through Will's mind. Then the moment he'd lost sight of her. He knew he should be looking for the rest of his party, but he couldn't—not until he found Cora.

"William!" Antonio said, emerging from the dark crowd, the youngest girls on either of his arms.

"Oh, good," Will said, his eyes drifting over them for a second. "Have you seen the others?"

"Andrew and Vivian were right behind us. They're somewhere near. What of Cora? Hugh and Felix?"

Feeling strangled, Will shrugged and turned in a slow circle, hoping the moon would rise and he'd be able to see more faces....

Felix arrived, helping a limping Yves along. Five minutes later, Andrew and Vivian, Hugh, and Claude reached them. But still there was no Cora.

People were congregating, drinking and laughing, as others streamed down the streets, heading home or out to bistros and bars. Will ran his hand through his hair as he frantically searched faces. "C'mon, Cora," he muttered. "Where are you?" Art arrived, then set off again when he learned Cora was still missing.

Will refused to think she might have been taken, kidnapped. They'd left their attackers behind them in Paris, right? But even letting the question run through his mind made his heart pause for a moment, then pound painfully in his chest.

"Yves, are you up to watching over the women?"

Yves nodded, looking a little weak, but Will knew he carried a pistol underneath his jacket. Will looked to the men. "Andrew, Hugh, you two head right and see if you see Cora. I'll go with Felix and Claude to the left. She has to be here someplace."

They hurried along, searching every face they could in the dark, slowly making their way around the gray arches of the arena. Will's heart sank when they met up with Andrew and

Hugh coming from the other direction and they slowly shook their heads.

"All right," Will said, refusing to lose hope. "Maybe she's back with the others already. Let's split up again, take another look. Call her name as you go. Maybe she's just standing a bit out of view...."

The men separated, and Felix and he took turns calling her name. Here and there, jokesters would pretend to answer in falsetto voices, making them pause in hope. Over and over, Will turned and stepped forward, praying that they'd find her just around the next bend.

When they reached the rest of the group again, his heart felt as if it were in a vice grip. Cora wasn't there.

—◇◇◇—

~Cora~

For a minute or two I could see his head towering over the others, but then I lost sight of him. Only the view of the tunnel exit gave me hope. At the end was freedom. A place I could once again find my footing. Control my own path. Breathe.

We burst out and separated, all still running, frightened we'd be trampled by those behind us. I lifted my skirts and ran with the rest. But then people were pausing in groups, gasping, laughing, patting one another on the backs in congratulations for having escaped the potential goring and the more likely death at the hands of their fellow man. I didn't have to speak French to interpret what they were saying.

Police were arriving, blowing shrill whistles. Injured people were tended to. I milled among the small groupings in the dark, still trying to catch my breath and slow my hammering heart, trying to make out faces. I was looking for Will, my family, anyone from our traveling party. I couldn't see any of them. And there were hundreds upon hundreds of people about.

Two men came up to me, both tall. *"Mademoiselle? Êtes-vous perdue?"*

My eyes shifted from one to the other, and the hair on the back of my neck stood on end. I wasn't certain of what they said. They might've been asking if I needed help—but my mind flashed to the time in Paris when Will and I had been followed, pursued. Did the men seem familiar? In the dark it was hard to tell.

And then five young men, our young friends who'd sat in front of us in the arena, moved around me, separating me from the two newcomers, facing off with them, flicking out their chins, barking quick words in French and gesturing for them to be on their way.

Once the worrisome men were gone, the five turned to me, bending their heads, all asking rapid questions of me at once in broken English. "Mademoiselle, what are you…Where…your escort? Are you lost, my friend? We…help?" Their manner was solicitous, not threatening, and I melted in relief. Will wouldn't like it, but I decided to trust them.

"Mansion Mantin?" I asked hopefully. I needed to get back to the mansion. It was the only place I could be certain I'd find the others, in time. Here by the arena it appeared hopeless, especially as it seemed that the bullfighting match had been declared over, and more people streamed out, grumbling and disheartened, but all curious to see what had transpired with those who had fled, as if we were the new choice in entertainment.

"Mansion Mantin? Oui, oui, Mansion Mantin!" said one of the young men, offering his arm.

Another came to my other side and offered his arm as well.

I cast one more glance around, wishing there were gas lamps alight nearby. What if Will had been hurt? Or another in our group? Would they panic when they could not find me within reach? But here…it was impossible. It was best for me to go to the one place I knew they'd eventually head—the mansion.

I sighed and took one man's arm and then the other's. "Mansion Mantin, mes amis."

CHAPTER TWELVE

~Cora~

My companions sang on the way, pausing to do a few steps of a dance with me. I laughed, and the tension that had held me eased as I gave in to the moment, appreciating that God had made a way for me to get to safety here in this strange city, where I spoke precious little of the language. We turned one corner and then another, the crowds thinning to just a few people here and there.

I craned my neck, looking for the mansion, thinking we ought to have arrived by now. But the men continued to chatter at me, and their antics distracted me. We ended up at the doorway of a cabaret, and I paused in confusion, looking up and down the street as the men gestured me in. "No, no," I said. "Mansion Mantin. You said you'd take me back to Mansion Mantin."

Two gestured to the door and held up one finger. *"Un verre du vin,"* one pleaded. *"Juste une."*

I sighed and frowned in frustration. Perhaps they were confused. Perhaps there was someone inside that spoke English who could better aid me. Or a taxi-cab driver...

I felt a warning wash through me. No. I needed to get back. Now. Will would be so worried.

"No," I said, turning around and walking to the curb, looking one way and then the other, trying to find the arena or some other landmark to help me get my bearings. "Mansion Mantin," I insisted as two of the men came to either side of me.

"Oui, oui," said one resignedly. He said something over his shoulder, and the others went inside, leaving me with just the two of them. A shiver of fear ran down my back. Without the camaraderie of the group, the atmosphere felt distinctly different. "Mansion Mantin," said the second man, pointing down the street. There wasn't another soul in sight, only a lone motorcar driving away, in and out of the creamy circles of light cast by the street lamps.

I frowned, my trepidation increasing.

"No, merci," I said, deciding that I'd be better off going inside and finding help there than trusting these two, whose easy smiles had faded to determined, intent expressions. I turned to enter the cabaret.

"*Comme ça,*" said one, turning to walk backward, away from me. He hooked a thumb over his shoulder. "Mansion Mantin?"

"No, merci," I repeated, reaching for the door handle.

At that moment, the other man covered my mouth with his hand, wrapped his arm around me, and carried me toward his companion. Together, they hauled me into the alley beside the cabaret and down into the dark recesses. I saw other men at the end in silhouette, and

I redoubled my efforts to get away. But it was no use. The two had an iron grip on me.

When we reached them, one flicked a lighter and held it up to my face to see me, and in that moment, I knew what I thought I'd known as soon as we entered the alleyway.

It was the man from Paris and his companion. Our kidnappers.

He smiled and laughed under his breath, saying something to the men who held me without looking away from my face. He leaned closer to me and then perused my body from head to toe. He flicked his fingers, indicating that he wanted me brought along. Another man grabbed my waist and put a cloth over my mouth. I tasted the medicine in it before I realized I was inhaling…and then I was out.

I awakened later in the back of a motorcar and, realizing I slumped against a man, quickly sat up. I blinked heavily, dizzy from the remains of whatever they'd drugged me with. I tried to make sense of what I'd seen in the near dark.

Art Stapleton sat beside me.

"Are you all right?" he asked, his voice honey thick with concern.

"What—? Where—? Art, what happened?" I asked, putting my hand to my head.

"You were attacked," he said, turning to look over his shoulder out the back window. "Luckily I'd caught sight of you with those men and was a couple blocks away when I saw you hauled into the alley."

"How…how did you get me away?"

"I didn't do it alone. Our driver helped me waylay them." I saw him nod to the front seat and then give a shrug as we passed a street lamp. "My pistol trained at the head of the leader helped convince them."

"I…I don't know how to thank you." Madly, I tried to figure out how he and the driver could've held off five men and managed to squire me away—unconscious. It made no sense. But I was so relieved to be away from them that I pushed away my confusion.

"No thanks are needed. I'm only glad I happened to be the one who found you first. Everyone was so worried, back at the arena."

"Is everyone else all right?" I asked, thinking of the girls, Viv, the men….

"Yes, yes. Everyone is present and accounted for. They'll likely return here any moment. Ahh. Here we are. See? Safe and sound." We pulled up in front of the mansion, and my remaining mad fear— that Arthur was somehow involved with the kidnappers—dissipated. If he were involved, he wouldn't bring me back. It made no sense. The only thing that made sense was that he told the truth…he'd saved me.

And for that I was sincerely grateful.

He got out, paid the driver with a wad of cash, and came around to help me out. "Can you stand?" he asked.

"Yes, yes," I said, but even as I did so, I sagged against him, almost falling from a wave of dizziness.

"Easy, there. I have you." He picked me up then and carried me up the stairs. We reached the front door just as Will and Claude were stepping out.

"Cora!" he cried. "What is it? What's happened?"

"She's all right," Art said, carrying me past. "She was attacked. But I managed to free her."

He carried me into the front parlor and laid me down on a settee. Felix, Hugh, and Andrew followed us in, all demanding to know the details of what had happened at once. Apparently, Viv was up with the girls, trying to settle their nerves after our trying night.

"It was the same men, Will," I said, staring at him. "From Paris. They followed us here. Two of the men from the arena grabbed me and took me into the alley, where *they* were waiting."

Will paced back and forth, listening to me. "We have to go to the police."

"You could," Art said, going to a crystal decanter and pouring himself a drink. "But it will do you no good. They're more corrupt than the mob in this city."

"No. *No.*" I knew what this tour meant to Will now. It meant his entire future—either continue as a bear, trustworthy and capable of leading other groups, or go back to school to become an architect after collecting his check at the end of the tour. It wasn't his fault that he shepherded children of the copper kings—targets for determined kidnappers. *It's not his fault.* I couldn't tolerate it if we became the end of all hope for him. What would he do? Where would he go?

. And what chance would there be for the two of us?

I gestured for Will to come to sit beside me, and reluctantly, he did so, as tense as a caged tiger. "Will, nothing's changed."

"Nothing's changed?" he sputtered, a flush rising on his cheeks. "Cora, they nearly had you."

"Nearly. But we knew they were there all along, right? We have proper guardians. Who could have predicted that things would go awry at the bullfight?"

"It doesn't matter. The only thing that matters is your safety. And I wasn't able to secure that tonight."

I pursed my lips. "A hundred different things could endanger us. Our fathers know that. Heavens, we could be killed at home or anywhere, Will. Thrown from a horse. Drowned like those on the *Titanic*."

His eyes narrowed, and he put his hands together as if praying and tapped his lips with them. "What exactly are you saying?"

"I'm saying that we tell the girls that I was lost and that kind men from the arena helped get me home." I looked at each man in turn, ending with Art. "Which is the truth."

"Of a sort," Andrew said with a snort, running his hand through his hair.

"You want to continue this tour more than anyone, Drew," I said.

"Not if it means Vivian is at risk."

"Were they targeting you?" Will asked. "Did they come after you, specifically?"

"I don't know," I said, shaking my head, accepting a glass of water from a butler. "Honestly, I think they were seeking any of us alone, lost."

"Not us fellows," Felix scoffed.

"I don't know. I assume they're after ransom," I said. "Why wouldn't they take any one of us? I think if we are to continue, you fellows have to assume you're just as much a target as we are."

"I'd dearly love if they would give me another chance at them," Andrew said with a snarl. "I'd show them what a university boxing champ can do if he's not blindsided by cowards. The cretins, going after our girls…" His protective inclusion of me warmed me a little, even in the midst of his diatribe.

"I say we go back to that cabaret, see if those gents are still there," Felix said.

"Yes!" Andrew seconded.

"They won't be there," Art said calmly. "They were likely gone before our Cora was even face-to-face with her would-be kidnappers."

"They told us where they lived!" Felix said, pacing. He threw one hand forward. "They were cheering for that one bullfighter from…"

"Listen," Art said soberly, "don't you think it was all a lie? A setup from the start. I saw them pay off others in those seats as we entered, but I figured they only were after better seats than their own. But then they invited you home for a party afterward, did they not?" He shook his head and sipped from his glass. "I'm telling you, it smells of a setup."

Will's head was in his hands, his fingers rubbing his scalp. He looked up at me again, his hands rubbing his face, his eyes running back and forth, as if visualizing what could have happened to me.

"Will," I said lowly, pleading with him. "Don't end it here. I want to go on. Finish our tour." *I want to see what else there is for us.* I hoped he could read my intent in my eyes. "If you send word that we've been attacked again, our fathers will only tell you to bring us straight away to Vienna, yes? They are already en route. Let us get there, and we can discuss what's next, together with them."

He took a deep breath. "Are you certain? The fastest route to your fathers' sides," he said carefully, "may be to return to Pierre's. Richelieu could provide additional security. We could send word to your fathers to meet us there. They'll likely be coming through Paris anyway, boarding a train en route to Vienna."

Felix let out a groan. "I no longer wish to return to Paris. If we're going to continue traveling, let us go on."

"Agreed," Andrew said.

Hugh considered them lazily and then searched my eyes. "I'm in."

I breathed a sigh of relief and then looked to Will.

"Are you certain, Cora?" he asked, now silently pleading with me. "The last thing I want is to see you or any of the others come to harm."

"I'm certain." I swung my legs down and sat up straight. I knew I must look a sight, but I wanted him to see me stronger, more assured. "It's really a sort of adventure, yes? A part of our tour. Seeing what lengths people might go to. I consider myself more educated because of it." I cast them all a wry smile.

Hugh laughed softly at my words, as did Art. "Come now, young bear," I said, fighting the urge to reach for his hand. "Lead us on?"

He shook his head and smiled in wonder at me. "Only if you promise me not to go anywhere without escort."

"I promise," I said. But even as the words left my mouth, I knew we were both thinking of that moment when the crowds parted us and there was nothing we could do about it.

CHAPTER THIRTEEN

~Cora~

Back in my room, I looked at my reflection in the mirror. My hair was in disarray, my careful knots gone. I glanced down and saw that the pocket of my jacket was torn and my skirt was smudged. I leaned forward to look into my own eyes, wondering if I'd just made a fatal decision. Memory of the man's grimy hand over my mouth, the feel of his iron grip…I shivered, just as Anna entered.

"Help you change, miss?"

"Please." Every muscle in my body ached as the maid hurried over to help me take off my jacket and then helped me slip out of my blouse and skirt.

"Miss?" she said, holding my arm, eyes wide with alarm. I looked down and saw what she did—the four bruising lines of a man's fingers. "What happened to you?"

"Pay it no mind, Anna. Just part of my adventures this evening."

"Are you certain?" she asked, still holding my arm, reaching for my face, apparently seeing something else there.

"I am." I pulled away and turned to reach for my nightgown. How many times were people going to interrogate me tonight? My decision to stay was made. Right? I threw the lace-trimmed gown over my head and yanked it down, wanting only to slip under the covers and try to dream away the worst of tonight's memories.

Anna wordlessly helped me into bed and covered me. "Anything else, miss?"

"No, thank you, Anna."

She turned and blew out the bedside lamp, stiff with obvious frustration that I hadn't elected to confide in her. She made her way out of the room. I resisted the urge to call her back, to tell her every detail and make sure I was making the right choice. Was I endangering her life too? Memories of the dead butler back at Pierre's chateau rose in my head. I turned over and closed my eyes tight. "Give me wisdom, Lord," I whispered. "Is this the right way? Is there any other? Without harming Will's future?"

But truth be told, I wasn't ready to give this up either. When would I ever return to Europe in my lifetime? If I went my own way, and Wallace Kensington went his…if we parted now, as I wished, would I ever find out if there was something of merit growing between me and Will? Between me and my siblings?

What would my parents, Alan and Alma, tell me to do?

My stomach rumbled. From hunger or agitation?

I felt so confused…so lost. Thinking about returning to Pierre's sprawling chateau. The danger in my kidnapper's eyes. His glee at having me in hand. And wondering again how Art freed me… Then thinking of my parents again, of sitting down to a meal with them and taking part in quiet conversation, wisdom etched into their thoughtful words. I had to send them a telegram soon.

On and on my thoughts went, some connected, some not, until I was once again out of bed and slipping into my most comfortable gown. I brushed my hair, pulled it into a quick knot, and shoved several pins through it. I bent to loosely lace up my boots and then quietly stepped out of my room, well aware that it was past two in the morning.

Downstairs, I made my way to the kitchen, past Hugh and Felix, who were up playing cards in the parlor. I was *really* hungry. Starving. The luxurious hors d'oeuvres we'd had before entering the arena had been lovely, but hardly a meal. I glanced down the hall. Given the hour, the cook was no doubt asleep or gone for the night. But that didn't have to stop me from making something.

The kitchen was vast, with electric lights, white marble counters veined with blue, and white cupboards. I reached into a drawer and pulled out a knife, then strode to the end to the ice locker and opened it. If we were renting the mansion, we could do as we wished, couldn't we? Especially when all I wanted to do was make a meal.

The walk-in ice locker was huge. And cold, with four massive blocks of ice in the center, covered in straw. I reached for a lamp and lit it, casting the shelves in a warm glow. I reached for an empty basket from the floor and went to the far end, where all kinds of meats hung on hooks—a slab of beef, a lighter-colored slab I thought might be veal, and links of sausage.

I reached up and cut away three sausage links, then cut two hunks of meat on a butcher's board beside them. When I had those in my basket, I turned to collect eggs. Outside the locker, I bent to grab onions and a loaf of bread, potatoes, and carrots from bins that lined the pantry wall. I almost dropped it all when Art walked in.

"Cora?" He lifted his hands. "Sorry. I clearly startled you."

"I couldn't sleep," I said, swallowing around a lump in my throat. I had nothing to fear from this man. I was simply jumpy. "I was hungry. Thought I'd make something that tasted like home."

"Ahh, I see. I can't sleep either," he said, going into the ice locker and emerging with a bottle of milk. "Mind if I lend a hand?"

"That depends," I said, forcing playfulness to my tone even as I continued to struggle with an odd sense of fear. It was ridiculous. This man had saved me! I handed him several big potatoes and lifted a brow. "Peel these for me, would you?" I said. "And do you know how to light a French oven?"

"I think so," he said, setting down the potatoes and glass of milk and turning to the oven. He fiddled with a knob and a match, and a moment later, I heard the roar of flame.

Art set to peeling potatoes, and I reconsidered my plan now that it appeared someone would share my meal. But meatloaf was what I had to have. My mouth watered at the thought of it. It'd been ages since I'd had a meal that reminded me of my parents, of home. And tonight I was bound and determined to have it.

"So tell me…do all the Kensingtons cook?"

"I have no idea," I said. "But as you've discovered, I'm rather new to the clan. And I've been cooking all my life."

He lifted his eyebrows but remained silent as he peeled, as if he found that fascinating.

I quickly diced the meat and fed it through a grinder, then mixed it with the sausage, freed from its casings. *Perfect.* I dumped the mixture into a big bowl, then turned to quickly chop two big onions, and afterward sliced a dry baguette, which I then crumbled. I added the eggs, Worcestershire sauce, red wine, a jar of crushed tomatoes, a bit of sugar, salt, and pepper. I walked down an impressive row of spices in bottles on a rack, pulling out the cork to sniff each one, and added those I thought might be good, feeling like a scientist, experimenting. Then I rolled up my sleeves and started mushing it all together.

"If I may be so bold as to inquire, how is it that you came to join the Kensingtons on this tour if you've not long been part of the fold?" Art asked, still peeling.

"Wallace Kensington insisted," I said. "And truth be told, I've been glad I came."

"Even after tonight?"

I paused and considered his words. "Even after tonight," I said. "It's been good for me to be on this tour, in many different ways."

"As in finding a rich beau like Lord Richelieu."

I smiled, even as I felt a pang of guilt. "Lord Richelieu's pursuit has been exceedingly flattering, but no, that is not what I speak of."

"No? Then what?"

"I...I think I've discovered parts of myself that I didn't know existed."

"Your newfound wealth?"

I frowned and shook my head. "No. I am not to be an heir of Wallace Kensington. This tour—the fine clothes, the opulence—it's all rather temporary. And that's fine, I assure you. No, the thing I appreciate is that I keep finding I have greater strength than I thought I did. So much yet to learn, and a passion for doing so. It makes me rather excited to resume Normal School."

He paused and looked sideways at me. "You intend to become a teacher?"

"I do."

"A daughter of Wallace Kensington as a teacher?"

"A daughter of Alan and Alma Diehl, a teacher," I corrected with a soft smile. "My path as a Kensington will not be the same as my sisters'."

"You seem rather certain of that," he said doubtfully.

"That's because I am." I pulled down two loaf pans from a shelf and divided my meat mixture, forming fat loaves.

"Where do you want these, mademoiselle?" Art asked, lifting his bowl of clean potatoes.

"There, please," I said, waving toward the counter. I bent and slipped both pans of meatloaf into the oven, then turned back to begin chopping the potatoes.

Will opened the door and peeked in, apparently alarmed that there was noise coming from the kitchen. "Cora! Do you know what time it is?" he asked, looking alternately elated and aghast to see me in an apron, working. His eyes shifted to Art, and he seemed to compose himself. "Wh-what are you doing?"

"Making meatloaf!" I said brightly, waving to the kitchen table where the servants ate each day. "Take a seat. I'll have supper ready in about an hour. You're probably as famished as I am."

Hugh and Felix peeked over his shoulder. Hugh entered first, then Felix. "You're *cooking*?" my brother asked.

"I was hungry," I said.

"Why not summon the cook from her quarters?" Hugh asked.

"Because *I* wanted to cook. I'm hungry for home. Or a taste of it, anyway, especially after our mad adventure tonight. We'll have meatloaf and mashed potatoes, and if I can get them done, carrots!"

"I can help," Will said, looking at me with new respect.

"That'd be wonderful," I said.

Side by side, we set to washing, peeling, and chopping as the others settled around the table and shared stories of the evening, laughing now that the danger was past.

Will leaned closer. "I was so afraid, Cora," he whispered. "I'd be…lost if anything happened to you."

I felt some of the jagged pieces inside me begin to shift, settle, at his words, helped by the homey smells emanating from the oven. "I'm sorry too, Will," I whispered back, putting the last of the potatoes in a pot and then moving over to the sink to cover them in water. "I didn't know what to do," I said, passing by him. I placed the heavy pot on the stove and turned on the gas and then, as Arthur had done, lit the flame beneath it.

"I know," he said, sliding the sliced carrots into a sauté pan. I went back to the ice locker and brought out some butter and put a thick slice in with the carrots, adding tarragon, salt, and pepper.

"There you are!" Lil said, entering the kitchen with Viv. All we were missing were Andrew, Nell, and the detectives. "We couldn't sleep and found all of you missing! Yves said you'd disappeared in here."

"Welcome," I said with a smile. "I'm making dinner for breakfast. Some food ought to help settle all of our stomachs." The girls sat down with the men at the long table and accepted glasses of milk.

"I've never thought of it," Felix said, crossing his arms as he looked over the potatoes and carrots and took a long, deep breath through his nose, appreciating the scent. "You, cooking. But I suppose it makes sense."

I gave him a wry grin. "This life of leisure has only been mine for about two months," I said.

"You had no cook at your home?" he asked, arching a brow.

"Just my mother and me," I said.

"Tell us of that, Cora," Hugh called, shuffling a deck of cards he'd pulled from a jacket pocket. "Of your home out on the range."

There was no trace of humor in his voice, only curiosity, and as I turned to face him, I saw the others watching me with equal interest. They'd never asked of my life before. I smiled, poured myself a glass of milk, and then sat beside Lillian on the bench. "Our ranch was in the shadow of the mountains, two hours outside of Helena by train. It has been in the Diehl family since my great-grandfather homesteaded it, but it's a hard place to make a go of farming. Dry, windy, dusty, rocky," I said with a smile.

"You sound as if you loved it," Vivian said, her delicate brows pulling together in confusion.

"I do," I said with a little shrug. "Every bit of it. Or I should say, I *did*..." It was gone now, long sold to the Kensington empire....

"Did?" Art asked.

"We lost it. Or rather, Wallace Kensington kindly offered to purchase it so my papa could get some much-needed medical care in Minnesota."

"So Father's offer was a blessing," Viv said.

I considered her. "In most ways, yes."

"The farm...was it large? Successful, once?" Felix asked, popping a bite of bread in his mouth.

"Neither, really," I said with a little laugh. "But it wasn't our success that made it good, made me love it." I paused and looked about at them, trying to figure out how to convey all that was in my heart. "It's all I've ever known. It's *home* to me. The hill with the tree I climbed every day as a girl. The schoolhouse that gave me my first taste of knowledge. The church and the town, filled with people I love and people who love me." I looked around at them tentatively and was startled by what I saw there. Intrigue. Wonder. Confusion.

"But now your place is here with us," Vivian said. "You'll discover a new definition of home."

Her words startled me, even though she wasn't the first person to voice such thoughts. But in them was not warning as I'd come to expect when we'd first set off on our journey, but invitation, hope. Could it be that my sister truly wanted me nearby, for longer than this tour?

"That...that remains to be seen. I have plans for after the tour. But I'd dearly love it if what we began here could continue in some form," I said, the thought crystallizing even as I spoke. I met her gaze and saw her eyes narrow. She'd perceived my doubt as a slight, and I wondered if any of them had ever been told no, faced any sort of rejection at all. After all, to be invited into the Kensington circle would be what every society girl longed for.

They had friendships, but intrinsically different than mine. Lives, brushing past one another, in their finest. Struggling for power. Vying for attention. Protecting their own. Judging others. There was some of that in our small town life, too, for sure. But I knew, then, that I'd been blessed with something that these around me had never had. My community was—*had been*, I corrected myself, feeling a pang of loss—like family. It felt vaguely like a play, actors each taking their place onstage. But they were hungry for something real. Hungry for what I knew, experienced. Had taken for granted.

I lifted my chin, startled. Because it made me feel settled, truly settled among them, for the first time, even if it wasn't all perfect.

———◇◇◇———

~William~

With every story Cora told, Will fell a little more in love with her. They stayed at that kitchen table until dawn lit the sky, eating her delectable meatloaf and mashed potatoes with dark gravy. Listening spellbound to her stories of wading into waist-high snows, a rope tied around her, to tend to the animals. Hoeing trenches in the soil until her hands blistered and bled. Helping her father break a mustang and breaking her arm and clavicle instead. "We never could make that horse take a saddle," she said with a regretful smile.

Lil and Vivian's mouths fell open so far that Will idly considered tossing bits of bread in them. The rest were equally intrigued, speaking only to ask her another question. It was as if they were afraid that Cora would remember her place and clam up again, when they wanted to know more. Hugh continued to look at her as though she were an exotic animal he'd like to capture and keep as a pet. Felix had nothing but respect in his eyes. Likely the Kensingtons and Morgans had never met anyone who had worked as hard as Cora had in life other than servants, and they had never stopped them to ask what their lives were like.

Art, too, asked question after question, keeping the stories going and retrieving his Kodak so he could take her photograph by the stove.

"Honestly, Art, why would you want a photograph of me in the kitchen when you've taken so many of us out and about? Among all the fine landmarks we've seen? And look at me. I'm a mess," she said, touching the messy knot of hair on her head.

"You're as beautiful as ever," he said, already finding her in the viewer. "Charming. Pick up that wooden spoon, would you?"

"We're resorting to props now?" she asked with a wry grin.

"It's part of the story, don't you think?" he said, clicking the button attached to a wire. He straightened and wound the film. "One more?"

But then the cook came in for a cup of morning coffee, in a fresh dress and clean apron. When she spied what had happened to her kitchen, she cried, *"Qu'est-ce que c'est que ça? Qu'est-ce qui s'est passé ici? Pourquoi est-ce que tu n'es pas venu me chercher?" What is this? What has happened here? Why did you not come and fetch me?* The cook turned on them then, fury in her eyes. "Out! Out!" she said in English. Sharing surreptitious glances, they hurriedly slunk out of the kitchen as if they were young children caught with their hands in the cookie jar. It mattered not that they were paying to rent the mansion. The kitchen was clearly her domain, and they'd entered uninvited.

Cora paused beside Will in the doorway and looked back. "Ask her if I would be permitted to stay and help clean up, would you?"

Will hesitated as the woman grumbled, carrying the pot of dried-up mashed potatoes to the sink. *"S'il vous plait, est-ce que nous pouvons aider à nettoyer?"*

"Non! Out! Out!"

Will lifted his brows and hurried out and down the hall. The others were saying their good nights at the stairs and separating, all likely recognizing their weariness and the late hour. Will reached in his pocket for his watch and groaned. It was five in the morning. They had only a few hours before they were to board a train north, likely all bleary-eyed and grumbling.

But he wouldn't have traded it for anything. To eat Cora's food. To hear her stories. To see how she captured her siblings and their friends just by living her life well. He itched to grab her hand and pull her into an empty room and kiss her. To hold her and hope for the chance at forever. He had a vision of a small city apartment, and Cora making her meatloaf—just big enough for two.

CHAPTER
FOURTEEN

~Cora~

We boarded the train a few hours later, all of us with dark shadows beneath our eyes from our late night. I wished I could sit beside Will. That we were traveling alone—just the two of us. I daydreamed about him putting his arm around me, and me nestling in to doze. But instead, I pivoted on my heel and sat where I knew I'd be expected—beside Vivian, across from the girls—feeling his eyes following my every move.

All the men and I were on alert, searching each face, ready for our enemies this time around if they dared to come near again.

"I must admit," Vivian said, "your meal last night was exactly what I craved. It tasted of...America."

"It did," I returned with a smile. "Thank you for joining me."

"I haven't stepped inside a kitchen since I was but a bit of a girl," she confessed in a whisper, "tended by my governess."

"Never?" I asked, trying to determine if she was joking. But she was serious. "What would you do if your cook took ill? Or you found yourself alone, without aid?"

Vivian laughed. "Well, I suppose I'd simply have to survive on what I could until another cook could be found."

I stared at her a moment. Even after these weeks together, these children of privilege could at times take my very breath away with their assumptions. So much they took for granted. "Or I could teach you how to cook a few items so that you might never find yourself at a complete loss."

There was conflict in her eyes. Part of her clearly wanted to accept my offer; part of her clearly thought it was preposterous.

"Consider it, Vivian," I said, before she could say no. "I think you'd make a decent cook." She was certainly particular enough....

"I'd like a lesson!" Nell said, her round cheeks ruddy with excitement.

"As would I!" Lil said.

"Good," I said, as the train whistle blew and, a moment later, the train began to move out of the station. "At least I have two students. Where shall we hold our lesson? Switzerland? Austria? Or Italy?" I grinned, thinking about what was ahead of us yet, and feeling as privileged and audacious as Vivian for once. What a gift this trip was. How wide my world had become in the space of a few short weeks.

I closed my eyes, thinking through all we'd seen, all we'd experienced...and again and again, my thoughts came to rest on Will. Will in Montana. On board the *Olympic*. Dancing with him in England. Crossing the Channel, the wind in his hair...

On and on again, my memories of him went through my mind, like Arthur's photographs, until I at last gave in to sleep.

———◇◇◇———

I awakened hours later as we neared Lyon. Vivian had fallen asleep too, as had the girls across from us. Vivian yawned and stretched, both of us feeling a bit awkward when we realized we'd been dozing for so long. But then we realized the men had done the same. The night before had taxed us all. There was an odd intimacy in it that I equally chafed against and wanted to embrace. I stared out at the passing farms, a man driving a wagon piled high with hay. Did I want to be a part of this family and their friends...or not? More and more, I found connection and ties with them. But was that a good or bad thing?

And if I settled in more deeply with them, where did that leave me and my parents? I stared out the window, thinking of Mama and Papa, cascading between concern for my papa and his health—especially after seeing Stuart alive and well one day and then gone the next—and what I had to admit as anger that lingered still toward my mama. She'd lied to me for so long about who I was...which I understood in a certain measure, and not at all in the next. When we were reunited, there'd be much to discuss.

I stared out the window and thought about that some more. How much of my reluctance to return home and face my parents' duplicity drove my desire to stay on this tour? And how much did my mad desire to stay near Will keep me from dissolving in fear that we hadn't left our kidnappers behind in Nîmes for good? Was I even in my right mind? And yet, and yet...for the first time in a long while I felt steady. Strong. More myself. *Me* again, somehow.

Will rose and stood in the aisle, supporting himself by holding onto the nearest seat as the train car continued to lurch and sway. He waited until he had our attention. "We're approaching Lyon," he pronounced it the French way, as *lee-uh*, which I found exceptionally attractive, "a venerable old city with, yet again, Roman roots. As we travel I suspect you are beginning to get a sense of the scope of the Roman Empire. At one time it stretched all the way from Britain across Europe, from southern Egypt to the Middle East.

"Lyon was a natural trade city situated on the banks of not one but two rivers, and, like Paris, she is divided into separate *arrondissements*, or neighborhoods. The city has the modest remains of a Roman theater, but nothing as grand as what we saw in Nîmes or what we'll see ahead of us in Italia. But this city was the starting point of all central Roman roads throughout Roman Gaul."

"Enough with the history, William," Hugh called. "Are there cabarets?"

Will cast him a warning look and went on. "Lyon is famous for her *cathedral*," he emphasized the word, "the lovely St. John, known as St. Jean here, with medieval bones; the sprawling park—the largest in any city in France; and the Lumière brothers, who've made such advancements in film...." Will continued his tour lecture as we drew near, speaking of another cathedral situated high on a hill, of the fact that the Roman emperor Caracalla once resided here, and of the funicular railway in Lyon—the world's first—that we would ride tomorrow. But as he spoke, I kept waiting for him to meet my gaze, feeling a thrill run down my arms each time he did, no matter how briefly.

Will closed the hotel door quietly and was surprised to find me in the hall, waiting. "Cora!" he said, half smiling. His eyes shifted down the empty hall.

"It's all right," I said, giving him a conspiratorial grin. "Everyone is changing for supper."

"Good." He crossed his arms as if he didn't trust himself not to touch me. Leaning against the wall, he stared at me as if he wanted to memorize every inch of my face. "Cora, are you well? I mean, since the attack in Nîmes, I've so longed to—"

"I'm fine, Will. Truly."

"When I think of what might've happened had Art not come along…"

"But he did. It's okay. And perhaps now they will give up pursuit of us and move on."

"Or become more determined than ever. Promise me you'll take great care to stay with the rest of the group."

"I promise."

"Because if anything happened to you…" he whispered, leaning so close to me I could feel his breath in my hair. "After losing my uncle…Cora, I—"

I leaned back and searched his eyes with mine, hanging on his words, and then abruptly straightened, belatedly seeing Andrew and

Vivian reach the top of the stairs and turn in our direction. They came down the hall toward us, arm in arm, and I wished for the hundredth time that Will and I could do the same.

"What news, William? Did you make arrangements for supper?" Andrew asked.

"Indeed. They're expecting us about eight. I'd advise you to take advantage of our afternoon respite and catch up on some of the rest we lost last night."

I reluctantly parted ways from Will with Vivian, having no tangible excuse to linger, and we chatted about what we planned to wear that night. It seemed surreal, my sister inquiring about which dress I might don, when two months ago she could barely tolerate being in the same room with me. But try as I might, all I could think about was Will and seeing him again.

"Rest well, Cora," Viv said, leaving my side.

"And you as well," I said. I slipped my bag from my elbow and fished out the key, turning it in my lock, then closed the door and leaned my forehead against it, fighting the urge to peek down the hall and see if William was still there, talking to Andrew. Just one more look…

But they'd left too.

That evening, Anna was finishing an elaborate knot in my hair when we heard a knock on the door. She placed the comb—laden with pearls and rhinestones—in my hair and then scurried over to answer it. "Miss Kensington," she said, bowing her head in deference and opening it wider so that Vivian could enter.

I watched in the mirror as Vivian strode in and looked back to Anna. "Might I have a moment alone with Cora, Anna?"

"Of course, miss," she said, bobbing a curtsy and moving straight to the door.

Casually, I clipped on an earring and reached for the other, watching as Vivian drew closer. She looked lovely in her lavender evening dress with heavy beaded lace across the shoulders, sleeves that reached to her elbows, long gloves, and her hair done up.

She stood behind me, meeting my gaze in the mirror. "Cora, I don't know who you think you are fooling."

"Pardon?" I said, frowning at the sudden change in her.

"You. And William. It is plain as day that you have eyes for each other."

"Will and I?" I scoffed, my heartbeat tripling. I gave my head a little shake and slowly turned on the stool to face her. "Will and I... we understand each other. You've mistaken friendship for something more." I knew if she reported to our father that we were involved, Will would be fired and sent home without payment. Wallace Kensington would consider it a grave offense.

She peered down her nose at me. "You are certain? Because Father would disapprove of you carrying on with him, even more than he would of your entanglement with Pierre de Richelieu."

Not that it is any of his business whom I choose to carry on with, I thought. But instead I forced a small smile. "Obviously. And if it assures you any, Pierre is to meet us again in Vienna." Even as the words left my lips, I felt a twinge of guilt.

She smiled a little then in admiration. "You certainly have managed to get under his skin."

"I don't know why. We have so little in common."

Vivian sighed. "Why be concerned about that? He's fabulously rich, attentive, and clearly enamored with you. Not to mention handsome. Why not simply accept your own happily ever after? Is it not what every girl dreams of?" Her eyes narrowed as I searched for a response. "Unless you have some sort of draw to William…"

"Vivian. Will and I are *friends*. Are we not allowed to be friends?" I smiled innocently. But I was careful not to claim that was all we were. It wasn't truly a lie if it merely went unsaid, was it?

Her dark eyes searched mine. "Of course you are," she said, straightening her gloves. "I only wanted to be certain you were clear about Father's expectations."

"The only expectations Wallace Kensington laid out for me were that I was to go on this tour, try to find my way with you and Felix and Lil, and then return to my schooling." I pulled off the cork on my powder jar and then dusted my face with a brush.

In the mirror's reflection, I saw her pause in the midst of straightening the seam on her long glove and stare at me. "Oh, no. This is but the beginning, Cora. You may call yourself by your old name, but you are a Kensington—it may as well be branded on your forehead. What Father wants, Father gets." She sniffed. "Now that I know you, I've come to accept his wisdom in this. But this tour is only the start. Your destiny is in remaining with us."

I turned to face her. "Everyone keeps telling me that. But my deal with our father was very clear. I go on the tour; he sends me back to school."

"It wouldn't be appropriate, a daughter of Wallace Kensington off to be a country bumpkin schoolmarm. No, sister," she said, shaking her head slowly. "You've already drawn the eye of Pierre de Richelieu. Your story shall be far more grand than what you have previously envisioned."

"Vivian, since when did you become so concerned about me and my future? You have wanted nothing more than for me to be gone from your life at the earliest possible moment." I turned to face her again, wanting to fully see her reaction.

She shrugged. "I decided I have enough room in my heart to accept you. And Father has more than enough money for each of our inheritances."

"Oh, I don't—"

"Just don't do anything to disrupt our tour," she interrupted, shaking a warning finger at me. "If those horrible men who continue to follow us aren't enough to do so, you taking up with the hired help would certainly draw Father's ire and summarily end this trip." A hopeful smile grew across her face, and she looked to the window. "I think Andrew has aspirations for Venezia to ask a special question...."

My mind spun with all the different ways her words irked me. "So Venezia shall be the place?" I muttered.

"Truly," she said with an excited nod, moving on as if she hadn't just offended me in five different ways. I thought it a bit sad that there would be no surprise in their proposal, just relief that the engagement everyone knew was coming had finally come to pass. Hardly the romantic ideal but, I supposed, a typical point of passage for their set. Marriages arranged and long anticipated, mutually agreed upon, as planned as any other legally binding arrangement. Had Vivian and Andrew really ever had a choice? Or had it always been assumed they would be together, the eldest child of each copper king's family?

"Do you love him very much, Vivian?"

She looked at me with confusion. "What?"

"You are in love with Andrew, then," I said, rising and turning toward her. "For you to be so excited, I assume you are in love with him."

She paused for a telling moment. Then, "I am quite fond of Andrew. I always have been." Her tone and stance told me that her walls were once again firmly in place.

"I…I'm glad," I said, making myself leave it at that, even though I longed to say more. Was fondness enough to make a marriage?

She gave a curt nod. "Are you ready? Shall we go down together?"

"Certainly," I said, reaching for my bag and following her out, still thinking about what made a strong marriage. What had Wallace Kensington's marriage been like, that had caused him to have an affair with the maid? Had their union too been based on "fondness"? But then, my own parents had been nothing but acquaintances when they met and moved to Dunnigan. And that had turned into a deep, abiding love and respect. Could not Vivian's marriage turn into something similar?

I forced a smile and listened to her chatter about her finds shopping that afternoon with Andrew, having ignored Will's entreaties for them to rest. Apparently she was shipping home some antique silver that the dealer swore once belonged to a cousin of Napoleon, as well as some beautiful silks for new dresses. But once my eyes found Will, waiting in the foyer at the bottom of the stairs with the others, her voice—and her warnings—faded away. He stared up at me in admiration, a tiny smile on his lips.

I am not fond of him, I thought. *We are not merely friends.*
I am in love. God help me. I am truly in love.

CHAPTER FIFTEEN

~Cora~

"What do you think you're doing?" Andrew said, cupping my elbow as we strode behind the rest of the group along the marble floors of St. Jean the next day.

"Pardon me?" I asked, glancing up at him in confusion.

"With Vivian?"

My confusion deepened. I looked ahead and saw Vivian between Lil and Nell. "What?"

Andrew steered me into a small side chapel and faced me. He looked so angry I took a step backward and felt the cool wall behind me. He crossed his arms and leaned toward me. "What did you say to her? Last night?"

"Last night?" I stammered. I immediately remembered our conversation. But what of that could I relate to him? Without stepping on his toes—or Vivian's?

"Yes. Last night," he hissed.

I stared at him blankly, wanting him to think I had no recollection.

"Don't pretend innocence, Cora," he said, placing a hand on the wall behind me and pointing at my chest. "You've interfered. Just what scheme are you cooking up in that pretty head of yours?" The veins in his temples bulged.

"S-scheme?" I sputtered. "Andrew, to what do you refer?"

"Yesterday, we had a lovely afternoon together. *Then*," he said, practically spitting the word, "after one conversation with you, she's wondering if we ought to take some time. Have some distance. *Entertain other suitors*."

He looked like he wanted to strangle me right then and there. She'd said what? I was aghast. I hadn't meant to—

"Miss Kensington? Mr. Morgan?" Antonio said, standing in the center of the chapel's entrance. "Is there a problem?" While his words were polite, his burly arms were crossed, and he cast a murderous glare at Andrew.

"I was only having a word with Miss Cora." Andrew immediately dropped his arm and stepped away from me. He wrapped a hand around his neck and rubbed it, meeting my gaze with a look that said, *We're not finished here*. A shiver ran down my neck and back as I passed him and Antonio and rejoined the group. They had paused at another chapel, two down. Will's eyes filled with curiosity, but he kept to his topic at the massive painting above the altar. But I couldn't concentrate on his words, only the brooding arrival of Andrew, five paces away. And then the smirking grin of Hugh on my other side.

It was just what I didn't need. Both Morgan men with an untoward interest in me. What had I done? My chat with Vivian had been all of a couple minutes…and she'd seemed so *settled* on the idea of them together.

I groaned inwardly. If I were the cause of disunion between the Kensington and Morgan families, there'd be misery to pay. But then I clenched my teeth. What if I had caused her to examine her heart? Was it not appropriate to ask such questions? Was I not serving my sister rather than cultural and societal expectations? Surely Wallace Kensington himself would support such a process. After all, if he did not fear acknowledging me as his blood kin, then how could he fear his eldest making a wise choice in marriage?

Perhaps that would change his mind about insisting I remain entrenched "in the fold," after we got home.

My eyes shifted to my half sister as we moved toward the doors to leave. For the first time, I recognized that she was sticking firmly with the girls rather than walking beside Andrew, as she had every hour of every day we had been on tour. Outside, they paused to pose for one of Art's photographs.

I took a deep breath. Because despite my internal rallying, my efforts at justifying my actions, I knew that I was in a whole new pot of boiling water.

"Cora, Cora, Cora," Hugh said with a devilish grin, leaning toward me as we went back outside. "What have you done now?"

"I don't know," I said, feigning ignorance and reluctantly looking toward him as we walked. "Perhaps you can tell me."

"You don't know?" he said, cocking a brow. He made me wait several seconds, reveling in my agitation. "Vivian has turned away from my brother's pursuit."

"Surely you are overstating it."

"Not at all, my sweet, innocent friend." He took my hand and wrapped it through the curve of his arm as if we were, indeed, old friends. "I love it when you get that look of surprise in your beautiful blues."

"Hugh, really..."

"So, how did you manage it? In a matter of hours, they go from practically engaged to barely speaking to one another. What did you say?"

"I doubt it was anything I said.... Perhaps it's just a spat. Surely they'll be back together by tomorrow."

"Do you think so?" He pursed his lips. "I don't know. Dear Drew seems quite distraught. And Vivian...well, perhaps you're right. Maybe all she seeks is the thrill of my brother pursuing her in earnest again. Don't all women want that?"

"Not all women."

"No?" He pretended to consider me and my words, then dismissed it. "No. Every woman likes to be pursued. I bet you yourself get a little thrill each time I come near."

"I thought we were past this, Hugh," I said, forcing myself to keep my hand on his arm.

"Past it? I hope not. Our flirtations have been one of a few things that have made this entire tour of interest to me. But now, this, with Drew and Viv... You provide all *manner* of entertainment, Cora."

I thought on that a moment. I hoped he was only being his cocky, jocular self, exaggerating for effect rather than being truthful. Because if he saw the moments between us—moments I found barely tolerable—as the apex of his journey? Then that was simply sad.

"Hugh, I need to know." I glanced over my shoulder and saw Andrew and Antonio walking together, talking, Andrew slope-shouldered and shuffling in his step. "What exactly happened between Vivian and Andrew?"

"She asked him if he loved her."

I waited a moment. He clearly liked making me ask for more. "And he said…?" I asked tiredly.

"He asked if *she* loved *him*."

I sucked in my breath. "Poor form on his part."

"Indeed. For what my brother has in knowledge, he lacks in wisdom—at least in the ways of men and women. I suppose I got all the good looks and understanding of how women work, in my family." Again, I resisted the urge to pull away when he leaned toward me, and instead looked ahead to Will, who was glancing back at us in concern. I gave my head a little shake, silently telling him not to worry, and he turned his attention back to Lil, beside him.

"And so?"

"And so?" Hugh repeated wryly.

"Hugh. What is their plan?"

"To spend some time apart. To think on it. Search their hearts. And decide if they truly belong together."

"Goodness," I said, still a bit overwhelmed by this turn. All on account of such a short conversation with Viv? Or a sleeping dragon awakened by a butterfly's passing?

"You should know," Hugh said. "My brother can get rather volatile when he's angry."

"Are you…*warning* me?" We neared the funicular railway station.

He pursed his lips a moment. "Just that you should stick with the group. Don't go where Andrew can corner you alone again. Especially if he's been drinking."

I frowned. I'd never seen Andrew overly imbibe. That was more the realm of Felix and Hugh. "How is any of this my fault?" I whispered as we got closer to the others. My heart was pounding. Because while Hugh liked to play with my emotions, he seemed earnest in this warning.

He turned to me and leaned toward my ear. "You, dear Cora, appear determined to delve into matters of the heart. Don't you know that we Morgans and Kensingtons prefer to keep things on another plane altogether?"

I avoided Andrew all night, as well as most of the others in our party. I kept to myself, forcing myself to eat something, then quickly making my excuses of a headache as some of them went to the Lumière cinema for a moving picture show, and the others went to a local dance hall. "I'd like to turn in early," I said, meeting Will's searching eyes. "I'm exhausted."

He nodded and let me go, clearly reluctant. Antonio escorted me to my room, waiting until I had locked the door behind me. I didn't even call upon Anna, glad to undress myself, unpin my hair, brush it out, and slip into a nightdress, then burrow under the cool sheets and blankets of my big bed. Because I *was* unaccountably tired. Weary from the bones out. Tired of trying to think through every word, every action, and what the repercussions might be.

And within seconds of laying my head on the pillow, just as I was thinking I'd never sleep, with all that was on my mind, I was.

Hours later, I dreamed of knocking, pounding at my door. Someone calling my name. I opened one eye and sat up, turning up the flame of my bedside lamp and then going to the door, still wondering if I was dreaming.

"Cora!" he said. "I must see you!"

It was Andrew.

"Andrew, it's far too late. I shall see you in the morning."

"Come out! Come out this instant!"

I could hear the slur in his voice. And Hugh's words came back to me. About his volatility. Particularly when he'd been drinking. As if to emphasize the truth of Hugh's warning, he banged on the door so hard, the whole thing shuddered. I took a step back.

I glanced at the lamp in my hand. I was shaking so hard, the oil was sloshing around in the well at the bottom. "Tomorrow, Andrew! We'll speak tomorrow!"

"Come out here, Cora! Please!" I heard his voice crack. He paused. "Please. Just a word." Could he truly be weeping?

My heart paused a moment and then pounded. What had I done? Why had I interfered? The man was clearly devastated.

"Just a moment, Andrew." I moved to my bedside table and set down the lamp, then pulled on my dressing robe. I went back to the door and opened it a few inches. "Andrew?"

"Just a word, Cora," he said, his shoulders shaking. He was leaning his head against the wall, inches from the door. He wiped his nose and cheek with one serpentine swipe of his hand and arm and looked at me with such pain, such brokenness, that my heart broke for him.

"Andrew," I begged him. "Go to Vivian. She'll see that you love her."

"No," he said. "She won't. She wants something from me that I cannot define. Something even she cannot define. It was you. You planted some seed in her mind...." He searched my eyes, and in that moment, his own hardened.

My internal alarm moved me to action a moment too late. I tried to slam the door, but he wedged his foot in and then pushed it open, sending me sprawling. I fell on my hip and elbow, sliding across the polished floor and moved to try to get up. But he was there, yanking me upward, clenching both my arms in his powerful hands. "What have you done?" he spat at me. "What have you *done*?"

He shook me so hard my teeth rattled.

"Andrew, I didn't mean to. Please...you've had too much to drink—"

He let out a cry and this time pushed me up against a wall, his fingers digging into my arms. He leaned his beet-red face down toward mine. "How dare you tell me I've had too much to drink! Who are you to come into our lives and get between us? What do you hope to gain? Why are you bent on destroying our future?"

"I hardly think I've destroyed anything," I said, finding strength in my own fury. "If my innocent question was enough to do so, you had no semblance of a foundation for a marriage! Come now, Andrew. Look at yourself. What are you doing?"

"Yes," Will said from the doorway, every line in his face speaking of warning. "What *are* you doing?"

Art was beside him.

Andrew looked at them, to me, and then back to Will. "I needed a word with her." He released me and took a step back.

"In the middle of the night? Menacing her so?" He strode over to us.

"This is none of your business, William," Andrew said. "I will be done here in a moment."

"No," Will returned evenly. "You are done now. Go to your quarters and sleep off whatever you've imbibed this night, or Art and I shall drag you there."

Andrew looked over Will's shoulder to Art. Behind him, several of the hotel's guests in nightcaps and dressing gowns peered from their doorways to see what the fuss was about. Andrew let out a sound of disgust and shook a finger at me. "Make it right with Vivian. Immediately."

"The only one who can make it right with Vivian is *you*, Andrew," I said.

His eyes widened with renewed anger, and he lifted his hand to slap me, but Will was there, grabbing his wrist and twisting his arm behind him. "To bed, Andrew. Now," he seethed, forcing him from my room.

Art, halfway in my room, turned to the gaping people in the hallway. He spoke to them soothingly, his tone clear, even though he spoke French. He was probably telling them it was all over, to go back to their rooms. Slowly, grudgingly, they turned and did as he asked, while he stood there, a hand on either side of my doorframe, as if standing guard.

After a moment, he threw a wry grin over his shoulder and cocked his head. "You certainly know how to rile people up, Cora Diehl Kensington."

My knees felt watery beneath me, and I shakily reached for the back of my dressing table chair.

"Whoa there," he said, hurrying over to me and grabbing my arms, helping me sit down.

When I winced, he belatedly realized he held me where Andrew had. If I'd had bruises from the kidnappers, what would these be like come morning? Vaguely, I reached up and ran the fingers of my right hand over my left arm.

"Sorry. I wasn't thinking," he said, kneeling before me. "Do you need something? A glass of water? Something stronger?"

"No, no." I looked to the empty doorway, longing for Will to return. I wanted him here. Him to take me in his arms. Not this man with his inquisitive eyes.

"I've messed things up," I said with a sigh. "Again. We were all getting along so well."

"Who?"

"Me and my siblings. They were accepting me, trusting me… and now this."

"Seems to me that it's Morgan who has an issue with you. Not your siblings."

"Trust me," I said dimly. "It won't take long for the Kensington ire to follow."

"I take it you came between Andrew and Vivian."

"Not on purpose. I merely asked Viv if she loved him."

Art laughed softly. "You truly are new to this whole set of society, aren't you?"

I cast him a look of irritation. "Don't mock me, Arthur. I'm not in the mood."

He quickly schooled his expression. "Forgive me. But you do seem to walk into trouble after trouble…."

"Cora?" Will said from the door, looking at me and Art, then back again. He stepped closer. "Are you all right?"

Just seeing his face made me feel so relieved I wanted to cry despite myself.

Art looked at us and rose. "I'll see myself out."

We should have refused him. We shouldn't have been left alone. But neither of us spoke.

Art smiled a little and departed, but he did not close the door. Will, frowning in concern over me, followed him and quietly shut it. We met in the middle of the room. I threw myself into his arms, clinging to him, and he wrapped his arms around me, cradling me against his chest. "Are you all right?" he asked, stroking my hair. "Did he hurt you?"

"No—" My voice broke. I was crying, knowing that it was more than Andrew's attack. It was the trauma of this night on top of our last night in Nîmes. It was all too much...Too much. I shook my head and tried to gather myself. "I'm fine. Just shaken. If you and Art hadn't come when you did..."

"It's all right, Cora. Shh. I'm sorry. Andrew will be better tomorrow. He'll have a beast of a headache. But he'll be better." He backed away a bit to cradle my face and gaze into my eyes. "Trust me," he said. "Andrew has to figure out some things. But I think he will. It's just that..."

"What? I—"

"You took something from him. Regardless of whether you meant to do it or not," he said quickly, seeing that I was about to defend myself. "He sees you as the one that set this ball rolling." He ducked his head. "Granted, it needed to roll. Before an engagement happened. But I'd wager no one has ever taken something away from Andrew Morgan, all his life."

He smiled then. Because we both had had things and people taken from us. And this…the normal course of life put everyone on an even playing field. In time.

"They might…they might resume their relationship. Tomorrow."

"I'd wager it's likely," he said, leaning close, brushing away my tears. "But in the meantime, you've made them think about things they should have been considering all along." He kissed me then, tenderly, reassuringly, on either side of my face. "About what it means to care." He gave me another kiss, softly, this time on the lips. "About what it means to be devoted." And another…"About what it is to love." He used his thumbs to wipe away more of my tears, but his eyes never left mine.

I stared up at him, wondering if he was saying what I thought he was saying.

"I love you, Cora Diehl Kensington," he whispered, his hands tightening on either side of my face. He shook his head, his eyes becoming desperate. "And I don't know if I can continue this ruse. Pretending that you are merely one of my seven clients, when every moment, all I want to do is to sweep you away. If only I had the means…if only Uncle—"

He paused and ran a hand through his hair. "Please know that I'd declare myself to your father today if I could. I'd tell him I could no longer act as your guide. Because I wish to court you as your intended. But my uncle…"

"What is it? Are you not his heir? Have you not come into your own means?"

"A pauper's means," he said bitterly, backing slightly away from me. "I inherited nothing but debt. Even after we sell everything he had, I'm liable for more." He looked at me, pain in his eyes. "I need to see this tour through. To the end. Collect my pay, *then* tell your father of my intentions."

I took his hands in mine. "I love you, too, William. And I understand. Truly. It's only another six weeks, this tour. Surely we can last that long. You can collect your pay. I can get my tuition check. And when we're home, nothing can keep us from each other. Not even Wallace Kensington."

He smiled and leaned his forehead against mine. "Do you really think it's possible?"

"Yes. *Yes.*"

"What of…Pierre?" he asked, both guilt and fear crossing his face.

"I wanted to tell him in Carcassonne. But with all that went on…I will send him word. Tomorrow. I promise. Now, please. You must be away. If anyone were to find you in here…"

"I know," he said miserably, making no move to depart. After a moment, he groaned, pulled me into another long, tender hug, and then forced himself to turn away and go to the door. "Lock it as soon—"

"Wait." I pulled him aside and then peeked out the door and down the hall, looking both ways. Making sure no one yet lingered in the hall, I pushed him out and practically slammed the door in his face, then leaned against it, smiling. "Good night, Will," I whispered, knowing he couldn't hear me. Not that it mattered.

He loved me.

William McCabe loved me.

Part II

~GENEVA~

CHAPTER SIXTEEN

~Cora~

The next day, I posted my farewell letter to Pierre—which both pained me and relieved me—and we left France behind. It felt symbolic to me as we crossed the border into Switzerland, as if I were closing the door on whatever wild dreams I'd had about Pierre, too, and could focus on the future. On Will, I thought with a smile. I only hoped the letter would reach him before he set off to meet me, or that might prove to be awkward.

I tried to sit next to Vivian, hoping we could share a quick conversation, but when I patted the seat beside me she ignored me, choosing to sit by herself. Perhaps she was vexed with me as well, I thought, for getting her beau riled up into such a state. It mattered little. Once we got to Geneva, I'd find a time and place to talk to her and find out what was happening in her head...and heart.

We traveled through deep mountain valleys filled with tidy Tyrolean buildings—with bright white, stucco walls framed by big brown timbers and bright red shutters—and past shepherds driving herds of sheep and cattle from one meadow to the next. The train track made a serpentine path through the snowcapped peaks and over frequent, frightfully high arched stone bridges where waterfalls cascaded below us.

We all sat by the windows, gazing out in awe, mesmerized. Even Montana, with her glorious mountains and lakes, could not compare to this alpine glory. Gradually, we began to descend again, arriving in Geneva midafternoon. She was a pretty city, with obvious wealth behind her—every building had a perfect facade and gleaming glass in its windows. Streetcars ran meticulously on schedule, Will said, appropriate for a city known as much for her skill in crafting clocks as she was for banking and international diplomacy.

He led the way out of the train car, then toward taxicabs that took us to a gorgeous, sprawling hotel on the shores of Lake Geneva. Women strolled in crisp white linen, parasols above their heads, dapper-looking men at their sides. And out on the water was one sailboat after another, like a scene out of a painting.

"Ahh, yes, the Genevans do enjoy a proper bit of sailing," Art said, pausing beside me. "Did you know Lake Geneva is the biggest freshwater lake in Europe?" He lifted his camera. "Do you mind? You're as pretty as a picture there with your parasol."

"If you're so inclined," I said. Did the man never reach the end of his film?

He hovered over the viewfinder. "Would you mind looking back out over your shoulder, toward the water? I like your face in profile."

I did as he asked, feeling a tinge of a blush at his words. And yet I sensed no interest in a personal pursuit from him. He merely was concerned about his photographs, it seemed. With each stop I thought he'd leave us, but now he was securing sailing vessels for us tomorrow, and I'd heard Vivian say something about him having contacts in Vienna.

"Perhaps I can arrange a way to get us all out on the water tomorrow, to take part in the regatta..." he said, still peering into his viewfinder.

"Is there anywhere you do not know people, Art?" I asked, considering him. I wondered how he could be away from his business for so long. Or was he merely another young man of the well-to-do set, free to travel the world on an unlimited budget?

"I do know a good number across Europe," he said, pursing his lips. "I grew up coming here and have fostered many good relationships over the years. It's good for my business."

"What is your business? If I may ask," I said. I'd seen a typewriter among his luggage and knew he spent a fair amount of time in the local telegraph office, but he spent more time developing his photographs and traveling about with us, as far as I could see.

"I deal in people," he said with a grin, winking at me. "The interweaving of lives. The intersections of our stories."

I frowned in confusion over his cryptic answer, but he was already moving on. He gestured again toward the water and then patted his chest. "It does a body good to be by such a lake or sea, don't you think?"

I couldn't restrain my smile, turning to fully look at it myself. "Indeed."

"Maybe Andrew and Vivian will find their way back to each other," he whispered. He looked outward. "It's irresistibly romantic."

I glanced up at him. "Do you believe they will?"

"I do."

"I hope you're right. Because right now, neither of them is speaking to me."

He gave me a wink. "It will work out. Come on. The others are already inside. Surely William has our room assignments by now."

He offered me his arm, and together we walked up the wide marble steps, entering the grand lobby of the hotel. Inside it was posh, luxurious, with attendants at the counter in full black-and-white livery. The biggest crystal chandelier I'd ever seen dominated the center of the ceiling; gorgeous brocade and velvet couches and chairs and settees in groupings invited guests to come and sit for a while and look out through vast banks of windows to the veranda and blue lake beyond.

"Cora, you can follow this bellman and Anna to your room," Will said, handing me a key and gesturing toward a young attendant and my maid. "Please join us here in the lobby in two hours. We are to attend an evening garden party."

I agreed, and we set off toward the big, curving staircase carpeted in red. Another series of windows alongside the stairs showcased the view of blue upon blue, and when we reached the top, the bellman led us down one hall, turned a corner, then down another. "Your key, mademoiselle?" he asked in heavily accented English. Here in Geneva, they spoke as much French as they did German.

I handed it to him, and he quickly unlocked the tall door and entered, holding it open for me and then Anna. He moved past me and set down my two valises, then went to the windows and pulled aside the long, thick curtains, letting the sunshine stream in. Swiftly, he pointed out the hidden en suite bathroom door, as well as the door to my maid's room, each cleverly papered to blend in with the rest of the wall. He disappeared for a moment and returned with a silver tray, on which was a pitcher of water, glasses, lemon slices, and a plate of cookies. "Anything else I might get for you, Mademoiselle Kensington?" he asked, straightening his white gloves.

"No, thank you." I fished a coin from my purse and handed it to him.

"Ring for anything you need," he said, pausing near the door and pointing to a pulley. "We'll be at your door within a minute or two."

"Thank you."

Anna shut the door behind him and turned to me. "It's a grand hotel, is it not?"

"Truly." Every time we checked into someplace new, I remembered being escorted from my beautiful room in Syon House in England to the servants' quarters after the hosts learned of my scandalous parentage. Would I ever be free of that? It always made me glad to be staying in a paid room rather than relying on the kindness of distant relatives or acquaintances who might pass judgment on me and find me wanting.

I strode toward the windows and gazed at the whitecaps blowing across the water. It was sunny but quite breezy outside, no doubt to the delight of the many sailors upon the water. "Do you think Arthur was serious?" I asked, looking at Anna over my shoulder. "That we might be able to sail tomorrow?"

"No doubt," she said, moving toward my valises. "Now let me see to your garden ensemble for tonight. And if tomorrow is to hold some sailing for you, you'll need something ironed for that as well."

"Thank you, Anna."

She pulled a neatly folded pile of clothes from a valise, sorted through them, and selected a white linen blouse and a straight navy skirt. "What do you think? For tomorrow? I can fetch your white hat from the trunks."

"Perfect."

"And how about your light blue dress for tonight's garden party? It's so pretty with your eyes."

"Again, that would be perfect."

Someone knocked on the door, and Anna went to answer it. Outside, a bellman held a vase with a bounty of beautiful, long-stemmed red roses in a crystal vase. "Flowers for Miss Cora Kensington," he said.

"You can set them there," Anna said, gesturing toward a small, round mahogany table between two wing-backed chairs.

"Of course," he said. Anna took care to tip him, and he exited, closing the door quietly behind him.

But my eyes ran across the gorgeous blossoms, a perfect ruby red. "Have you ever seen anything so beautiful?" I asked her.

"No, miss," Anna said, eyes round with awe. "There must be three dozen flowers in that vase!"

I spotted a small envelope in the midst of all the foliage and reached for it. I tore open the flap and slipped out the tiny card. *Look upon these flowers and think of me*, it read. *As I'll be thinking of you.* I smiled. Had Will done something so extravagant as this? When funds were so short? I tapped my bottom lip with the edge of the card and then read it again. *How irresponsible and reckless of him... and romantic...*

"Who sent them, miss?" Anna asked, pausing with my clothes over her arm.

"I don't know," I said. "There is no name."

"But you have a guess," she said with an impish smile.

"Indeed," I returned dreamily. It was smart of him not to sign the card. If one of my sisters happened to come to my room and see it...

"Well, get a little rest in, and I'll be back to see you into your gown and re-pin your hair."

"Thank you, Anna." I pulled off my gloves and unpinned my hat, setting both on a shelf in the armoire. Then I sat down on the edge of the bed, unlaced my boots, and lay down. I thought it wise— her suggestion I nap—but all I could do was stare at the roses again and again and think, *He loves me.*

———◦◇◦———

I hurried down the staircase, eager to join the others in the gardens, where they were gathering for the party. From snatches of conversation about me, I gathered that today had been the first of several days of racing, and tomorrow afternoon was to be a leisurely sail for which all of Geneva would turn out. I eagerly looked from face to face, looking for my travel party, but most of all, Will.

A group of several gentlemen turned to watch me pass by, but I paid them no attention. I only wanted to see William and thank him for his grand gift. *There they are. At least Lil and Nell and Vivian are here.* I tried to adopt a more subdued, demure expression once I made eye contact with Viv. The last thing she needed was my giddiness in the face of trying to figure out whether she was in love or not. "Good evening, ladies," I said, drawing near. I didn't miss the quick, wary glances Lil and Nell shot in Vivian's direction.

Lil and Nell put on overly cheery grins, while Viv at least managed to smile in greeting. "Did you all get a little rest?" I said.

"Who could rest?" Lil said, bouncing on her toes, her ringlets bouncing with her. "I can't wait to go sailing. Can you?"

"No," I said. "I'm very excited about that. I've never been on a pleasure boat before. Have you?"

All three shook their heads. Sensing that this might be the only opening I might have, I took Vivian's arm. "Might I have a word with you, Vivian?"

She paused and then nodded, and we stepped a few paces away from the girls. "Vivian, I'm so sorry that our conversation the other night seems to have led you into some trouble with Andrew. I never thought—"

"No," she said, lifting a hand to her temple. "It is I who am sorry, taking it out on you. It's all right, Cora. You simply asked me a question I was unprepared to answer. And it seems that Andrew was unprepared as well."

I leaned closer to her. "You still care for him?"

She nodded quickly. "Of course."

"But you are not certain you love him."

She paused and then slowly shook her head. She looked up into my eyes, cocking her head. "We've always been together, really. From the time we were toddlers, our mothers always talked about us getting married someday."

"And so it was simply…assumed?" I took her hands in mine. "Vivian, you must not feel entrapped. You are a beautiful woman of poise and class. Surely, this small separation will make Andrew examine his heart, and he'll discover he loves you. And if he does not, he doesn't deserve you!"

Vivian slipped her hands from mine and bit her lip. "It is not that simple, Cora. Father *wants* this."

I considered her tone for a moment. It said that I couldn't possibly understand. Because we were raised in such different circumstances? "Regardless, in a union of any sort—whether between farmers or the well-to-do—God ordains that it is love that binds us, does He not?"

"I am fond of Andrew." There was a measure of defensiveness in her tone now. But I couldn't keep from saying what I thought I must—what I thought no one else dared. Simply because the copper kings wanted it to be so…

"Vivian, I understand you are fond of him. But what of his quick temper?"

She frowned at me, and I could tangibly feel her slipping away. "Many men have quick tempers. A lady simply learns to manage it. I think it rather attractive, actually. He's so *powerful.*" She looked over my shoulder and scanned the crowd. I followed her glance and saw Hugh and Andrew approaching.

"Vivian," I said, catching her hand, my desperation to reach her rising. "You're fond of him. But I'll ask it again. Do you *love* him?"

"Sometimes, Cora," she said with a sniff, "it is not love that is required of us, but other things."

She left me—feeling utterly confused—as she went to Andrew, offering him her hands and then her cheeks for him to kiss, one and then the other, in the European style. His eyes shifted over to me, with a mixture of suspicion and triumph. He'd not bothered to apologize for last night—not even a note of regret. Perhaps he didn't even remember it, given how much he'd imbibed.

I stifled a sigh. It was up to them, not me. And if their rift had been bridged, at least Andrew likely wouldn't come after me again if he had a few too many glasses of champagne at the party.

Were the Morgan and Kensington patriarchs so powerful that they forced even their children to kowtow to their wishes?

"Did I see roses headed toward your room?" Hugh asked, sidling near.

"Perhaps." I gave him a brief smile, then looked through the crowds, hoping to see William.

"A secret admirer?" he asked. By the lilt in his voice, I knew he knew more than he was saying. I quickly scanned his face, worried for a moment that it had been he who had sent the arrangement.

"It appears so," I said. "It was unsigned."

"Well, that *is* mysterious," he said.

"Indeed." I squinted up at him, studying his expression. "Hugh… did you send them to me? To toy with my emotions?"

"Me?" he said, bringing a hand to his chest, his eyebrows arching in surprise. "No, my dear. I require at least a kiss before I send such an extravagant gift to the women in my life," he said. "Now that can be arranged…."

"*Hugh.*"

"All right," he said. "You are truly in the dark as to who might have sent them?"

"A bit," I hedged.

"Something tells me you'll know before the night is over." He turned to shake hands with Felix, and, a moment later, Art and William joined us too, followed by Yves and Claude. I smiled at Will, and his eyes flashed with curiosity at my bold manner. Quickly, I looked away; at least he'd know I was thankful for his grand gesture. I hoped there would be dancing at the party and he'd find an excuse to take me for a turn on the floor.

Together, our group moved out of the hotel and down the front walk, then to the right, toward the private gardens and beach. I was thankful that the wind had died down, leaving the water fairly still, the boats moored just offshore, others in slips down in the harbor a half mile distant. The city spread upon the hills below, reaching higher and higher to mountains above. And down here, by the lake, there were orderly lines of trees and hedges. A tent had been erected, and inside were elegant tables full of food. Waiters circulated among the guests, bearing trays with glasses of champagne and sparkling pink soda water.

I selected a glass of the soda, taking a sip. It tasted sweet, of raspberries with sugar.

"Come, Cora!" Lil said, coming to take me by the hand. "The dancing has started, and no one will ask us to dance if we're hiding up here in the tent."

"You two go on," Nell said, a plate of food already in her hand. She appeared to have more interest in the mounds of food on the buffet table than any dancing. "I'll join you in a moment."

Two gentlemen watched us pass, open admiration in their eyes. "You look beautiful tonight, Lil," I said, glancing over to my younger half sister. "Is that a new dress?"

"It is, but you know as well as I that those men were watching you pass, not me."

"You never know," I said, smiling at her. "You've grown up while we've been on tour. You're coming into your own. Soon you'll have your own suitors."

"Maybe," she said, her cheeks drawing a pretty blush at my praise. "Though Father will have a say in who will be welcomed at our door."

"Well, Father isn't here now. What's to keep a Kensington girl from a little innocent flirting?"

Her green eyes—so unlike mine and Felix's—went wide with surprise and delight.

We reached the edge of the park where it bordered the lake. The sun was setting now, casting lovely reds and oranges into the sky, and mirrored in the water. The rows of electric lights extended out onto three floating platforms, where a string quartet was playing a lively tune and couples were already dancing. "Oooh, look," Lillian said, pulling my attention to the right.

I followed where she pointed. A juggler was sending seven balls up and into an oblong circle above his head; then, every third ball, he caught one behind his back. The small crowd gathered around him clapped as he took off his shoe and added that to the mix.

"And there are games!" Lil said, pulling me forward. I looked around and saw Antonio following behind us. As usual, we had our guard, which comforted me more than irritated me in this distracting new environment. Antonio would make certain no harm came to me or Lil. I could simply enjoy the party.

Lil and I did our best to toss beanbags through a board with five holes, failing miserably at the task, then we went on to watch a magician atop a wide, overturned barrel. His eyes moved over us, and he smiled. He beckoned Lil closer, and we stepped forward. "M'ladies," he said with a British accent and a gallant bow. But when he straightened, he frowned at Lillian. "Are you American, miss?"

"Why, yes," she said.

"Is it your custom to wear coins behind your ears?"

"What? I don't have—"

But he was already reaching up to her ear and pulled a gold coin from it.

"What... How did you...?" she said in delighted wonder, fingering the gold coin a moment before handing it back to him.

"And My Lady of the Blossom," he said, looking to me. He leaned closer, and I smelled it before I saw it. A red rosebud. He grinned and handed it to me, and I furtively looked around for Will. Had he arranged this? Or was it a coincidence?

We moved on to the next station, a game of Pin the Tail on the Donkey. Lil and I were both blindfolded, turned several times, and sent in the direction of the target. People laughed and shouted at us, mostly in French and German, which didn't help us at all, of course. We called out to each other and eventually found our goal and pinned our "tails" on. I lifted my blindfold to see how I did, and there, at the top of the target, was a long-stemmed rose, sitting atop it. "Lil, did you see who put that there?" I asked, turning to peruse the crowd, looking for Will.

"The tail?"

"No, the rose!"

She shook her head. "Wasn't it there all along?"

"I don't think so," I mumbled, disappointed when Will didn't appear. I edged closer to Antonio. "Did you see who pinned the rose there, Antonio?"

He gave me a confused look and glanced to the target. "No. It wasn't there before?"

"No. I don't think so." Maybe it was my imagination. I simply had roses on my mind, and I was paying more attention to them than any of my companions were. It was an odd coincidence, nothing more.

The two young gentlemen who had watched us pass earlier were suddenly before us. "Ladies," said one in a heavy German accent. "Might you favor us with a dance?"

Lil smiled and ducked her head, blushing, but I looked from one to the other and then glanced over to make sure our guardian was still in place. "Certainly. We would have your names first, however."

"I am Gebhard Schlict," said the younger one, his eyes shifting to Lil in open admiration. He had fair hair and beautiful blue-green eyes. "And this is my cousin, Sebastian Schlict." His relative was taller, with sandy hair and brown eyes, pleasing enough to look at and friendly in demeanor.

"We're glad to make your acquaintance," I said, giving them a small curtsy. "I am Cora Diehl Kensington, and this is my sister Lillian."

"You are Kensingtons?" said the younger man with a bit of awe in his tone. He shared a look with his cousin. "You are kin to Wallace Kensington, of America?"

"One and the same," I said, wondering over the strange wave of pride I felt at the instant respect the Kensington name commanded. In the short time the name had been mine, I'd certainly come to enjoy that.

I took the older cousin's arm, and we made our way down to the floating platforms, walking across a gangplank to enter the least crowded one. The men spoke excitedly of their family enterprise mining in the Alps, and they wondered if our father accompanied us. They barely hid their disappointment when we let them know he did not, but still they managed to lead us gallantly through a turkey trot and then a waltz as the last rays of the setting sun gave way to the gathering dark.

When we exited and thanked our partners for the dances, I spied Will, high on the hill beside Art, near the tent. He smiled at me and lifted his champagne flute. My stomach rumbled, and I thought it might be a most excellent time to return to the tent for food. But a servant came up to me then, a red rose in his hand. "Pardon me, mademoiselle," he said, with a crisp bow. "My lord bids you follow the trail," he said, gesturing back behind him. Even in the growing darkness, I could see the meandering trail of red rose petals up the grass to the top of the hill. "Your lord, is it?" I asked, taking the rose from him and looking for Will again. He had disappeared. Was he waiting for me at the end of the trail? I grinned, and, seeing that Antonio was absorbed in keeping watch over Lil, who was still chatting with the young, blond Gebhard, I turned and slipped away. A moment alone with Will, to thank him, would be so lovely....

I picked up my skirts and hurried up the grassy knoll, ignoring Hugh's questioning gaze as I passed. The trail extended into a gazebo, illuminated by a gas lamp. I hesitated and looked back over my shoulder. The nearest people were now twenty yards away. "Will?" I whispered. I tentatively climbed the steps into the gazebo.

A man in a formal black jacket leaned against the far railing, deep in shadow. It took me a moment, but before he had taken three steps, I knew he wasn't William.

"Mon ange!" Pierre de Richelieu said, his face the very definition of joy as he strode over to me, hands outstretched. "Forgive me. I simply could not stay away."

CHAPTER SEVENTEEN

~Cora~

He took my hands in his, kissing me on both cheeks as he smiled at me. "You look surprised to see me. You received my gift of the flowers, yes?"

"Th-those were from you?" What an idiot I'd been. To think that Will could afford such a gift, given his circumstances.

"But of course! Who else would they be from? Do you have so many admirers you cannot keep track of them? Why, certainly you do!" He grinned, and I had no choice but to smile back at him. He embodied exuberant pleasure, ease. And he was so pleased to see me, it was infectious. But I could not seem to find my tongue.

"Forgive my largesse," he said, gesturing toward the trail of petals. "But I do love a dramatic, romantic moment." He lifted my hands to his lips, kissing the knuckles of one and then the other.

"Oh, how I have missed you since you left, my sweet! Nothing has been the same since we parted. Nothing."

"P-Pierre," I stuttered, "did you not receive my letter?" Even as I said the words, I knew it was impossible. There hadn't been time.... He probably left before—

"Your letter? No." He shook his head in sorrow. "What did it say?"

"Pierre," I said, aching over what must be said, all over again, and finding it twice as hard in person. "You are so lovely. So kind and generous. But you and I..." I shook my head. "I simply don't think we are meant to be together."

He frowned, inhaled and held the breath, lifting his chin. He studied me and then slowly exhaled, nodding. "Cora, we are just beginning to explore what we might have. Would you stamp out a sprout before you'd yet seen its flower?" He shook his head. "I hear your heart, dear one. Your doubt. But I cannot let you go so easily." His eyes searched mine, and he lifted a hand to cradle my cheek.

I stared up at him, wondering what else I could say...to tell him without it becoming a knife wound, slashing his heart....

"Cora?" Will asked, behind me.

I turned slowly, feeling vaguely nauseated. He'd certainly seen. Seen Pierre speak to me in such a caring manner, caress my face. "Will," I said, feeling caught and unaccountably guilty. "L-look who's here!"

Pierre moved past me to shake Will's hand enthusiastically. "Imagine my good pleasure when I received word that you were coming to this hotel! I despaired I'd never find you!"

"Yes, well," Will said, shooting me a confused glance, "that is fortunate." He paused, and a flash of displeasure washed through his eyes. "I understood we wouldn't enjoy your company again until we met in Vienna."

"As did I!" Pierre said gleefully, his eyes still solely on me. "Happily, I was able to revise my plans."

"What a nice surprise," Will said, no note of joy in his tone. Pierre appeared not to notice. Or ignored it. "How long might you sojourn with us before Paris calls you back? A day? Two?"

"No, no, no, my friend," Pierre said, clapping him on the back. "I have two weeks before I must tear myself away." He spoke to Will but smiled at me. "I've arranged to meet Cora's father in Vienna to discuss a certain business venture. It's become clear to me that nothing could have greater import."

"Speak with my f-father?" I said.

"Yes," Pierre smiled, clearly pleased. "It came to me, after you departed. That Montana Copper might be the perfect partner for a certain business enterprise of my own. Monsieur Kensington telegrammed me in return, suggesting a rendezvous in Vienna. It is perfect, no?"

No, I wanted to say. *No, no, no!* He continued to smile at me, then at Will. "I would very much like to travel with you to Vienna and perhaps as far as Venezia."

"You showed us great kindness in Paris and beyond, Pierre," Will said, as polite in his tone as a servant, now, "but I regret I must say no. It is against our policies to accept any other travelers, being in the employ of our clients' fathers, solely to care for their children."

"But what of Arthur Stapleton?" Pierre asked, his forehead wrinkled in confusion.

"I welcomed his continued company as an additional man to guard the women in the group, but I'm certain we've left our ne'er-do-wells behind in France. Art intends to part ways with us in Vienna. Where you yourself can rendezvous with Miss Kensington again, as well as her father." He turned to wave Claude near, obviously preparing to depart and yet not wishing to abandon me without escort. "I shall leave you two to your evening." He reached over and offered his hand to Pierre again, careful not to look my way, and shook it. Then he turned to rush down the stairs. I followed after him, pausing at the top, wrapping my hands around a gazebo pole.

"William," I said.

He halted, looked up to the sky, and then turned partway back to me, as if he had to force himself. "Yes, Cora?"

"Will, we need to discuss—"

He shook his head, glancing at Pierre. He didn't want him to know. If Pierre found out, the others would too, most likely. "There is nothing more that needs to be said." His tone was overly bright and polite. "It is a beautiful night. And your dashing admirer has come to call. Don't let me interfere."

His eyes searched mine. Did he doubt I'd sent the letter? Anger flashed through me as he turned to walk away.

Pierre wrapped his hands around my shoulders and gently turned me, even as he glanced at Claude. "If our time is to be so short, let us get back to *us*," he whispered, "and me telling you how I missed you every moment of every hour of every day since I left your side."

―○◇○―

~William~

He strode down the hill, avoiding the groups of people as he fought the urge to break into a run, to tear his tie from his neck, his jacket from his back. Fury surged through him, dismay at Cora's betrayal, rage at himself for not taking a stand, regardless of what would ensue. The thought passed through him that Richelieu hadn't had time to receive the letter, or if he had, that he was here, bent on convincing her to reconsider.

He shook his head. What did it matter? He was not free to fight for her. Claim her. Drive Richelieu off back to Paris. His hands were tied. Tied! He took a champagne flute from a passing waiter's tray and swallowed it in one gulp, then walked directly to Antonio. "You knew he was here," he hissed in his friend's ear, grabbing another glass of champagne and downing it in similar fashion.

The older man studied him a moment and then looked back over the crowd. "And you need to cease imbibing. It isn't our place as guides. As to Miss Cora…William, given your financial straits, would it not be best to simply look the other way? For both of you?"

Will grimaced and moved his head as if the man had hit him, forcing himself not to react for a moment. "Did you invite him here, or did Cora?"

"Neither of us *invited* him." He waved his hands in agitation as only the Italian could do. "But is it not best? Your uncle did not wish for Cora to lose her heart to Richelieu, but he knew it was far more dangerous if she lost her heart to you." His dark eyes bore into Will's.

Will sighed heavily and turned away, clenching and unclenching his fists.

After a moment, Antonio said, "It will pass in time, my friend. It will hurt like the devil for a while. But in time, you will see that it is best. People like the Kensingtons…they do not welcome people like us as anything but hired help. And Miss Cora—she has enough to manage without you…*complicating* her life further, no?"

Will thought of ten things he wished he could say. Half of him wanted to fire the man now. Half of him wanted to weep, accepting his words as wisdom. But instead, he blurted, "I need the evening. You will see to our clients?" He cast a furious look in Antonio's direction, but he wasn't awaiting permission.

The older man nodded even as Will turned away, striding to the trees and, once there, rushing down the hill, eager to enter his hotel room.

To lock the door. And seal the rest of them out.

———◇◇———

~Cora~

I edged away from him. "Please, Pierre. I…I need a little time. To think." I paced back and forth, before him.

"*Mon ange*. I know our lives are so different…but must they be? Why could we not live for a time in Montana and a time in Paris? Bring together what was once so separate? Weave together an entirely new life—part yours, part mine?"

"Pierre, it is hardly appropriate to speak of such things—"

"But if we cannot speak openly of the problem, how might we ever come to a solution? It is a dam in our river, no? We must get past it in order for the river to meet the ocean, no?"

I sighed and lifted my hand to my forehead. "You simply don't—"

"Perhaps we live in neither Montana nor Paris. Perhaps we live in New York. Or London…"

"Pierre."

He smiled and stepped closer, reaching up to touch my chin, but I shied away. He sighed and rested his hand on his chest. "I see that we've lost hard-won ground. Perhaps you feared what your father would say when he learned of our romance?"

"What? No…"

"Well, rest assured. I have declared my intentions to your father, and he was most receptive. He says that we can speak of it in person once we all gather in Vienna."

I felt my mouth drop open. He had written to Wallace of his intentions? My mind spun. Was it not an unwritten rule that there were to be no romantic entanglements while on the tour? Or was I merely a commodity that could be bartered off to a wealthy business partner? I thought of Vivian's betrothal to Andrew—was that, too, a means of securing his partnership with Morgan?

"Come, *mon amie*," he said, taking my hand and leading me down the steps of the gazebo. "If you will not allow me to kiss you, I at least wish to dance with you until the musicians cannot play another note." He tucked my hand around his arm and led me, in a daze, to the bottom of the hill and onto the dance platform.

And as we waltzed, I slowly eased into his charms, one after another, the delight of being in his arms through a dance—how he made me feel as if I were floating, treasured, a delight—with every word, every movement.

But over and over, I wished it weren't Pierre who held me, but Will.

CHAPTER EIGHTEEN

~Cora~

I awakened angry. Angry that Pierre had ignored my protests, so certain that he was right, and I was wrong. Angry that Will had walked away from the gazebo, assuming the worst of me. Was I any different from my sister, swayed by the men around her? I sat up with a groan, pulling my sleeping cap from my head as I stared at the huge bouquet of red roses, each blossom spreading like a morning welcome from Pierre. What had delighted me yesterday brought me nothing but misery today. They reminded me that Pierre was here and Will was far from me.

Anna knocked and then entered without waiting. Her eyes widened at the sight of me. "Did you not sleep well, then, miss?"

"Is it that obvious?"

"A bit, yes," she said, going to the hall door and, after retrieving my breakfast tray, returning to set it on the table in front of the roses. "Bad dreams?"

"No," I said with a humorless laugh. "Bad thoughts upon waking. Over and over again."

She frowned as she poured me a cup of tea and stirred in a spoonful of sugar, just as I liked it, then handed it to me. "Many would welcome the arrival of a suitor such as Lord Richelieu. Is it the memories of the attack at his chateau that plague you?"

"No," I said quietly, sipping from my cup and then watching a piece of tea leaf adrift on the surface.

"Is it the man himself that dismays you?" She went over to the window and drew back the curtains. "Has he treated you poorly?"

"No. He is a gentleman. Charming from head to toe. And handsome to boot."

She returned to my side, arms crossed, eyebrows in a wry arch. "So you want someone offensive and rude and disagreeable. And ugly, if at all possible."

I smiled. "Of course not." I searched her face. "But I do want someone more...real. Sturdy. Regular. Not Prince Charming." I gestured to my room. "All this comes to an end for me, Anna, come fall. I return to real life. No grand balls. No grand meals. No fine *maid* seeing to my every need," I said to her with a nod. "Normal School in Montana. A boardinghouse room. A meal made on a small wood stove. A job, eventually, on the prairie. And that's fine with me. It truly is. It's who I am."

I knew I said the words for myself as much as for her. To remind myself. Or was it to convince myself? Regardless of what my father might want?

"May I?" she said, gesturing toward another chair.

I nodded and moved my feet, making room for her.

She looked at me as if trying to choose her words. "I suspect you are already different from who you were once, miss." She swallowed hard and rubbed her hands together. "One cannot experience what you have and remain unchanged. You wish to remain who you were out of loyalty to your mama and papa." She paused and studied me.

I stared back at her, waiting for her to finish.

"But miss…you know this time is a gift. And perhaps the road you once thought was the right one for you might be more difficult to find if you retrace your steps." She crossed her ankles. "I came to work for the Kensingtons when I was just fifteen years old and their children were just out of diapers. Even as a maid, my life was changed because of it. I lived in a boardinghouse once. But now? I favor the servants' quarters in the grand palaces we get to see. I favor the adventure. I favor the new turns my life takes each year in the company of my employers. I am different. Might you, miss, be different too? More than you care to admit?"

I frowned at her words but kept silent, thinking them over. I supposed I had been fundamentally changed in some respects, even though I was the same in others.

She reached out and took my hand. "You've been given a chance few of us would ever dare to dream about. You're living a fairy tale. Why not consider the prince, too? Why cast him out before you've even had a chance to see what you can discover about him through courting?"

I looked to the window, then back to her. "Because I've already given my heart to another."

She frowned, and I almost winced at how hard she gripped my hand. "T-to whom?"

I stared back into her eyes until understanding reached them. She lifted a hand to her mouth and shook her head, her face becoming a shade paler. "No, Miss Cora. You cannot." Her eyebrows knit with worry. "Do you not understand? It is one thing for a man of Monsieur Richelieu's standing, his wealth, to pursue a Kensington daughter. But our young bear?" Fear rounded her eyes. "No, Cora. You must end that in all haste. Because if Mr. Kensington discovers it, he will destroy William. Destroy him."

I pulled my hand from hers, my heartbeat picking up its pace. "Surely, you exaggerate—"

"No. *No*. Miss Vivian..." Anna said anxiously. "She once loved a boy she'd known all her life. But he wasn't like Mr. Andrew. No, he was a miner's son, hired by the Kensingtons since he was little to fill the stove each day and stock each of the fireplaces with fresh wood and kindling. He always made Vivian laugh. Oh, how she laughed," she said, giving me a small smile. "But when Mr. Kensington found out, he had the boy's father fired from the mine, and he called in the rent on their home three months in advance. With no other mines hiring, the boy's family had no choice but to move on to look for work."

I frowned back at her. "That...that's barbaric."

"No, miss. That is power. Mr. Kensington believes he knows what is best for his children. And he had long known he wanted Andrew Morgan as Vivian's groom."

I laughed, the sound mirthless in my own ears. "He is wealthy beyond measure. But he is not God."

"Don't be so certain," she muttered, rising and going to my breakfast tray.

"He purports to follow God's lead," I said, following her.

"He does," she said, placing a scone on a plate and then a scoop of clotted cream. "He's devout. Faithful. And he oft says he owes a debt to God for his failings. But you see, that only lends more weight to his decisions. His desire to put things right, with you and your siblings, by sending you down the best road. And you, Miss Cora, perhaps even *more* than the others." She shook her head in grave warning. "No, while he sent you away once, he came to reclaim you. And now duty will convince the man that he shall see you restored in spades."

She handed me the plate, and I took it from her, numb, my stomach filled with knots. She waited until I met her gaze again. "Trust me, miss. If he's agreed to meet Monsieur Richelieu in Vienna, you'd best not interfere. What you must pray for is that the man comes up wanting in Mr. Kensington's eyes. And then he shall send him packing. But if it is because you have your heart set on William?" She shook her head. "Please. For his sake. And your own..."

I set down my plate with a clatter and strode to the window. "I refuse to be corralled. Trapped. My life is my own to live. Not his. He gave up any rights he had as my father when he sent my mother off on that train to marry another."

"Rights he reclaimed this summer."

"No. No! I agreed to the tour, and he agreed to send me back to school. To take care of my papa's medical care. See my mother settled in Minnesota again. We made a deal."

"And he will see it through. He might allow you your education, if he cannot dissuade you. Beyond that..."

Let him try, I wanted to scream. But her solemn expression made me fear not for myself, but for Will. Will, saddled with his uncle's debt and his own unrealized dreams of returning to school. To some-day becoming an architect. To continuing the family business as bear, if nothing else. I turned to the window, looking out at the wide silver blue of the lake under a bright morning sun.

And all I could think about was how my father would cut short every dream Will had, should he become the target of his wrath. The family's Grand Tour business, ended, when my father warned every wealthy associate that Will had tried to convince his daughter she was in love with him. The university, sending him a rejection letter, persuaded by a certain wealthy donor. One architectural firm after another, passing his application by in favor of someone else's, worried about incurring the wrath of Wallace Kensington or one of his cronies.

I lifted my fingers to my temples and rubbed.

I could see no way out.

My father could never, ever believe that there was anything at all between me and Will.

If I loved him, I had to turn him away.

---◇---

~William~

Pierre de Richelieu had managed to outdo Art's connections in the form of a more luxurious yacht the next morning. It was crewed by six men and owned by one of his friends in Paris. Every step of the way to the harbor, Will fought the desire to turn on his heel and walk away, wishing he were anywhere but there.

The man had swept in again and seemed to dominate their every moment, capitalizing on the hours until he had to formally part ways with Cora. A better boat this morning. A private tour that afternoon of the church so instrumental in Calvin the Reformationist's life. An irresistible invitation this evening for supper. A more luxurious car on the train in two days to Vienna. If a stolen moment with Cora was hard to come by before Richelieu's arrival, it would be triply hard to find now. And what was going on in her heart, anyway? All morning long, she'd barely looked his way, seeming to be pulled right back into Richelieu's enchantments.

His clients rubbed their hands in delight with each new turn of fortune, thanks to Richelieu, while Will fought the desire to wrap his hands around Richelieu's slender throat and squeeze....

"A fine-looking couple, aren't they?" Felix said, taking off his yachting cap to mop his brow of sweat, then replacing it. Will reluctantly looked to the stern, where Richelieu's arms were wrapped around Cora's at the wheel, as if teaching her how to steer. He bent down to say something in her ear, and she smiled, looking up to the sails. She looked so lovely, Will ached. *Look my way, Cora. Just look at me. Tell me it's all an act....*

"Will?" Felix asked.

Will remembered himself and met his friend's gaze.

"Uh-oh," Felix said. He glanced to the stern of the boat and back to his friend. "Are you...are you pining for my *sister?*" he whispered.

"What? No. No!" Will let out a scoffing laugh and then dug his toe into the wood of the floorboards, as if trying to dislodge some dirt. "I'm only envious of what she seems to have discovered with

Richelieu. You get to our age and you start to have thoughts about finding the right girl and settling down, you know?"

Felix's eyebrows arched in surprise. "Not me," he said, clamping a hand on Will's shoulder. "And you are far too young to be having such thoughts yourself." He forcibly turned Will to look out upon the lake. "Imagine," he said, sweeping a dramatic arm across the water, "all the fish in the sea, that many women, just waiting to meet us. How could we settle on just one before we've met them all? How would we know we'd met the best one?"

"Felix, this is a lake, not a sea."

Felix pushed him away. "You know what I mean."

Will nodded. He understood what Felix meant, even if he did not agree. What he described was eternal dissatisfaction—perpetually wondering if there might be someone better waiting around the corner. What he'd found with Cora…he'd thought they had found ultimate satisfaction. Peace. Understanding that they belonged together, that they had what it took to be together forever. And yet, now they were clearly not.

He dared to glance back at the wheel and caught Cora staring his way. Flustered, she immediately looked away to the water. She almost looked frightened. But she'd been looking. *She'd been looking.*

Will turned to watch the waves too, fighting a mad urge to grin. Perhaps all was not lost. Perhaps she was only playing the game her family expected her to play. But why the fear?

All he needed was a moment to catch her alone. *Just one moment, Lord*, he prayed, *to know the truth.*

CHAPTER NINETEEN

~Cora~

The next day, as Will stubbornly insisted, Pierre reluctantly left for Vienna. And the following day, our group was on yet another train, this one on a short-distance, narrow-gauge track up to the famed mountains above—with names like Eiger, Jungfrau, and Mönch. For two hours we wound our way steadily up and into the mountains, each valley and her surrounding peaks becoming progressively more dramatic.

"It's like being on the top of the world," Lillian breathed.

"Like heaven!" Nell added.

"I think of the sea as more like heaven than this," Hugh said, gesturing outward, then rubbing his upper arms as if cold. "Give me sand between my toes and women in bathing costumes, rather than a proper coat and scarf, any day."

"Master *Morgan*," Antonio barked, even as Vivian shook her head in disgust. I looked out the window, remembering how he'd once looked upon me in my bathing costume and how I'd endeavored to never wear one near him again.

"Forgive me," he said, pretending to be contrite even as he shared a grin with Felix.

Our entire party was dressed in borrowed trousers and boots, and with coats and gloves stowed in the compartments above, we were ready to meet our ice-trekking guides.

Will sat up front, looking out, never glancing my way. He was angry. And I didn't blame him. How would I have felt, watching him cavort and flirt with another woman these past days?

"So," our young bear said at last, turning in his seat, not daring to stand, so much did the train sway and lurch. "What thoughts have you had on the Reformation and our 'Protestant Pope,' John Calvin, since seeing his church?"

"It is hard to imagine," Vivian said. "The change within the church at large. Of death threats, solely for what you believe..."

"America is unique in her stance of freedom of speech, as well as freedom of expression, in faith matters or otherwise," returned Will. "The Reformation was but a hundred and fifty years after when the pilgrims set off for the shores of America, craving the ability to make their own choices without threat of censure."

"It was poor form for those churchmen, threatening them so," Andrew said. "What does it matter where a man worships God?"

"But we've seen already in our travels," Will said, "that it matters a great deal. Right? With faith comes power, and with power, money, and with money...corruption. Not that the Reformationists were blameless. Calvin himself watched at least one heretic burned in Geneva." He crossed his arms. He looked happy and relaxed in his role as bear, teaching. Natural. Except for the fact that he wouldn't look my way. Not that I wanted him to…not really. How was I to explain myself? My reasoning? In a way he'd understand?

"Who'd he see burned in Geneva?" Lillian asked.

"Severtus. He was a Spanish physician that many claim discovered pulmonary circulation of the blood. He was an astute debater and loved a good oratory discourse, especially if he could challenge the theologians. But when he denied the Trinity, he found he'd tread upon holy ground, and in territory where heresy was a capital offense—even if the definitions of heresy shifted on the sands of the border—he soon found himself destined for the stake."

"They burned him for that?" Hugh asked.

Will nodded. "Calvin pleaded with the authorities to cut off Severtus's head, considering it more humane, but they refused."

"Could he do nothing to change Severtus's mind?" Vivian asked, hand at her chest.

Our young bear stroked his chin, as if trying to remember the exact story. "I believe he tried. But Severtus only laughed."

"He should've stayed in Spain," Felix called.

"Ahh, there he would've been burned at the stake as a younger man, most likely," Will said. "The Spanish were behind the Inquisition, remember?"

"They took heresy a bit too seriously, in my opinion," Hugh put in. We all ignored him.

"Did Calvin know Martin Luther?" I asked, before I remembered I didn't want Will looking my way.

His eyes met mine, and he paused a moment. "I don't believe so. Calvin became a Lutheran, of course, when he first turned from his Catholic beginnings. It was the only choice at first—you were either Catholic or Lutheran. But I think the closest he came to Luther was in meeting Philip Melancthon, Luther's compatriot. Calvin signed the Augsburg Confession, as revised by Melancthon."

"I thought Calvin was the father of the Presbyterian Church," Vivian said.

"His influence was felt primarily in the Swiss Reformation, and his ideas were just a bit different from Luther's in terms of church government," Will said. "But his ideas spread across Europe. In the eighteenth century, the Scots really took hold of it. It was there that the Presbyterian Church was truly born."

I looked out the window, watching as our train chugged through a tiny village with wide, low buildings, smoke curling out of the chimneys. Even now in the midst of summer, it was chilly this high up. The snow was only a few hundred feet above us. Or were those glaciers? Glaciers made me think of the mountains that cast sunset shadows over our farms back home. Even in the middle of a hot summer day, you could see glittering snow high above.

Thoughts of it sent pangs of homesickness through me, and I wished I could go home—even for a day—to go to the barn to stroke Sugarbeet's velvety nose and sneak her a carrot. To sit at the dinner table with Mama and Papa. To go to church and see all the faces—old and young—I'd known all my life. I was weary. So weary. Of all the newness. Of all the change. I closed my eyes. *Oh, for a bit of familiarity...* And yet even the thought of home seemed removed, dreamlike. Was what Anna said true? Was I already irrevocably changed? Could I never go home? Feel settled in such a place again?

We passed a tiny white church with a bell tower, and I wondered if it was Catholic or Lutheran or Presbyterian or something else entirely now. Back home, in the cities, there were Baptist and Methodist and Congregationalist options, too. And as my eyes searched the startling, picturesque mountain ridges, I thought how sad it all must make God, that His people were so divided, so separated when it came to matters of faith. As with so much else that was right and true in life, we got stuck in the particulars and lost sight of what was right and true in the first place—we concentrated on the things that divided us rather than the things that unified us. Love. Grace. Peace.

I remembered being in that massive cathedral in Paris with Will, and my eyes shifted to his back. We'd both felt such a kinship with the Holy in that place…I was sure of it. Will was turned forward again in the front seat, leaning with his elbows on his knees, swaying with the motion of the train. I knew he was a man of faith, a man who sought God. I wondered then what Pierre believed. I had no idea where he stood on matters of faith. I shook my head and turned back to the window. It startled me that I did not know, nor had bothered to find out. Back home, most everyone went to church. But I knew here, in Europe, it wasn't always the case. Did Pierre even believe in God at all? And might that be enough to dissuade my father from insisting I accept his pursuit?

———◇◇◇———

After a hearty lunch of beef stew and crusty bread in a cozy alpine inn, we met up with our guides. We rode in the back of a wagon pulled by oxen up a long, steep hill. We women had been given the option of staying behind with Yves and Claude—waiting in the warm inn, sitting by the fire while the men hiked the glacier—an option none of us took, since we all were excited about this adventurous excursion. From the top of the hill, we would begin our hike up and onto the nearby glacier, a force that had been shaping these mountains and valleys for thousands of years and was slowly receding.

Our guides slipped hobbled nail straps around our boots, tied us together with ropes, from waist to waist, and handed us poles for balance. We climbed a series of rickety makeshift ladders to the top of the glacier's edge, a hundred feet above us. Despite the exercise, I was glad for my split skirt and the warm woolen leggings Anna had insisted I wear, as well as for my gloves, scarf, and coat. It was frigid, challenging work, and I wondered how my sisters and Nell were doing behind me. We were arranged from the biggest to the smallest of us. One big guide of about fifty years of age, his face wrinkled and weather-beaten, led the way, just ahead of Will and Andrew. Just ahead of me was Hugh. Behind me were Vivian and the girls. Two younger men—the leader's sons?—brought up the very end, perhaps staged there to help the women.

I resolved I would need no assistance. It was exhilarating, being here, so near the top of the mountains, on top of this ice set in place by the hand of God thousands of years ago…. Along the two miles we walked, we saw cirques—rounded carvings in stone and ice, like massive, natural amphitheaters. We saw ridges hewn into razor-sharp tips, and valleys in sweeping, rounded rivers still filled with the last vestiges of glacial meltings.

The sun, high and bright, warmed our heads, even as a cold wind chapped our cheeks and noses. Behind me, Vivian grumbled about what it might do to our complexions, but she kept up with the slow, sure pace our lead guide set. At one point, we paused in an ice cave with a wide, curved roof of blue and a rivulet running along the bottom. The farther back we went, the darker blue it was. We turned to look back out. I didn't think I'd ever forget that perspective—of the smooth, Mediterranean-blue ice framing the most picturesque alpine view I'd ever seen…a green valley, a swath of red wildflowers on one hillside, far below, and mountain upon mountain above her.

"Smell that?" Will said, and we all inhaled.

The odor made my nose twitch. It was a particular, earthy, mineral-rich scent.

"That is what a few on the *Titanic* said they could smell before they hit the iceberg. It's unique, is it not?"

"I don't believe it," Hugh said with a scoff. "How could they smell it above the scent of the sea?"

Will shrugged. "Believe what you wish. I, for one, think it possible."

And I agreed. It was a smell that made an imprint on the mind—like the loamy mud on a riverbank, or soil just turned on the farm come spring, or the grassy smell of manure. As we exited the ice cave, thoughts of the smells of home made me wonder over just how far I was from Montana. Never in my life had I thought to come this far, experience this sort of adventure. What joy it would be to relate to my students, my stories! To plant a seed within them that might grow into a desire to explore, experience such things themselves. So many never left their hometowns in Montana. So few even went to Butte or Billings or Helena. I myself had never left the state before Wallace Kensington came to call.

As we hiked on, heading toward another viewpoint, I got lost in thoughts of my biological father. Was it true? Would he truly keep me from returning to Normal School, from teaching? When we had agreed on it? When it was my heart's desire? I understood that he might attempt to keep me involved with the family. In truth, I continued to warm to that idea. But to keep me from meaningful work? The means to provide for myself? Or, worse, force me into a union I didn't want? I didn't want to—

A scream behind me made me look up, right before I felt the ice give way beneath me. I saw the guide ram his ice pick into the glacier and whip more rope around it, even as I heard his younger compatriots do the same behind us. They were shouting, in German, words we didn't understand. Not that we could do anything. We all slid to the end of our ropes, wincing as we came to an abrupt jolting stop, like a giant's necklace of human bodies, separated by a length of rope. I gasped for air, hanging over a ledge, a deep crevasse beneath me. My heart pounded as I craned my neck, looking for the bottom. I couldn't see it. *If these ropes give way, we'll*—

"Cora…are you all right?" Hugh asked over his shoulder to me.

"I…I think so," I said. The girls were crying behind me. The men were all shouting at once. Vivian was quiet.

"Viv? You all right?" I asked. I tried to turn to see her, but I could not. And I was struggling to breathe, the rope was so tight around my abdomen.

"Lil!" I cried when Vivian didn't respond. "Is Vivian all right?"

"Her head…" the girl said, tears thick in her voice. "I think she must've hit a rock."

I closed my eyes and grimaced, then felt the tug of rope. They were already hauling us up, I thought with relief as I moved a few inches. There was more shouting above, the men below quieting, perhaps all trying as hard as I was to take the next breath.

"We can't haul you up this way!" Will shouted, from somewhere above us. "It's too much weight! Hugh, do you have your knife on you?" I remembered that the men had all purchased Swiss Army knives while we perused a glove shop, and then we had all gathered in a watch shop.

"Yes! I think I can reach it!"

Will's face appeared fifteen feet above us. "I know this will be frightening, but Hugh, I need you to cut the rope between you and Felix. We need the group divided in order to be able to pull you up."

Hugh groaned and lifted his head, fear radiating from him. "Hold on, girls," he called. Lillian whimpered above me. I swallowed hard. I knew what was to come when he cut the rope. We'd go swinging deeper into the crevasse....

Despite myself, I cried out as he finally sawed the rope apart and we slid again, sweeping into a vertical line down and into the crevasse, as the others swept away from us.

I heard Hugh gasp as he hit the crevasse wall, and then I hit it too and slid downward, my hip and then leg catching just as we came to a stop. I screamed as my calf lodged between two planes of ice. Hugh dangled beneath me, pulling my leg deeper with his weight.

I turned my head and looked down at him. We still couldn't see to the bottom of the crevasse. I fought to study his face instead of the horrific drop beneath him. "My leg...I'm caught, Hugh."

Above us, the guides began to haul us up, and I cried out as I felt my body twist and the movement wrenched at my leg.

"Stop! Stop!" Hugh shouted, his voice echoing through the crevasse in eerie fashion.

I grimaced and looked down at him. "I think we're in a predicament," I said, trying to add some levity.

Hugh just stared at me and then swore under his breath. "We need another rope!" he screamed.

Fifteen feet above us, Lillian repeated his words, fear in every syllable.

"You can't wiggle it free?" Vivian asked, apparently conscious again.

"No," I said. "It's really lodged." Even now, I could feel my toes going numb, the circulation cut off. Dimly, I thought about the burned heretic Severtus and how he'd discovered pulmonary circulation.

"What's wrong?" Felix called, from twenty feet away, already moving as they hauled him toward safety, his boots against the ice as if this were simply a mountaineering pleasure excursion.

"Cora…she's stuck," Hugh said, gasping for breath, the rope probably digging into his diaphragm.

"Hang on!" Felix called. "I'll tell them what's happening and we'll get to you in a minute."

None of us answered, each just trying to stay calm and concentrate on breathing. Could it be? That I'd come so far, experienced so much, just to die here? Stuck in the clutches of a glacier's fingers? I laughed under my breath. Never had I thought I might share my last moments with Hugh Morgan, of all people. Felix was shouting for a rope. I thought I heard Will translating.

A moment later, another rope slapped my right shoulder. Hugh grabbed hold of it. "Thank God," he muttered. I turned my head and watched him fashion a seat out of it and slip it around his legs. He yanked on the second rope, testing the tension. "All right!" he shouted. "Hold on to me! I'm going to move to the second rope and release the tension on Cora!"

He moved, trying his best to not pull at me, but some tugging was inevitable. I squeezed my eyes shut and sucked in my breath as my leg wrenched again. But then there was sweet relief. No more pulling. I tried moving my leg, hoping that now that I was free of Hugh's weight, I could escape the trap, but to no avail.

"Take me up five feet!" Hugh shouted.

He was immediately beside me, his knees against the ledge that held me captive. "Well, I confess when I'd dreamed of a moment alone with you, it wasn't here."

I laughed, knowing he was trying to make me smile. And I welcomed it, even if it was Hugh. "How did you know how to do that with the rope?"

"We Morgan boys have done our share of mountaineering," he said, as if surprised that I didn't know such things. "Last summer we trekked fifty miles of the Continental Divide in Montana."

"Really?"

"I need a third rope!" Hugh called upward, ignoring my question, concentrating on the task at hand. "And an ice pick!" He looked back at me, his eyes deadly serious. I didn't think I'd ever seen him like that, so in charge. Yet so compassionate. "We need to cut Vivian and the girls loose, so that we're only dealing with your weight. Then we can get you free."

I nodded, trying to gather enough saliva to swallow. He watched me and then reached for a canteen on his belt. "Here. Drink."

I took it from him, unscrewed the lid, and did as he asked, grateful for the cold water that slid down my throat. I could hear Lil and Nell crying above me.

"Your leg," Vivian said from above me, twisting to look at me but unable to stay in one position for more than a moment. "Is it broken?"

"I…I don't think so. I think it's simply stuck. But *really* stuck."

The third rope arrived. Hugh slipped his canteen into his belt loop and fashioned another loop out of it. "Here. Slip it around your shoulders and under your arms." I did as he asked, and once it was in place, he yanked on it. "Rope three is secure around Cora!" he called.

He pulled his knife back out and looked at me. "I'm going to cut the girls loose."

I nodded and watched as he sawed at the taut rope, the wisps of each strand fraying and catching the sunlight from above. Finally, he got through it, and the girls cried a little as they shifted left with me no longer tethering them. "Take them up!" Hugh called.

They immediately began separating from me, and I felt a new shaft of despair, a peculiar sense of loneliness that made me glad that Hugh was with me. *For the first time on this entire tour, I'm glad I'm with Hugh Morgan.* It made me laugh, within. God had an odd sense of humor. *It couldn't have been Will, Father? That would've been far more agreeable.…*

But despite my whiny prayer, I had to grudgingly admire Hugh and his sure, strong movements. As the girls disappeared above us, one of the younger guides repelled down to us, ice pick in hand. He paused beside Hugh, then grabbed hold of the ledge and yanked.

"Yeah, I tried that," Hugh said in English, but the young man was already moving on, examining the placement of my leg in the small gap, measuring with his hand how deep I was lodged within it.

Without another word, he pushed Hugh to the left, right by my head and out of his way, then pulled the pick from his belt. He dug the toes of his nail-tipped boots into the ice, bounced on them a bit to make certain he was secure, then pulled back the pick in order to strike.

I gasped and closed my eyes. Hugh shouted and grabbed hold of my shoulder. But then I felt the impact, directly below my calf. I opened my eyes to see him lifting for a second swing and quickly shut them again, unable to watch as he rammed down again, into the ice, as deadly certain as if he'd done it a thousand times. *Perhaps he has*, I thought, turning to stare into the blue cliff at my left, rather than see him lift that pick again. I didn't want to remember the strike that ultimately led to that fearsome metal nose piercing my leg....

After fifteen more strikes, I felt the ice give way, and I cried out as I swung left, directly toward Hugh.

Our guide shouted something upward in German.

But I was wrapping my arms around Hugh, clinging to his jacket with my fingers, terrified we'd fall again.

"It's all right, it's all right," he soothed. He smiled at me, waiting for me to look up and into his eyes. "Now this is more like it," he said, the cavalier, roguish glint back in his tone. "Cora Diehl Kensington, at last in the right man's arms."

I gasped for breath, wanting to laugh and cry and scream at the same time. He was only teasing me, slipping back into his rogue act. But I'd seen it—that glimpse of humanity. And I knew that I couldn't distrust him any longer. Not after what had just transpired.

"How's the leg?" he asked.

I gingerly turned my ankle and wriggled my toes. "Numb…but I think it's all right." I shook my head in wonder.

"Good," he said, smiling. "Take her up," he called, lifting his face.

The guide beside us repeated his order in German, and I was immediately moving. But my eyes stayed on Hugh. "Thank you," I said.

"You're welcome."

I reached the top, and the girls immediately surrounded me, hugging me and all talking at once in excited and relieved chatter. I limped a couple of steps, and Will was there, then, beside me, bending to look into my eyes, one hand out to catch me if I fell. "Are you all right?"

I looked up into his eyes and saw that he looked pale. I nodded. "I think it's just numb from getting lodged. It feels dead, like a lump of flesh rather than a foot."

He nodded and, without asking, swept me up into his arms.

"Will, really, I think I can walk. I just need a few minutes."

He turned, and I saw Andrew examining Vivian's bleeding head. And then Hugh, emerging from the circle of glad embraces. "Typical," he said, waving toward us. "I save the girl, but who ends up with her in his arms? William McCabe."

The others turned to smile at us, but their eyes went back and forth between me and Will, as if seeing us for the first time as Hugh had always seen us.…

Together.

CHAPTER TWENTY

~William~

"Put me down, Will," Cora whispered urgently as the rest of the group watched them. But at that moment, he didn't care who saw them. He wanted her in his arms, to kiss her and touch her, to reassure himself that she was here. Whole. Well.

He carried her to a boulder that emerged from the ice and set her upon it. He kneeled by Cora's feet and carefully lifted her boot in one hand, watching her face. She winced, and he immediately paused. "That hurts?"

"Only because it's starting to get some feeling back. In the form of a thousand needles."

"But you don't think it's seriously injured? Not even a sprain?"

"No. I don't believe so."

Will gently set it down. "I almost lost you today," he said quietly, so only she could hear, touching her knee and casually lifting her foot again as if continuing to test it. "And I don't ever intend to do that again." He looked up at her. "Having you down there...so far from me..." He turned his head and gave it a little shake, fighting an embarrassing tear.

"Will," Cora said, gesturing toward her foot as if they were discussing it, rather than something else. The rest of their group did not need any more cause to guess that something was happening between the two of them. "I sent Pierre that letter."

Will looked over his shoulder at the group and then back to her. "And he received it?"

"No. There hadn't been time. But I told him, Will. Told him I didn't think we belonged together."

"And he said?"

She sighed. "He thinks he can convince me to reconsider. He's already spoken to my father about his intentions. And Will...I'm afraid. For you. That if we try to pursue this thing between us..."

The others were making their way to them now, so Will hurriedly searched her face. "Cora, listen. I was a fool for walking away from you the other night in the gazebo. A fool for not telling Richelieu that you are *mine*." He squeezed her hand, but she only looked alarmed.

"It would've been unwise," she whispered. "For some mad reason my father's decided to hear Pierre's request to court me. I think it might be a means to secure a deal. But Will, if you get in the way of that, my father will likely blame us and do everything he can to stand between us...."

With the others upon them, Will rose to his feet, and she tentatively did the same. She grimaced, still feeling some pain, even as the guides wrapped a new rope around her waist, then Will's. They were singing, clearly rejoicing that they were bringing all seven of their clients back to the inn.

"I assume residual pain is good," Will said. "It must mean the circulation is returning."

"Which is far better than the alternative," she said. "Even if it is a form of torture."

"Would you like me to carry you this time?" Hugh asked, stepping up beside her.

"No," Will said. "I shall see to her. I think you've done enough." He offered him his hand. "If it wasn't for your skills with the ropes, we might not all be standing here. I'm grateful, Hugh."

"Yes, well," Hugh returned, "if our guide hadn't been as talented as he was with the pick, some of us would likely *still* be down there."

Will turned to shake the guide's hand, and then the others, thanking each of them. The group circled together.

"Are you all right, Vivian?" he asked.

"Fine, fine," she said, characteristically brusque and strong. "Head wounds always bleed a lot, as I understand it."

"Impressive, Miss Vivian," Art said, finding her in his Kodak and taking a photograph.

"Arthur Stapleton!" she said, touching her disheveled head in alarm.

"Rest assured," Will said, "this is, by far, our most adventurous outing. After this, your greatest risk shall be avoiding a dirty motorcar or an unsavory partner on the dance floor."

"I hope you jest," Felix said, bending to frame his own photograph of a pointed mountain peak above them. "This has been the most grand day of the trip, in my book! What an adventure!"

"Well, I can look into some other touring options," Will said to him. "For you. Without endangering the women."

Felix smiled and clapped him on the shoulder.

"So the women are to be held in an ivory tower?" Cora asked as they fell into line again, trudging back toward the inn. "While the men venture out? That sounds rather dull."

"Really, Cora?" Vivian huffed. "After what we've just been through?"

"I didn't come all the way to Europe to sit in my room. I came for just this sort of experience." She bit her lip. "I would not choose our harrowing fall again, of course. But coming here? To see all of this?" She glanced outward. "I wouldn't have missed it."

———◇◇◇———

~Cora~

Two days later, we arrived in Vienna via the blue Danube River, steaming past quaint villages that climbed the hillsides and castles that once controlled trade upon the waters. I paced for hours along the wooden deck, anxious about what was ahead of me from both Pierre and my father. And try as we might, Will and I could never seem to steal a moment to ourselves. When I was alone, someone was with him. And when he was alone, I was invariably accompanied. It was enough to drive me mad, looking for an opportunity around every corner.

I had to see through what was ahead of me without further word from him, I decided, watching as the paddlewheel turned, water churning down below as the sun set to the west of us. It sent golden shafts of light through the mountain passes, which made the water a deeper shade of blue, the hills a richer shade of green. I heard a footstep behind me, and my heart quickened. I hoped it was Will, at last.

I looked up and over my shoulder, then away, not wanting him to see my swift disappointment. Hugh. Not Will. *Hugh*.

"So I take it, given that cold reaction, you were expecting someone else," he said, leaning his elbows on the rail. He raked his fingers through his brown hair, pushing it from his eyes.

"Not at all," I said, forcing cheer to my voice as I stared at the rotating wheel. "Have you fully recovered from our mountain adventure?"

"I have. And you, my Lady of the Crevasse? I would've been sorely dismayed, had we lost you."

"Oh?" I mused. "In some ways, I think you all would be far better off without me here. I simply make things more complex."

"Which is exactly why we need you. Who else will entertain us? Make us wonder whom you shall choose—young Will, The Penniless, or young Pierre, The Prince. Of course, there's always a third option. *Moi*."

I narrowed my eyes at him and sighed. "Really, Hugh. Don't you grow tired of trying to bait me?" I gestured about us. "Is this not enough to keep you entertained? The luxury? The excursions? The new people, new lands? Why must you come after me?"

He shrugged again. "You're close at hand." He turned partway to me, leaning his side against the rail and sweeping his hair from his eyes again. "Your cross to bear, and all that—having to cope with me. I simply find it entertaining. The rags-to-riches girl, suddenly drawing the attention of every rich bachelor we pass, as well as our junior bear, still in rags. Before you give your heart to him, you ought to think long and hard."

I hesitated, shocked at how plainly he spoke. "Why? Do you hope that I might cast you a new glance?" I couldn't believe my audacity, my forward manner. But I had to know what drove him. And how to stop it.

He shook his head, and in that moment, there was such sorrow in his movement, such hopelessness in the cavalier tilt of his shoulders, my heart lurched. "Me? No," he scoffed. "You and I would clearly be a mismatch. And I'm naught but the second son, a playboy, a misfit. My father looks down his nose at me. Why should you not do the same?"

I frowned a little at the pain that shadowed his tone. "Hugh, I…I don't look down my nose at you. But you…you've hardly *invited* respect from me. Yes, you saved me in that crevasse—for that I'll be eternally grateful—but you have not been a *friend* to me. Not truly."

"I know," he said, turning to face the water wheel, both forearms on the railing now. "I'm sorry," he said, looking at me from the side. "I'm a creature of impulse, I fear."

"Impulses can be curbed, controlled," I said.

"Perhaps," he said. "Maybe if I had a drink…"

I shot him a quick look of dismay, and he smiled. "I'm joking! Goodness, Cora, perhaps it's you who needs a drink."

"Hugh…"

He stood up and lifted his hands in surrender. "I understand. I've pushed too far. Anyway…friends? Might we be friends?" He offered a hand, as if to shake mine as men did.

I straightened and faced him too. "No more manipulation? Taunting?"

"No more," he said earnestly.

And so I shook his hand. "Friends," I said, but even as I said it, I wondered if it would ever be true.

———◦◇◦———

~William~

Will felt as if he were crawling the walls of the river steamer. He'd been unable to find a moment to speak to Cora, and he was desperate for a word from her, to find out what she was thinking, feeling, before they reached her father. And Pierre de Richelieu again.

But now it was too late. He'd walked the decks and even considered knocking on her cabin door—but he could not come up with any plausible reason for disturbing her, especially if Vivian answered. They'd reach the docks within the hour. He paced back and forth in his small cabin, squeezing his hands together. What was done was done.

A knock sounded on his door, and he opened it.

Antonio looked at him in surprise, probably due to how quickly he'd opened it. "Will? We'll gather for the lecture on Vienna's history, up on deck?"

"Of course," he said, pretending that he'd remembered all along that was the plan. "Let me finish my packing and get my coat."

"Good. I shall go and collect the others."

Will forced a smile and nodded, closing the door and leaning his head against it. How could he keep up the facade? Even if it all didn't come to a head here in Vienna? How could he pretend he felt anything less than he did for Cora?

Part III
~VIENNA~

CHAPTER
TWENTY-ONE

~Cora~

The summer season was at its height when we reached Vienna, the city of music, with outdoor concerts for the public and private concerts every night. She was a grand old city, full of baroque buildings. But despite Emperor Franz Josef's best efforts, more modern, sleek buildings were making their appearances, inspired by architects subscribing to the "form follows function" philosophy. This city, too, we learned, had Roman foundations, with both illustrious and scandalous stories. Later, Richard the Lionheart was kidnapped here en route home from the Third Crusade and ransomed for enough to build the newer southern walls.

"Those walls stood for quite some time," Will lectured, frowning a bit, which I thought made him look rather distinguished and thoughtful. "But then the emperor thought it best to give way to expansion, so he decided the era of needing a wall for protection was over. Vienna became the seat of the Austro-Hungarian Empire and was ruled by the Habsburg dynasty from 1273 onward. It's been an astonishing run, really. That long, for any royal family. They've weathered much, but from what I can see, the emperor is losing touch with his people, and it cannot last much longer."

I stared out the motorcar window as the big trees of the Ringstrasse swept by me, and thought about old men of power and meeting up with my father again. And Pierre, the son of so many generations of power…

"Are you fretting, Cora?" Vivian said, nodding to my hands. I realized I'd wound a handkerchief into a knot, worrying it with my fingers.

"What? No. No. Only…thinking." I met her eyes. "All right, perhaps I'm fretting a bit."

"Father responds best to respect."

I knew she meant it as a kindness, her words of advice, a means to aid me in what was to come, but I had to swallow a sharp retort. I nodded, hoping I appeared grateful, then looked out the window again.

Did I have it in me to respect the man who had taken everything I knew, everyone I loved, and then placed me in an entirely new world, with people and places I was begrudgingly coming to love? It still wasn't clear to me how I was to treat him. What I wanted from him. And part of it was that I needed to know if what Anna said was true—had it all been a ruse to get me on this path in the first place? So that when the walls became so high around me I had no choice but to stay?

I resolved to find that out.

The driver pulled off of the Ringstrasse and onto another main thoroughfare. Here, the estates reminded me a bit of the Richelieu chateau—with wide manicured lawns; perfect gardens; and beautiful stone mansions with long windows and steep copper roofs tinged turquoise from a century of rain. Our hosts, descendants of the Habsburgs—and a business associate of my father's—had agreed to house us all. As with other places we'd stayed, we merely took up a small portion of the hundred-plus rooms.

We were greeted by the Baroness Grün, an American by birth, who looked as elegant as her name, with her blonde hair swept up into a pearl-encrusted clip, long fingers tucked into perfectly white gloves. She wore a delicate pink afternoon dress that clung to her slender body. She walked with chin up, her arms poised as if for a portrait, and greeted us with a demure, dignified air. But her keen eyes shifted from one to the next of us, taking us in, taking stock. After her crystalline blue eyes met mine for a long moment, I felt a bit unbalanced—as if she'd pulled the very core of who I was out. I wondered if everyone else felt the same—that the woman was so keen, she *knew* something key about us after but a moment.

Servants were assigned to each of us, carrying our luggage and showing us to our rooms where we would stay for the next few days. The decor inside was Rococo, with gilt mirrors and ornate chandeliers all down the hall. Walls papered in a gorgeous Danish blue were lined by thick white moldings, and golden cherubs peeked out at us from each high corner.

"Here is your room, miss," said the servant in a thick German accent. He was about twenty years of age and as perfectly poised as his mistress. He opened the door for me, and I walked into the sprawling suite, past a massive four-poster bed covered with a thick tapestry canopy and with the most sumptuous pillows I'd ever seen. Past the bed was a full sitting area with two couches and a chair on either end, a table between them. And on either side of the window was one of a matching set of Queen Anne chairs.

Through a tall white door with a gold knob was a sprawling bathroom, complete with a long white tub, a separate shower—something I'd never tried—and a water closet and sink. My whole house in Dunnigan could've fit inside that portion alone.

"It is acceptable, miss?" asked the servant.

"More than acceptable," I said to him. "It is lovely. Thank you."

"It is my good pleasure. Your maid will find her room right next door," he said to me, never looking at Anna. "The baroness wishes for you all to gather in the garden at five. Tonight you shall enjoy a concert and party."

"Thank you," I said and then watched him slip out the door, as quiet as a ghost.

Anna looked around the room and then studied the painted ceiling, a picture of two large, naked women cavorting about the clouds. "We've landed in another palace," she said, moving toward my trunks to fetch the right gown for the evening's events.

"Indeed." I went to the window and looked out. The palace was shaped like a large U, and my room looked down on the entry. From here I'd be able to see everyone arrive. I'd be able to make certain I made the right choice as to what to wear. It was perfect, really. And given that my father was a business associate of our hosts, I hoped I'd be protected from any ill treatment.

But my father was somewhere here on the premises. Something told me that nothing like what had transpired at Syon House would ever happen with Wallace Kensington around. It both comforted and alarmed me that he was here. The sooner we had a conversation, the better. I needed to know how deeply tied to Pierre de Richelieu he was and why he would entertain the man's pursuit when we were sent out with explicit directions not to fall for any of Europe's "playboys." Perhaps he was eager to see me joined with anyone at all respectable, given my scandalous start and my humble upbringing.

"Miss Cora?" Anna asked, obviously not the first time.

I turned and looked at her. She was holding up my pink gown, the one I associated with Pierre and Paris. I shook my head. "I'd like another."

"But this one is so beautiful on you!"

"How about the blue?"

She stood there, frowning at me. "Are you certain, miss?"

"Very." I turned away, back to the window, disliking my superior tone but unable to stop myself. I felt so…disconcerted. "I need to find Mr. Kensington," I said.

"You don't wish to rest for a bit?"

"No. I need to see him." I looked over my shoulder at her. It was partially her fault, really. The ideas she had planted. The fears.

She averted her eyes and lifted the blue dress. "I'll just give it a quick press and be back."

"Thank you," I mumbled, turning to the window. I watched as a horse-drawn carriage passed by, beyond the front gates, a couple out for a romantic ride on a pretty summer afternoon; and then three motorcars as they drove in and more elegantly dressed people emerged, greeted by servants. I didn't spy the baroness again.

I discovered my silver-haired, distinguished father with Mr. Morgan in the library, each with a cup of Vienna's famous coffee. They rose to greet me, holding my hands and kissing my cheek as if I were close kin. Seeing me stare at my father and then look to the ground, Mr. Morgan made his excuses and departed, promising to see us both in the coming hours.

A maid wordlessly appeared with a new china cup and set it on the tray for me. "Cream or sugar, miss?"

"Both, please," I said. I accepted the cup from her and sat back in the chair Mr. Morgan had vacated.

"You are looking well, Cora."

"I am well, thank you. What news have you of home?"

"Fine news, grand news, really," he said, settling his cup in its saucer. "Alan was discharged from the hospital, Cora. He and your mother have settled into a beautiful little cottage not far from your grandparents. My man tells me that they have planted a garden."

I inwardly tripped at the mention of his "man"—a spy?—but then smiled, my heart picking up at the thought of Mama and Papa, content, well, and settling in. "That is the best news possible," I said, hand on my chest. "Thank you," I said earnestly. "For seeing to their care. Most especially for Papa."

He waved me off. "Not at all. It was the least I could do. I was in Dunnigan right before we left to make the crossing. Came across this in the general store…" He rose and went to a box sitting on a side table. He brought it over and handed it to me.

I recognized the box immediately, even before I saw the Jaspers logo on the front. I looked up at him, loathe to open it. I felt unaccountably guilty, even if I'd not known it was from him.

"It was a *gift*, Cora. For your sixteenth birthday. You weren't to sell it."

I sighed. "I sold it in the hope that we could plant a crop and save the farm."

He studied me with those eyes so like my own, for a breath, then two. "You are a fine woman, Cora. It takes a mountain of mettle to sacrifice your own desires for the good of those you love." He reached down, took the box from me, and flipped open the lid. Then he slid the multi-strand necklace from it and went around the chair to clip it around my neck. "But you needn't resort to such measures. No daughter of mine shall ever have to sell her jewelry to pay for necessities."

I looked up at him as he came back around the chair. I knew the necklace was perfect, matching the pearl clasps at the shoulders of my blue gown, as well as the pearls that Anna had wound into my hair. "Thank you," I whispered, trying to find my voice again. I was unaccountably glad to have the necklace back. A treasure lost, now found. I inhaled, remembering the reason I had been so eager to see him. "But it…it's hardly the sort of thing I shall wear once I have a proper teaching position."

He paused and clamped his lips together. "You may be surprised how often you may have the opportunity to wear it," he said casually, picking up his cup and sitting back into his chair. He looked over the rim of his cup at me as he sipped. "You're as pretty as a picture, Cora Kensington."

"I prefer Cora *Diehl* Kensington," I said quietly.

"No matter," he said, giving me a dismissive wave. "As fine looking as you are, in claiming my name—in whatever order you wish—it was inevitable that you'd draw the attention of Europe's finest."

"You speak of Pierre de Richelieu."

"Indeed. He sent me a rather long, persuasive letter, Cora. I had the opportunity to meet with him in person last night. He is quite taken with you and wishes to court you in earnest. And while I resisted the idea of any of my daughters taking up with a man on the Continent, it was primarily because I didn't want some cad with empty coffers luring you in with his dandy ways and grand, old home, only to break your heart once your funds were locked in his family's bank vault."

I frowned in confusion. I had no funds. No dowry. No inheritance.

"But this Richelieu…he is far from penniless," he went on. "He is a rather astute businessman, eager to bring Montana Copper's resources to France and beyond. I was impressed, in spite of myself."

"I admit that Pierre *is* rather impressive," I said. "It's inescapable, really. But—"

"No, no, no!" he said, waving a finger toward me. "You may not dismiss him out of hand. Not this one. There is far too much to be gained in our relationship."

"Our…*our* relationship? I confess that I am rather confused. I thought—"

"Do not do anything to dissuade him. At least not yet." He gave me an aggravating wink as if I were but a small girl ready to do anything her daddy requested. As if I were in on whatever plan he had in mind. But along with the studied playfulness was an edge of power, the subtle threat that I should dare not do anything but what he asked of me.

"I am quite fond of Pierre. He is a good man. But you see I—"

"Fondness! A lovely way to begin."

"No, you misunderstand me. I do not wish to lead him on. Not when I—"

"It is not 'leading him on' to simply receive his attentions."

I gaped at him. "What would you call it?"

"I'd call it the ways of polite society. Call it what you wish, but do not dissuade Pierre from his pursuit. Not yet. Do you understand me? It is most vital that you follow my direction on this, Cora. *Most* vital."

"But I—"

"My girl," he said, rising and coming to me, putting his hands on either arm as I contemplated the words... *My girl.* "This deal... what we could *make* in working with Richelieu..." He shook his head. "It is far more vast than you can imagine. You must do this. You must not send him off brokenhearted when this deal could bring all of us—everyone in the family—"

"Father!" Vivian cried, entering the library. I stifled a frustrated sigh and took a sip of coffee, knowing that my opportunity to find out more had just officially ended.

Felix and Lillian were right behind her, Lil hugging him with genuine affection, Felix smiling and shaking his hand. "Good to see you, sir," he said.

"Is that a new necklace, Cora?" Lil asked, reaching up to touch my strands.

"Yes. And no," I said gently.

She frowned at me in confusion. "It's just like one Father gave me and Vivian on our sixteenths."

Vivian peered at me as if she could pry the truth of it from my eyes. "A gift from Pierre, then?"

"No, it's from Father," I said, meeting her gaze with what I hoped was a challenge in my own. "He sent it on my birthday. He just retrieved it from Montana for me."

"Ahh," she said with a sniff, lifting her chin and wrapping her arm through mine. "No need to be defensive, Cora. I was merely curious."

Wallace looked over at us, our arms entwined, and grinned. He clasped his hands together. "How delighted I am to see my girls together." He came over and wrapped an arm around us, hugging us to him, surprising me. "This is exactly what I had hoped would happen. The tour has drawn you together."

We pulled back, and it was Vivian's turn to look defensive. It was true—our travels and adventures and experiences *had* drawn us closer—but neither of us was quite ready to commit to anything beyond it. Not yet.

"There they are!" my father said, turning fully toward the door. I froze as Will and Pierre entered together. What was I to do now? Here? Before I'd had the opportunity to speak to my father…

Wallace greeted Pierre with a handshake, taking his hand in both of his. Pierre then moved immediately to me, taking my hand and kissing it as he studied my face. He held it as he straightened and searched my eyes. "Cora? These few days have felt like weeks in your absence."

"You are too kind," I said, feeling the heat of my blush climb past my jaw.

"Not kind—only happy beyond measure to be with you again." He smiled and placed my hand on his arm. We turned together toward Will, who had just been clapped on the back by my father. Wallace was congratulating Will for getting us safely through such difficult circumstances and offered his condolences for the bear's passing.

I could not look him in the eyes. Would he understand? Why I had to play this out a bit longer? For his own good? Only until I could figure a way out. A path that didn't include Wallace Kensington destroying Will piece by piece...

<hr>

I managed to extricate myself from the others and sat in the gardens for a while reading. Or rather pretending to read. But after an hour of my mind spinning, flitting from one thought to another, I was just beginning to relax, inhaling the heavy, sweet scent of the roses on the breeze, feeling the heat of the morning sun warm my gloved hands, appreciating the utter quiet...when I saw Pierre on the far side of the garden.

I hurriedly looked down at my book, pretending I hadn't spied his approach, working out what I wished to say to him. Regardless of what my father said, I couldn't stomach being less than truthful with him.

He paused five paces away from me, then straightened, studying my face, which was partially hidden by the wide brim of my hat. He held his sketchbook in one hand. "Ahh, mon cherie. I've disturbed you."

"No. No, Pierre. Please. Come sit," I said, patting the stone bench beside me. "I've wanted to speak with you in private."

He came over and sat beside me, taking my hand and kissing it. "While I am more than glad to have a moment alone with you, Cora, I did not come to talk."

"No?" I asked in confusion, wondering if he meant to steal a kiss instead.

"No," he said, quirking a smile. He cocked one brow. "I'd hoped to sketch you again, *mon ange*."

"But Pierre…"

"Uh-uh!" he said, quieting me with a smile. "Speak not." He rose and walked five paces away again, looking me over. "Exactly. Stay right there. You may read if you wish."

"You give me that permission, do you?" I added a smile to my teasing words.

"But of course."

I wondered what I was doing. Slipping into such an easy, flirtatious manner with him. He always seemed to bring it out of me, every time. And I couldn't deny that it felt good. To simply give in to that joyfulness, for once. To not feel everything with the weight of a thousand stones. For a bit, I gave in to the fantasy. What would it be like to accept Pierre's pursuit? Give it full sway. To get engaged. Marry. Live at Chateau de Richelieu. Each successive thought made it seem all the more preposterous.

"Something amuses you, mon cherie? Your smile is…mysterious."

"Amuses me?" I started. "No. *Amused* isn't how I'd describe it."

"Ahh, something you don't wish to share," he said, still sketching. "Head up a bit, please. No. Too much. Yes. There." He continued with quick, long strokes of his charcoal, then holding up his thumb and squinting his eye in my direction.

"Where did you learn to draw, Pierre?" I asked, turning toward him.

"Uh-uh!" he cried, and I belatedly remembered I was to hold my pose.

"Forgive me." I grimaced and tried to resume my previous position. But sitting still, all I could think about was what I needed to say to him. I struggled to remain in position when my body called for pacing.

Eventually, he answered me. "I wanted to be an artist when I was young."

"And you must have been."

"No. Not as I wished. My father would hear nothing of it. Being an artist, you see, is a craft of the bourgeoisie, not of the aristocracy. Supported as a noble exercise, but not as a noble vocation, at least not in my family. We are of…uh, the sort that supports artists. We do not become them."

"Oh," I said with a heavy sigh.

"I learned to draw from friends, those I sponsor as a patron. When one is a patron," he said with a little laugh, "your artistic friends suddenly become very patient in answering questions as a tutor."

I smiled with him. It was in keeping with his generous personality that he would help struggling artists. "Well, at least you can express yourself this way now. As a man grown. You didn't get to make your choice earlier, but look at you now—a successful busi-nessman *and* an artist."

"Yes," he said, but his tone did not entirely agree. My heart went out to him. Had he been shoved into an unhappy role by his father too? Was that part of what drew him to me?

"Pierre, may I look up?"

"One…moment… There. Now, cherie, you may look where you wish." He stared at me, and yet his gaze was that of an artist, respect-fully examining lines and distances.

"Pierre, did that make you sad? Not being able to follow your dream? To be an artist?"

"It is as you say…I *am* an artist. Only as a hobby. Not as a craft. It is all right," he said, old sorrow softening his eyes as they met mine. "One makes compromises to honor their family."

I stared hard at him then. Was he saying what I thought he was saying? Did he know my father was pushing me toward him? That it wasn't my choice? I had to know. And I had to be honest with him. No matter the cost.

He looked to his sketchpad and continued to fill in some detail, then eyed me again. But his gaze was once again distant.

"Pierre, I am in love with another man."

There it was. Out in the open at last. I dared to take a breath as his charcoal stilled a moment, then moved again in soft, even strokes.

"I know, cherie." He gave me a quick, small grin. "It is my hope to show you that you might love me, too, in time."

I frowned. Did he not understand what I was saying? "My father's intentions…he wishes to seal your business deal. Use me to keep you close."

He bit his lip, still sketching. Then he met my gaze. "I think you are wrong. He is not adverse to utilizing your place in my heart to accomplish his goals. A man such as Wallace Kensington does not accomplish what he has without being a bit ruthless, no? But I believe he desires nothing more than your happiness. We have spoken of my desire to court you. And he asked me the questions of a loving father, not a businessman trading a commodity."

"I see," I said. And I did then. Wallace Kensington was incredibly adept at what he did. Manipulating all within reach to do exactly as he bid. Anna's words came back to me. The miner's family, sent away, just to keep the son from Viv. It was as if he were a master chess player, moving all the pieces into just the right spots in order to capture the queen. Except this time, the queen was me.

And somehow, Wallace would feel good about his methods, because I'd be married off to a man of means…the years of struggle in Dunnigan magically rectified.

"Cora," Pierre said, coming to sit beside me. A gardener looked up from trimming the roses and then hurriedly glanced away. Beyond him, Yves kept watch over me, casually, purely there for the job, but without any untoward interest. In the far corner, Arthur was taking pictures of two young society girls—his latest photographic interest. Pierre took my hand. "Truthfully, would it be so awful? To be both rich *and* loved?"

I laughed, then, at his words. Really, how could I take issue with either? Who in their right mind would? And one laugh took me into another. Until tears streamed down my face. He waited through the whole thing, patient, kind, never irritated by my foolishness—and in that moment I knew that I did care for him.

Just not as I cared for Will.

"No, Pierre," I said at last. "It is not a bad thing to be both rich and loved. I believe it is all many people aspire to. But for me…I am meant to be loved, yes. Rich?" I shook my head and waved about me at the expansive gardens, the mansion. "This is extraordinary. A dream, in many ways. But that's *it*, right there, I think. It feels too much like a dream. Not real. Not something you can reach out and touch…or at least hope to hold for long."

He set aside his sketchpad, took my hand, and placed it over his heart, his eyes deadly serious now. "Do you not feel that? My heart? Am I not real?"

I sighed. There was no way to convey to him what I was feeling. "You can't understand, Pierre, not really. This is your world, the only world you have ever known. So while it feels very real to you, it's because it *is*. It's because you *belong* here. You've always belonged here." I lifted a hand to my forehead. "I'm not explaining this well."

"*Non,*" he said, tracing my face with a feather-light touch. "You are. Perhaps I need to journey to your world to fully understand. To Montana." He hitched his shoulders back and put his thumbs in his waistband. "Wear chaps and spurs. A cowboy hat."

I giggled, trying to picture him there. "Not all Montanans wear such things."

"No?" He frowned, but a teasing smile crept into his eyes. "That is most disappointing." He released my hand from his chest but kept it between the two of his. "I must come, though. See what so ties your heart to that land. Perhaps I will fall in love with it too and never return to Paris."

I shook my head. "Don't you see? That would be wrong too. This is where you belong, Pierre. I mean, you are welcome to come, but you would find what I have here. It is lovely. Intriguing, being in a place that is not your own. But in the end, it is *not* your own, and you have no choice but to find your way back to what is."

"Not all do as you say. Some find their way. In a foreign land. And in time, it feels as home."

"I suppose so," I said.

"Don't give up yet, *mon ange*," he said, bringing my hand to his lips and giving my knuckles a tender kiss. "You have been honest with your feelings. I knew from the start that William would give me—" He laughed when I looked up in surprise. "Oh no, cherie, it is no secret that William is the one who draws you. But I am not as convinced as you that he is the right man for you. That he is a better match than I, for you. So…you've been honest. You've had your say. I have heard it, no? I shall never claim you were unfair to me, untruthful. But I beg you to do as your father asked and simply give me more time to win your heart. If what you share with William is right, true, it will stand the test, right?"

"Oh, I don't know," I said, shaking my head in confusion.

"It is always wise to give big decisions time, Cora. To not rush them. And in giving this more time you obey your father's wishes and make sure you are making a wise decision."

I stared at him for a long moment. "I…I suppose that's true."

His grin spread across his handsome face, and he leaned over to give me a slow, tender kiss on the cheek. "Thank you, cherie. For granting me a bit more time. That is all I ask. See? We are all happy now. Me. You. Your father."

I nodded, feeling a bit dazed. What had just happened? It had not gone at all as I'd envisioned. And there was one person Pierre had not mentioned in his list of those who were happy.

Will.

Pierre stood and bid me adieu, promising that he'd be the first to request a dance after the concert, and then he walked away, whistling.

I saw his pad and picked it up. "Pierre! Your sketchbook!"

He turned and nodded, remembering the forgotten book, then sidled back toward me. As he did, curiosity got the best of me, and I peeked at his illustration, then turned it in my hands to really take it in.

It was as perfectly executed as the one he'd made of me on the boat in Versailles. But this time, he'd sketched in a perfect rendition of himself beside me. Like two young lovers perched in the rose garden, which I supposed, in some measure, we were.

"See, cherie," he said, with a half-pained smile, "it looks right. The two of us together, yes?"

I handed him the sketchbook and gave him a smile. "You are incorrigible," I said with a shake of my head.

"What is this word, incorrigible?" he said, pretending his perfect English didn't cover it. He tore the page from the book and handed it to me.

"Impossible. Outrageous."

"Ahh, perhaps, cherie, perhaps." Then he turned on his heel, whistling again as he left the garden. But he'd accomplished what he'd been after.

The romantic image of the two of us together was both in my hands and in my head.

─◦◇◦─

~William~

As much as he tried to keep his eyes from her, Cora seemed to appear in his line of vision, everywhere Will looked.

Two tables over during the garden supper, he glimpsed her in profile again and again, but she never looked his way.

During the Haydn concert, when she closed her eyes, her pale brows lifting in glory and furrowing in angst, as if feeling the power of every note.

And afterward, on the vast patio in the gardens, where the dancing went on for hours, and she spent much of it in Pierre de Richelieu's arms, every moment of which made Will seethe with jealousy.

Antonio sidled up beside him and perused the group. "Perhaps she is putting on a ruse, the means to keep a certain someone out from under her father's fury," Antonio said, lifting a dark, bushy brow in Will's direction.

Will ran a hand through his hair, considering it. Was that it? Was she simply protecting him? Getting through this visit with her father and Richelieu so that they could find their hidden moments again in Venezia and a life together beyond the tour?

He glanced over at Wallace Kensington chatting with a table full of men and considered the possibility. Did he dare walk over there? Declare himself? Declare his intentions toward Cora? What would happen then? Would he be summarily excused?

His eyes roamed over the crowd, back to Cora and Richelieu, now dancing a tango. He had to look away—and not because of

Cora's lack of expertise. But because another man was holding his girl in his arms. In far too intimate a fashion.

Go. Speak to him.

Now? Now? It's not right....

Now.

Will turned toward the tables, rather than the dance floor, and Antonio grabbed his arm. "What do you think you are doing?"

"Speaking to her father," he said, looking from Antonio's hand on his arm to the man himself.

"No, Will. *No.* Go, cut in. Dance with Cora. But do not speak to Mr. Kensington."

"Don't you see?" Will hissed. "I have no choice. It's now or never. Richelieu has made his move. I have to make my intentions known, or Wallace Kensington will forever see me as an interloper, a cad, not a man of merit."

Antonio turned to block his way. "Listen to me. *Listen to me,*" he said, tapping Will's chest with each word. "Richelieu is smooth. Charming. And smart. They've talked business. And yes, they've likely spoken of courtship, but, Will, the man has had two days with him."

"What of it?" Will asked, throwing his hand up in the air. "Mr. Kensington knows me, too. I've been in his home! I'm the guardian of his children...a *proven* protector."

"And now he'll see you as a predator, not a protector. One he trusted to keep his distance. You failed him. We are here, in Richelieu's backyard, his field of battle. Look at him. Take a good long look at him." He turned sideways to peruse the dance floor, and Will followed his gaze until he found Cora and Richelieu. For the first time, he focused on the man, not the woman, watching Richelieu as he smiled over Cora's shoulder at one person after another.

"You see what I see?" Antonio said, under his breath. "He knows them. He knows them all. Business contacts. Perhaps even kin. Now look at Mr. Kensington. Do you see him? How he's watching Richelieu? He *likes* Richelieu's connections with these people. They're already talking business, Will. Richelieu is greasing the right wheels, so that Montana Copper's surplus might be imported to France."

Will eyed him even as his heart sank. Such an arrangement had to be worth hundreds of thousands of dollars. Even millions.

"Why do you think Kensington is suddenly entertaining a request for courtship for one of his daughters when he was explicitly against such a thing when he bid them bon voyage?"

Will rubbed the back of his neck and sighed, defeated. His chest felt empty. Hollow. "It's done, then," he said, every word devoid of hope. Then anger surged. He turned to face Antonio again. "I don't even get a chance? A chance to declare myself?"

"No," the older man said gently, putting a hand on his shoulder. "No, my friend. Because then you would not only end up without the girl, but without a future. A man such as that…" He paused to look over at Wallace, then back to Will. "One does not cross a man such as that, unless one is ready to walk forever with a limp."

CHAPTER
TWENTY-TWO

~Cora~

Looking over Pierre's shoulder, I saw Will beside Antonio, turning ragged eyes on me, and I quickly looked away. I didn't want him to see it in my face—my inability to take a stand. To force my father to hear me out, to see that this romance was impossible…or to dissuade Pierre from his pursuit.

"Cherie?" Pierre asked, frowning down at me and then whispering in my ear. "What is it? You have lost all concentration."

"I have," I said. "I confess that I am not in the right mood for the tango. Might we pause for some punch?"

"Indeed." He put his hands on my waist and smiled into my eyes. "Or something stronger?"

"Punch would be good," I said, suddenly thirsty. The last thing I needed was a glass of champagne. Not with all that was transpiring before me.

"I'll be back in but a moment," he said, tracing a knuckle down my jaw line in a quick, intimate move.

I nodded and smiled, as if I didn't wish to draw away. But as I watched him go, I noticed Will observing me and felt my face flush in embarrassment. What must he think of me? Allowing Pierre such advances, when he knew my heart was with him? I wanted to run away into the gardens, far from everyone's questioning gaze. Because the truth was, I wasn't sure what to think or what to do. Every way I turned seemed wrong.

I hurried past the crowd, to the edge of the garden, aware that Antonio trailed me, keeping me within view but also keeping his distance.

"Are you well, Cora?" Art asked as I passed. Plainly I looked as dizzy as I felt.

"Fine, fine, thank you," I said, forcing a smile.

In moments, I was blessedly alone, except for my silent guard twenty paces away. *Lord, I need Your guidance*, I prayed silently, looking toward the rising moon on the horizon, thinking of the moon above Carcassonne, when Will had finally kissed me, and another, over Paris, when Pierre had done the same. Two so very different men who had offered me different kisses, each winsome and special.

Show me, Lord. Show me what I am to do. The best way out of this mess. The path that will hurt both the least.

What was I doing? I wasn't this person! I was in love with Will. He was the one who held my heart. The one with whom I belonged. And yet to break it off with Pierre would incur the wrath of my father…and Will would bear the brunt of that.

If we were to have a chance, I had to convince my father first that I didn't belong with Pierre or in Paris. That my heart was heading home, regardless of what I might be leaving behind here. This was all completely fantastic—a dream—but my heart was in Montana. Home.

"Your punch, Cora," Pierre said, suddenly beside me, and I whirled so fast I almost upset the cup and sent it spilling over his sleeve.

"Cora!" he said in alarm. "What is the matter?"

"Oh, Pierre," I said, wringing my hands. "I'm so sorry." I took the cup from him and quickly drank it down, my mouth like cotton. "I think…I think I should retire. My head is throbbing, and I am not feeling at all well." It was true, in part.

"Certainly," he said, his kind eyes tracing my face. "I shall see you in and—"

"No! No," I said, belatedly softening my tone, regretting practically yelling at him. "Antonio is just over there. He's more than capable of accompanying me. You stay here and enjoy the party. I'll see you in the morning?" I asked, bringing what I hoped was a bright smile to my face.

He lifted my hand to his lips and kissed it slowly. "Most assuredly," he said, but his eyes held storm clouds of worry.

I turned from him then, and Antonio saw me heading toward him. He met me halfway. "Turning in already, miss?"

"Yes, Antonio. I have a terrible headache."

"I am sorry to hear that. Should I send for a doctor?"

"No, no. Nothing that a cup of mint tea and a night's slumber can't ease."

"I see." He offered me his arm, and we strolled toward the garden entrance of the huge mansion, nodding to one guest after another as we passed.

I struggled with the desire to say something of my predicament to the older man, my guardian. I knew Antonio was well aware of what was transpiring between me and Will. And yet to tie anyone else in further might prove disastrous for him, too.

"Did you have a nice evening, Miss Cora?"

"Fine, thank you. Wasn't the concert lovely?"

"Indeed. Some of the finest music in the world here in Vienna. Tomorrow there shall be a Strauss concert, and the next night is the baroness's ball. They shall showcase Mozart and Beethoven, music written right here in the city when they lived here."

The ball.

I'd forgotten there'd be another, here. While we'd attended many parties with dancing, there hadn't been a formal ball since Pierre's masquerade. "I…I don't have a gown."

"No worries," he said, patting my hand. "Vienna is the city of one ball after another, all season long. So many that there is a street with nothing but shops for both gown and costume rentals. We shall find everything you and the others need tomorrow morning, with plenty of time for adjustments before the party. The appointment is already set."

"Oh, that's grand," I murmured, trying to infuse enthusiasm into my tone. "Grand."

"It truly is," he said, opening the door for me. "If you enjoyed tonight's concert, the next one, and the ball…will be a delight."

"Are we to dress in period gowns for the ball again?"

"Indeed," he said. "And even though the music of Mozart and Beethoven shall be featured, the period the baroness has chosen for this summer's ball is nineteenth century."

"Victorian?" I said in surprise.

"Indeed," he said, lifting a bushy eyebrow as we climbed the stairs. "A personal favorite of hers."

"Well, at least it shall be different from Pierre's," I said. "And without the heavy, dreadful wigs."

"There is that."

But there'd be corsets for certain, far more constrictive than our more recent renditions. It made me feel faint already just thinking of it. Even if I did like the idea of wearing a beautiful, full-skirted gown.

It was with some dismay that I realized we'd reached my suite. I'd been lost in thought about what colors I would look for and necklines that I might favor. When had I become the sort of woman who was so captivated by fashion? I'd begun the summer with two dresses to my name!

"Good night, Antonio," I said wearily, tired of everything, everyone, most especially myself.

"Good night, Miss Cora. I shall send a maid with your mint tea."

"Thank you."

I slipped inside and closed the door, leaning my head against it for a moment, relishing the lack of conversation, bustle, eyes on me. The only sounds now were the murmur of voices and laughter below in the courtyard, the roar of an engine as someone departed. I turned up the gas lamp at my bedside, preferring its softer, warmer light to the garish electrical light of my overhead fixture, and then I padded over to the window as I took off my long gloves and reached up to release my necklace.

I watched as another vehicle was loaded with guests bent on an early escape. They roared off. All along the massive courtyard—perhaps three blocks long—were carriages and motorcars, with servants milling about, waiting to be summoned.

It'll be a long night of noise, I thought with a sigh, thinking about those who'd stay until the wee hours before returning to their homes, reluctant to leave the bountiful buffet tables and circulating waiters. Anna arrived then and pulled shut my curtains, helped me out of my dress and into my nightgown, then unpinned my hair and brushed it out. As she worked, I stared at my reflection in the mirror.

Would I miss such pampering when I got home? I thought not. It was all so much work, this lot of the wealthy. Changing one's clothes two to three times a day, planning the social schedule, making certain everyone was attended to, making polite conversation with people one would never see again. I'd rather do hours of chores than see through this nonsense day after day. A pang of homesickness struck so hard I almost groaned.

"You all right, miss?" Anna said, peeking at me in the mirror as she brushed.

"Fine, Anna. Thank you. Just dreadfully tired."

A knock sounded at the door, and she turned to go and answer it. A moment later, she was back with my tea, setting it on the edge of my dressing table. She then turned to the gigantic bed, folding down the covers and sheets. "Is there anything else you'll be needin' tonight, miss?"

"No, thank you, Anna. Good night."

"Good night, miss."

I took my cup in both hands and leaned against the chair back, studying my reflection in the mirror. In my plain nightgown, without jewels, my hair down, I felt more myself. More like the Cora I used to know. But I really wasn't that girl anymore. I'd never be her again, if I was honest with myself. Cora Diehl felt like a distant memory—a treasured memory, but far, far from my present reality. And as much as I tried to marry my past with my future, I couldn't quite see them melding. Could I truly go back to Normal School in Montana and settle in with the girls there? Would they treat me differently once they knew that Wallace Kensington had reclaimed his long-lost daughter? Would my professors? Would I feel different? Or would I slowly recapture my sense of self? Who I was before all this began?

I took a long, deep breath and turned my lamp down so low it was almost completely dark in the room. I rose from my chair and went to the window. I pushed aside the long, velvet curtains and leaned my hip against the low sill and sipped my tea, watching guests leave and a few latecomers arrive. I observed how they interacted with one another, with the servants, and I admired the ladies' gowns and the men's fine black jackets and crisp white shirts. I felt a part of them now, able to make my way among them. But not truly one with them.

Did that leave me as a woman without a country? A people? Would this journey leave me lost rather than found? My eyes went back to the servants and rested on one driver. He leaned against his motorcar, hat drawn low, even as he looked up to the mansion, toward me. His head never moved, but there was something oddly familiar about him—about his stance, cavalier, relaxed. I glanced down, making sure I wasn't visible, and then backed away from the window, realizing that with the lamp behind me, my silhouette would be clear, if nothing else.

Stupid, silly twit, I berated myself, moving to the lamp and bringing the room into utter darkness. It was so dark, there was more light from outside than in the room itself now. Tentatively, I moved back to peek out to the courtyard again. The man was still there, staring up at my room. I was sure of it. My heart began to pound when I realized from where I knew him.

The man from Paris. And Nîmes.

The ringleader. The one who had tried to kidnap me twice.

I couldn't be certain—with the hat, the relative darkness—and yet I was. My mouth dropped open, and I froze, waiting for him to move. Another driver walked up, had a few words with him, and he shoved off, casually strolling away. So it hadn't been his motorcar. That had only been the means to stop and find my room, wait for a glimpse of me…or my sisters. He took ten paces, then turned, gave me a casual salute—as if he could see me, as if he knew I was there—and continued his relaxed walk out of the courtyard.

My hand went to my throat. He was here. He'd followed us. Was he insane? There'd be no way he could get to us, with Will, Antonio, and the detectives keeping watch. And now my father and Mr. Morgan… *That's it.* He'd been waiting for the right moment to edge near again. Somehow…for some reason, our fathers' arrival had pushed him to it. The question was, why?

A more expedient track to payday, if one of us was held for ransom? Or was he so angry with me for foiling his plans twice over that he'd now targeted me?

Back home on the farm, I'd been fairly adept with a rifle, driving off coyotes, the occasional bear. I itched for the weight of my papa's rifle in my hands, the chance to squeeze off a shot, hitting the ground five feet to the man's side. I wanted to make him run, make him fear ever coming near me or mine again. But instead, here I was, helpless. Like a lioness caught in a zoo cage, close to her prey and yet hopelessly separated. I went over to the desk and took hold of the sharp, pearl-handled letter opener, and then went back to the window.

The man was gone. Quickly, I strode to the lever by my door that would ring the bell for Anna. Will and the others had to know what I'd seen. She came a minute later, her hair hastily tucked into a nightcap. "Miss?"

"Fetch William, will you, Anna?"

"What is it, miss?" she asked, her eyes narrowing.

"Trouble," I said.

------◇◇◇------

~William~

He ran to her room, and when he saw her, pacing, ashen, hands trembling, he longed to take her in his arms. But he couldn't. Not with Anna there. Instead, he kept a respectful distance. He folded his arms and bent his head toward hers, seeking her blue eyes, which were wild with fear. "Cora. What is it?"

"He's here, Will. The man from Paris. The one who tried to kidnap me after the bullfight."

"What? Are you certain? Where?"

"I saw him from the window just a bit ago. He was outside in the courtyard, watching."

He went to the window, searching the grounds. There were about twenty motorcars and three horse-drawn carriages outside. And many men. He scanned each one, then looked to her. "Are you certain?" he asked again. "It's rather dark out there...."

"He had a hat on and was pretending to be a waiting driver. It was *him*, Will," she said.

She seemed sure, but he had to know before he raised the alarm. "And you hadn't fallen asleep? Perhaps dreamed it?"

"William, I have yet to go to bed!"

He raised his hands, palms to her. "All right. I understand. I just had to be sure." He paced back and forth, running his fingers through his hair, rubbing his face, thinking. "He wouldn't dare make a move on us again," he said, mostly to himself. "Not with our added protection." He stopped and looked at Cora and Anna. "But I'll make certain there are more men on watch tonight, all night. Don't worry. Every one of you will be under guard."

Cora had her arms folded as if cold and gave him a quick nod. "Thank you."

"Of course. And...I'll have to tell your father."

She nodded again, more slowly this time, then heaved a sigh. "He'll triple our guard. Or put us on the first train and ship home."

He gave her a hopeless look. They'd done what they could to get this far. Perhaps this would be an answer to prayer, in a way. The means to get Cora out of Pierre's clutches and back home, where he might have a chance to see her…as long as this fellow didn't trail her all the way to the States and try and nab her there. He bit his lip, anxious at the thought. Surely he wouldn't go as far as that. And surely Mr. Kensington wouldn't leave Cora without a guard of some sort.…

"Do you feel comfortable seeing yourself back to your quarters?" he said to Anna.

"Of course. It's not me they're after," she quipped.

"No!" Cora said, wringing her hands. "Anna…would you stay with me tonight? Here? There's plenty of room in that big bed.…"

Anna paused a moment, clearly taken aback by such a request from a lady. "By all means, miss."

Will went to the door and looked over his shoulder at them. "I'll return if I learn anything. Otherwise, try and get some sleep, and know you will be safe."

"Thank you, Will," Cora said, coming over to him. After watching her all evening with Pierre, he didn't know if he could tolerate her proximity. Not when he couldn't take her in his arms. He had to physically make himself turn the knob and slip partway out rather than touch her.

"Lock the door behind me, Cora," he said. He just wanted to be certain.

She nodded, and he left, striding directly down the hall, urgency tightening his every muscle. Yves was already on watch at the end of the hall. Fortunately their clients were all in one massive wing, all doors visible. After he made certain that all were safely in their rooms for the night, he'd put Claude on the far end of that same hall. In the wee hours, he and Antonio would relieve them. No one would be slipping past a sleeping guard tonight.

He half ran down the wide staircase and out the garden doors. The party seemed to have picked up steam rather than waned, and for several anxious moments, he could not find any of the men.

Hugh was on the dance floor, a pretty young woman in his arms. Will tried to catch his eyes as he turned her. Will gestured for Hugh to join him as soon as the song was done, and with one eyebrow cocked, Hugh gestured his assent. Will moved on to find Felix. He was laughing with Arthur and three young women. "Felix, excuse me. May I have a word?"

"Sure, William," Felix said. He made his apologies and followed him away from the group, and as the song ended, Hugh came over too. Art trailed behind.

"The man from Paris, the one we believe organized the attack on us and tried to kidnap Cora again in Nîmes," Will said, "Cora thinks she saw him, watching her room from the courtyard."

"You jest!" Hugh said.

"I'm afraid not."

"What will it take to dissuade this louse?" Felix said.

"I wish I knew."

The young men frowned and then quickly looked around, fists clenching.

"I need to find your fathers," Will said. "And I need you to get to your rooms until we have a plan."

"They'd never attempt to take us," Felix said. "Not here. Besides, it will be the women who are in the most danger. And I believe that all but Viv have retired for the night."

"Or is that what they wish us to think?" Will returned. "Please. Help me find your fathers, and we'll make a plan together."

Hugh grabbed his arm. "If our fathers know there continues to be this sort of danger, our tour is through."

"If there is danger, our tour might end in a far less desirable way. It was one thing when we hoped we could leave them behind in France...another to suspect they've followed us all the way here."

"Why show his face?" Felix asked. "It makes no sense."

"I don't know," Will said.

"I saw Father this way," Felix said, tossing his head over his shoulder to the right. They followed him through the crowd, and then, when they got close to Mr. Kensington, respectfully waited for the man to finish his conversation, while searching every face in the crowd, many impossible to make out in the darkness.

After a moment, Wallace turned to them, his cane in his hands. "Gentlemen?"

"Mr. Kensington, do you know where we might find Mr. Morgan? We need a word with you both. Immediately."

Mr. Kensington shot him a look of warning. "Lead the way, McCabe. I hope this is as vital as you're making it out to be."

They collected the elder Mr. Morgan, sent Andrew to see Vivian to her room, and then gathered in a small sitting room near the foyer. A cheery fire crackled in the hearth, and Mr. Kensington stood stock still before it, staring at the flames as Will told him—and the others—what he knew. It irked Will that Richelieu had seen them departing and followed them in uninvited. But Will supposed it was best that he be informed too. One more man to keep Cora safe... even *that* man.

Arthur had offered to excuse himself, but Will wanted him there. After all, he knew, better than many of them, exactly what this fellow looked like since he'd rescued Cora in Nîmes.

"Why would he show himself to Cora?" Mr. Kensington asked.

"I don't know," Will said.

"Is she his target, then?" Mr. Morgan asked. "Not our youngest children?"

"I don't know," Will repeated.

"Could she be hysterical? Imagining things?" Mr. Kensington asked, rubbing his forehead and looking to Richelieu. "After the trauma she endured in Paris…"

"Cora is rather levelheaded, Mr. Kensington," Will said. "She is not given to undue hysteria, and truly, if that were likely, it would've happened before now, I think."

Mr. Kensington stared at him and then nodded, looking back to the fire. He scratched his beard. "What the devil is he after? It makes no sense to show his face before striking."

"Perhaps he likes a game of cat and mouse," Will guessed. "Taunting the mouse before he strikes."

"No child of mine is a mouse!" Mr. Kensington said lowly.

"Of course not, Mr. Kensington," Will said. "I only meant—"

"I know what you meant," Mr. Kensington said with a weary sigh, tossing up a hand of dismissal. "And you're most likely correct."

"There are really four choices," Will said, looking at both fathers as Andrew joined them. "We add more men, a guard for every one of the Kensington and Morgan children, and we carry on with the tour.

Or we continue as we have, if you feel that is adequate guard—and we switch up our itinerary—perhaps escaping them. Or we could alert the authorities—"

"Bah," Mr. Kensington said. "They'd likely accomplish little other than wasting our time and stirring up newspaper fodder."

"Right. Then there's the last option," Will said. "We pack our bags and return to the States, cutting short the tour."

Mr. Kensington eyed Mr. Morgan, then looked back to Will. "What would your uncle advise?"

Will cocked a brow and crossed his arms. "We've never come up against a situation such as this. But I believe he would leave it to the two of you. Only you can make such a decision when there is a clear and present danger to your children."

Mr. Morgan turned and looked up to Will. "What would you do…if they were your children?"

"Father, I—" Andrew began to protest, but his father shushed him with one hand.

Will considered him. "Mr. Morgan, your children are a target whether they are abroad or home in the States, are they not?" His eyes flicked to Kensington and back to Morgan. "Is it not best to deal with this adversary here and now?"

"You mean…draw him out," Mr. Kensington said.

Will nodded, an idea taking form in his mind. "Yes. We hire more men. But we hire men really good at keeping to the shadows, blending. Men who will help us keep watch and come to our aid if we are attacked."

"You speak of laying a trap," Mr. Kensington said.

"With our children as bait?" Mr. Morgan asked, looking wan.

Will looked each man in the eye and nodded, hands on his hips. "Yes."

A slow smile spread across Kensington's face, a measure of respect in his eyes. "I like it. We draw them out and deal with them. Once and for all."

"You let the world know that no one messes with a Kensington or Morgan and comes out unscathed," Will said. "The mouse becomes the cat."

The diminutive Mr. Morgan nodded slowly. "As long as there are a good number of guards, whether visible or hidden, I'd agree." He raised a finger. "But I am not leaving you until this is dealt with. Even if it means I travel all the way to Rome with you."

"As will I," Mr. Kensington said.

Will stifled a groan. How would he keep his feelings so under wraps that even Cora's father would miss his care for her? "I understand," he managed to choke out.

"We should keep it from the younger girls," Mr. Kensington said. "I don't wish for them to lose sleep, nor for them to go about their days in fear."

"Plus, they'd give the plan away," Hugh said. "They'd never be able to pretend to be at peace if they thought the same men who tried to take them in Paris were back and bent on getting to them here."

"Agreed," Felix said.

It was the only way. To be free of the threat. Once and for all.

But as Will led them upstairs to the hall that would be guarded through the night, his heart pounded at the thought of that man daring to show his face to Cora. Watching her for how long? For what purpose?

Will hoped he'd be there when the man made his move. Because Will dearly wanted to show him what happened when he dared to mess with the woman he loved.

CHAPTER
TWENTY-THREE

~Cora~

I awakened wishing I had another five hours in my bed. I knew my sleep had been fitful through the night and had likely kept Anna awake. But I was so glad for her company. Had she not stayed with me, I doubted I'd have slept at all.

Anna had slipped away early, whispering that she was off to see to her own toilette and to fetch some breakfast for me, as well as a fresh gown. Word came with the breakfast tray that our tour was not to come to an abrupt end as I'd assumed. There was another plan in place.

After a meal of pastry, fruit, cheese, and the dark coffee Vienna was famous for—a remnant of the Turks who once tried to invade her—made more delectable with a dollop of fresh cream, I slipped into the ivory day suit that Anna had chosen for me, along with a big camel-colored hat tied with an ivory ribbon. I pulled my jacket straight and examined my reflection in the mirror, wishing I could wash away the dark circles under my eyes.

Resolving to excuse myself for a nap after our ball costumes were chosen, I went to the door and found William waiting outside, leaning against the far wall. He started when he saw me, and then in three strides was in front of me, reaching out to take my hands—then, obviously thinking better of it, folding his arms instead. I dropped my own hands awkwardly to my sides, glimpsing Antonio on one end of the hall and Yves on the other. Will's gaze covered my face like a caress. "Cora, we'll see this through. Together. Know that there will be many men keeping watch over you at every moment, both seen and unseen. We intend to draw out the men who wish to harm you and deal with them at once."

"Draw them out," I said, fussing with the finger of one glove that was slightly twisted. Had I heard him right?

"Once and for all. You cannot live life always looking over your shoulder—the Kensingtons and Morgans."

I looked up at him, understanding him better now. "You want us to pretend as if we don't know that we might be in danger. Make them come after us."

His jaw clenched. "Yes. But I promise you, you will not be alone when they do."

"*If* they do," I corrected. "And until then, we'll be stuck in this glass bowl. Never having the opportunity to be alone. To *talk*," I said, giving him a meaningful look. There was so much I needed to tell him. So much I needed to talk through with him. But there was never an opportunity. And now there'd be even fewer chances...

"Yes," he said miserably. "Exactly. All the more reason to draw them out and have this done with, yes?"

I nodded, and he took my arm. "We do not intend to tell Lil and Nell," he whispered as the others emerged in the foyer.

"Why?"

"We fear they would tip our hand."

I understood their intention, even agreed with it, but keeping such a secret from the girls chafed at me. Vivian looked about as weary and dazed as I felt—with one glance, I knew Andrew had told her the plan—while Lillian and Nell were excited, chattering about the gowns they hoped to find at the costume shop. When Lillian looped her arm through mine as we walked down the stairs, asking me what was wrong, I told her I'd simply stayed up too late the night before. "Let's find just the right gowns for the ball quickly," I said, giving her hand a pat, "so that we can return for a good rest this afternoon."

I saw that our fathers were in the foyer, along with Felix, Hugh, and Andrew. Vivian went to Andrew and took his hands, and he bent to give her a kiss on either cheek. Viv accepted his overture with grace—but with any joy? It was impossible to tell.

We all moved outdoors, loading into the motorcars. I was in the last one with Arthur, Felix, and Lillian. As we pulled out onto the main thoroughfare, I glanced over my shoulder through the small window to see if anyone was following us. There were other motorcars, of course, but were they those of additional guards or our assailants, or were they merely other Viennese? I'd go mad trying to figure it out.

The costume shops were in a poorer district, but Antonio had been right—the stores lined one side of the block and the other—and it was so clogged with traffic, we had to park several blocks away and return on foot. Men's costumes and formal wear were in just a few shops and separated from the women's—each with a strict rule of the opposite gender not entering the other—so Will and the other guardians had to be content with guarding both the front and back entrances as we girls moved from one shop to the next.

Vivian was the first to find her gown, a lovely mossy green that cinched up at her tiny waist and cascaded in enormous tiers. The bodice was low cut and swept from shoulder to shoulder in a wide arc, the sleeves tightly covering her arms. "It's perfect," I said, looking her over in appreciation. "It's the exact green in your eyes!"

"It is," Lillian agreed with a quick nod, already trying on her third gown, this one a deep yellow. She stepped up on the tailor's bench, took a quick glance in the mirror, shook her blonde head, and then flounced off.

"But, Lil," I said, "that's pretty!"

"No! It's not right!" she called over her shoulder.

Vivian met my gaze. "We'll be here all morning. This is the girls' idea of the most fun possible."

I smiled and relaxed as I went back to rummaging through dress after dress on the rack that appeared to be close to my size. "I can't blame them, really," I said, pulling out a ruby red gown and then shoving it back, thinking I'd never have the courage to wear such a garish thing.

Vivian lifted a corner of a dusty-rose-colored gown from the other end, her skirts so wide over her hoops, they brushed against my legs. "This would be a pretty color on you." She brought it all the way out, holding it in front of her, modeling it for me.

"It's lovely," I said. "But that neckline!"

"They're all that low, Cora," she said, lifting it to me. "Go on. Try it on."

"If you think it might work," I said. I stopped by the front desk, and a grumpy woman who spoke little English handed me a hoop skirt and corset, pointing me and one of her maids into a dressing room with all the finesse of a cowboy herding a cow into a corral. I supposed I couldn't blame her, I thought, alone for a precious minute as I undressed. Dealing with uppity women all day, all bent on finding the perfect dress for a single ball, would be enough to drive anyone mad.

I stood there in nothing but my underthings, wondering how the maid would know when to come in, when she knocked on my narrow door. "Come in," I said.

She slipped through the door, closed it, and then grabbed hold of the corset, wrapping it around my waist. With quick fingers, she pulled it back and forth, getting it settled on my figure, then immediately set to lacing it. Disgruntled with my movement, she sighed, took my hands, wrapped them around a post, put her hands on my shoulders, gave me a look in the eye that said *stay*, then returned to the lacing. She was ridiculously good at it, I thought with chagrin, waiting until I exhaled each time to tighten the next level of lacing. Then she bent, leaving the hoops in a cascading circle at my feet.

I stepped in, and she lifted the hoops, the smallest just fitting around my hips and above it, cinching a waist ribbon to secure it.

She turned to the gown and threw the heavy silk over my head and outstretched arms, then pulled it down, keeping my back to the mirror as she fastened one tiny fabric-covered button after another behind me. When done, she straightened the tiny cap sleeves, which just barely covered my shoulders, and slowly turned me toward the mirror. I gasped and then covered my mouth, embarrassed by my vain reaction. But it was truly beautiful. A desert-rose color that made my skin look golden, healthy, and contrasted nicely with my eyes. The corset and bodice had done their job, giving my breasts a lift and my waist a cinch. The silk had a slight sheen to it, and the skirt was as wide as Vivian's, with a dramatic waterfall effect of gathers all around.

I gestured toward the door, so I could show my sisters and Nell, and when I came out, the younger girls clapped excitedly while Vivian gave me a dignified, knowing smile. I was startled to recognize a bit of pride in her eyes, rather than her customary competition. "*You* fished it out of the pond," I said in appreciation.

"No man will be able to keep his eyes off you, Cora," Lil said, running her fingers over the beautiful silk.

"No, they won't," Nell said, her brown coils of hair bouncing as she shook her head. "You're beautiful. Not that you need any more men noticing you, what with Monsieur de *Richelieu* doting upon you."

I stepped up onto the tailor's bench and looked in all four mirrors, thinking of four men looking upon me. Pierre. Will. My father. And the mysterious man who had tracked us here. To each, I'd appear slightly different, I thought, my eyes flicking from one glass pane to the next. A conquest to conquer. A love to be honored. A daughter to win over. A prize to collect.

Who would take my arm, in the end? I thought distantly, feeling vaguely helpless. The thought of it made me want to run again, refuse them all. Take matters into my own hands.

I was my own woman. They could not make me what they wished. I would allow what *I* wished.

Nell's words rang in my head. Pierre was glorious—dramatic, handsome, perfectly attentive. But he was a fantasy. I was no Cinderella. I belonged in no castle. It was Will who held my heart. I turned to look out the front window and saw him outside standing guard, his broad shoulders daring anyone to try to get past him. He was real. True. Right. Able to walk beside me in this world as well as in *my* real world. He alone understood me. Where I came from and where I could go.

And being away from him was making me feverish. We had to find our own moment alone soon....

I stepped down from the tailor's bench and was walking back to the dressing room when I paused beside the matron at the front desk. She was reading a paper. I bent and peered at an article, catching the English words "Montana Copper" and "Dunnigan" in the first sentences.

She set it down and looked at me, her grumpiness fading with me in her gown. *"Schön, schön,"* she said, waving up and down at me, looking pleased.

"Oh! *Danke,*" I said, assuming she was saying something complementary, by her expression. I knew less German than I did French. "May I?" I asked, gesturing toward her paper.

She frowned in confusion and then waved at it as if to say "go ahead," and I picked it up, scanning the article. The headline held the words "Montana Copper" and the first line of the article mentioned Dunnigan. It was all in German, and I could not understand any more of it, but as my eyes ran from the company name to my hometown's name, my heart sank as I reread the words, again and again.

Instinctively, I knew it could not be good. What exactly had my father been up to while I was traveling the world? I stood up straight, staring at a rack of gowns, not seeing them, only seeing the mountains that lined my papa's property, now with Wallace Kensington's name on the title. "He couldn't have," I whispered, shaking my head. "It's impossible."

"May I?" I asked the matron, gesturing to the paper, hoping she understood that I was asking if I might take it with me.

She frowned at me and shook her head, speaking in rapid German. Apparently she was not yet done reading it and felt no need to bend over backward for her clients.

"Cora?" Vivian asked from across the room. "Are you all right?"

"Yes, yes," I said, dodging her questioning glance. I hurried into the dressing room and swallowed an urge to scream as the maid began the long, laborious task of taking the gown and corset off me. Only the release of the corset brought me some relief. I struggled to breathe, slowly and steadily, trying to gather my wits. I had to find a translator. And a copy of that newspaper, before I made incorrect assumptions.

Don't jump to conclusions without the facts, my papa always said. But I was jumping, leaping....

And where I landed was a deep, deep hole.

—◇◇◇—

~William~

Cora and Vivian found their gowns at the first stop, but Lillian and Nell were proving far more difficult to please. The men had their rented costumes in order too, and all were scheduled to be delivered in the morning, clean and pressed. Vivian accompanied the girls into the next shop, but Cora lingered outside with the men, looking one way down the street and then the other.

"Cora?" Will asked quietly, wondering what she sought.

"Is there a newsstand nearby?" she whispered.

"Around the corner. Why?"

"Might you purchase a paper for me? Today's?"

He cast her a wry grin. "Aim to practice your German?"

"Something like that," she said. "Just see if you can purchase a copy? And get it to me?"

"Of course," he said, giving her a deferential nod. Their eyes met and held. Will forced himself to turn to Felix and begin a conversation lest Mr. Kensington's keen blue eyes discovered them together.

Three shops later, the youngest girls found their gowns—Lillian's reportedly a pale yellow and Nell's a dark, ruby red—and they were finally free to return to their cars. Will casually glanced across the street, glad to see the two men in top hats smoking cigars and chatting, lingering as if waiting for wives inside the costume shops. Will knew them as Bruno and Ludolf, two of the additional guards who had been hired. Women came out of the shop beside them, and the men turned to follow them, as if the ladies were indeed their wives.

Antonio had told him the other two guards around back were dressed as street sweepers, industriously working.

They were some of Austria's version of Pinkerton detectives, and their stated goal was to be as invisible to the troop of Kensington and Morgan travelers as they were to their pursuers. "If we do our job well," their boss had told Will that morning, "you will find it difficult to see us, discover us, and just when you do, we shall switch out the men for others. But know this," he'd added, raising a stern finger, "we shall always have four men within direct reach. You are not alone in your task. On that you have my word."

They came on the baroness's highest recommendation, and Will thought he had little choice but to trust her. But it made him antsy, not knowing exactly where all his men were at any given time. To whom he could reach out and call for help. He preferred the rank-and-file soldiers he had hired in Yves and Claude, the detectives from France. Still, he knew that if they were to draw the potential kidnappers out, this was how it would have to be played.

After high tea in the elegant Grand Hotel Wien, with enough scones and tiny tea sandwiches to hold them all until supper, they stopped at the Schönbrunn Palace. Will forced himself to run through the litany of lessons that he knew his uncle would have expected him to recite, feeling a bit melancholy as he thought about the old man. But only the younger girls seemed to be paying attention, the rest constantly fidgeting, their minds on the bigger issue at hand, no doubt. It was with some relief when they returned to their cars to head back to the baroness's mansion.

With everyone accounted for, Will spied a paperboy on the corner and belatedly remembered Cora's odd request just as he was about to enter his motorcar. "Hold on a moment," he said to his driver, jogging to the corner to purchase the paper. He hurried back, searching for the hidden detectives, but could see none about. There were men with children, women…then he saw the two in top hats, strolling toward them, as if they had all the time in the world, and he smiled in relief. *Probably heading to their own motorcar to follow us.*

He opened the door and jumped into the front seat beside his driver and gave him the nod to take them home. And as they drove, he scanned the front page of the paper. His eyes rested on the headline Cora had obviously seen.

Montana Copper Strikes Gold, it read in German. His eyes moved downward, rapidly translating most of it. A dusty, forgotten town named Dunnigan. Cora's hometown. The recent discovery of both gold and copper in her hills. Several farmers on the brink of bankruptcy, soon to be very wealthy men. But most of the property had been purchased over the years by none other than Wallace Kensington.

He read and reread the lines, thinking he'd imagined it. Will closed his eyes and rubbed them, a sudden ache making them throb. Had the man really done it? Purchased the Diehls' property out from under them? Moved in when Alan was weak, sick? Sent them on to Minnesota, and Cora here, in order to get them out of the way?

CHAPTER
TWENTY-FOUR

~William~

He avoided her as they entered the mansion, refusing to meet her questioning gaze and keeping the paper firmly tucked beneath his arm. They had to find a moment. Alone. Together. So he could break this to her as gently as possible.

"We are to meet the baroness at six here, dressed for the evening concert," he called to the group. "Have a good afternoon of rest. If any of you have need of me, I shall be taking my leisure in the mansion's library."

Cora's eyes flashed, meeting his. She had understood. Above her, Mr. Kensington and Mr. Morgan were already climbing the stairs, apparently more than eager to take their rest, with the others following behind, Cora beside Lil. Given a measure of luck, no one but Cora would come to the library. *A word, Lord. A moment*, he begged silently. But deep within, he hoped for much more.

She arrived an hour later. He was up on the second level of the magnificent library, in one of several small alcoves not fully visible from the areas below. He was pretending to linger over a section of books about ancient Greece when he sensed her arrival. He looked over his shoulder and saw Antonio scan the library, spot him above, and then take his position by the door. Cora brushed past him and saw Will then too and immediately went to the mahogany ladder, climbing up to him.

"You on the hunt for a tome about ancient Greece too?" he said, in case anyone was coming in after her.

"Perhaps," she said, with a small smile. He slipped his hand around hers and pulled her around the corner, into the alcove, away from Antonio's eyes.

They stood there for a moment, tentative and awkward, each knowing there was too much to say and not enough time. But there was one thing he had to know.

"Have you given in, then, Cora? To him?" Will asked, his tone laced with pain.

"No, Will," she said, sorrow in her blue eyes. "Pierre…he's lovely. But he's not the one my heart wants."

His heart leaped. They stared at each other as if to memorize each other's face. It had been so long. So long since they'd had a moment alone. "Cora," he breathed, daring to pull her close.

"Will," she whispered back, her face inches away, inviting him in.

After a long, searching kiss, he pulled away with a groan, knowing that if they were discovered, everything would become much more complicated. "What are we going to do?" he asked, every word an ache.

"My father insists I accept Pierre's bid to court me," she said, taking a step away as if guilty. He held her hand, stubbornly refusing to release it. "And if I don't, I'm afraid my father will figure out that *you* are the cause of my resistance."

"Cora. I so wish to speak to him about my own desire to court you."

"You mustn't!" she said, her eyes widening. "If he finds out about you and me…"

"He won't," Will said, pulling her close. "Not yet anyway. Not until he can't hurt either of us. Don't worry about me, okay?"

"I do, though," she said, taking his other hand. "I do. Pierre already guessed that it is you who holds my heart from him. How long until he tells my father? Or how long until Wallace sees it himself, traveling with us?"

"We only need to take increased care." But the fact that she'd told Richelieu of him, of her true feelings, made his heart soar, even as a dark cloud of fear entered in.

Her eyes echoed what her words had said—by some miracle, it was he who still held her heart.

"Cora, there's more we must speak about…." He turned away from her to lift the folded paper from the alcove table, then slowly turned back, knowing that what was to come would hurt her deeply.

"What is it?" she asked, sounding a bit faint. As if she knew already.

"They discovered copper, Cora. And gold, too. In Dunnigan. Your father's wealth shall quadruple with the stores they figure are in the rock below."

Her lush lips parted, and air came out in a *whoosh*. He grabbed hold of her arm and turned to sit her in a chair before she fainted. "Cora, breathe. Breathe," he said, taking a knee and stroking her arm, then holding one of her hands between both of his, against his chest.

Her eyes were flicking back and forth, as if she were trying to make sense of it.

"He didn't," she muttered. "He couldn't have...he wouldn't...." Then her gaze stilled, suddenly, staring straight ahead. She lifted her chin and rose. "I have to go see him. Now."

"No, Cora. Consider the consequences."

She ignored him. Simply picked up the paper and made her way down the narrow ladder as if she'd completely forgotten he was there.

He groaned in frustration and followed her down the ladder and out the door, Antonio beside him.

"What is it?" Antonio whispered.

"Disaster," Will said.

She scurried up the stairs and down the hall, directly to her father's suite, where she paused, squared her shoulders, and then knocked on the door. A footman answered it, gave her a small bow, then turned to announce her. Will followed behind, not waiting for an invitation, leaving Antonio to guard the door.

Mr. Kensington was sitting in one of two large wing-backed chairs by the window, his welcoming smile quickly fading when he saw Cora's frown. His eyes moved to Will, as if seeking an explanation, but Cora held the paper in front of him, the article visible on the top. "Explain *this* to me, *Mr. Kensington*."

Wallace gestured to the footman to leave them in privacy, and the man did so at once, quietly closing the door behind him. He then glanced at Will, but Cora interceded. "No, I want him here." She shook the folded paper in her hand again. "Tell me. Tell me I simply do not know enough German to properly translate this."

The gray-haired man took the paper from her and scanned the article a moment, then tossed it to the table. "It's true. I was going to tell you, but the drama of late has kept our attention on other topics."

Her lips parted in astonishment. "Wh-what? How...how could you do such a thing?"

"What? Turn a plot of dirt into a profitable mine?" His hands spread apart. "It's what I do!"

"By taking advantage of your own daughter?" Cora asked. "And the people who reared her for you?"

The older man's eyes moved in agitation to Will and then back to Cora, as if he didn't appreciate being called to account, especially in front of another. "Perhaps we should speak of this in private," he said.

"No," she said, more riled up than Will had ever seen her. "He stays. He is my friend, my *guardian*," she said, leaning slightly toward her father. "A role you don't seem to understand."

"Cora," Wallace said with a sigh, gesturing toward the other chair. "Sit down."

"No, thank you," she said, crossing her arms. "Simply explain it to me. Please."

"Cora," he said again, leaning back, his elbows on either arm of the chair, and steepling his fingers. "Sit *down*." He stared back at her, his blue eyes brooking no argument. "I refuse to have this conversation unless we do so in a civil manner. What would your mother say?"

"How dare you mention my mother at a time like this!"

"Cora." He kept his tone low.

Finally, Cora lifted her chin and demurely sat down on the edge of the chair, as if she intended to remain there for the shortest possible time. "You stole that property out from under my papa, knowing all along what it was worth."

He studied her face. "Is that what you think of me?"

She shifted in her seat, the movement so small Will almost missed it. But something told him Wallace Kensington had not. "You are well known as a ruthless businessman," Cora said. "You saw an opportunity. You took it. No matter who it harmed."

"I delivered your parents from a property that was bleeding them dry. When I arrived, your papa was at death's door. You know him, Cora. If he had spent another week on that farm, it would've killed him. He would have rallied, risen, and died walking those fields, trying to coax something of a harvest out of that wretched, drought-ridden soil. He's stubborn. Determined."

"Almost as stubborn and determined as you."

"Almost," Mr. Kensington allowed, locking eyes with her.

"So you waited until he was too weak to fight you. Until we were all too weak to fight you."

"I know it must seem that way to you."

"How else could it seem?" she said, letting out a little laugh and shaking her head. "In short order you had my folks on a train to Minnesota—"

"Where they have found *health*, peace."

"And me on a train to the lake—"

"Where you began the grandest chapter of your *life*."

"And the title to my father's farm—my *grandfather's* land—was in your hand."

Wallace clamped his lips shut, waiting her out.

"Did you ever truly want me?" she asked. "To be a part of your family? Or have I endured all this—made my siblings endure all this—so that you could get me off the property too? So you could become twice as wealthy?"

"It isn't as it seems, Cora...."

"Isn't it?" she asked, rising, her voice rising too. She was clearly close to tears. "Here we are in Vienna. While your men drill into the ridge my papa walked for years. For *years*."

Wallace's nostrils flared. "He was a farmer! He would've never dug into that ridge, Cora. You know as well as I that he would've stayed married to the soil, never looking beyond it." He took a deep breath, splaying his hands. "Alan's a good man, true and faithful. But he has no vision, nor did he have the means to do anything else to—"

"Stop. Stop it." She lifted her hand to him, shaking her head. "You may not steal from an ill man and then speak poorly of him. You may not!"

"I did not steal from him! I made something from nothing. All in an effort to—"

"How can you say that?" she asked, furious tears streaming down her face. "He was barely well enough to sign his name to that title. And you asked him to do so, knowing all along what was under that rock. Did you not?" She paused, searching his face. "Did you not?" she repeated.

He looked at her, and for the first time, Will glimpsed helplessness in the older man.

She let out a scoffing laugh and shook her head again. "I am sending Pierre home. I will not lead him on so that you can add to your despicable kingdom of wealth!"

"No. You are not," he said, rising.

"I am. I care for him, but I do not love him. And unlike you, I do not use people to get something from them."

He stared at her. "You already told Pierre that he does not hold your heart."

She raised her head in surprise.

"Yes, he told me," Wallace said. "But you may not send him home. It is up to him, what he does with your words. And he chooses to try to convince you of your folly. It is my desire you give him the chance to do so."

Will dug his fingers into his palms as he forced himself to stay silent.

"Pierre has always gotten what he went after," Cora said. "Just as you have. But that doesn't mean he gets *me*."

"You will allow his attempt to win you, at the very least."

"No. I won't."

"You will. Or we shall end this little tour, and the entire clan shall be heading home to Montana. And our deal to send you to school? It shall be null and void, since you did not complete the tour…." He looked to the window, every movement speaking of weariness. "I should probably do that anyway…end it," he muttered. "Before you or the rest are in any further danger. But this deal with Richelieu is more important than you realize." He looked at her, appearing ten years older than he had a moment before.

Her mouth dropped open, and she wiped furiously at her tears. "You would hold even my sisters and brother against me? Threaten to turn them against me by ending the tour early?"

"Only because you've left me no choice, Cora. It is the only way I see to stop you from making a decision that will harm the whole family, including *you*."

"You are…" she said, so softly that Will barely heard her, "reprehensible." And with that, she turned and rushed out of the room.

Mr. Kensington heaved a sigh, turning to the window, hands on the end of his cane like a crutch, then looked over his shoulder at Will. "Well, go after her, young man! Make certain she is all right. And see that you get her to see my side of this."

Will needed no further encouragement. He ran after her and, pausing, heard her sobbing somewhere close. He walked down the hall and found her in an empty room. He knocked softly, letting himself in, and then closed the door behind him. She was leaning over a desk, her torso shaking with her sobs. The sound of it threatened to break Will's heart.

"Cora," he said, coming beside her.

She turned to him and threw herself into his arms. "Oh, Will," she said, crying and crying.

He held her, stroking her back, her hair, until her tears were spent. Then he led her to a chair, sat her down in it, and passed her his handkerchief. He knelt beside her, his hand on her knee. Waiting.

Ready to do anything at all he could to alleviate the pain. "I'm sorry, Cora. I know this is difficult to bear."

She shook her head, blowing her nose into the handkerchief. "Don't you see? He's getting exactly what he wants! I am but a pawn in his game!"

"I know it appears as such but—"

"Are you…" she said, her brow furrowing. "Are you taking his *side*?"

"I'm only saying that perhaps you ought to—"

"What? Do everything he says? Don't tell me you fear him too. Oh, wait. You do. You're just as much a pawn as I."

Will drew back, stung by her words.

"I'm sorry. Forgive me," she said, shaking her head. "I am not myself."

"No," he said, rising slowly. "You're not."

She came to her feet too and wrapped her arms around his waist, laying her head against his chest. "I'm sorry, Will, so sorry. I'm all twisted inside. Confused."

Will put one hand to her back, and one to his head. "As am I."

"I don't know which end is up."

"That, I understand," he said. He gazed down at her, waiting for her to look up, and when she did, the jagged end of his anger melted.

"We can get through this, right?" she sobbed. "Somehow? Some way?"

"Somehow. Some way," he promised.

But deep down, his heart sank. Because he had no earthly idea how.

CHAPTER TWENTY-FIVE

~William~

With their female clients all in their own quarters and their young male clients watched over by Yves and Claude, Will wandered out to the garden that night after the concert, attempting to sort out his thoughts. He again battled the urge to tell Mr. Kensington of his feelings, his desire to court Cora. But the threat of the tour ending early, and perhaps not receiving the promised bonus—his only hope of paying his uncle's bills and returning to university in the fall—bound him as surely as if he were gagged and tied to a chair. *What have I to offer her anyway?* He had no apartment to return to; the bank had probably claimed it by now. If he professed his love and Antonio was right—if Kensington, in a rage, blocked him at every angle—how could he even support them? His only option was to continue as a bear, escorting Grand Tourists. But the memory of her on Richelieu's arm was enough to turn him inside out.

Will spied him, then, as if summoned by whispers of his innermost thoughts. Richelieu wound past the hedge of fat, fragrant roses and sat down on a bench across the path from him. Will nodded in greeting but could not summon the strength to form a word. Richelieu was a good man. Kind. Truly, he could not come up with a decent reason for Cora to turn him away, other than one.

He loved her and wanted her for himself.

"Let her go, man," Richelieu said, looking up at him, his hands gripping either side of him. His tone was not unkind. "She's better off with me. We both know it."

Will studied him, only the ridge of his brow and nose and chin visible in the moonlight. He pretended confusion. "I'm sorry?"

Richelieu sighed and leaned forward, forearms on his thighs. "There is no need to feign ignorance," he said gently. "I know the truth of it. I do not fear the fact that she cares for you. Because she cares for me, too."

Will mirrored his stance, leaning forward too. "Does she?"

Richelieu paused a moment. "Perhaps I'm deluding myself. The ways of women are somewhat of a mystery, are they not? All I ask is that you give her some distance to sort out her truest feelings."

"I am hardly in a position to pursue her. If only I had the luxury of such a convenience..." he said, failing to keep the bitterness from his tone.

Richelieu let out a scoffing laugh. "You do not even recognize your own advantage. Close to her, every day, from morn to night. Sharing new experiences and seeing new vistas together." He shook his head and threw out his splayed hands. "Add to that the allure of a forbidden affair—when her father, currently suffering her renewed disfavor, has explicitly asked her to entertain *my* affections.... No. It is up to you, Will. If she is meant to be with you, she will continue to resist my pursuit. But if she is meant to be with me, if you allow her some distance—of the heart, even though you are in such close physical proximity—she might see me with new eyes. Might you not allow her the grace to choose between us?"

Will stared at him, thinking through what he was saying. Was it fair to tie Cora to him, when it seemed so completely hopeless? Truly, he could not see a way for them. Not until the tour was over and both were home and free of Wallace Kensington's power—if there would ever be such a time—and he was free of Stuart's debts.

Wasn't true love able to weather all?

And yet wasn't true love also unselfish? Wanting only the best for the other person?

Richelieu seemed to sense his internal shift. "So you'll allow it, then. A bit of distance. Both of us will soon find out about Cora's truest feelings."

"Is it truly fair, though?" Will said, finding his voice. "Two suitors can only both be considered when both show up at a lady's door. If I give her 'distance,' as you suggest, how is she not to take that as rejection and fall into your arms?"

"Distance makes the heart grow fonder, they say," Richelieu said.

"They also say, 'Out of sight, out of mind.'"

Richelieu took a deep breath. "Give me the chance. If I'm not the right man for her, even by becoming, how you say, *within sight*, then she will send me home."

Will swallowed hard. *Lord, wisdom. I need Your wisdom....*

"Consider it, William," Richelieu said, rising. He reached out a hand, offering it to Will. "Isn't it fair? To wager that the right man will win her heart?"

He couldn't risk it. Declaring himself to her father. Not yet. Not without bringing them both down. They just needed more time. More time...

Will stood up, even though his knees trembled beneath him. And then he reached out to shake the nobleman's hand, feeling vaguely like Judas.

————◇◇◇————

~Cora~

I hovered in the ladies' salon for as long as I could, powdering and repowdering my nose. But I finally reentered the grand baroque hall that contained what had to be two hundred men and women dressed in Victorian finery, many of whom were taking instruction on a unique waltz that allowed for the wide hoop skirts the women all wore. I could feel the lingering glances of men as I passed but ignored them, not wishing to invite any of them to approach.

I searched the hall for a familiar face, eager to avoid my dreadful father, wishing I could dance with Will—who seemed distant today—but giving in to the fact that it would probably be Pierre with whom I danced this night. I spied Lillian on the arm of an attentive, rather wolfish-looking blond man and watched as they turned. He bent to say something in her ear, and she giggled and flashed a smile at him even as she blushed prettily.

The hairs on the back of my neck stood up. Was I merely feeling protective over my little sister? Or was it intuition—a godly warning that this might be one of our attackers?

"My, you look lovely tonight, Cora," Art said, nodding to me as he and Hugh approached.

"Indeed," Hugh said, looking me over from head to toe.

I shook my head at him. "I was about to say you two looked like fine Victorian gentlemen, but perhaps that's only an apt description of *one* of you."

"Come now. A man cannot be blamed for his masculine appetites," Hugh said, waggling his eyebrows.

"Go. Find someone with whom to dance before you say something we both regret," I said. He was incorrigible, but I was beginning to recognize his act. His role, as if it were a mere script. Did everyone in this crowd have a role to play? Was anyone allowed to be as they were, created by God, following His lead? I looked to Vivian dancing with Andrew and thought of her onetime love for a servant's son. Andrew, dutifully seeing to his intended but simmering beneath the surface. Felix drifted by, a beautiful woman in his arms, and I suddenly could see him ten years hence, still dancing, still moving, still resisting our father's desire for him to make something of himself—but even his role as a playboy seemed just that...a role. I glimpsed Will for a moment. He was leaving the hall. I thought of his desire to be an architect, his desire to be with me...neither of which seemed entirely possible.

Even we girls now played our parts as bait. I again found Lillian and her dance partner, drifting toward me as the music played on.

What was it about him that troubled me? It was good for her to enjoy a man's attention for once. She looked lovely and was of age to accept suitors. Perhaps that was it...I simply saw her as my little sister, just discovered, not a woman grown. But this man was looking at her as if she were ripe for the plucking. Just as Art had looked at her, these past weeks.

I eased a bit when I saw Antonio, arms crossed, not ten steps away, intently watching them both. His expression made me smile—he was as filled with consternation and wariness as any doting father. I made myself take a breath—as best I could, anyway, given the tight corset I wore.

"Ahh, there you are, mon amie," Pierre said, smoothly coming to my side. "I was beginning to think you'd disappeared into the hedge labyrinth outside." He gave me a quick kiss on the hand and a devilish smile. He knew well enough that it would remind me of our chase in his hedges in Paris and our kiss in the gazebo....

I forced myself to smile back at him rather than cower in a puddle of embarrassment and blushes. I allowed my eyes to wander, searching the doorway for Will, waiting for him to reenter. But he did not return, or I'd missed his entry and he was lost in the crowd. Perhaps he had taken a position out of my line of vision. Pierre confidently offered his arm. "Would you care to dance, Cora?"

I looked again to Lillian twirling in a circle around the blond man, her color high. *Oh yes, she is taken with this one.* It'd be good to draw near and find out more about him. "I'd be delighted," I said to Pierre. He immediately gave me a tiny bow and then led me to the dance floor directly beside Lillian and her partner just as the dance ended.

"I do not believe we've yet been acquainted," Pierre said to the man, reaching out a hand.

"No, I believe you're right," said the man, pushing back a shock of blond hair in a rakish move that reminded me of Hugh. He reached out to shake Pierre's hand. "Nathan Hawke, esquire, of New York."

"Pierre de Richelieu," he answered with a half smile, "of Paris."

Mr. Hawke glanced down toward me, and his smile faltered. His hand went to his heart. "Forgive me. You gave me quite a start, miss. Have we met before? You look terribly familiar."

Lillian took my arm and smiled up at him, clearly wanting to get back into his line of vision. Did she think I might try to steal him from her? "This is my sister, Miss Cora Diehl Kensington."

"Miss Kensington," he said, recovering his manners. He bowed and took my gloved hand, giving it a quick kiss. "A pleasure to meet you. I was born in Helena, so your sister and I have been reminiscing. Apparently, we share an affinity for the mountains of our onetime shared home." He smiled down at Lillian, giving her a quick wink.

"Helena?" My heart leaped at the mention of a city in my home state, instantly making me feel more at ease with him, and yet I bristled at his brazen wink. "What a small world." Perhaps that was why I appeared familiar to him. Maybe we'd even passed each other on the boardwalk in town. "What has brought you to Vienna?"

But the conductor had begun the prelude to the next song, and everyone hurriedly lined up for the dance. Nathan studied me and then leaned forward to whisper, "We must speak of it and more," as if it were a secret and I was the only one privy to know. I bristled at his assumed intimacy.

Pierre and I settled into a familiar two-step, and I tried to relax. I was being silly. Nathan Hawke was not a kidnapper. Our kidnappers favored the shadows and surprise, not an overt introduction. And he was from America. I was in one of the finest halls of one of the finest cities, on the arm of one of the world's finest men, in a gown I could have only dreamed of as a girl.

But as we passed Lillian and Mr. Hawke, I saw his eyes trailing after me. Not as a potential suitor, but with the look of a troubled friend. I lost them in the crowd as we turned, and then my vision began to tunnel, even as the song came to an end.

"Cora?" Pierre asked, strengthening his hold on me. "Where are you?" He gave me a wry look that held the faintest edge of anger. "Certainly not with me."

"Forgive me," I said. "I confess there is so much in my head, that I feel a bit dizzy."

The anger dissolved, and he turned me away from the floor, wrapping a strong arm around my waist—a move explicitly reserved for dancing. But I was grateful for it, as my knees felt like jelly. "Are you ill? Would you like a chair?"

"No, no," I assured him. "Please. Just a cup of punch? It's no doubt the costume keeping me from a full breath."

"Ahh," he said, giving me a quick appraisal, shaking his head as he glanced at the beautiful dress. "Come with me."

His tone brooked no argument, so I meekly followed him and took one of several empty chairs he gestured to, feeling very much like the girls of old who would fall onto fainting couches and be awakened with smelling salts. "I will return in a moment," he said but his tone said, *Stay here.* His protective manner both warmed me and made me bristle. I brought a hand to my head. What was the matter with me? Did I not want a man to watch over and care for me?

"Are you quite all right?" Nathan Hawke stood before me. "You look terribly peaked."

"I am feeling a bit faint. Pierre set off to fetch me a cup of punch. I'm sure once I catch my breath I'll be fine."

"You need a bit of air in the garden," he said.

My head jerked up, offended by his demanding tone, so out of place.

"Make your excuses," he said lowly as Pierre appeared, ten paces behind him. "Come away to the garden for a bit. The arches in the far corner. There is something you must know. Now."

I frowned even as he tipped back his head and laughed, as if I'd said something hilarious. Then, with a small bow, he moved away to meet up with Lillian again and offer her a cup of punch.

"Cora? What did he say?" Pierre asked, frowning at my expression and then looking after him.

"He said he wanted to meet me alone in the garden. He said he has something I must know."

Pierre's frown deepened with rage. "The scoundrel! I'll tell you who will meet him there. *Moi*."

"No," I said, reaching out to place a hand on his arm. I smiled and laughed lightly. "Besides, who are you to take umbrage at his request? Did you not meet me alone in a garden once?"

"You were not being courted by anyone else as I recall," he said, relaxing just a bit at the memory. "I knew I had to make a move before anyone else spotted the budding rose." His kind eyes washed over my face, and I knew then the honesty of his love. It took my breath away, and I hurriedly took a sip of the tart, blood-orange punch. Pierre turned to find Nathan Hawke bowing before Lillian and then departing, leaving her looking more than a bit dashed.

·"Pierre, what if he is connected to the kidnappers? Might this be our chance to flush them out? I could go and meet him as he requested. With you and Antonio in the shadows. If he makes any untoward moves—for any reason—you two would be right there."

His brow lowered. "If you intend to expose yourself, there will be more than two of us in the shadows. I will not allow you to come to any harm. And if this Hawke has companions who await him…"

I shivered, remembering the iron-strong arms of the men who'd accompanied my kidnapper in Nîmes, and hurriedly agreed. "But you must remain hidden until we know his intentions."

"Are you certain?" he said, his eyes now rife with worry. "I do not like it. Placing you in the center of potential danger."

"It is a chance to be free of these men, once and for all, yes? And what harm can truly come to me if you and three others are on all four sides of me? Go. Alert the others. When you give the signal I will go to him. At the first sign of trouble, come to my aid." I squeezed his arm. "I will be fine."

He leaned close enough that I felt the heat of his whisper on my ear. "I will not let you out of my sight. Give me five minutes to get the others in position." And then he was gone, leaving me to wonder if I truly had the strength to do what I'd offered.

But if there was one thing I had in common with Wallace Kensington, it was this—I wanted the men who threatened us gone.

CHAPTER
TWENTY-SIX

~William~

Irritated, Will eyed Richelieu as he approached. Had he not removed himself from the dance hall? Was he still too near to Cora for the man's comfort?

Richelieu gestured to a corner where they could speak in private, and regretfully, Will could think of no reason not to hear him out. "What is it?" he asked as soon as they were alone.

"It's Cora. She's been approached by an American named Nathan Hawke. He insisted she meet him in the garden. He says he has something he must show her. She is intent on doing as he asked in order to see if this might be a ruse of the kidnappers."

Will's eyes narrowed even as his heartbeat doubled. "You left her? Alone?"

Richelieu met his gaze with a stern look of his own. "Only so that I might find assistance in forming a guard in the shadows. Given that you feel as I do toward her, I thought it prudent you be among them."

Will lifted his chin in admiration. The man cared for her enough to bring in the man who would care for her more than any other, even though it meant he'd be closer to her than he liked. His grudging admiration grew. *He loves her. He truly loves her.*

"Let's go," he grunted. "I want Antonio and Yves in on this too."

They entered the dance hall and quickly found their men. Will knew that there were others in disguise around them. He prayed they'd be keeping as close an eye on their clients as their fee dictated they would. He worried that this could be a ruse to draw their attention elsewhere, so that the kidnappers could take Lillian or Nell. He paused beside Claude and bade him to promise to keep an even closer eye on those two. Vivian was still accompanied by Andrew, and well aware of the threat, so he fretted less over her.

He saw Cora slip through the French doors that opened upon a wide marble veranda and out to the gardens. On the far side was a curved garden portico, with two rows of covered arches extending from a tall fountain like welcoming arms gesturing inward. She began making her way there. "I'll go to the far side," he said to the men. "Antonio, you go to the left, Yves to the right. It makes sense that you, Pierre, would be among the gardens, catching some fresh air."

The men nodded in agreement and edged apart, filtering into the crowd as if intent on reentering the party, and through it entering the dark gardens from separate directions. Will wished he carried a pistol as the others did, rather than the dress cane. But he knew if he had the opportunity to grab hold of any man who dared to try to take Cora, his fists would be the only weapon he needed.

He saw her reach the fountain just as he edged past the end. Flames danced in gas lamps at every arch, casting a warm, romantic glow and deep shadows throughout. Was the man simply after a romantic tryst? He smiled grimly. Even that would come to an unhappy end if the man attempted it. Will hopped over a four-foot-high hedge and then crouched over, looking around. Confident he was alone, he moved back toward the arches from the other side, stealing close enough to hear the click of Cora's heels on the stone floor of the garden patio.

He spied her through a hole in the hedge, and for the first time all night, he allowed himself the luxury of gazing upon her in the splendor of her Victorian finery. The dusty-rose color made her skin appear creamy, her blue eyes brighter. Tendrils of hair from her curling knot atop her head had escaped and teased the edges of her long neck. She paced back and forth a bit and then seemed to make herself still, half hidden in the shadows. She looked so comely, so inviting, he had to force himself to stay where he was and not go to her himself. *Oh, to be a welcome suitor of Cora Diehl Kensington…*

Her head came up, and then he heard what she had—footsteps as someone approached. She greeted a fair-haired man he assumed was Nathan Hawke. Will tensed. But the man paused a pace away from Cora and looked about, as if as nervous as she.

"Forgive the intrigue," he said. "It's only that I knew you would want to know of this as soon as possible. And in private." He reached inside his jacket and drew out a folded magazine from a pocket and handed it to Cora. What was this? A ruse to distract her? Will's hands clenched.

"My sister, who just arrived this morning from New York, brought it with her."

Cora, casting him a confused look, turned to lift the magazine toward the lamp. "*Life*? What has this to do with me?"

The fellow bit his lip and then gestured to it. "You'll see. I'll leave you to find out. I'm sorry, Miss Kensington. You seem like a nice woman."

She frowned and watched him depart even as Will's frown deepened. He warily looked around, wishing he could see better in the dark. Were the others approaching?

Cora took a step toward the light and paged through the magazine, then abruptly stilled. He heard her gasp. And then Richelieu's shout as she fainted.

———◇◇◇———

~Cora~

I came to in Pierre's arms, recognizing with some alarm that we were still in the garden. In a moment, I remembered what had stolen my breath. The magazine...

"Please," I said, scrambling to my feet. "Let me see it."

"Come inside, Cora," Will said, handing the magazine to me. "Where we can peruse it in private."

By his grim tone and expression, I guessed he'd seen the spread on the inside too. "Postcards from the Grand Tour," the headline screamed. And beneath it, photo after photo of me and my companions—some in seemingly compromising situations. Quotes from us, out of context. He offered his arm, and Pierre offered his, too. I took both, still feeling woozy and short of breath, my vision tunneling in and out. They shielded me from the gathering crowd of concerned partygoers, telling them that I needed to rest as we made our way inside and up to our quarters in the mansion.

My father glimpsed us and rushed over. "What happened?"

"Bad news, I'm afraid," Will said through gritted teeth. "Might you attend us upstairs, sir?"

"Certainly."

I swallowed my complaint, suddenly feeling nauseous, and he and Mr. Morgan fell in behind us. Andrew and Vivian, too. We left the girls and Hugh and Felix to dance. There was time enough for them to learn of this latest development.

"Ring for Anna," Will grunted to Pierre. Pierre moved to the lever by my door and pulled as Will helped me to a chair. "She needs to get out of this infernal dress. She can't breathe," Will hurriedly added, blushing at the implications of his statement.

Anna appeared immediately, slightly out of breath. "Anna, can you help her out of her gown and into something a little lighter?" Will asked. "She just fainted."

"Of course, sir," she said with a bob. She closed the door behind the men and quickly helped me out of the rose gown I'd been so anxious to wear, and into a loose-fitting day dress. She poured me a cup of water and forced me to drink it as I spread out the magazine on the chest of drawers and turned the pages. Six pages of postcards—literally postcards of our trip, photographs that Art had taken all along—with captions such as "Castle Diving with the Bear-in-Training," a photograph of me and Will about to leap into the Rhône. "A Quiet Moment Post-Rescue," a photograph of Will hovering over me, pale and wet, in my bathing costume…in my bed. Interspersed was titillating copy about our pasts, our recent meeting, and much about our rich, rich fathers. I groaned and shut my eyes.

"Oh, dear," Anna said, looking over my shoulder. She edged closer. "Oh *dear*," she said again.

After I'd scanned all six pages, I went back to the first and found his name. I knew it before I saw it, of course, but here, in the pages of *Life*, Art was known as A. W. Stapleton. This was why Vivian had recognized his name. Listed in the front, he appeared to be a regular society reporter for the magazine, a monthly I'd seen her read. Beneath the headline, a line read, "Part One of Three." I turned to the cover. It had been published a week prior. What other photographs had he taken since he'd sent this off? It could only mean that for the next two months, we'd await more horrifyingly intimate invasions of our privacy.

My eyes narrowed, and I fought the urge to track him down here and now. How could he use us in this manner? Travel with us, befriend us, then betray us?

With a trembling hand, I pinched my temples between my thumb and middle finger, now able to breathe but with a headache building into a rage. "All right," I said, mostly to myself. "We must see it through. Let's get on with it."

"Another sip of water, miss," Anna said. "I won't have you fainting again on my watch."

I forced down another swallow and then strode toward the door. Outside, the men straightened. "Come in," I said, gesturing toward the couch and two sitting chairs that flanked a wide, short table. As

Will passed, I flashed the first spread of the magazine to him so he was warned of what was to come.

He hovered over my shoulder and slowly brought a hand to his mouth. I thought I heard him groan, as if barely holding back a cry of outrage.

"Let me see it," my father said, lifting a hand.

I hesitated a moment, as if I were but a small girl holding on to a stolen toy. But it was no use. Even if I refused, he'd find another copy shortly. I lifted my chin, took a breath, and passed it over.

He studied me a moment, pulled on a pair of spectacles, and then spread the magazine open on the table, so that both he and Mr. Morgan could see it.

"Oh, my," Mr. Morgan said, as my father's face became deadly still.

A vein in my father's temple bulged. His skin became red, making his gray beard appear all the more white. He turned the page, paused a moment, and then turned another. Slowly, ever so slowly, he looked up at Will. "How…how could you allow this?"

Will shook his head. "A terrible error, sir," he said, splaying out his hands. "Art met up with us on the train…he was staying with Pierre's sister on the Rhône…." He cast a desperate look over to Pierre. I knew he wasn't trying to cast blame, only explain why we'd trusted Art.

Pierre shrugged. "Arthur's family has a vineyard. My brother-in-law has worked with them for years. I knew he was a writer, but he seemed to be on the Continent for family business, not as a journalist. A grave mistake," he said, bringing a slender hand to his chest and bowing toward the elder men. "But surely, your family is accustomed to such attention, no?" He shrugged. "At home in Paris, my family and friends are often photographed and written about."

"Bah," said my father. "Reports of parties and balls and meetings. That is acceptable. Expected. But not anything like *this*." He lifted the magazine and shook it. "This is an invasion of privacy. And he makes our children appear as nothing more than drunks and loose women. And *you*…you, our young bear, have much to explain."

I winced over his words. It was an overstatement, but I knew what he meant. The photographs were largely of our time in the south of France. A photograph of Hugh and Felix in the cabaret, clearly inebriated, each with arms around women. Me in my swimsuit, from behind, on the edge of the wall. Will, far too close, in my bedroom, after the accident, making it appear that we were all alone. There were other photographs too, far more sedate. The ones we'd known Art was taking. Posing at famous monuments. Dancing at a ball. Picnicking. Dining at a fantastic table suitable for kings and queens. All in all, it painted a rather comprehensive picture of the first part of our journey. But it also made us look spoiled, careless, wanton.

"At least he wasn't with us in England or Paris," I tried.

"Why? What horrifying things transpired there?" my father bit out, rising. "What is yet to come? What will we see in the coming months, from the time he was traveling with you, taking photograph after photograph?" He turned to face Will and tapped him on the chest. He was a foot shorter than Will, and yet he was as intimidating as any giant. "I trusted you, boy. I *trusted* you."

Will winced. "The photographs are skewed, sir," Will tried. "Far worse than reality."

"Are they? Were you not in my daughter's bedroom? Look at that photograph!" he said, gesturing toward the magazine on the table. "See for yourself! And in others, too. It's as plain as day that you think the sun rises and sets around Cora." He sighed and fell heavily into his chair. "It's completely inappropriate."

Will's face blazed with heat. "It's only inappropriate if I fail to admit it's true." He glanced toward me and then back to my father. "I've fallen in love with your daughter, sir. And she with me."

Wallace stared up at him, clearly infuriated. "You dare to admit it!"

"Yes. I've yearned to speak to you plainly about it, particularly when Pierre made his attentions known."

"But you didn't."

"No. I didn't."

"Because you knew I'd fire you in an instant."

I held my breath. Was this truly happening?

"Yes, sir," Will said, clamping his lips shut. "Because I knew you would."

"You were right," Wallace said slowly, seeming to regain some control. He took a long, slow breath and pinched the bridge of his nose.

For a moment, I hoped, hoped he'd see—

"Pack your bags, William. You are not welcome near me or mine again."

Will wavered, almost as if he didn't believe what Wallace had said. "You can't do that, sir."

"Father, I—" I began.

"I cannot? Why not? Have you not made untoward advances toward my daughter?"

Will looked to me and then back again. "Nothing that Pierre de Richelieu has not done himself. And I assure you that—"

"Pierre de Richelieu is not my employee. He is not the man I entrusted with the safety of my daughters and son, as well as my friend's children. *You* are." He stared up at Will.

Will paused.

"Have you kissed her?" Wallace went on.

"Father, really—" I tried.

"I *have* kissed her," Will said, then turned to me. "I *love* her. I want to marry her."

I sucked in my breath. He wanted to marry me? My heart leaped.

"Well, you can bury that dream right now. You are on your way out of her life. This instant."

It was Will's turn to take a breath. He gathered himself, straightening his shoulders and facing him again. "I believe that is up to Cora to decide," he said slowly. "Since I am no longer your employee."

"Do not challenge me further," Wallace said, pointing a finger at him and shaking his head. "You will regret it."

"I'm afraid I must. I love her, sir. I love her. Surely you understand it. Were you not in love with Cora's mother?"

Vivian gasped.

"Get out!" Wallace said, his voice shaking. He rose and pointed to the door. "Get *out*."

"Not unless Cora comes with me."

"Cora is not coming with you."

"I'm not?" I asked, almost to myself. It wasn't until all eyes were on me that I realized I'd spoken aloud. I swallowed, wishing I could take another drink of water to ease my suddenly dry mouth. I looked around to each of them, hesitating over Pierre, over my father, but then resting my gaze on Will. William…it had always been Will. "I love him, too."

My eyes found Wallace Kensington's again. Eyes so like mine. But pain edged them. "Oh, my dear. This is a sorry turn of events. But you cannot follow where your heart leads you. Not here. Not now."

"I cannot?" I was beginning to gain strength as my anger grew. Who was he to dictate such things? He could control my summer, but not my life….

"No. Not this time." He took a seat again, appearing older.

"What is to stop me?" I said, taking Will's arm. "So my tour comes to an end. So you will not fund my return to Normal School. I shall work for a time and fund my own schooling. I am grateful for this opportunity, but my life is my own."

Wallace shook his head and rubbed his face with both hands. "No, it is not," he said gently. "Nor is William's. His uncle died, severely indebted, leaving Will liable for those debts. Some of them are to me. But I can call them in tomorrow."

I stilled. "You would leave him penniless? On the streets?"

"I would. If you force my hand."

I glanced up at Will, wanting to be sure he was as certain as I. He gave me a grim look of helplessness, clearly not wanting to drag me into such dire straits. "Then I shall be penniless with him. Together, we'll find our way."

Wallace laughed. Then laughed again, his amusement gaining steam. "No, my dear. You'd be far *worse* than penniless."

I frowned in confusion. What could be worse?

"You'd be a millionaire who chose poverty," he said.

"I...I beg your pardon?"

"Your farm in Dunnigan. The mines beneath the hills on the western edge...you read it for yourself. We struck both gold and copper. You are rich beyond your dreams."

"You mean you are rich. You hold the title."

"We hold it together. Along with your mama and papa," he said, casting out a hand in dismissal and leaning back in the chair, crossing one foot over his other knee. "I did not rob it from you, as you supposed. I *included* you in the wealth." He tapped a finger against his lips. "But you see, dear daughter, I took some precautions in adding you three to the title. You have access to a fair amount of the funds for the next two years, enough to keep you all very comfortable. But people new to money should never have too much access. I am the controlling partner, able to buy you each out for a dollar if I decide to. And rest assured," he said, leveling his gaze on mine, "I will buy the three of you out if you displease me."

My mind spun. I was rich. Rich beyond my dreams. And so were my parents, after all these years. But only if I agreed to be one of my father's puppets. "That is...monstrous. You attempt to control my life by threatening my...my *parents*?"

"That is *insurance*. All with the desire to do right by all three of you. Given time, maturity, you will see it from my perspective."

I repositioned my hand on Will's arm, drawing strength from him even as I felt my argument losing steam. After these last weeks with my siblings and the Morgans, I knew how money could corrupt, but I also knew that it was a gift. And my parents...after all these years, the thought of them comfortable, at ease, with more than enough in the bank… "You knew I might walk away from it," I said softly, looking to my father, "if it was only me."

"I knew you'd be passionate enough to do such a thing, yes. But I knew you wouldn't be selfish. Or in the end, foolish. I pray I was right."

"You were," Will said. He turned to me and took my hands. "I love you, Cora. But you cannot walk away from this." He shook his head, miserable. "Not this. Not when I have nothing at all to offer you. Not when it affects your folks, too."

My cheeks instantly flamed with anger, even as my heart sank to my stomach. "So that's it, then? Once again, I have no choice but to do exactly as Wallace Kensington dictates?"

My father remained silent, as did Will. The others shifted nervously. I dropped Will's hands and wrapped my arms around myself, feeling abandoned, lost, as confused as the day I learned I was a Kensington.

Wallace stood up, and Mr. Morgan followed. "We leave in the morning," my father said. "I will secure transit to Venezia and beyond. After reaching Rome, we'll board an ocean liner taking us directly home. Our time in Italy will be cursory, but at least the tour won't be entirely over," he said. "But it *will* be over before another *Life* magazine goes to press."

And with that, it was done.

As ugly and yet as beautifully complete as the day I'd met Wallace.

CHAPTER
TWENTY-SEVEN

~William~

"A word, McCabe," Wallace called as Will strode down the hall to his room. The older man said something to Morgan, and his partner scurried off, leaving them alone.

"Please," Wallace said, reaching him and gesturing into a small salon.

"Have we not said all there is to say?" Will asked.

"Indeed we have not."

Will frowned and followed after him. Wallace took a seat, but Will chose to remain standing by the fireplace.

Wallace sat back and studied him a moment. "I know that you must find all this devastating, but it had to be done."

Will took a deep breath. "I stand behind my words, sir. I might never gain your blessing, but I intend to court your daughter. Just as soon as I settle my uncle's debts, you can expect me."

"No. You are to exit her life right now and never return. For her sake. Her parents'. And yours, too."

Will shook his head. "I can't promise that."

"She'll lose everything, McCabe, as will her parents. You would do that to her?" Wallace coughed and looked to the door and then back to him. "You and Cora both know I loved her mother. I did. And while it ripped out my heart to see her married to another, to send her off on that train, I did it because it was best for her and our child. Alma would never have been accepted in society as my bride, even if I'd chosen to divorce my wife and leave my children. I could not continue to subject her to a role as mistress. Not when I loved her. Do you love Cora in such a manner, William? In a way that compels you to sacrifice for her?"

"Well, of course, but I hardly see how my relationship with Cora compares with your relationship with her mother."

"Truly?" Wallace said calmly. "Was not your love forbidden? Illicit? Explicitly against the contract written between me and your uncle?"

Will's face burned. Well he knew the rules. Stuart had driven them into his head time and time again. "That was a contract signed by my uncle, not by me."

"And yet assumed by you after his death, correct?"

"In a sense, yes," Will said dimly, knowing he had little ground on which to stand.

Wallace pulled a packet from his jacket pocket. "I am giving you enough to get home to the States. Find a job. Pay your debts. Get back to the university if you can. But stay out of Cora's life." He paused, his blue eyes searching Will's. "Come," he said, more gently.

"You know it's the right thing. Do it, Will. If you love her, do it for her."

Wallace pressed the envelope toward Will, and Will considered his options, one wild thought after another shifting through his mind. As much as he loathed it, he could see no way forward without a dollar to his name, and Wallace Kensington knew it. "I'll pay you back, sir," Will said, his fingers closing around the envelope. "Every cent of it."

Wallace smiled, victory etched in the lines of his face, and Will quickly turned away, resisting the powerful urge to strike the older man. But as he left the mansion, his every thought turned to Cora.

And how he must somehow, some way, find his way back to her.

~Cora~

"Is he gone, then?" I whispered to Antonio, taking his arm as we left the baroness's home for the last time. I felt as if I were stumbling forward in the dark, even though bright morning light flooded the front entry. How could we be separating? After so much time spent together, it felt impossible, like it would tear me in two.

"William might not be with us, but he is only as far from your heart as you choose." He turned sad brown eyes toward me as my heart sank. "In time, it will make sense again, my young friend."

"You're certain?"

"I believe so, yes."

"I do wish I had a bit of your confidence." After a restless night's sleep, I awakened feeling more dizzy and bleary-eyed than I had before. Had everything I thought happened really transpired? It seemed impossible. But still, I kept hoping against reason that he'd appear as we all said farewell to the baroness and drove to the train station. Did he understand why I had to do this? For my parents? To protect him? Or did he think me weak, giving up on him, us... walking away? Did he think I feared poverty? After all we'd shared?

We boarded a private train car, as dutifully polite and quiet as schoolchildren on an expedition headed by a stalwart headmaster, my father. Antonio was the only man my father chose to keep on, given his knowledge of Italy and her language. The rest had been dismissed and sent home, replaced with four new guards. Their unfamiliar faces only increased my sense of isolation.

I dodged as Pierre approached—clearly wishing to speak to me—with a shake of my head and mouthing the words *not yet*. It was too soon. I was too raw, and I feared I'd say things I'd regret. Gracious as ever, he gave me a little bow, pain in his pretty green eyes, and I retreated to the small cabin that I was to share with Vivian. I closed the door, sat down on one of the two berths, and with a shaking hand, withdrew the copy of *Life* from my valise. For the first time, I read every word. Art Stapleton had taken numerous quotes from all of us out of context, reporting them truthfully but skewing them to make them all the more entertaining for his readers. He set me up as a rags-to-riches heroine, drawn at one time to our young bear, then to the "Prince of Paris," and back again. It was not entirely untrue. I knew it. But he'd made me out as mindless. Heartless, even. And the photographs were damning evidence to support his case.

I wept, then, in a swirl of painful humiliation and fury over his betrayal. I'd considered Art a friend and felt that loss keenly. Had any of it been real? His interest, his camaraderie? Or had it all been a ruse to become closer to me and the rest of the Kensingtons and Morgans? Had I simply been a dunce, through and through? It seemed impossible that I'd so misread him.

My eyes traced the photographs of Will's earnest face, knowing he loved me. Not as an heiress, but as Cora Diehl, finding my way in my new world as a Kensington. Just as Pierre loved me, I thought, looking at his photograph, too; he pursued me before he even knew I had wealth of my own, after he knew of my mother's indiscretions and my own base birth. Never had he hesitated. He was always so sure, so stalwart in his pursuit. It was hard not to be taken by that determination. I didn't know why Pierre de Richelieu had set his sights on me, exactly, but he appeared to be in it to win my heart.

I reached into my valise for a fresh handkerchief, my old one now wet with tears, and touched another paper. Glancing down, I saw it was the sketch Pierre had made of us in the garden, entwined like young lovers. I had to admit we looked right together, as he envisioned us. Peaceful, playful. And something had shifted between us in the hours since I had learned that I was a partner in a sizable mine with Wallace and my parents. An heiress.

Even though my heart longed for Will, my life was now more on Pierre's plain, the valley between us bridged. At least in terms of wealth.

An heiress, I repeated silently. As if my life could not become more convoluted and confusing than it already was...I was now potentially very wealthy. As wealthy or even wealthier than my siblings and their friends. I could see the genius of my father's plan. I was not taking any of my siblings' inheritance; Wallace Kensington had engineered an inheritance that solely belonged to me and mine. There was nothing to divide me from my siblings in this; it would only bring us closer together. Just as the wealth gap was bridged with Pierre, so it now was with Felix, Vivian, and Lil.

I flopped backward to my pillows, feeling the walls of Wallace Kensington's fortress close in around me. How was I to stop something that was irrefutably doing some good things, too?

—◇◇◇—

~William~

Will had hovered in the shadows, unable to let Cora go without seeing her board the train for Venice. How he longed to run out, pull her into his arms, promise her he'd come for her soon. Beg her not to give up on them. *Please, Lord, let her know. Confirm that my heart is in her hands. That I am gone, but not forever...* Over and over he prayed such prayers as he steadily pursued two goals: to figure out who was truly behind the kidnapping attempts, and to track down Arthur Stapleton.

The man had disappeared sometime during the baroness's ball, as if cannily aware that he was about to be exposed as a traitor. Interloper. Betrayer. Art had robbed him of precious weeks with Cora. Given her father reason to hate Will. And given Pierre de Richelieu a frustrating edge to win her back.

A butler told Will that a driver of the baroness's had taken Art away last evening with his luggage packed. After Will watched the Kensingtons and Morgans depart—feeling every turn of the wheels as a screw tightening in his heart—he walked toward the stables, now converted to house three luxurious motorcars. It felt dreadfully wrong to be apart from Cora—from any of his clients, really. At the end of the season, he usually welcomed the separation, but here, now…had his uncle been alive, this surely would have killed him.

Ah, Stuart, how I've messed things up. I'm sorry, so sorry. He felt the burn of shame on his cheeks, and he paused beside the stables, letting his head rest against the cool stones for a moment as he gathered himself. But anger gave him the strength he needed. Hadn't Stuart himself made a mess of things, leaving his estate in disarray, his debts seemingly insurmountable? How had he continued to spend, giving Will so little, when he knew the bills on his bookkeeper's desk?

But as soon as the bitter thoughts entered his mind, so did the tender memories of Stuart taking him in as an orphan, without hesitation, giving him everything he could. Raising him as his own. Leaving him the business, if he wished to take it—providing there would ever be another client.

Will's only choice was to make it all right. And swiftly. Then and only then could he see the way clear to his future. A future he dearly hoped would include Cora. And it began with finding Arthur Stapleton. Somehow, he knew the man was the key.

He took a deep breath and turned to enter the stables. Three cars were inside, two of them beneath protective blankets, one with her hood folded back, a man turning a wrench around a bolt within. "Owen Goering?" Will called.

The man looked up and straightened a bit. "I am Goering," he said in German.

"Good, good." Will came closer, considered offering him his hand, but then saw the dark oil that covered the driver's hand. "I am a friend and guest of the baroness's, William McCabe."

"Yes," he said, wiping his hands on a rag. "I've seen you about, sir."

"Last night, you took Arthur Stapleton away from here. I need to know where you left him."

"The Hotel Sacher, sir."

"The Hotel Sacher. Did you see him check in?"

"No, sir. But I handed his bags and trunks to a bellman."

"Good. *Danke.*"

"*Willkommen.*"

Will left the stables, fighting the urge to run all the way to the grand old hotel. He planned as he went. He wanted word to reach Art that the Kensingtons and Morgans had fled and for Art to believe Will had gone with them. If Kensington had accomplished what he hoped, they'd reach the train with no word of their intended destination. If God would only grant them this one favor, winding through the Alps, they'd lose anyone who dared to pursue them.

Will prayed his plan to escape the kidnappers would work. Above all, he wanted Cora to be safe. And he could not wait to get his hands on one of the men who had hurt her—Arthur Stapleton. Then he would do his best to track down the man who dogged them and make sure he never took a step in their direction again.

Upon reaching the hotel, he went directly to the concierge and asked for a pen and card. Swiftly he wrote a note intended to draw Art out, and asked a bellman to get it to Arthur Stapleton's room. "Within the next five minutes, if possible," he said, peeling off another bill from the wad that Kensington had given him to get home.

The bellman scurried off, and Will sat down on a vast, curved, upholstered lounge in the center of the lobby to wait for him.

Ten minutes later, Art appeared, looking relaxed with his collar open at the neck, his jacket unbuttoned. He walked over to Will and kept his gaze. Will rose, fighting to keep his composure.

"You were our friend," Will ground out.

"I am still your friend, if you allow it."

Will was in motion before his thoughts caught up with his fist. He punched Art and sent him sprawling, then went after him. Women screamed. Art half rose, blood spurting from his nose.

A bellman blew a whistle, and a second sounded a moment later as Will pummeled Art's face. Art let out a guttural cry and pushed him away with his legs, sending Will hard against a nearby sculpture of a woman, tipping it over. He winced as the sculpture's hand dug into his shoulder before shattering beneath him. But he was rising, intent on going after Art again, when he saw two policemen clamp down on either of Stapleton's arms. A moment later, two others did the same to him. He tried to wrench away, but it was no use. They had him.

"He attacked me!" Art cried.

But the manager was speaking in rapid German with another policeman, waving in their direction, then over to the broken sculpture and spattered blood across his luxurious carpet. "Bring them," the fifth man said to the guards holding Will and Art, "and we'll sort it out at the station." The four officers immediately hauled them out of the lobby, past women with handkerchiefs to their mouths, hands over heaving breasts, past men with frowns of dismay and protective stances.

This, Will thought as they loaded him and Art into the back of a barred wagon—a jail cell on wheels—*wasn't how I'd planned it.*

But what was new? Nothing seemed to be going his way. He stared helplessly through the bars to the wide Ringstrasse that had borne Cora's motorcar to the rail station.

No, nothing at all seemed to be going Will's way.

CHAPTER TWENTY-EIGHT

~William~

The police chief let them sit in separate cells, side by side, for hours.

Or rather, he let Will pace, and Art sit and dab at his bleeding lip and cover his bruised eye with his hand, as if the eye ached.

"So you didn't *really* wish to speak with me," Art said at last, watching him pace.

"I did," Will responded, turning to face him, hands on hips. With the bars between them, he couldn't go after him again. "I wanted to know how a man we all thought was honest and true could be an out and out liar. A user. But then when I saw you, I knew I wanted to deck you too."

Art shrugged. "If you see a journalist as a liar and user, so be it. I do not. I write it as I see it. And if you do not wish to be written about, live life as a hermit."

"You are not a *journalist*. A journalist would've made it clear that he was writing a story about a group on the Grand Tour. Received their permission. Not covertly gathered his information, catching his friends at their weakest, using that weakness to create a more titillating story."

"Vivian recognized my name. Adrien said I liked to gather stories."

"You know as well as I do that she recognized it but could not place it. And that we missed that casual reference! How do you do it, Art? How can you stand yourself? How can you sleep at night?"

"It's a job, Will. Something I figured you'd understand. Do you love everything about being a bear?" He paused and then smirked. "Clearly not. But do you do your job well anyway? Of course. Because that is what is expected of you. Just as my editor expects the same of me."

"You crossed a line, Art."

"I did," he said, dropping his hand with a sigh. "But you have to admit it came together in one compelling story. My editor telegrammed me yesterday. They had to go back for a third printing, sales are so good."

Will shook his head. "What are you expecting from me? Congratulations?"

"No. Understanding."

"For using your friends? For being less than honest?"

"Did you not do the same? Use the Kensingtons and Morgans as a means to an end? To remain close to Cora? *You* be honest. Once your uncle died, everything in you wanted to head home to the States. But you stayed. Because you wanted more time with Cora. And the payday at the end of this tour."

"I had a job to do. I had to see it through."

"A job to do. You had to see it through," Art repeated. "That was my experience too. No matter how I came to care for you all. I had to see the job through."

"Why? Why?" Will sputtered. "Why not go and be the man Adrien portrayed you to be, sowing goodwill across the Continent on behalf of your family and vineyard? Why not see to that task over this?"

"Because I do not want only that task." Art stood and paced away, running a hand through his hair and turning back to him. "I want my own task. To be my own man. Not simply follow the dictates of my father."

Will let out a groan and waved an angry hand in the air. "So you are but one more wealthy son striving to make his own way in the world? I'm so weary of men like you! So weary! Do you not know what you have? What you've been given?"

Art considered him. "I thought you were free. Your own man. But you are as constricted by those who have gone before you as I am, are you not?"

"Indeed," Will bit out. "But without the fat bank account to fuel my way. Worse, I'm saddled with debts. Some of which are now held by none other than Wallace Kensington."

"There's a way, Will. Lead me to them. Gain me access so I can finish the third part of my story, perhaps even a fourth, and I'll cut you in. My editor has already offered me bonuses if this series continues to gain steam and—"

"You expect me to help you?" Will stared. "Yes, I want to make my own way in life. I want to be free. But I shall not get there across the backs of my friends."

Art sighed and sat down on the edge of his bunk, head in hands. "You need to help me, Will."

"No, I do not. I intend to keep you as far away from my former clients as possible. In my book, you and the louts that tried to kidnap Cora are on the same level, Art. I'm going after them next."

"They're already ahead of us. Another reason for you to lead me to them."

Will stilled at his deadly, defeated tone, his words laced with knowledge. "You know who tried to kidnap Cora."

Art shrugged.

Will moved to his side of the cell and met his gaze. "Tell me, man! What do you know?"

"I don't expect you to understand this. Will...I hired them."

"You what? *You!*" Will shrieked and vainly tried to grab him, longing to ram the man into the hard steel. He pushed against the bars as if he could bend them, until his rage passed. "You *hired* them?" he said, panting. "When? Where? Any *why?*"

Art spread out his hands. "In Paris. I came across your party at Pierre's ball. Saw that he was taken with Cora and knew there was a story brewing. When I saw how you were smitten too, it was all the better. But I needed something more. An edge of danger. Intrigue. And a reason to tie Pierre to you all for good. To feel responsible for you."

"So you hired the men to attack us?" Will said, feeling as if his head were about to burst. "The butler died in that attack, man! He died!"

Art's head was back in his hands. "I never intended them to go as far as they did. But once they knew who you were, they knew there was an even richer pot of gold at the end of the Kensington rainbow than I could offer."

"No, no, no," Will groaned, walking away, hands on his head. "It's impossible."

"I only intended this to be a onetime event, in Paris. Some chasing. Maids tied up. They were to get close to you all but not actually touch you. No one was to die. You have to believe me."

"But then they showed up in Nîmes...."

"And I paid them off. I thought we were done. Through. That it was over and you all were safe. I stayed with you as far as Vienna to make sure. And then our man showed his face here, to Cora, because she'd recognize him. He wanted me to know he was still around. Hoped I might have to provide additional funds to get rid of him for good. Sure enough, he contacted me."

Will paced his cell, hands on his hips. His heart leaped in his chest. It was far worse than even Arthur thought. Was it possible they knew already? News of the Dunnigan strike had been in the papers. Had the men put two and two together? Or found another means of information? "No, no, no," he muttered. "They can't know yet. Not yet."

"Know what?" Art asked.

"Nothing!" Will barked. He wouldn't give Art more fodder to write about if he could help it. "Who is he? What will it take to end it?"

Art heaved a sigh. "I'd say there's only one way to end it forever," he said, shooting Will a meaningful look. "His name is Luc Coltaire."

It was Will's turn to take a seat and slump over, head in hands. "At least that's one reason I can be glad the Kensingtons and Morgans left. Gotten away. With luck, they'll shake Coltaire from their trail."

"I wouldn't count on luck. I would count on this man's skill to follow among the shadows. I've never seen anything like it. I hate to say it, but I'd wager he's likely on whatever train your clients are on. Right now. And waiting for the right opportunity to take Cora, or another." Art paused. "There's only one way I can see us intervening before Coltaire does something foolish."

"Let me hazard a guess. It involves you writing more of your story."

"Yes," Art said carefully. "And no. Will you hear me out?"

Will heaved a sigh, searching for his own ideas, but there was no way Wallace Kensington would even let him near Cora again. "I'm listening."

Part IV
~VENEZIA~

CHAPTER
TWENTY-NINE

~Cora~

As we moved from a train that wound through the mountains to another train that descended into the rolling hills and fields of northern Italy, and then to a ferry across a lagoon, I decided my mind and heart had settled into a numb paralysis—as if they'd taken on too much and could endure no more. And that was all right by me. I accompanied my siblings and friends, our fathers, Pierre, Antonio, and our new guardians, nodding politely and answering any direct questions. But mostly I allowed the journey itself to wind around me like gauze on a wound. Cradling me, holding me, until I could begin to feel and think on my own again.

Sailing across the silver-green water to Venice, I fell in love with the uniquely salty scent of the Adriatic, feeling as if I were taking my first full breaths in weeks. I leaned against the small ferry's rail and watched as sailboats skipped across the water, narrowly avoiding the more stately steamers. Across the lagoon, in the distance, white-tipped, alpine mountains like those we'd crossed marked the northern border of Italia. It felt good, so good to be on the water again. It brought back memories of being on the *Olympic*, and then on the Channel in that sailboat....

"Ahh," Pierre said, edging near. "You look as you did that first day I met you."

I smiled softly, daring to glance his way, feeling melancholy. "I was just thinking about that." On that day, so much had begun. So much stretched before me as possible, exhilarating. I shook my head when he stepped closer. "I can't, Pierre. I'm too...raw. It's too soon."

I left him there, moving to the other side of the boat, knowing I was probably hurting him. Why was he so stubborn? When he knew my heart was with Will? When I'd said as much? Was he hoping I'd give up on Will? Soften toward him in Will's absence? I didn't mind if he felt the full measure of my displeasure. Even if it had been my father who had orchestrated this recent series of events. How could he agree with my father's decision to send Will away? Did he so lack the confidence that he could win my heart, with or without William McCabe in the picture?

Venezia was a colorful mishmash of earth-toned three- and four-story buildings and church steeples, dense and constant, one on top of the other. But when we reached the mouth of the Grand Canal, or *canalazzo*, as Pierre called it as he dared to move to my side of the boat again, my mouth dropped open. He came around me to see my face, and I couldn't convince myself to look away from him or cover up my joy. Here, the palaces lined the canal on either side and ran straight into the water. They were grand—some covered in colorful mosaics, others built in a clearly Turkish-inspired style. There were palaces of pink stone and others of white. "Palazzo Oro," Pierre said, gently gesturing toward one shining with gold.

"You have been here before, then?" I asked, trying to let go of some of my anger at him. Anger was simply so…wearying.

"Mmm, many times," he said. "All my life, really, several times a year. But each time I enter, she is a wonder anew."

"Oh, Cora, aren't they stunning?" Lil asked, clapping her small hands in excitement and moving to my other side. "And we get to stay in one!"

"Indeed," I murmured. "Simply stunning." Palace after palace was before us, each with four levels and many with a Turkish flair at the top of the windows—a delicate, curving swoop. It was almost as if we were entering Constantinople rather than Venezia.

"The palazzos are hundreds of years old," Pierre said to our small group, "and some clearly show the ravages of time, but considering their age and how they were built, they're something of an architectural wonder."

"How were they built?" Andrew asked from behind me. "Given the sandy soil of a lagoon?"

"Atop thousands of pilings driven into the soil, ten, sometimes twenty feet deep. San Marco, the basilica we'll tour this afternoon, was built atop a hundred thousand pilings. Most of these palazzos are on at least ten thousand."

"Good grief, man," Felix said, "that must've been a business in itself, importing all that wood."

I shifted uneasily. Did Pierre feel he had to fill Will's role as tour guide? I had to bite my tongue as he went on. I wanted to tell him that he had his own strengths, his own charms. He did not need to assume Will's as guide.

"Venezia was a trading force for centuries. Almost everything came through here. Crusades were outfitted, armies set sail, and Venezia?" He shrugged and lifted a brow. "She capitalized upon it, of course. Her founders arrived here destitute, but their great-great-grandchildren became some of the world's wealthiest." He looked out to the canal. "Yes, you, my friends, are on waters that ruled the world for a very long time."

"Do the pilings not rot, there in the water?" my father asked.

"No," Pierre said. "I'll give you an example. When the bell tower fell in '02 and they went to rebuild it, they found the thousand-year-old pilings in as good a shape as ever. The waters here…full of minerals—they seem to enhance…uh, become like rock, over time. It happens with trees." His forehead wrinkled as he searched for the right word.

"Petrification," Andrew supplied.

"Oui," Pierre said with a relieved nod. "A *petrification* process that makes them stronger than ever."

"I must say that you do quite a good job filling in as bear," Lil said, taking Pierre's arm. I stiffened and turned away. No one could fill Will's place. No one. I knew it was silly. Pierre was simply trying to help us, engage us, answer our questions. This was a city he knew well, and we were to stay in a palazzo owned by one of his friends. But I could not help feeling defensive on Will's behalf.

The ferry stopped at a dock, and we disembarked and waited for the servants to gather our luggage. Then Pierre set off, leading us through narrow alleys and down a crowded street so thick with people we could barely move, then through a tunnel and into a tiny piazza, with a well at the center and buildings all about, one of which was a large white building to our left. Pierre went to the gates and rang a bell that we could hear clang within, high up. "From now on, we'll come and go from the palazzo via the waterway," Pierre said. "As her owners once did."

A manservant came to the gates and, after a word in Italian with Pierre, allowed us entry. We walked through a tiny portico and garden, then through a huge, tall door into the foyer. Out of the sun and surrounded by stone, it was blessedly cool. I walked forward, drawn by the light, and my mouth again parted in wonder. The entire center of the palazzo was open to the sun, forming a square courtyard that extended four stories high.

Antonio turned to direct the servants on where each person would be and therefore where they should deliver the luggage, while the rest of us congregated around Pierre. I moved over, happily allowing others to put some distance between me and Pierre. I was overcome by my agitation again, despite my best efforts. "This bottom floor was where the merchants saw to all their business," he said. "The next floor up was where they lived, as well as the third. The fourth floor was usually reserved for servants. Now, as families struggle to maintain the palazzos—for they are costly—many rent out the third and fourth levels, or *pianos*, as they call them, electing to live on the first and second. But back in Venezia's heyday, that would've been impossible. Because all day, every day, the gates to the canal would have been open, and in many buildings, goods would enter and exit, an active trade business."

"Where does that trade occur now?" Andrew asked, making me want to throttle him. I was about to scream from the lectures. Lectures that should have been Will's to give.

"Mostly on the mainland." Pierre reached out to run his hand along the smooth stone of a column. "Venezia now echoes with the wonder she once was; she serves as a reminder of how power comes and goes, no matter how great."

He said the last with such a gentle tone that it almost sounded like introspection, thawing a tiny bit more of the chill building within me. He clapped his hands together. "Well, then, my friends. Let us all go and rest before we begin exploring, no?" He pulled out his pocket watch, looked around, and said, "Let us meet here again in two hours. That should give you each enough time for a rest, and then we'll go and tour San Marco and I'll take you to my favorite *trattoria* for some supper."

"That sounds delightful, Richelieu," my father said. "I can't tell you how grateful I am, you setting this up for us."

"Not at all, not at all, my friend."

I left then, not meeting his eyes, eyes I could feel trailing after me. If I looked beyond my own resentment, I grudgingly had to admit that he was an excellent guide, with an intuitive sense of when to wax on and when to cut short a lecture. No doubt it served him well in all his business and political endeavors. I hurried up the stairs after Anna, eager to be free of him and my father for a bit. No doubt I wouldn't be able to avoid Pierre for long. Soon we'd need to speak, and speak frankly. The trouble was, I couldn't seem to figure out which end was up. I liked him, cared for him, but my heart was Will's. More and more, I was sure of it. And yet my father had hog-tied me to Pierre. So how was I to speak about what I couldn't get straight in my own head?

"Cora! You're down here! Next to me!" Lil cried, waving me down the hall to the end. "Wait until you see it!" She practically ran down to me and looped her arm through mine. We entered my room, and I laughed with delight. The tall windows on the far wall were open, light curtains blowing in the breeze. We could hear the wash of water, the shouts of boat captains below, before we reached it. What was more, there was a small patio outside and a narrow door with a rusted brass knob allowing us access. Lillian squealed and led the way out, pulling me by the hand. "Come, come! Look! It runs the whole length of the palace! We can come out here tonight!"

"It's lovely," I whispered in awe. For the first time on the tour, I wasn't thinking about what might be next, but rather how long I might be able to remain. Because, oh, how this place invited me to linger, pause, *heal…* Looking one way and then the other along the canal—here a long, wide curve with buildings disappearing around the bend—and behind me at yet another beautiful bedroom boasting a big four-poster bed laden with pillows and a thick comforter, I couldn't imagine anywhere else I'd rather be. If only Will could be here with me, I decided. And Mama and Papa. Then it'd be perfect.

The thought brought me up short. Because try as I might, I couldn't imagine Mama and Papa here with me. In this palazzo. They'd be lost, intimidated, ill at ease. And that scared me. *How will I ever feel at home with them again? Now that I know more of the world? Possibility? Potential? Promise? Or am I forever changed?*

I walked along the narrow porch, dragging my fingers along the polished limestone, wondering if the mine, the sudden wealth, would change them, too. Open them up to all I had experienced. *Bring us together again.* It was all enough to make my head throb.

"Lil," I said, taking her hand in mine. "Would you excuse me? I think I need to lie down."

"Of course," she said, green eyes twinkling. "I'll return to my room this way!"

I smiled at her glee, and we parted. When I closed the porch door and shut out the canal's traffic noise, the relative silence eased me. The room was massive, housing the bed, two chairs and a dresser, an armoire, and a table with a pitcher and bowl—there was no water closet, I saw—and I felt swallowed up in the space.

I sat down on the bed, pulled off my suit jacket, and then bent to unlace my boots, suddenly feeling every ounce of weariness in my body. When the second boot dropped to the thick carpet atop the marble tiles, I flopped to my back, looking up to the fabric draped across the rods above me, then over to the ceiling. It looked like it'd been damaged and repaired over the years, now with a painting of clouds across its surface. I stared at them, imagining myself home, on the farm, beneath the tree out back, and it took me some time to remember what it felt like, smelled like.

But after a while, in my head and heart, I was back in Dunnigan, and at last I slept.

———◇◇◇———

"Miss Cora. Miss Cora," Anna said, shaking my shoulder. I groaned and reluctantly felt my dream slip away. I had been with Mama and Papa, outside the little country church, talking with the neighbors about what everyone was bringing to the picnic. Waking to find I was in Venezia, the sound of water overtaking the sound of my dreams—wind from the mountains—was jarring and left me feeling a bit unbalanced. Wary.

"My, you must have been weary indeed to have slept the way you have," Anna said, going to open the curtains a little wider and allow the last bit of afternoon sun in. "I came in an hour ago and found you so asleep I thought I'd better give you more time."

"Thank you," I said, forcing myself to sit up and yawning. "I think I might've slept the whole night through, given the option."

"Yes, well," she said, "you've had some frightfully short nights. Perhaps you'll catch up on your rest here."

So she'd noticed. My late-night pacing. My inability to sleep past sunup. Combined, they'd left me with far too little sleep. Back home, I'd gone down with the sun.... For a moment, I considered giving in to my drowsiness and returning to my dreams of home.

"Miss Cora?" Anna asked, obviously for the second time.

"Oh. Pardon me?"

"I wondered if you'd like a fresh suit for your afternoon outing."

I looked down at my skirt and blouse and knew I must have appeared rather rumpled. But what did it matter, really? Who was I to impress? Did I not want Pierre and my father to accept me as I was? Why would I pander to their attentions? I rose and turned my backside to her. "Am I presentable enough?"

"Let me just give your skirt a quick press. Given that you took off the coat, I think we can make do."

"It will be dark soon," I said, smiling as I unbuttoned the skirt and stepped out of it. "So no need to work too hard at it."

"Lucky for us. I'll return in two shakes of a lamb's tail."

"Thank you, Anna."

"Not at all, miss. I laid your brush and powders over there on the dressing table." With that, she disappeared.

I pulled out a small watch from my pocket and flipped open the cover. I was to meet the others in fifteen minutes. *No wonder Anna urged me to see to my own hair.* I sighed and forced my swollen feet into my boots, laced them back up, and walked over to the dresser, a small stool before it, a mirror above it. I laughed when I saw my reflection, my hair a catawampus mess after my long nap. It was to Anna's credit that she had not laughed aloud when she saw me.

Moving quickly now, I pulled out the twenty or more pins and brushed out my hair in furious strokes, wincing as I hit one knot after another. Then I elected for a simple knot atop my head that I'd mostly hide with a big hat. In a minute, I had it in proper order, and the hat pinned atop it. Anna arrived with my skirt, buttoned me up in back, and I scurried out of the room. I was reluctant to depart this sea-kissed sanctuary and looked forward to returning—evening above the canal would be rather magical, I thought.

I was the last to arrive in the courtyard, and my father gave me such a long look, full of chastisement for being tardy, that I narrowly resisted sticking my tongue out at him. Hugh, also at the back of the group, edged closer to me, his hand in front of his mouth, laughter in his eyes. "What kept you?" he asked in a whisper. "You were so late I thought you had stolen away"

"I was hardly off cavorting," I whispered back. "I was napping."

"Ahh, beauty rest for the beauty, eh?"

I rolled my eyes at his idle flattery. "One does what one must."

"Well, then," my father said, "let's be off. Outside on the canal are several gondoliers. They shall take us down to *Piazza San Marco*."

Hugh offered his arm, and I accepted it. "So it appears you've chosen the prince over the pauper?"

"I have chosen no one, no matter how my father wishes to choose for me. Pierre and I are…friends."

"Come now, Cora. There is no such thing as a friendship between men and women."

"No? Then what are we?"

That caught him, and he paused as we stepped down the stone stairs to get to the small pier outside. "More than friends, I think," he said, holding the door open. "More bonded, after all our adventures together."

I smiled at him as I passed. Who would have ever guessed that I would one day think Hugh tolerable? Almost…endearing? I sucked in my breath as we came outside and I saw two gondoliers on either side of the narrow pier, with three more maintaining their position just a bit away. The long black boats were elegantly slender, with a gentle curve to them and a fancy decoration at their stern. The boatmen stood on the back, rhythmically turning their long oars in a small circle on one side to keep them in place.

Hugh went first down the walkway, gallantly offering me his hand. I accepted, given that in my long, narrow skirt and high boots, it'd be a horror I'd never live down if I fell in the water. He'd fished me out of an icy crevasse; I didn't need him to fish me from the turquoise waters of the lagoon. At the end of the walkway, the gondolier offered me his hand too. *"Per favore,"* he said, gesturing down and into a seat for two decorated with red cushions. Gingerly, I stepped into the gondola, adjusted to the rocking sway of it, and then made my way over and onto the seat.

Hugh came after me. "Do you mind?"

"Not at all," I said. *Better him than Pierre.*

One of the new guards, Nario, climbed in with us, and our gondolier moved off, making room for the next to be loaded. On the other side of the pier, Vivian and Andrew departed, with another guard named Pascal playing the chaperone. Lil rode with Felix and Antonio, and Nell with both fathers. They didn't have guards with them, but I noticed our gondolier waited for the others, then set off behind Pierre, while Vivian and Andrew's brought up the rear.

My eyes scanned the other boats nearby, knowing that other burly, newly hired guards had to be about. In a moment, I spotted one on the opposite side of the Grand Canal, trailing us, and the other on the side we'd just left.

I wondered if I'd imagined the whole thing in Vienna, seeing our attacker in the dark. Why would the man show his face to me in the courtyard if he didn't intend to do anything about it? Maybe it had just been a man who looked terribly similar to the first, and he'd spied me in the shadows and was simply flirting.

No. It had been him. I knew it. Hadn't he been pretending to wait by a motorcar, when it turned out he wasn't a chauffeur at all? That was hardly the action of an innocent man....

"Penny for your thoughts," Hugh said, nudging me. "I'd ask Nario here, but the man is as talkative as a monk who's taken a vow of silence."

The detective gave Hugh a small smile and then resumed his duties, looking about. I smiled too, thinking about a silent movie with all its subtitles. What would it be like to read the subtitles of Nario's thoughts, along with the rest of the group on tour? *Rather handy*, I decided.

"I was just wondering if it's truly needed, setting guards about us, when we've seen neither hide nor hair of the interlopers here."

"That's the trouble with such scoundrels," Hugh said, uncharacteristically sober in his response. "They show neither hide nor hair until they want to take yours."

I shivered, as much from his serious tone as from his words.

"Ahh, there, there," he said, reaching to pat my hand. "Don't fret. You are more than protected. No need to fear what happened in Paris or in Nîmes here in this beautiful city. If they attempt another attack, Nario and I'll simply hold them under this smelly lagoon water until they drown, won't we, Nario?"

Nario gave him another smile, but I frowned. "You think it odorous? I think it smells uncommonly fine," I said, inhaling deeply. "Fresh. Teeming with *life*."

"You *would* think that," he said with a laugh, his brows knitting together high on his forehead. He pushed aside the hair falling into his eyes. "I truly have not met a girl like you before, Cora." He lifted his hands. "No, no. Don't get your hackles up. I'm not making a play. I promise. Clearly, you have enough men doing that."

"Then what?" I said, teasing him now. "Are you my *friend*, by chance?"

He lifted one brow and perused me. A smile spread across his face. "Yes, maybe it is possible to be friends. Now."

"Now?"

"Yes. Now that I know I couldn't possibly claim your heart, and you never had any interest in claiming mine."

"You never wanted my heart, Hugh Morgan."

He laughed, the sound mostly breath. "True. I simply had my eye on snagging a kiss from those pretty lips."

"You are incorrigible."

"Indeed," he said agreeably. "But you see, that is what is necessary for men and women to be friends. A complete lack of interest in anything other than honesty."

I pulled off my right glove and trailed my fingers in the water, remembering doing the same on the Gardon beneath the magnificent Pont du Gard, when Felix had been making fun of our grumpy oarsman and Arthur was taking photograph upon photograph of us.... Perhaps Hugh was right. What got in the way of peace, friendship with Will was a constant desire, deep within each of us, for something more. Something that seemed impossibly distant. Was it truly possible? For us ever to be together? Or had my father managed to seal off every avenue of reunion? I wondered how Will was, where he was...how he'd manage to get home. To find employment... *Please, Lord, take care of him. Show us both Your way. And what we are to do.*

There were many gondolas upon the water. We went under a wooden bridge heavy with foot traffic, men and women carrying boxes and large items on their backs. Then we turned the corner, and a huge white church with several lovely domes on her roof was on our right. We passed what appeared to be the entry point to the Rialto, guarded by walls and a cannon. On our left, a pink and ivory palace appeared, and beside her were two obelisks, a lion atop one and a saint with a crocodile on the other. Farther in, beside the palace, was the most exotic, amazing church I'd ever seen, with onion-shaped domes climbing to the sky above her. And across the small piazza was a huge bell tower. The one Pierre had mentioned? The *campanile?*

"Oh!" I said, over and over, every time we saw a bit more. It was as if the city herself was coaxing me out, back to life, back to myself.

Our gondolier pulled up alongside a series of small wooden piers, and we got out, smiling our thanks. Pierre pointed up to the obelisks we passed and the statues atop them. "One is of Saint Theodore, the patron saint of the Crusaders and all who go to war; the other, of course, is the winged lion, or Saint Mark." We followed him, walking past the beautiful arches of the Palazzo Ducale, or the doge's palace—the duke of Venezia's home then out and into the wide expanse of the rectangular piazza, what had to be one of the grandest squares in all of Europe. To our right was a tall, beautiful clock, which appeared to have ceased working, the gilding of her arms, as well as a blue paint, faded by the constant sun and wind and rain. On three sides, the palazzo was lined by huge public buildings and on the fourth, San Marco. We all turned and gazed about us in wonder.

After all we'd seen on our travels, nothing quite rivaled this. I felt like I was on the edge of an empire. *In more ways than one*, I mused.

Flocks of pigeons landed and waddled around, collecting seeds that tourists threw out for them. Some landed on people's outstretched arms and hats. I shuddered at the thought. I knew well enough what pigeons roosted in, from back at the farm. It was not charming. It was disgusting.

"You'll see the grates all along the piazza," Pierre said, pointing to the flower-patterned holes in the stone tiles beneath our feet. "Venezia is prone to flooding. They call it *acqua alta*. So they dug channels beneath the piazza, allowing for the water to flow when it must, then drain away as quickly as possible."

"What do the Venetians do when it floods?" Lillian asked.

"Use their gondolas all the more," Pierre said with a smile. "These shops that line the square, the church—all of it closes. But eventually the water recedes. It always does."

"How awful!" Nell cried. "I'd hate it if this all was lost to the seas!"

Pierre looked about. "I think that a city as old as this is not going to crumble and fade without a fight. Now come, let us go see the church."

We followed him through the square again, pigeons scattering and flying off like a parting wave, toward the massive church. She reminded me of a ghostly silver cloud, grayed with age, but with glimpses of former grandeur. Above each doorway was a mosaic. One here of warrior saints. The next of the cardinal virtues. Over the central entry was a mosaic of Saint Mark in winged lion glory. We entered beneath that one and climbed two steps into a wide, covered entry, then several more steps up and into the church. I wondered if all the stairs kept the water out.

Once inside, I gaped yet again. Because high above us was dome after dome containing the most elaborate mosaics I'd ever seen, with a predominant theme of gold. So much gold, the domes glittered like a million jewels. The style was clearly influenced by the East, sitting here on the edge of the Ottoman Empire, but with Christian symbols and saints. Below our feet were huge blocks of costly marble and granite in purple, green, red, and white. But it was the ceiling that captured my attention, shimmering even in the dim, strained light.

"They call it Chiesa d'Oro, Church of Gold, for a reason," Pierre whispered in my ear. He straightened and stood beside me, so near that his fingers grazed mine. "It is magnificent, no?"

"Magnificent, yes," I said with a smile, hoping it softened the sting as I moved my hand away from his.

"Are you so angry, mon amie?" he whispered, still looking upward, as if we were discussing the artwork above us. "Do you resent me being here?"

I considered his words. Angry and resentful, yes. But was any of it his fault? Not really. It was my father's. Solely my father's. And Pierre was being nothing but sweet and respectful, even if he was clearly pressing his suit. "I…I don't think so. Not with you, Pierre. But I'm afraid it's coming out that way. Can you forgive me?"

"But of course. You have been through quite an ordeal. It is a testimony to your fortitude that you have carried forward with such grace."

"You are more than kind, Pierre." I hesitated, trying to figure out what I could say. And couldn't. "But, Pierre, I—"

"Non, non," he said, bringing a finger to his lips, then pointing upward. "Leave it to God, will you not? Here in His house. Ask Him what you might do."

He slipped away then, ignoring, I thought, my whisperings of his name. His suggestion surprised me. Did he do so because he sought God's leading too? Or because he knew I might find peace in His answer?

"Miss Kensington?" asked Pascal, gesturing to the others, who were far ahead of us now. He was clearly anxious for us to remain close together, where we could be more easily guarded.

I reached the rest of the group, and together we admired the huge altar screen of gold and icons up front while inhaling air redolent with incense and beeswax. For the first time in what felt like weeks, I tried to settle into prayer, a true communion with my God, rather than the hurried, desperate prayers that had marked most of my journey. I slipped onto a kneeling bench and leaned forward, bowing my head, hoping my clear stance of prayer would shield me from my companions' interruptions for a moment.

After a breath, then two, then three, I thought I had it.

Lord, Lord, I need You. Please, draw near to me. There is so much for me to sort out…so much for me to decide. So much I don't understand. What would You have me do? What is right? What is wrong? And is Will the man You've placed in my heart? Or is that merely some sort of rebellion against my father, who wishes for me to be close to Pierre instead? Do I hold him at arm's length because he is not the one You have for me? Or because I do not wish to do as my father asks?

I forced myself to remain steady, quiet, unmoving, trusting that God would see me through. That He would answer me. Breathing in the scents of incense and beeswax. The less desirable, passing scent of perspiring tourists.

But the answer I got wasn't the one I'd hoped for, prayed for. Nothing clear and succinct. Only a vague sense that I was to wait… and trust.

I wanted answers. If I was to do as Wallace Kensington instructed. If it was wise to accept the wealth already in my name. If I was right to choose Will over Pierre. But instead He seemed to be advocating, pressing me toward pausing, breathing…waiting. And as much as I disliked such an answer, I couldn't deny the steady, solid *rightness* of it. *Good*, I decided as I took a long, deep breath. So much of this summer had such a mad pace. Pressing, pressing, pressing. Why did I give in to it? Why did I not wait on Him? Why did I feel compelled to choose on any front? Why could I not settle in and enjoy this time for what it was—the trip of my life—and see what came of it? On all fronts?

For the first time that day, I felt as if I could breathe. As if this, this was what God was leading me to. Waiting, abiding, resting. Enjoying what was rather than fearing what might be or resenting what had come before.

I opened my eyes and stared up at the gilt crucifix, so overtly gaudy and foreign, it almost interfered with my concentration. But I focused on the body, the image of my Savior, and thought about what He wanted for me. To trust. To rest.

I will wait, I prayed silently. *Lead me, Lord. Lead me on.*

I rose then, slowly, aware that both Pierre and Pascal were at opposite corners of the kneeling bench behind me, respectfully allowing me to finish, and it thawed my heart all the more. When Pierre took my arm, I allowed it.

After we'd traversed the whole church, Pierre led us up a steep flight of stairs. Up top, we could get close to some of the golden domes and see that they were made of millions of tiny squares, each one meticulously laid. I put my hand across a span and did a quick estimate—there had to be a hundred just in the space of my palm.

"We could visit a mosaic studio," Pierre said. "Would you like that? The art form is still alive and well here in the city."

"Truly? I'd love to see such artists at work." I turned and moved on, as if even more intrigued by the mosaics than I was before, but he stayed right with me.

"It took thousands of men hundreds of years to complete them," Pierre said, looking up and about when we paused again under the next arch. "I'm told that even now they employ seven mosaic artists solely to repair and tend to them."

"They're marvelous," I said. "It really is the most beautiful church we've yet seen." I dared to look up at him and found him staring at me, his heart in his eyes, full of hope. I felt my heart shift—from guilt? Or desire?—and edged away. I was tired of feeling vulnerable. So very tired of feeling as if I moved with the sea, as if I had no anchor. And Pierre de Richelieu made me feel just that, at times. Weakened. Liable to drift one way and then the other.

We paused beneath another massive arch inlaid with thousands of tiny mosaic tiles and looked up at the image of Christ, hands out, as if welcoming us. "Where do you stand, Pierre, in regard to God?"

He smiled, even as he gazed upward. "Beneath him," he quipped.

"But in your everyday life," I pressed, allowing him to take my arm as we moved on. "When you're not traveling or romancing foreign women," I said with a smile. "Do you attend church? Do you pray?"

He gave me a playful frown. "This old church has brought to mind very serious questions for you, mon amie."

"They *are* serious questions," I said lightly. "To me."

He was silent for a few steps and then stopped. "I believe in God. But my life is far too busy to attend more often than on Christmas and Easter." When he saw my expression, he rushed on. "But that doesn't mean that I would keep you from going anytime you wish."

I stared into his eyes and saw the earnest hope within them. The concern that this would be a final dividing line between us. I knew God wanted something different for me than a man who would only be nominally interested in matters of faith. I knew I wanted something different from a man with whom I'd share a life.... Could that be awakened within him? Or was this yet another point of caution?

I hurried ahead of him, across the old wooden walkways the priests and mosaic artists presumably used to light the old chandeliers and tend to the elaborate ceilings. As I turned the corner, I looked down to the church floor, my eyes studying thirteenth-century stones in the image of beautiful flowers and peacocks and urns and geometric patterns. A man caught my eye as I passed a massive column, and I looked back.

I froze.

The man from Paris, from Nîmes, from Vienna. Here. In this church. Staring up at Lillian and Nell.

"You!" I yelled, the word reverberating around the hushed, cavernous sanctuary.

"Cora?" Pierre asked, turning to look where I did as he passed by the column.

But the man was on the move, hidden now from his view.

"Pierre," I cried, hurriedly turning him around and pushing him toward the stairwell. "It's him, Pierre. The kidnapper." We got to the other side of the column and leaned over the railing, just glimpsing the man as he rushed out the front door.

"Remain here," he said, "with the girls." He broke into a run, bumping past an elderly man and dodging two women as he gestured frantically to the detectives and guards.

I went to the girls, took both by the hand, and pulled them into the biggest room, which was milling with people. No one would dare grab them here, now.

"Cora?" Nell asked.

"Cora, what is it?" Lil said.

"Nothing, nothing," I said, pasting on a smile. "I only wanted to be certain you saw the diorama here of the basilica. Is it not amazing? The detail?"

"Yes," Nell said. "But why so excited about it in miniature when we're in the actual, grand building?" she asked, gesturing around us.

"I'm just amazed at the detail," I said, walking around to the other side. "Look at how they've formed the columns!"

"Cora," Lil said, hands on her hips. "What has gotten into you? And where are the others?" she asked, looking around.

"All right," I said, giving up, leaning in closer toward them. "Here's the truth of it. Remember the man who attacked us in Paris, and me in Nîmes? The one who was in charge? I saw him in Vienna. We didn't want to alarm you. But I just saw him here, below us."

Nell gasped and put her gloved hand in front of her rosebud lips, while Lil's eyes rounded in alarm.

"Rest assured, our men are in pursuit of him as we speak. Perhaps even now, they've corralled him at last and our shadow will cease to follow us, haunt us." I scanned the crowd, and my eyes rested with some relief on one burly guard looking about, an expression of pure consternation on his face as he spoke to Mr. Morgan and my father. At least they *all* hadn't disappeared.

"Why would he be *here*?" Nell whispered. "Did he think he could get one of us in this crowded place?"

"I don't know," I said. "But we're staying here until Pierre or Antonio comes for us."

But just as I said that, the large tour group returned downstairs, leaving us almost alone. I looked around in alarm. Even the big guard and our fathers were no longer in view. Had they given chase too? Vivian and Andrew, Hugh and Felix had to be halfway around the church by now, exploring the narrow tunnels that intersected the entire upper floor, too far away to hear our call. I left the girls behind me and went to the stairwell, hoping I'd see Pierre coming.

What I saw instead stopped my heart.

Our attacker. With another man behind him.

I backed up and closed the door, sliding the bolt across. A priest ten feet away started shouting at me in Italian, but I ignored him, scurrying over to the girls. "Go!" I cried. "Run! They're coming!"

We lifted our skirts and ran down the tunnel, then across a narrow wooden bridge that took us around the edge and toward the very back of the basilica. I kept looking for places to hide, other avenues of escape, but saw nothing. Our best chance was to find the others—or another large group.

I glanced over my shoulder as we turned a corner and gasped... the men were still after us. And gaining. "Go, Nell, go!" I said as the girl slowed, panting. Where were those other guards? Had they joined Pierre in the chase somewhere outside? Had the man slipped away and doubled back without them recognizing it? I turned and slammed a flimsy wooden door shut, latching it with a rotten crossbeam, knowing it'd take our pursuers less than a minute to get through it.

Visions of them in Paris, coming through the door with an axe, ran through my head as I urged the girls forward. The next passageway stretched ahead of us, dark and eerie, as I heard the splintering of wood behind me. "Go, Lil!" I cried, my hands on Nell's shoulders. We ran into the darkness, praying it would lead us to an escape, but then I saw Lillian pulled to the right and Nell to the left, their cries quickly muffled just as rough hands took hold of me, too. I writhed and fought my attacker, until I made out his voice.

It was Pierre. Pierre! I immediately stilled, and he turned me in his arms, hugging me to his chest, even as he shielded me from anyone coming down the passageway. They'd done it. Used us as the bait in an attempt to trap the snakes. As I'd agreed. Pierre held me close, stroking my back, and I recognized that he smelled of soap and something warm, like cedar. I tried to take a step back, but he kept me close, still. As a precaution? Or because he enjoyed the excuse?

The girls and I were trying to be quiet and listen with Pierre, Antonio, and Nario, but we were panting so hard I could hear nothing but my own breath and the rush of blood in my ears. As my eyes adjusted to the dark, I saw that another guard was with them. I hoped we'd drawn the men into our trap. That the kidnappers would come after us, right where our men could catch them. Once and for all.

But no one came. I wanted to cry with disappointment as Pierre lifted my chin, finger to his lips, and then walked down the passageway with Antonio right behind him, perhaps wondering if our pursuers had gotten sidetracked, even lost. Or had they sensed danger and turned tail to run?

I wanted it over. I didn't want to live my life always looking over my shoulder, afraid, even if it was the girls he was after, not me. I loved them, I thought with a start, looking over at them and then welcoming them into my arms like frightened little chicks. *I really love them. Not just my sister, but Nell, too.* And the thought of it made me angry, fierce, like a mother bear whose cubs had been threatened.

CHAPTER THIRTY

~Cora~

Given the traumatic experiences of our day, Pierre did not press his request to take us to the trattoria that eve. Instead, we sat with the others after a somber supper at the palazzo as my father paced before a raging fire in the palazzo fireplace, raging himself. "We were to lose them in deviating from the planned itinerary! How the devil did they find us? I will not have this go on and on. We need to find these men and make sure they are imprisoned before our children are endangered any further!"

Pierre took my hand, obviously wishing to bring me comfort, and I allowed it. We had slipped away to Venezia with no one knowing where we were to go. Our previous itinerary had dictated stops in Milano, Torino. How had they found us? Unless it was impossible to slip from their vision, escape them…unless they'd always had eyes upon us, every step of the way. I shivered, and Pierre looked at me with concerned eyes, resting his other hand atop mine. "I still believe it is wise to force them to ground, sir," he said to my father. "Once and for all. You and yours cannot live in fear that at any moment they might be attacked. People like this need to be shown that you are the lion and they the prey, not vice versa."

"I am coming to believe that that will be our lot," Wallace said gravely. "To be prey, never safe." He nodded to the men who ringed us. "We are too well known, particularly since the release of those photos in that cursed magazine."

I winced, knowing that accusation was tossed in my direction. I burned within. Hadn't I intuited that Art had had less-than-honorable intent? Or was Wallace merely blaming me for embarrassing him, compromising the family name, being the source of that which sent us on the run? I let out a scoffing laugh beneath my breath. *If you hadn't had an affair...if you hadn't come to claim me in Dunnigan...*

His head jerked up, and he stared hard at me, almost as if he'd heard my thoughts. For a moment, I wondered if I'd spoken them aloud. But then he was conversing with Morgan in a whisper, conspiring over yet another plan. But my own words echoed through my head. What *would* have happened had he not come to claim me? We would've likely lost the farm. My papa would have likely died. My mama might have never seen her parents again. I would not have had the means to return to Normal School. And I wouldn't have known my siblings. My friends. William. Even Pierre. I wouldn't have lived a life I knew, deep down *knew*, I was meant to live.

Wait...and trust, God had urged me. I'd gotten this far, hadn't I?

Slowly, I stood up. "I have worked from sunup to sundown, fighting weeds on the plains in order to coax wheat to life. I have helped a mare birth twin foals. I've dug through ten feet of snow in order to fetch wood to see us through the night. The strength within my blood is a strength we all share, and I, for one, will not back down from men such as these."

My guards, my family, the Morgans, and Pierre stared at me with a mixture of horror and respect.

"We should do as we did before," I said. "Go about our lives. And when these men make their move, we shall be ready for them. Are we not well guarded?"

Antonio arrived in the doorway, looking red-faced from the stairs as well as chagrined. He tossed a magazine and newspaper to the side table. "It's out, if they bother to check the newsstand and can read Italian. About Cora's holdings in Dunnigan. Her own wealth. 'Dirt Farmer's Daughter Strikes Gold...and Copper' is how the headlines read."

All eyes moved to me as my heart sank. Because with words like that out there, I suddenly wanted a whole army around me.

———◦◦◦———

Fortunately, I felt better in time. So when Pierre sent word, asking for me to meet him downstairs, I obliged. His eyes lit up as I entered the room, and he came to me, taking my hands in his and kissing both my cheeks. His eyes went to Anna, who took a seat in the corner of the room and pretended to lift a book to read, giving us some semblance of privacy, then he looked back to me. "Please, mon amie, sit with me for a moment?"

"Of course."

He sat down beside me, inches away, so close that our knees touched as he turned toward me. "Are you well? I worried for you...

knowing now that this man is in Venezia and may double his efforts to come after you. Cherie, know I will stay close to you. I will not allow you out of my sight for one—"

I stood abruptly and rubbed my hands together. "No," I said. "That is not necessary."

His face fell into a frown. Perhaps he'd hoped this new threat would help me decide, even push me into his arms. "I...I must know...would you prefer for me to leave? Perhaps I should give you some time to ponder. To consider...us. Perhaps it was wrong of me to hope that if we had but a few weeks alone, you would see me as a viable beau."

"Oh, Pierre," I said with a weary sigh, sitting down again and taking his hand. Half of me didn't want him to go; half of me did. But if he did...would Wallace truly punish me? My parents? Will? And yet...it was not at all fair to Pierre to lead him on. "I've always considered you more than viable. You are as Art dubbed you—a Parisian Prince. But Pierre, you have to know...this..." I waved back and forth between us. "This is still more my father's doing than me following my heart."

He listened to me intently and then lifted a gentle hand to my face, stroking my cheek with his index knuckle. "But it may soon become your own heart's desire, yes? If I wait? If I remain patient?" He smiled, but there was hurt in his eyes. Because I could not give him an honest chance. Because my heart was still tied to Will's.

"Forgive me, Pierre, for bringing you pain," I said. "It's the last thing I wished to do."

He lifted my hand to his lips. "If it takes pain to hear you say my name in such a tender way, bring forth the whip," he said, kissing my bare knuckles. His lips lingered there, kissing my hand again and again, watching me as shivers ran up my arm and neck. I wondered if Anna was watching. If she was aghast at my forward, fickle nature.

I pulled my hand from his, regretting my weakness, my fear, my eagerness to assuage his angst by simply ending it. Even if I sent him away, would Will and I ever have a real chance? Given the barriers my father had created? And if not, would I regret it, in time? Was this part of why God wanted me to wait, rest? To not rush into anything, even a decision? Pierre was so earnest, so dear.... "You confuse me," I whispered at last.

"That is good," he whispered back. "For if you were not confused, then you would be decided. And until I know that you will decide for me, I am in no rush at all."

I rose suddenly. "I must retire for the evening. Good night, Pierre."

"Au revoir, mon amie," he said, giving me a gentle smile, not reaching for me, as if he knew such a move would send me running. "Until tomorrow."

CHAPTER
THIRTY-ONE

~Cora~

After sailing to Torcello, the birthplace of Venezia, we'd been invited
to a count's home along the Grand Canal to dine that night before
attending the Teatro la Fenice, an opera house known the world over.
I was so weary, I thought I might fall asleep in my consommé, but
as I donned one of my prettiest gowns and Anna did my hair, I felt
a resurgence of spirit, eager to see another palazzo along the canal,
as well as to experience an opera. The count sent many gondolas to
fetch us, and my father insisted I ride with Pierre, alone, en route to
the palazzo. "Simply do as I've asked for once, Cora," he said when
I opened my mouth to suggest I ride with the younger girls instead.

I frowned but accepted Pierre's arm, wondering if this was a new
attempt to bait the trap, to draw out our would-be kidnapper. Why
did the men not confide in me? Did I not deserve to know, more
than any other, if I was indeed their target? And did I truly wish for

a life as a "target"? Who else might come after me, once the world knew me as a true heiress? I had a very serious desire to board the next ship for home and take my lumps as they came. If it weren't for my father's threat of removing my mama and papa from the deed if I didn't do as he said...

I studied the water as we headed out. Who was to say that he would truly do it? Did he not desire a harmonious relationship with me? One between me and my siblings? Why had I kowtowed to his every demand? Did I not have rights of my own?

"Pierre," I said softly.

He turned to me. "Yes?"

"Do you know of a good estate attorney here in Venezia? One who might be able to advise me of my rights in regard to my new holdings in America?"

He considered me and my request for a moment and then gave me a single slow nod. "What is it you wish to know?"

"Many things," I said, turning back to the water. "Many, many things."

"May I be of assistance? Advice?"

"Perhaps," I said gently. "In time. Or perhaps this is for me to find out on my own."

The water reflected the coral and pink tones of the setting sun, giving the canal a particularly soft, romantic look. The gondolier followed three ahead of us, pulling in toward a magnificent white palazzo with long windows along the first three levels and smaller ones on the fourth *piano* as well. Two men in Arabian dress awaited the guests, assisting us out and onto the stairs that led to the receiving hall. Admiring their silk turbans and balloon-like pants flowing in the wind, I felt as if I were entering a home even more exotic than any other I'd yet visited.

Pierre took my arm, and we climbed the stairs, which opened into a courtyard, much as it did in the palazzo in which we were residing. But here, the occupants had filled every inch of the walls with rich, dark oil paintings, and in the walkway in front of the paintings was sculpture after sculpture.

Pierre pulled me toward the Conte and Contessa Biviglio, our hosts for the evening. They were homely nobles with bulbous noses and wide bodies testifying to long, languid evenings filled with delicacies and ample wine. But their smiles and welcoming manner did nothing but endear them to me. "Ah, it is the newest Signorina Kensington," the count said, bending to kiss my hand. "You honor us, attending our dinner."

"It is you who has honored us with your invitation, Conte," I said, smiling into his brown eyes.

"You shall be the talk of the evening, my dear," he said, patting my hand and looking over my face as if I were another sculpture he could acquire.

"Oh, but she already is!" laughed the countess, gesturing widely, guileless. "Here on the arm of our friend Pierre, as well as in the pages of magazines and newspapers."

"It seems my Cora is destined to steal the world's stage," Pierre said, casting me an admiring glance.

"Just do not let our opera star hear such things," whispered the countess, moving on to greet the others behind us.

I giggled. "Far be it from me to ever challenge an opera star for center stage," I whispered to Pierre.

"No?" he said, bemusement in each handsome line of his face. "You cannot carry a tune? Is this your one fault, *mon ange*?"

"One of many," I said with a light laugh. I glanced over the crowd and stopped when I saw Lillian and Nell speaking with a tall blond man. Nathan Hawke. The man we'd met in Vienna—the one who had given us his sister's copy of *Life*. "Let's attend my sister, shall we?"

Pierre readily agreed, and we moved toward the trio.

"Ah, we meet again, Miss Kensington. This time under happier circumstances, I trust?" Nathan said, bowing toward me and Pierre.

"Indeed. I think we're all eager to put that evening behind us."

"Understandably," he said with a gentle smile. He cast a flirtier smile in Lillian's direction. "I was more than delighted to find that I'd run across my newest friends here in the city of love."

Lil bit her lip and smiled, blushing prettily under his gaze, but my eyes narrowed as I studied him. He seemed charming, kind, but what was he really after? A man as handsome as he could pick his own bud among the gardens. Why my sister? Because of her name?

Pierre turned to take two flutes of champagne from a passing servant, and I checked my thoughts. Since when was I so protective? I searched the crowd again. Since I feared that man had come after my sister and her friend? Or since I decided I loved them both? The flood of emotion in my heart threatened to overwhelm me, and with sudden tears, I looked for Felix, over to Lil, then on to Vivian, Nell, Hugh, and even Andrew.

It was as if God had spoken directly into my heart. I wasn't ready to leave them all. Indeed, I wanted to be with them to the end. And beyond, back home in Montana. As much as my father wished for me to embrace a relationship with the Kensingtons, I wanted it myself. But how was that to be accomplished when I so hungered for the chance to make decisions of my own? To carve my own path rather than simply dutifully follow the dictates of my father?

Wait…and trust.

I watched as Nathan whispered something into Lillian's ear and she smiled up at him with adoration in her eyes as he passed her a glass of champagne. Was he not far too old for her? Where was my father, anyway? Why wasn't he looking after Lillian as he did for me and Vivian?

Vivian moved into our circle then, clearly intent on ferreting out the same information I'd been considering drawing from this Mr. Nathan Hawke. I breathed a sigh of relief. Viv had the tenacity—and the place in our family—to do what I could not. Warn Hawke to tread very carefully with our baby sister…

I turned with a smile to acknowledge Pierre's gesture toward the others, now filtering to a far room to be seated for dinner. "He's not here, our enemy," he whispered in my ear. "Rest, mon amie, and enjoy." But all through our many courses, from the salted sardines to the mussels in rich broth, from the delicately cooked beef to the pasta flavored—and colored—with oily black squid ink, my attention was on Nathan, who was flirting with my sister at every turn.

It wasn't that Lil was ugly. She was slender, and comely enough with her bright green eyes. But I'd been in social circles such as this all summer long. And I'd never seen a man as devilishly handsome as Nathan Hawke take up with a girl like her unless there was money involved. The same went for beautiful women taking up with plain-looking men. Generally speaking, it was money, and on rare occasion character, that bridged the gap. At some point tonight or tomorrow, I intended to find out just where Hawke had hailed from and what his prospects were. And what Vivian had found out.

He took a sip of wine and saw me staring at him. He lifted his goblet in a small, silent toast, giving me a warm, inquisitive look. I continued to smile, letting him think that I was silently flirting back, all while my mind was full of Vivian tearing him apart piece by piece. But my heart went out to Lil. The last thing I wanted was for the girl's tender heart to be shaken by the conniving wanderings of a man such as this. What had been his true intentions when he handed me that copy of the magazine? Truly to warn me? Or had he simply viewed it as the means to worm his way into our lives?

I had to caution Lil. Make sure Vivian had shaken some sense into her. A girl without a mother was apt to drift in her later teen years, like a ship without a rudder.

We finished with our fine meal, letting the tart crystals of a raspberry sorbet slide down our throats, and then rose to make our departure back toward the theater. The opera would begin in but an hour, its star long departed after her appearance over cocktails. Separated by twenty or so people, I saw Nathan dare to put his hand on my sister's lower back and bend to whisper in her ear again. He leaned back, cocked a brow, waiting expectantly, and after a moment, she hurriedly nodded, smiling shyly up at him. What was this? A proposal? For what?

They made their way to the edge of the crowd, and when a man began coughing as if he were choking, drawing nearby attention, Nathan grabbed Lil and pulled her into a dark side hallway.

I gasped and took Pierre's hand, yanking him with me.

"Cora? What is it?"

"Come!" I whispered over my shoulder. "That scoundrel has spirited Lil off for a kiss, I'd wager!"

Pierre laughed, the sound warm and low. "One can hardly blame a man for stealing a kiss from any of the Kensington women...."

"Pierre!"

"All right, all right," he soothed. "Be at peace. Let us see to your sister's honor and be on to the opera. It will be a night she'll likely remember forever, regardless of what's actually transpired."

But as we entered the dark hallway, I blinked in surprise. My skin prickled in fear.

Because it was empty. "Where'd they go?" I whispered, rushing to the end. There was only one door, and my hand went directly to the knob.

"Hold, Cora," Pierre said, all trace of amusement now gone. He tucked me behind him and reached into his jacket pocket, pulling out a small revolver. I shook off my surprise over his weapon as he opened the door. We saw that it led down a set of stairs and heard the lapping of waves; it was a sort of servant's entrance to the canal. A small lamp illuminated a part of a gondola bobbing on the waves.

Pierre hesitated. "Perhaps he only wished for what I myself wished—a gondola ride on a beautiful eve with his lady. Alone."

"Only you would gain my father's permission first, yes? I doubt this one has." He wasn't one of the kidnappers. It was impossible. This was innocent...in certain measure.

Antonio appeared behind me. "Have either of you seen Miss Lillian?" he said.

"Yes. She disappeared down here. With Nathan Hawke."

His bushy eyebrows lifted. "Well, regardless of his intent, Mr. Hawke is about to be relieved of her company. Will you permit me?" he asked Pierre, reaching for his own pistol and passing us.

"Stay here," Pierre said to me, turning to follow Antonio down the dark stairs.

Wringing my hands and fighting the desire to follow, I watched them descend, crouching to see better.

But then a hand clasped over my mouth, and strong arms dragged me back into the dark hallway. A man quietly closed the door to the canal and flipped the lock, then turned to face me, still held in the iron grip of another.

I knew who it was before he fully turned. My kidnapper.

He smiled into my eyes. "Hello, Miss Cora. Did you think you could outrun me forever? Bring her," he said cavalierly to the man who held me, turning to walk down the hallway, back to the main portion of the palazzo, whistling, hands in his dress jacket's pockets. He looked like any other nobleman at our table that night.

I prayed that any of the men would come around, looking for us, for Antonio. I glimpsed a small crowd of people to my left, their backs all turned. Had the others not yet missed us? Or did our guardians think we'd simply become lost in the crowd leaving for the opera, somewhere among a hundred gondolas?

My enemy looked one way and then the other, then bent to light a cigarette, giving my captor a casual wave to move ahead. The man held me so tightly against his chest I could barely breathe, my toes inches from the ground. We moved right and through a hidden door and then brazenly past several servants all absorbed in their tasks, their backs to us.

The man laughed lowly as we entered another hall. He looked down at me. I was breathing fast and furiously through my nostrils, trying not to pass out from lack of oxygen. "Miss Cora Diehl Kensington, I am Luc Coltaire," he said with a little bow. "After all this time, we'd yet to be formally introduced," he said to his companion, as if it was some great oversight. All humor left his voice with what he said next. "And now you shall come with me, on my arm, smiling. Or you shall see your little sister die."

Lillian. They had her.

"Come along quietly, and she will be released, unharmed."

I stared at him, feeling hatred so intense that my heart pounded. After a moment, I nodded.

"Good. Release her."

He stared hard at me as his companion let me go, waiting for me to try to run, to scream. But I merely straightened and pulled back my shoulders. He stared at me in wry admiration. "Shall we?" I said.

He laughed again and offered his arm. Begrudgingly, I took it, and we followed the huge man who'd held me out of the hall and down into a garden. From a side gate, we entered a narrow alley, the buildings so close together that we had to walk single file, me between the men now. A part of me was giving in to panic. But a larger part of me was surreally relaxed, relieved to finally be here. One way or another, my run-ins with this Luc Coltaire and his minions would end here, this night. Whether I lived or died, it would end tonight.

But oh, how I wanted to live...

Coltaire grabbed hold of my arm as we turned, three blocks down, and hurried over cobblestones and through long, arched tunnels, from one tiny piazza, an ancient well at her heart, to the next.

All of Venezia appeared to be sleeping—we spied few passersby. At one point I thought I heard a shout, and then another, but they were blocks away.

I prayed Pierre and Antonio hadn't run into more of Coltaire's men, that they'd turned and broken down that hallway door. Perhaps even now, our men were filtering through the streets, giving chase.

But if they caught us, would we lose Lillian forever?

CHAPTER
THIRTY-TWO

~Cora~

"Ahh, here we are," Coltaire said, pulling me inward as if inviting a long-lost friend home.

I blinked in confusion, seeing I was among five men and my sister. She was red-faced, her eyes swollen from crying, and she sat in a chair in the middle of the room. Nathan knelt beside her, patting her hand. So it was true. They had managed to kidnap them, too.

I moved to try to comfort her, but Coltaire blocked my way. "Uh-uh," he said as if chastising a wayward girl. "Not yet, big sister."

He slowly circled me, perusing me as if seeing me anew, as if every layer of my skin were made of gold. He came before me again and slowly let his eyes drift down my body and then back to my face. "I've waited a long, long time for this moment. Even more since Vienna."

"Leave her be, Coltaire," Nathan said, rising. He came between us and shoved Luc back a step when the man stubbornly refused to budge. Then he slowly turned to me. "You, my dear Cora, have proven a hard woman to track down."

And it was then that I knew Nathan was in on it…in with Coltaire. All along…*all along*. He'd even said he was from Montana, lately from New York. Obviously privy to my father's discovery in Dunnigan—my own holdings there, now. Giving me the copy of *Life*. Knowing it would help us trust him, all the while sending us into an uproar, unbalancing us. Giving them the opportunity to corral us and capture me. For what?

"What do you want?" I asked, looking from Nathan to Luc.

Luc crossed his arms, tapping his pursed lips with his fingers, then brushing his brown hair out of his eyes. "Just a small portion of your fortune, heiress. A fat payment will buy your freedom, and you shall be on your way, never to see me or Hawke here again."

Nathan looked at me too, awaiting my response.

"My father will never pay you."

"That's why this is so deliciously perfect," Nathan said. "He may not. But you will. You have money of your own." He moved over to Lillian and casually moved the hair that had fallen from her knot past her shoulder and let his hand rest there. I tensed, clear on what he threatened. "After I put your name together with you in Vienna, with that article in *Life*, I remembered where else I had heard your name. A newspaper from Montana, and a story about one of her newest, wealthiest residents…"

"You are a fool. I have no access to my inheritance. I only found out about it myself in Vienna."

"I can wait until you find the way," he said, running his fingers over my sister's clavicle. She whimpered and turned bright green eyes at me, pleading for me to bring it to an end. "We'll take a train to Switzerland together. The bankers are rather clever there."

I steeled myself. "Pay a kidnapper once, deal with others behind him. We'd never be free of your kind."

"Ah, you sell us short, Miss Kensington," Luc said. "Nathan and I will take this secret to the grave, won't we, Nathan?"

"Of course," he said with a languid smile. He continued to smile at me as if his secrets held many layers.

"And the others?" I said, looking to the other men in the room.

"They know it is wise to follow orders," Luc said, all trace of humor gone from his face.

"Who's to say I'd be free of *you*? What would keep you from coming back to me?" I dared to take a step toward him. "No. I shall not pay you."

He stared at me for a long moment. Then he pulled Lillian away from Nathan, forcing her to her feet, his hands around her neck, and drove her to the stone wall. He lifted her, choking her, ignoring me as I tried to pry his fingers from her throat, scratching at his arms. Her eyes bulged, and her face became bright red.

"Stop it!" I screamed, bodily attempting to push him from the wall, from my sister. But he was strong. Immovable. Lillian's growing stillness sent terror through me. "Stop it!"

Coltaire turned a casual eye toward me. "So you wish to fetch our money now?"

"Yes! Yes! Just release her!"

He dropped his hands, and Lillian collapsed to the floor, choking, croaking for air. I gathered her into my arms and looked up at him. "How could you? How could you be so...monstrous?"

They ignored my cries. Nathan went to the door. "Keep watch. The Misses Kensington and we have a train to catch. I'm off to buy tickets," he added with a smile. He sobered and pointed at Luc. "No more harm to the merchandise, you understand me?"

Luc lifted his hands and shook his bowed head, as if it was the last thing on his innocent mind. But just before Nathan departed, he gave me a slow, sure smile. I hated him. Hated him for drawing Lillian in, using her innocence against her. Hated him for using me. My thoughts turned to Pierre, our guards.... Would there be any way for them to know where we'd been taken?

Lillian clung to me, weeping in my arms.

"I was such a fool," she whispered, sniffing. "I'm sorry, Cora, so sorry."

"Don't worry, sweetheart," I said, hugging her close. "It's understandable. Confusing. I might've made the same—"

Coltaire went to the door, opened it, and peered out, Nathan now gone for several minutes. "Come on," he said, lifting me abruptly to my feet as another man lifted Lil. She cried out. "Quit it," he said to her. "No more of your sniveling. We have some walking to do."

Fear surged through me as they gagged us and tied our hands behind us. Where was he taking us? Didn't Nathan expect us to be there when he got back? But then I realized a move might be to our benefit. Surely if we came across any other pedestrians, they would see us in our finery and most of these men in their work clothes and notice that something was amiss.

A man in front searched the narrow street, looking both ways, then he moved out with us right behind him. They hurried us to a small canal and dumped us into the bottom of a gondola, a man sitting on either end. We immediately set off, not running across any others in this remote waterway, the apartments above us dark, their occupants slumbering. We passed block after block. Our boat joined a larger canal as the moon rose, but the two gondoliers we passed did not give us a second glance.

I wondered where they were taking us. I wondered how angry Nathan Hawke would be when he discovered he'd been used to capture us and then double-crossed. I wondered how all of this could possibly come to a peaceable end.

We pulled alongside a short pier, and one man lifted me and then Lil up to it. A second gondola bearing the other three men pulled in next. Two men took hold of my arms and led us down a small cobblestone street that ended at the doorway of what appeared to be an abandoned church. They pulled us in and shut the heavy door behind us. But my eyes weren't on the door.

They were on Will McCabe and Art Stapleton, dressed in black and white finery, as if they'd just set off for the opera house themselves. My heart leaped within me at the sight of the man I loved.

"Will!" I cried as Luc yanked me closer.

"You fool! Why bring *him*?" Luc said. Did he direct his question to Arthur? I frowned in confusion.

Art lifted a brow. "The disenfranchised bear, so easily dismissed by Kensington? The jilted lover of our own divine Miss Diehl Kensington, thrown over in favor of Pierre de Richelieu? Easy.

Justice. As well as his own earnings for his exclusive story. We all gain here, Luc. Now let us get on with it."

I searched Will's face, knowing it could not possibly be true, but he avoided looking back at me. Doubt edged in. *No, not my Will. It's impossible! Impossible!*

Art pulled a camera from his pocket. "Now be a good fellow, Coltaire, and light another lamp, would you? I need a bit more light to capture these two, bound and frightened as they are. Forgive me, Cora, Lillian. But I cannot resist recording this latest drama along the path of your Grand Tour. My readers will fight for copies."

Luc handed me to the nearest man and begrudgingly lowered another lamp and lit it, all the while keeping his eyes on Art and Will. Lillian was sobbing, and I wished I could go to her, but the man kept me in his grip. Luc turned to another of his men. "Take a look outside," he whispered. "Make certain we are yet alone." Then he called to Art, "Give me my share, and I'll be on my way."

Was he working *for* Art?

"Of course," Art said. "Simply put on this mask and pose with your victims, will you? Then you can be off, your money well earned."

Luc caught the mask he threw him, and his companion caught a second, while Art looked through the viewfinder of his Kodak. Could this truly be happening? All in an effort to complete his story? Again I tried to grab hold of Will's gaze, but he did not look my way. Because he was guilty? Or fearful that he would give himself away?

"Hold still," Art said, opening his shutter and holding his breath. He looked up at us. "All right. Now one without the gags."

Luc hesitated. "If they scream—"

"Only the dusty saints of this forgotten church will hear them. These walls are as thick as a tomb."

Coltaire untied my gag, letting his hands linger around my head. "Someday, we shall meet again, my sweet conquest."

"I shall be bearing a pistol pointed at your head," I returned.

He laughed softly.

"What of Hawke?" I added. "Were you too greedy to share the spoils?"

He paused. "Hawke's deal was potential. I knew Stapleton's payment was certain. I'm less a gambler than an opportunist," he said, turning me to face him and staring through a slit in the fabric of his mask. "Still," he whispered, glancing toward Will, "I have half a mind to kiss you before I go, just to test how *removed* Mr. McCabe truly is."

"If you try, prepare to leave your lips behind," I said through gritted teeth. "For I will bite them off."

He laughed. "You're not nearly as sweet as you appear."

"Cease toying with her," Art called. "Turn her back to the camera. Lillian, too."

After a second's pause, Luc did as he was instructed. Art took the photo and then pulled a heavy sack of coins from a belt beneath his jacket. "Gold," he said, tossing it to Luc. "Spendable in any country in which you wish to hide for a time. Dive deeply, Coltaire. I do not wish for our enemies to discover you. Nor hear from you ever again."

"A pleasure, as always, to do business with you, Mr. Stapleton," Luc said, bowing and pulling off his mask. But as he tossed it aside, I heard the distinctive click of Art's Kodak. Both Coltaire and his companion, also unmasked, stilled, but Art was turned toward Will, and appeared to be taking his photograph.

They turned to go, the door slightly open, when it burst inward. Antonio and Pascal came bounding in, tackling Luc's companion. Coltaire screamed his outrage, and our other three guards waded in, pulling Antonio off their companion, then Pascal. Antonio fired a pistol, and I took hold of Lillian and hurried her to the corner, hovering over her, our hands still bound but our feet free, shielding her with my back. A moment later, a man pried me away, pulling me backward so quickly I almost lost my footing.

As soon as his arm wrapped around my neck and he dragged me out, I knew it was Luc even without seeing him. Will kept step with us, threatening to strike him with his cane, hesitating as he watched Luc clamp down against my neck. Men behind him clashed, fighting, going down, entering the fray again.

Luc laughed. "So you are not as much the jilted lover as the disenfranchised bear, it seems," he tossed out. He was steadily making his way to the door, then out into the small square in front of the church. Did no one in Venezia remain up past sundown, other than those on the canal? I wondered wildly, looking about at the dark windows. Or did they merely fear to wade into such a tempest?

Coltaire dragged me down an alley, and we emerged on the grand, sprawling piazza of San Marco, her church's domes shining beneath the rising moon. In the distance, I glimpsed small figures beneath the basilica's entrance walking toward the Campanile, but we were too far away to call for help. We paused, both Luc and me panting heavily.

Without further warning, Will struck, hitting Coltaire on the arm that held me.

Luc cried out in pain, releasing me, and I hurried to and around Will. He lifted his cane toward our attacker. But when Coltaire growled and came after us, Will met him halfway. In seconds it was done, Coltaire on the ground and Will atop him. *"Polizia!"* he cried as Luc squirmed beneath him. *"Polizia!"*

"Give it up, Coltaire," Will told Luc. "We have you. On film."

Two policemen entered the square, down by the church, and ran in our direction. Will stood up, explaining what had happened, and they hauled Coltaire to his feet, his face a snarl. "This is not over."

"Oh, yes," Will said, stepping toward him. "It is."

An officer lifted his hand to Will, speaking rapidly in Italian. Gradually, Will pulled back and nodded at the policeman when he apparently asked him to come to the station with me, to file our statements.

We watched until they disappeared from the piazza, shadows disappearing among greater, wider shadows. And then Will pulled me into his arms, kissing my face, my head, my lips, as if making sure I was real, not an apparition. "I was so scared, Cora. So scared. That I would lose you. Forever."

"No, no," I said, smiling up into his eyes. "That'd be impossible, William McCabe. You came for me. In spite of it all. And I'm so glad. So, so glad."

CHAPTER THIRTY-THREE

~Cora~

Three days later

We were in the palazzo salon, having tea, when Will and Antonio escorted Art Stapleton in, hat in his hands.

Gradually, every man in the room stood. The veins in Andrew's neck bulged, and I knew he was itching to tear the man apart.

"Gentlemen, please," I said, lifting a hand. "Let's hear him out." He'd been missing since the night of our attack. Most of us had assumed he'd fled the city.

"Did you get another story filed, Stapleton?" Hugh sneered. "Is that why you show up now?"

"There will be one more segment in *Life*," Art said, "a story I sent two weeks ago, but no more after that. The only other pictures from my camera will be used by the authorities to prosecute Luc Coltaire and his men, or to tell my own story of duplicity."

"Sure," Andrew said sarcastically. "We believe that."

I set down my teacup, chagrined at my trembling, and rose and laid my hand on my brother's arm. Felix looked down at me. "Please," I said. "If I can tolerate his presence, can you not all as well?" It touched me, their defense. As much as they all felt exposed, used, we all knew I was the central focus of Art's stories.

Felix nodded slowly. "If Cora wishes to hear him out, I do too," he said, tucking my fingers more solidly around his arm. His gesture warmed me.

Art warily looked from Andrew to me and Felix and then swallowed hard. "There are no words, of course, to tell you all how sorry I am. And especially you, Cora. It started as a lark, really, a bit of drama in my mind. No one was to get hurt."

"But people did get hurt," Lil cried, bringing a hand to her mouth. "We did." Nell wrapped her arm around her friend's shoulders.

"A man died," Pierre said, his lips in a line. "A good man."

Art nodded, his eyebrows knit in contrition. "And for that, I'm sorriest of all. I'm heading to Paris to face the authorities." He paused, as if searching for the right words. "At first, you all were nothing but a story for me," he said. "And a good one at that. But after things went awry in Paris, I felt I must join you for a time to make sure Coltaire stayed away. But as I traveled with you, I became your friend. I know you all would never call me that any longer," he rushed on, "but I consider each of you friends now."

"Friends don't abuse their friends as you have," Felix said.

"I know," Art said. "Again, I beg for your forgiveness. But you see, by the time I was deciding that, I was in too deep. I was committed, my editor was sending me telegrams…"

"Spare us your woes," Vivian bit out.

"Right," Art said, clamping his lips shut. He pressed on. "I paid off Coltaire in Nîmes. I was hoping it would be the last of him."

"Or just another nice addition to the story?" Wallace said, hand on the mantle. All of this time, he'd been staring into the fire. Listening. Mr. Morgan, as usual, hovered nearby.

"It became both," Art admitted carefully. "But it was truly to be the end. Coltaire swore it was so."

"And then he showed up in Vienna," I said.

Art's eyes moved to meet mine. "Yes," he said with a slight nod. "And it was then I knew we'd never be free of him."

"Our only hope to nab them and put an end to this," Will said, "was to get to Coltaire first. To convince him that Art wanted one more dramatic segment for his story, at double the pay. Otherwise, Coltaire and his men would've continued to menace us."

"And then Nathan Hawke entered the mix," Felix said.

Art and Will nodded, and we all shared a sober silence. Hawke hadn't been seen since that last awful night either. When he'd been double-crossed by Coltaire. So…was it truly over? Or now, now that Nathan's true intentions had been exposed, would he stay out of sight, far from us? I sighed and looked to the window, again determined to never be trapped by the thoughts detrimental to what was now.

"You made mistakes," I said. "Dreadful decisions with terrible consequences. But all we can ask of you is what you are doing.

Apologizing and facing the authorities, then hopefully making better decisions in the future. Thank you for coming to us, Art."

The rest of the group looked at me in mild surprise as I took the lead, dismissing him. I could feel the heat of a blush at my jawline.

Art nodded and turned his hat in his hands. "If I could do it over again…" he began.

"But you can't, can you?" I said softly. "None of us can."

We were all silent for a bit. Then Art turned to walk away. My father gestured to Pascal, and the man followed him out. Art may have promised to do the right thing, but Wallace Kensington would ensure it was done. After the door shut, most of us sank to our seats again.

"It is time we go," Wallace said after a long moment, still standing beside the mantle. "Home, Cora. Where we belong." I studied my father. I knew there was a good part of him that thought he knew best, that he was merely looking out for me. But I was his daughter of a mere two months, truly. And everything was about to change again.

"I do not agree." I looked about at the rest of our group, then back to him. "You may have decided that the tour is over, but I wish to complete it. In a more restful, relaxed state from here on out."

"Impossible," my father blustered. "I will not allow it."

"You may wish to try and change my mind, but my decision is my own, Father," I said. "I have secured an attorney, and he assures me that I have good grounds to fight for my share of the Dunnigan mine, as do my parents. He's even assisted me in securing a small loan."

"It takes far more than you think to travel as you have," he warned.

"Then I shall travel in a more modest fashion," I said, looking to Will. He nodded once, assuring me. I returned my gaze to Wallace. "You cannot control me. I wish to know you as my father, not as dictator. I surmise that my siblings would concur."

I looked at Vivian, Felix, and Lillian, but their expressions spoke of doubt, fear. I smiled, gently. It had taken nearly losing my life—and fearing they might lose theirs—to realize how I felt about them. "You three may make your own decisions."

My father leveled a furious glance at me. "You cannot turn my family against me."

"That is not what I wish," I said softly. "My greatest wish is for you to see each of your children as the gift they are, not as a commodity to be managed, traded." I glanced at Vivian, but she turned away. "You, yourself, Father," I added, "are invited to join us as much as you wish. I wish to spend a week here, a couple of weeks in Tuscany, a couple of weeks in Rome, before heading back to Montana. But only after I stop in Minnesota."

I met Pierre's glance; it was pained, mixed with admiration. He didn't quite know what to make of this turn of events, what to make of me, even after I'd told him again that my heart was Will's and I was taking a stand against my father. Somehow, some way, we'd find our way forward as friends. I was sure of it.

Wait…and trust.

"It's been a grand adventure to date. I am so grateful to you all." My eyes found my father's again. "But these next steps, I propose we take on our own, as the self-possessed adults our fathers wished we would become along this journey. So…who shall join me?"

"I'm in," Will said.

"And I," Vivian said, with Andrew quickly echoing her. I glanced at him in surprise. Somehow, I'd thought this would be the last straw for the Morgans.

"And I," said Felix, Hugh, Lillian, and Nell as one.

I smiled even as my father continued to stare at me, Mr. Morgan rose, and the room stilled. Would my father lay down the gauntlet now? Begin to unleash his fury as he threatened? Will stepped forward and took my hand, and my father looked from our hands to my face. "You wish to lead, Cora? You think you know all it takes, to rule in my stead?" he said. He waved in the air. "Then you're welcome to find out. But don't come crying to me when you fall."

"Papa always said that when we fall, we gradually learn to stand on steadier feet," I said softly, meeting his unwavering gaze.

He clamped his lips shut.

"Wait and trust, Father. For I believe there are good things ahead," I said, looking about the room and then up at Will. "Good things indeed."

... a little more ...

When a delightful concert comes to an end,

the orchestra might offer an encore.

When a fine meal comes to an end,

it's always nice to savor a bit of dessert.

When a great story comes to an end,

we think you may want to linger.

And so, we offer ...

AfterWords—just a little something more after you

have finished a David C Cook novel.

We invite you to stay awhile in the story.

Thanks for reading!

Turn the page for ...

- **Discussion Questions**
- **A Chat with the Author**
- **Historical Notes**

Discussion Questions

1. Anna says, "We mustn't always pine after what we think we're missing.... Some things are just not ours to be had." What do you find you "pine after" that you think will never be yours? Why?

2. Cora thinks, "Moments belonged to those who acted. Not those who thought about acting." Have you ever faced a moment of glory, then overthought it so much that the moment passed? Or pushed through even though you were scared? Discuss.

3. Cora wonders, "How much did we do in life that was the result of what others around us demanded? Rather than what God was calling us to do?" Do you find that people around you drive you more than God? Why or why not?

4. The Grand Tourists encounter history that clearly depicts violence and hatred, much of it as a "holy cause." Do you think faith is an adequate reason to go to war? Why or why not?

5. Loss visits us all in some way—relationships, property, finances—regardless of whether we're poor or rich. Discuss how loss hurts but also can help.

6. Cora stubbornly holds on to her past as "who she is" and believes she will return to it. Have you ever left home? How did the move change you? Do you think someone can ever "go home again" and be the same person they were when they left? Why do we hunger for that at times? Discuss.

7. Do parents today still send their children on paths they believe to be right rather than allowing their kids to choose? What has been your experience?

8. Cora observes, "As with so much else that was right and true in life, we got lost in the particulars and lost sight of what was right and true in the first place—we concentrated on the things that divided us rather than the things that unified us. Love. Grace. Peace." What is an instance in your life where something good was destroyed by concentrating on the "things that divide" instead of the things that unite?

9. Cora wonders if her journey will ultimately lead to confusion rather than clarification: "Would this journey leave me lost rather than found?" How does wandering and exploring, either literally (e.g., a trip) or figuratively (e.g., thinking about things) help or hurt? Discuss good limits and ways to make the most of "journeys."

10. Have you ever prayed for specific answers and the only answer you received was "wait"? If so, how did you respond to that? If not, how do you think you would respond to that?

11. What do you think about being "equally yoked," in matters of faith, with a potential spouse?

12. The theme of doing as we are led, not only as our parents dictate, runs through this book for many characters. Did your parents encourage or even force you to pursue anything or anyone in your life? Did that work out well? Why or why not?

13. Cora decides she is to enjoy "what was rather than fearing what might be or resenting what had come before." Have fears of the future or regrets of the past ever kept you from enjoying the present? Discuss.

Chat with
the Author

Q: Have you been to all of the places described in *Grave Consequences*?

A: I wish! I spent some time in the south of France, so I had a decent feel for that part of the country, even though our Grand Tourists traveled much farther than I. But I've never been to Lyon, Nîmes, Geneva, the Alps, or Vienna. They're definitely all on my Someday List. For my research I relied on the Internet and guidebooks until I returned to my more familiar territory of Venice.

Q: You've stayed pretty close to home of late, compared to your travels of recent years. What's up with that?

A: I really wanted to see all these places in person before I wrote about them, and as a travel blogger, it would've had dual impact. But God encouraged me pretty clearly to simplify my life. I was feeling strung out, trying to cover too many bases, and travel, especially without my family, was a luxury of both time and money that could most readily be dropped for a while. So we put our travel blog on hiatus. I'm sure there are some fantastic trips in the future. But for now, God is directing me to focus on my family and friends. To stick close to home, as you said. When He's that clear, I've learned to obey. Wait and trust, as Cora heard. I'm doing the same.

Q: Speaking of that, are you good at waiting and trusting?

A: Ha! I wish. I'm an action-oriented person, a catalyst. I write novels because I like to control my fictional worlds and characters. But in this last year, as I've pressed into my identity as God's daughter, I've become hungry to find how He is working in my world and how I might join Him in it, rather than always trying to do my own thing and inviting *Him* into that. It's an ongoing effort to submit more and more to His will and His ways and find life more abundant. And you know what? I'm so excited. Because every day I press toward that goal, to live life more hand in hand with Him, to be an active, willing servant of the Most High, I find that waiting and trusting is met with joy-filled rewards.

Q: What's next for Cora and this group in *Glittering Promises*?

A: This series has an arcing theme of identity. And in this book, Cora's rediscovered her footing as an individual. What needs to happen next is for her to find out who she is as a daughter of the Father who will never, ever leave her. I think in that, she'll find her greatest security, allowing her to make critical decisions about her future, including her vocation and Will McCabe. But there will be some serious obstacles.... You'll have to wait to find out more!

Historical Notes

As with all my novels, I aspire to remain true to historical fact but reserve the right to craft the best tale possible, even if I have to bend the truth a tad. They do have bullfights in the old Roman arena in Nîmes, but I'm not certain if they did that routinely in 1913, or if bulls ever succeeded in jumping the barrier and attacking those in the stands.

There was a narrow-gauge railroad that went from Geneva up into the Alps and stopped in a tiny town near a glacier in 1913. I'm uncertain as to whether anyone would've trekked across it with a bunch of tourists at the risk of falling into a crevasse, but I'm continually surprised by what I find in my research, in both pictures and words. People have always been brave—and stupid—regardless of the era.

Life magazine was published in 1913, but I haven't seen anything like the photographic journal articles depicted in Art Stapleton's stories. At the time, tourists were just experimenting with the new Kodak and often sent home postcards made out of the prints from those cameras, which got me thinking about such a possibility. It wasn't based on journalistic standards of the time…it just became a lovely vehicle for complicating Cora's search for her truest identity by making her appear to be something she isn't. We fictioneers utilize what we can.

By and large, Grand Tours tended to be centered on meeting important people and seeing famous works of art and monuments.

To keep this series from becoming a monotonous travelogue, I've added an experimental factor (painting like the Impressionists, baking with a French chef, trekking across a glacier, etc.) that is entirely a figment of my imagination. I have no idea if the bears of the Tour would've favored such a thing, but if I were to take my kids today, I'd surely incorporate such things as painting, baking, and trekking to help them remember these fantastic, luscious places all the better. Wouldn't it be fun? Now I just need $50,000 to take my family away for a whole summer....

-L.T.B.

Acknowledgments

Many thanks to Traci DePree, the only person besides my husband (and a few amazing fans) who has read nearly all of my books (and edited almost all of them too). Thanks also to the amazing team at David C Cook, including Don Pape, Ingrid Beck, Caitlyn Carlson, Amy Konyndyk, Ginia Hairston, and Karen Stoller. Litfuse has been a terrific publicity partner too; I salute them. For French help, *merci* to Heather Broomhead, Megan Breedlove, and Jean-Philippe Feve! To all who have assisted me in crafting this project and getting the word out to readers, thank you.

STILL WANT TO KNOW MORE?

Find out more about Lisa, read about her journeys, and connect with her by visiting:

Web: LisaBergren.com

Facebook: Lisa Tawn Bergren and River of Time Series

Twitter: @LisaTBergren